COMPELLED

Written by Kevin Doyle

Dedication:

To the clan: Bryanne, Matthew, Spencer & Belle.
For Mercedes, who watches from everywhere.

PROLOGUE

The sun crested past its high noon position to transition the heat weathering on the side of the acreage house. The house was not far off the beaten path of a secondary highway but somewhat concealed by the line of trees and set back at the end of a worn, gravel driveway. The small acreage was nestled amongst pines, and its backdrop was of rolling hills that led to mountainous vistas.

Her parents' dream home was worth the extra drive for her dad, who loved the panoramic sunrises and vibrant sunsets. She found it beautiful but boring, as it was far from her friends. The hour-long drive in her old, unairconditioned car felt much longer. Rolling down the windows didn't help, as her slow car couldn't create a breeze, and it was far from fuel-efficient unless it was coasting downhill.

It was Sunday afternoon.

The teen lay on the couch in the living room, indulging her mind in a book. She sat up and clasped the novel shut with a quick snap and tossed it on the coffee table in front of her.

The story she was reading was dragging in the middle anyway, adding to her sense of boredom, compounded by her feeling of claustrophobia.

All this space, and yet she was feeling claustrophobic.

And bored.

And hot.

Her friends were an hour (or more) away. The small strip mall by the gas station was not. The strip mall was only about twenty minutes away. A short skip over the bridge was the strip mall with an ice cream store. It was a quaint little place of cool, nostalgic bliss. A trip there would relieve claustrophobia, boredom, and heat.

Jumping up from the couch, she bolted through the kitchen, snagged her keys from the rack, and shot out the spring-loaded patio door. Barney, the ever-faithful family dog, came flying after her.

Crashing through the door onto the front porch she almost knocked over her father onto his ass, forgetting her parents had been relaxing on the porch. The porch was the biggest selling feature. It was their little weekends, evenings, or whenever, sanctuary.

The tray of plastic glasses and jug spilled on the ground in Dad's surprise at her sudden exit, as he had been making his way inside for some obvious refills.

Go! Go now!

An urge, a need, propelled her.

She couldn't stop, instead tossing a quick "sorry" over her shoulder.

Mom was on her feet, calling to her. "Watch where you're going, young lady!"

Dad, recovering his footing, added, "And where are you going in such a hurry, Liz? Liz?"

"Ice Cream!" Liz yelled without slowing her pace or looking back.

"Ice cream is such an emergency?" He questioned. A bit flustered by almost being knocked over with the mess of plasticware at his feet.

"It is today!" Responding as she got in her car and pulled the driver's door closed, just in time to block Barney from making an uninvited ride-along.

With the key in the ignition, she cranked it hard, almost desperately, as if she were some girl in a "B" Grade horror flick that was desperate to escape a raving lunatic. As if expecting the car not to turn over and leave her vulnerable without escape. But in this real-life scenario, the engine fired to life effortlessly.

Liz slammed the gear shift into drive and pounded the gas pedal. A plume of dust and spraying gravel highlighted her exit. It was an emergency. At least it felt like one. She felt a desperation deep within and was anxious to get there.

"Well, she must have wanted some ice cream!" Mom commented, watching the dust plume settle.

"You think?" Dad replied. "I'm all wet from her sudden rush to satisfy a craving. She'd better slow down and drive safely! And bring me a treat to make up for it all."

The mom urged him inside. "I'll text her to get you something. Let's get you cleaned up and taken care of."

"Taken care of?" He looked at her with a sly grin.

"Well, we do have a minimum of forty minutes."

"In that car, it will be more like ninety." Dad chuckled.

"Then we have more than enough time," she joked while nudging him inside. "Because you only need five!"

"Ouch!" He acted pained by the remark.

"Just get inside!" The Mom gently encouraged him through the door with a slight tap on the rear.

"She better bring me some ice cream back as a recompense." He said over his shoulder.

"I'm sure she will, you big baby!"

Hunched forward, leaning her body into the steering wheel as if willing the car to go faster, Liz's little beater car shuddered as it barreled down the two-lane, secondary highway. *Was it a highway? Dad always said it was.* Liz figured it was just an ordinary country road. Her dad called it a highway to scare her into being careful. He had no trust in her driving skills.

Tires squealed as she gripped the steering wheel tightly. Exiting the turn, she floored the gas pedal, speeding toward the approaching bridge. The car bumped twice over the transition from tarmac to concrete.

Liz was afraid of heights and usually held her breath while driving over this high bridge. Today, as she brought the car to a stop, she pressed hard on the brake. Ahead through the windshield, she observed long tire skid marks that extended off the edge of the bridge where a section of the protective rail barrier was missing, creating a gap approximately the length of a car.

Before her was a nightmare—a plunge into icy waters below.

She didn't know the bridge's name; locals called it the "Suicide Bridge." Her dad introduced it this way, hinting at a long history. He often shared that at least 57 people had jumped off this bridge in the past century.

He joked that the bridge was a fisher of men. To her, it was a serial killer, claiming lives accidentally in winter and accepting jumpers without question in warmer months.

Liz was not focused on any of that today. Today, she observed that additional victims were being added to the bridge's incident list. She considered reaching for her cellphone to call emergency services.

Instead, she was opening her door and exiting her vehicle.

She was sprinting towards the broken edge of the bridge, and as she dived off the side, narrowing towards the soul-stealing river below, she realized she wasn't thinking at all. It was an Olympic-level dive slicing into chlorine waters. She pierced a river's topline and burrowed into cold and murky depths.

Her hands touched the bottom, and she grabbed a rock from its muddy refuge as her eyes caught the glint of headlights in their Willow-The-Wisp underwater sparkle. It was a car that had careened off the edge of the bridge. Resurfacing, she gasped for air and then swam under again. The current was mild, which probably saved her life. Anything stronger and her swimming skills would not have been able to cope.

Liz reached the windshield of the vehicle, pressed her face against the glass. Sadly, all that could be seen inside were the lifeless bodies of a man and a woman. Her lungs beat against her chest in a rhythmic request for air. Feeling hopeless, she pushed off the hood of the submerged vehicle and made for the surface. Still holding in her grasp was the rock she had grabbed from the river bottom.

Underwater again, kicking with everything she had to push herself down to the vehicle. At the driver's side, she looked inside again. With eyes and mouths wide, the adults inside were dead. To the side, something caught her eye. Liz slid down the side of the car to the rear passenger window.

Air! Her lungs pressured her.

Inside, a young girl was buckled in the seat. Eyes closed and not moving. Air! Now! Her lungs screamed for it, and Liz was forced to seek the surface. Gasping in sweet air, Liz felt suddenly confused at what she was doing, besides trying to catch a breath, besides freezing, and maybe crying. *That poor family.* She needed to get to shore and back to her car, so she could call the police. She reached the surface again. The face of the family flashed in her mind. The parents are floating in a state of death with their eyes wide open. The girl in the back seat. With eyes closed, mouth closed, there were a couple of bubbles coming out from the corner of her mouth.

Bubbles.

Air bubbles?

Rock in her hand.

Liz dove down at the car again. She went directly to the passenger side door and tried the handle a couple of times. The door was either locked or not budging due to the pressure. Liz began smashing the rock in her hand against the window. Once, twice, on the third time it cracked, fourth a larger radial spider web of fracturing occurred. The water numbed the impact of the rock against the glass. Heedless of the risk of breathing in the water, Liz screamed and smashed the window a sixth time. It shattered before her. She reached in, unbuckled the child, and pulled her out.

The scream had been a mistake. It expelled any reserves of oxygen she had, but she didn't even realize it and was deaf to the pounding in her chest. The seconds between grabbing the child and kicking to the surface were lost to an instinctive blindness of survival.

Breaching the waterline with a deep gasp of air, Liz pulled the limp body along as she swam towards the shoreline. The young girl's head bobbed listlessly, causing Liz to stop several times to adjust her position to ensure the girl's mouth and nose were above the surface. She didn't even pause to think that it may not matter. Liz kept moving forward, slowly drawing herself and the body towards shore, one single-armed stroke at a time.

Liz lay on the muddy shoreline on her side for half a second, catching her breath, facing the little girl who was lying lifelessly on her back. *Lifeless!*

Liz knelt over the girl, pinching her nose and blowing air into her mouth. She was doing CPR without any first aid training, mimicking the steps she thought were right as she moved to chest compressions.

"C'mon Lacey, breathe, just breathe, c'mon Lacey. You have to grow up to become a surgeon and save hundreds of lives." She said, unknowingly muttering to herself.

Later on, in a daze, Liz became aware she was wrapped in a blanket and sitting on a bed in the back of an ambulance. A female paramedic sat across her, checking Liz's vitals while a towering policeman leaned in from the open rear doors.

"You saved that little girl's life today!" The paramedic commended.

"Did you know the family?" The policeman leaned in closer to ask Liz.

"No," Liz replied shakily. She wasn't trembling from the cold; it was something deeper within.

The medic stepped back to provide some assurance to the shaken teenager. "You are going to be okay, there are no signs of hypothermia. Your parents have been called, and they are on their way."

The police officer took the opportunity to further question Liz. "You are a hero, young lady, and I'll be sure to let your parents know. I have to ask, what were you thinking? Weren't you afraid?"

Liz stared out of the open back doors of the ambulance, past the officer and into the beyond, in lost contemplation. She whispered. "I don't know. It was like I wasn't me. I just reacted."

If the officer had been leaning a little deeper as he asked his question, or if Liz had been looking at either of them directly in the eye, they would have seen a spasmodic shift, and a bit of flash behind her iris. Maybe it was just a reflection from the emergency lights beyond, or maybe it wasn't.

CHAPTER ONE

If the Ace budget Motel had regular housekeeping, and one of those housekeepers entered room 9, two-thirds down from the office on the first floor, they would have avoided the slow, screeching elevator. The elevator's grinding noise frightened anyone who used it, especially those with claustrophobia. Fortunately, the motel only had two floors. Unfortunately, there was no housekeeping service. The owner couple managed operations, with only the husband handling evictions for late checkouts or any overdue weekly payments.

If there was housekeeping, though, they would come across a 28-year-old man in room 9 who looked like he was dead on a double-sized bed.

The bed filled a good portion of the unit by being set in the middle of the room with one nightstand table, another worn chair by the curtain-drawn window, and a couple of steps away was the bathroom. The young man filled the bed, lying out spread-eagled in a crucifixion pose. It was obvious he had crashed or passed out, as his shabby jeans were still on, and he lay on top of the covers. He was awake but had been too skeptical of what might lie under the darkness of the covers and inhabit the bed with him. One of his legs hung off the side, and his shoe had dropped to the floor. He had immediately flopped onto the bed when he got back to his room, God knows when, but he had not slept. How much time had he lost staring at the ceiling? He was lost in the creases of his reddened palms as he brought his hands up to stare at them for another countless time.

There was dried and flaking blood on his palms. There was a small cut on his right hand that stung a little, but that cut would not have produced enough blood to explain his reddened hands. Most of this blood was not his. He flipped his hands over to view the soreness of the broken skin on his knuckles, this blood was mostly his. It wasn't the first time he had found blood on his hands without fully recollecting how.

Blood again.

The young man suddenly wretched, and something deep from his belly gurgled up into his throat with acidic fire. He jumped off the bed and rushed to the bathroom sink in case the bile from beneath made a second attempt to eject from his mouth.

It did not make a second attempt. He stared at his reflection in the mirror as he began to wash his hands. A scruffy face of a shallow beard and loose hair that hung just above his jawline stared back.

"Ely, what is wrong with you?" He questioned his reflective self, then looked down at his hands as he diligently scrubbed. "What is wrong with me?"

He looked back at the mirror in answer to himself. "I know what's wrong with me. I can never mind my own business. Just like last night." He squeezed his eyes shut from the memory.

So much weird stuff had happened in Ely's life that, as he got older, he was becoming an expert at being a loner. It was easier that way, keeping others at bay. Staring at himself in the mirror, Ely could not remember why he was at the shopping mall, or what he had been doing there before the moment when he bumped into his old work buddy, Jeff. The next thing Ely knew, he was agreeing to drinks and wings at a neighbouring pub.

The mall was a void in his memory, but last night, he remembered with vivid clarity.

Sitting in the pub, their talk quickly led to reminiscing of their workplace antics and then back to high school, it was easy to get sucked into a sense of normalcy.

Innocent enough, right? Just catching up on old times and watching a game, right? It should have been that way. It would have been that way if Ely's gaze didn't keep shifting to the couple off to the side. He was unaware of the game playing on the big screen, and his friend's words became a muffled noise.

The pub was only half full at best. It could only be assumed that most were regulars here and, for the most part, had congregated in the seats either at the bar or closer to the screen playing the game. A few filled tables at the outskirts of the establishment. A few, just like the couple at the small, two-person table close to the bathrooms. That couple kept pulling Ely's attention away to watch from the corner of his eye. The woman there was just an imp of a girl, raging red hair, and she sat at the edge of the chair so her toes could touch the floor. If she sat back, her legs would be dangling. He could only assume she got carded everywhere she went to verify her age.

The boyfriend was obviously of legal age, not just verified by his full beard or the fact that he was thrice her size, but his face said so. The creases on his forehead said so. They were having words, trying to keep it to the confines of their table, but Ely could see by the way he squeezed her arm, the little twist of his wrist, and the flex of that forearm that it was not a tender touch.

The crowd went wild as the home team scored, drawing Ely's attention back to reality.

"What a shot," Ely's friend said as he clinked his mug of beer against Ely's in a celebratory cheer.

"Great shot!" Ely replied even though he hadn't seen a thing.

"I can't believe it has been that long since you talked to your sister. She was a looker. Remember, I used to always bug you to set us up?"

"Oh, I remember. And I remember I told you never in a million years. We just don't touch base much often. My family has always been weird that way..."

Ely's head snapped to the side, back to the direction of the arguing couple. Nobody else seemed to pay attention to the argument. Except now the boyfriend was standing, leaning into the young woman, one hand on the back of her neck, the other squeezing her forearm low to the table.

"Hello, McFly? Are you even listening to me?" The friend was asking.

Ely wasn't listening. He was up out of his chair and moving. The only response to his friend was one word of excuse. "Bathroom!"

Ely, remembering, still stared at his reflection in the motel bathroom mirror, talking to that other self, the one that gets lost, the one that loses moments and time.

"I've always been a little impulsive."

Back at the bar, Ely was at the table of the couple. The boyfriend may have been giant to his girlfriend's size, but his size was deceiving from a distance. Up close, he was more than that; up close, he was a mountain to Ely. It didn't stop Ely, impulse was driving him, as he grabbed the meathead and shoved him back through the offsetting men's bathroom door.

"I've always been a little too reactive. It isn't being encumbered with a bad temper, there is no temper involved. I just react."

He threw a cupped hand full of water to splash onto his face in the hotel bathroom, snapping him to the present. "Most of the time, I barely remember. I remember the actions that didn't feel like they were mine, this time. I remember the words I said that were not mine. They just came out of my mouth."

He didn't dry his face, just let the water run down as he looked straight into the mirror. "I should have been intimidated. And I have no clue what I had been witnessing." He shook his head, and water droplets pocked the mirror.

The memory of the two men crashing into the bathroom came flying back, banging into the metal doors of the bathroom stalls. Being bigger, stronger, the boyfriend quickly pushed Ely off, creating a space between the two of them. Shaking off the surprise attack, the guy was visibly angry. With his size he was, he was not the type to back away from a fight.

"What's your problem, man?" The boyfriend engaged with Ely.

"I'm tired of watching you abuse her," Ely replied.

The boyfriend stepped back, taken aback. "What do you know about us?" He cricked his neck and curled those gorilla paws for hands into fists. "I'm going to teach you to mind your own business!"

Ely wasn't intimidated. "I can't play witness anymore!"

"I know how to make sure it never happens again," Ely said with a contorted rage, as his head twisted to the side and stared past the Boyfriend.

The two men circled each other.

The boyfriend pointed at Ely to give him a warning. "You've picked the wrong guy on the wrong night!"

"And you picked the wrong girl," Ely, but not Ely, snarled as he charged at the behemoth before him.

"You don't even know her!" The boyfriend grunted as the sudden attack caught him off guard, and off balance as Ely drove him into the side of the stalls.

"I know her," Ely retorted with fists hammering into the boyfriend's mid-section. "I know her...I know her!"

The sudden rage caused the boyfriend to slip back against the stalls, sliding down into a weakened position. But he was bigger, and stronger, and thicker than Ely. Even amongst the punches that were drilling into him, the boyfriend found his feet and arose to tower over Ely.

Ely continued to strike in a blind fury, repeating himself in rhythm with his punches. "I know her. I know her. I know her."

Ely was unaware as he was tackled by his boyfriend and kept beating his fists down in a blind fury, even as he was lifted off his feet and carried across the bathroom to be stunningly slammed into the rectangular mirrors above the two-sink facility. The mirror cracked in splinters, radiating from Ely's back impact. He slid down, bounced off the countertop sink, and thudded to the tile floor.

The Boyfriend drove his right foot into Ely's midsection in conjunction with yelling, "enough!"

Eyes wide open made it evident that Ely was not registering the pain. His hand slid out and grabbed a piece of the broken mirror that had fallen off with the impact. A nice little reflective shiv.

Believing he had put an end to this little charade, the boyfriend turned toward the bathroom door. Hearing movement from behind he turned and fell back against the wall, his arm stretched out and hand splayed in a defensive motion as Ely the little shit was there on his feet again attacking with a blade of glass.

Blood ran from Ely's hand as he gripped the blade and sliced back and forth, only catching air. The boyfriend had heard him, spun, and moved just out of range. Ely would have connected with an exposed throat as he whispered to nothing. "It never happens again."

Pressing in close, he chanted with his next strike, "Never again."

Luckily, for the boyfriend, Ely seemed to have horrible aim and missed a second time. He didn't want to risk a third and was about to scream for help or jump Ely when the bathroom door flew open. Ely's friend and the girlfriend raced in to see what the commotion was.

She was sick in the gut, having to stop her bully of a boyfriend from beating someone up for any senseless reason. This wouldn't have been the first time. Reasoning didn't come into play when he had done it to her.

In the present, Ely stared into the bathroom mirror at the stranger's reflection before putting his head down.

With his arms braced against the side of the sink, Ely slowly raised his head to look once more at the questioning reflection. "I did not know that woman."

"I've always been impulsive," he thought to his mirrored self, as if talking to another person telepathically. "A little too reactive."

He leaned in close to inspect and try to recognize himself. "It has gotten me into a lot of trouble over the years." He stared down at his hands. The one who had held the glass shard had a cut. "But last night, I was out of control."

Ely turned to pat his hands dry with the towel. The cut stung and throbbed with the slightest movement. "I wanted to kill that guy. I could have killed him. But the urge to do so, the rage, it was not my own. It was like I was being driven."

Moving out of the bathroom, on the floor before him was a duffel bag. It caught him by surprise. In that moment, he knew it was not the first time something like last night had happened. Ely looked at his cut hand again, then the duffel bag. He was garnering too much evidence to validate his crazy.

Grabbing the bag, he plopped onto the bed and pulled the zipper open to reveal that the duffel was filled with cash. Sometimes he was attacking abusers in a pub, other times he was blacking out and waking up in a strange place *(he never understood why he blacked-out)*.

A memory flashed in his mind's eye. He found himself standing in an alleyway, outside of an apartment complex. The building was older and run-down. Other residential buildings lined the narrow roadway that was littered with garbage dumpsters that seemed overflowing or unable to contain any refuse as garbage decorated the avenue. A young teenager was cradled in his arms. His right felt heavier and as he looked down the duffel bag dangled by its straps from his forearm.

The sound of sirens jolted Ely back. He moved to the motel room's window, peeking through the drape but saw no police or emergency vehicles. Realizing the sirens were from a flashback he couldn't recall, fear gripped him. More than fear, it terrified him that he was remembering something unknown. It felt like fleeting images from someone else's dream. Ely zipped up the duffel bag, recalling the events. These weren't just vivid dreams. He stood by the door, hand on the doorknob, hesitating. Should he go to the cops? He had no idea what he might have done. After last night, they were probably looking for him.

CHAPTER TWO

The small tourist town lay nestled amongst a wooded backdrop, and distant mountains offered a picturesque view of the horizon. In the winter, the town was overcrowded with skiers staying at the resorts. In the summer, it was overrun again by visitors coming to experience the awe-inspiring scenery of towering rocks, and maybe to see a bear or moose or two, while hopefully respecting the posted rules of "Do not feed the wildlife."

Right now, winter had melted away except for the snow caps still visible in the mountain range, and the evidence of such proved it wasn't quite summer, but the greening of the grass and vibrancy of trees showed it was not that far off.

As Sera commandeered her Jeep Grand Cherokee onto the main avenue, she was grateful there was no traffic, only locals.

It wasn't that she was a total recluse; she just got involved with her work, and being an author meant she only had to live in her head most of the time and deal with her publisher. Okay, she was a little recluse. She had a place in the city, but having lost her baby several years ago, she had pretty much made her cabin her permanent residence. It was the best way she could avoid having to be close to the baby room that she could never bear to touch, pack up, or erase the existence of her daughter. There were fewer memories here, which she used as an excuse. Truthfully, she felt more unreachable in her secluded cabin. People rarely dropped by, allowing her to ignore emails on bad days and turn off her phone when her loss made her want silence.

The main avenue was lined with hotels, restaurants, and stores catering to tourists. Sera turned right and drove down the next lane several blocks to the only grocery store in town. It was early, and there were not many cars in the parking lot. She selected a parking space and realized she did not know the store hours, hoping she had not arrived too early.

Out of her car, Sera's ice blue eyes glinted in the morning sun, and a slight breeze teased her medium-length, brown hair that cascaded just past her shoulders like a waterfall. Hitting the remote button lock on her key fob, she made her way towards the store entrance. A couple of people were exiting through the automatic doors as Sera approached. She had not arrived before opening hours, which was a relief.

Many locals lived within walking distance of the grocery store, so she should not have been surprised to see so few cars. It was a strange occurrence for her to be here at the beginning of the day. Nighttime was her active hours when she did her errands. During the day, she kept herself busy with work and household stuff. The quiet of the night left her with thoughts and growing sorrow, so she would either invest herself in work to keep her mind occupied or run errands. Recently, sleep was elusive. Her daughter's birthday was a few days away, which always made the thoughts of what could have been more prevalent and painful. Lack of sleep was having its effects.

Sera grabbed a basket. This was a quick stop for a few emergency items.

The line of five checkout lanes was just to the left. Only the first one was being commandeered.

The woman occupying it with the morning shift was obviously excited to see Sera as she waved to her enthusiastically. Maybe she was that excited to see everyone, acting as a store greeter from the first line of tills.

"Hey! Good morning!" The cashier said in accompaniment with her wave.

"Hey, yourself," Sera replied with less energy as she fitted the basket handles over her forearm.

The cashier was a woman of similar age to Sera, named Stacey. They were acquaintances, barely, considering Sera's social circle (basically non-existent social circle), but Sera had not seen her in ages, probably on account of Stacey having a morning shift, and Sera's nighttime preferences.

Sera moved closer to the cash register, making room for another customer who was just preparing to exit with a grocery cart full of bags. Stacey finished thanking the customer and wishing them an obligatory nice day before leaning back against the cash register and turning her focus to Sera.

"It has been a while, and that is all you can muster for your good morning. Somebody is not sounding too chipper!" Stacey commented in jest.

Stacey was harmless, and her sunrise exuberance was infectious to most. Not to bullet-proof in Sera's mind, you, but to most. And whereas Sera had a squarer face that held an aura of royalty, Stacey was at least half a foot shorter with a softer, oval shaped face embraced by black hair and striking emerald eyes accompanied by the cutest button nose that always made Sera wonder if it twitched as a mouse's would when she caught a whiff of cheese.

Sera lifted her basket. "Coffee and wine! That is all I need and all I am concerned with." She managed a smile. "Then I am covered off for breakfast and dinner."

An older man walked through the store doors, and Stacey waved her morning greeting before turning back to Sera. "The two most important meals of the day. So that's how you stay so svelte?"

"Fancy words," Sera joked.

"You should know, Miss Author Lady! Going that well, is it?" Stacey replied.

Sera leaned forward to half-whisper. "I think I got myself trapped on this project. I can't see the forest for the trees."

"So, you decided to come out of the forest," Stacey smiled quizzically.

A mother with her toddler sitting in the cart arrived at the top of the checkout lane and began unloading her groceries. A pang hit Sera at seeing the little girl, but she did not show it. She had become an expert at hiding emotions.

To make way for the customer, Sera backed away, holding her basket out to accentuate her announcement. "Yes, I did. Provisions were required! And your banter!"

Stacey paused, sliding the first of the groceries over the scanner to lean over the register and half yell in retort. "Banters free. Bags are five cents."

She resumed her duties of directing her attention to the mom and had an apologetic look on her face, with a little embarrassment for suddenly being so loud as she said. "Sorry!" And resumed scanning products.

***

Nervous of his surroundings, Ely slipped out of his motel room, wary of anyone around him who might take notice. The duffel bag was his only luggage. He wished he had a change of clothes, but he would have to return to his apartment for that, and he was worried that it was a bad decision. If the police were looking for him after the event of last night, he should stay away from home base for a while.

Moving down the street past a line of shops, he pulled his hoodie up to further conceal himself, just in time as a police cruiser came down the lane. Ely turned to window shop to avoid any glares from the officer's passing by.

They didn't stop.

Ely let out a long-held breath of relief. Maybe he was not on a most wanted list, yet!

He kept moving down the street like a drifting vagabond with no distinct purpose, no predetermined destination. He needed to move. It was all he could do to try to tame his increasing anxiety. The impulsiveness and situations he got himself into, almost in blacked-out states of mind, surfaced. He never had many friends. After the bar episode, he was pretty sure morphing or elevating that acquaintance to a friendship level was not going to pan out. Who could blame the guy who needs the stress of hanging out with someone so impulsive and, in the case of last night, explosive?

A young mom was drawing close with her two small children in tow. She held the younger boy's hand to keep him close and paid no heed to Ely as she passed. The mom was more concerned with calling back over her shoulder to have the lagging girl catch up. She must have been five or six years old and burst into a short sprint at the mother's stern warning.

The young girl ran by Ely, just as he thought, his impulsive moments were not endangering. Sometimes it was also a case of being in the right place at the right time. Either way, those moments were becoming more frequent.

The girl had passed him. She was out of eye line, but Ely was suddenly spinning on his heels and reaching out. He caught the back of the girl's coat, tripping, just catching her before she fell all the way forward. She would have been hurt with a face-first landing on the concrete sidewalk.

The mom spun at the short yelp from the girl, and came to her daughter's side, thanking Ely for the quick save.

He was on one knee to ensure the girl was okay, that he had not pulled too hard and inadvertently hurt her. She was okay. The mom was astounded at Ely's reflexes. He didn't let his expression show, but he was a bit surprised that he made that catch. And not necessarily in a good way. He felt like he was losing control of himself or just losing himself completely. Looking at the young girl, a strange reflection in her eyes made him think of his sister. They had not spoken for quite a while, but she was the one person who always accepted him as he was. She was the one person he could turn to, and he desperately needed to turn to someone.

***

Sera was on a mission. The pace she was moving could have landed her a spot on an Olympic speed walker team, but she did not care as she grabbed a couple of items to place in her carry basket. Coffee was the main goal, not a gold medal.

Finding the priority item, she grabbed a can of her preferred brand off the shelf and put it in her basket. Preoccupied with checking her basket against her mental list to ensure she was not forgetting anything, which was silly that she never wrote a list, grocery lists never fell in her line of accomplishments. And she never learned because she always inadvertently forgot something. She did not care what the "something" was today, just as long as it was not coffee. Too distracted with her basket when she rounded the end of the aisle at her race car pace, she drove right into an older gentleman.

The next thing she knew, she was on the ground with the contents of her basket scattering across the floor.

"I am so sorry," the old man said as he leaned in and offered his hand to help her up.

"It's okay," Sera smiled in embarrassment as she waved off his offer of assistance.

"No, no, let me help you," he offered again.

Sera shuffled around to start getting up. "It's okay. I can manage."

The old man pressed in closer, infringing on her space and ability to get to her feet, and she was sure a darkness washed over his demeanor. "Don't reject me now!"

For half a moment Sera froze, cocking an eyebrow at the old weirdo, before getting her wits back and more assertively replying, as she got up half waiving off her reaction and half waiving off the older guy's hand.

"Sorry, I'm good...I'm fine."

He was upright again, relaxed, and pleasant. "Okay, let me help you with your groceries then?"

They both began restocking Sera's basket. She side-eyed the man as he worked at helping her. Something strange had happened there, twinging at a memory. She had never met this man before, so she waved it off with a short chuckle.

He stopped in mid-motion, that demeanor again washing over him. "Are you laughing at me?"

This made her step back defensively. "No, of course not. I was just embarrassed at being knocked over and everything." She grabbed her basket and made to leave. "Thank you for helping me. Sorry for the fuss."

Checking over her shoulder as she turned down an aisle, the old man was still watching her.

Arriving at Stacey's checkout lane, Sera began emptying her basket.

Stacey looked up at Sera, happy to see her again. "Did you find everything okay?"

"Sure did," Sera replied. "Most importantly, coffee, and next is wine!"

Stacey began running things past the scanner. "Looks like there's enough junk food here that you'll be seeing the trees now. This helps you break through the wall of writer's block, does it?"

"Firstly, I don't think you are supposed to judge a customer's purchases, but yes, the wall I have hit is bigger than the Great Wall of China," Sera replied, waving her hand over some items. "That is what this stuff and the wine will be for."

The two women shared a laugh. The customer, before, had her back to them, bags in hand, and preparing to make her exit, she stopped abruptly unbeknownst to Sera and Stacey.

"You're a little early. Jerry's 'Wine and a Song' next door doesn't open until 10," Stacey advised Sera.

"Seriously? Kill me now!" Sera acted overly disappointed, and the pair shared a laugh again.

The other customer turned back to them, a little mad. "Are you laughing at me?"

Sera stopped laughing instantly, taken aback. This lady was acting similarly and saying the same thing as the old man, as she stammered a reply. "No, we were...it was just a personal, long-standing joke."

The lady resumed leaving.

Stacey made a face at Sera, hooking a thumb in the lady's direction. "Weird!"

"Right!" Sera replied, shoving the interaction off.

As she finished the transaction and prepared to pass the bags to Sera, Stacey suggested. "I can grab some wine later, save you the wait, and I'll bring it up?"

"That would be great. Are you sure it's not too far?" Sera asked.

"If I'm getting your cooking out of it? It's not too far," Stacey hinted broadly.

"I knew there would be a catch," Sera was about to laugh as she grabbed her stuff and made to leave, but thought better of it considering her last two interactions.

Outside, Sera went to the back of her car to store her groceries in the trunk, as she looked up from closing the tailgate, the lady that was before her at the lane was standing outside of her car, door open, but she looked frozen in place, and she was staring at Sera.

Weird, Sera thought to herself as she got in her car and started it. She didn't look over in the woman's direction again as she backed up and pulled away. She also ignored her rearview mirror for a while. If the lady was still watching her, Sera didn't want to know. The day had already maxed out its allotted quota of strange, and it wasn't even close to noon yet.

Back at her secluded little place in the woods, Sera got out of her car and began grabbing her groceries from the back. Staring up at the surrounding pines, Sera was grateful for this home away from home. Not so far off the beaten path, the forest area enclosing her made her feel secluded, but safe.

Generally, Sera felt safe. Sitting at her desk, staring at her computer screen for however long, nibbling at the cuticles of her fingers until they were red and raw, she had not accomplished anything on her manuscript, again, and the morning experiences she had with the grocery store strangers needled at her.

She was so lost in thought that she jumped out of her seat and elicited a little yelp when a phone rang from somewhere in the house. It was not her cell phone that sat beside her keyboard. It was the other one. The private one that she left plugged in and concealed within her nightstand drawer. The one that practically never rang. It was ringing now.

Out of her seat, she ran up the single flight of stairs and barged into her bedroom, hoping to be fast enough to answer the call before it went to voicemail.

"Hello?" Sera answered.

At a Greyhound bus station, Ely breathed a sigh of relief at the sound of his sister's voice. It was not common for her to pick up. Whenever he would call this number, she always had trouble locating the phone before it went to a messaging system, and he would have to wait for her to call back. This time she was on the ball. He wasn't in the mood for leaving a message and was half surprised to hear her as he prepared to cancel the call.

Ely looked around suspiciously at the bus station to ensure nobody was in earshot of his conversation. He rounded one of the travel buses to the opposite side of the passenger entrance and felt more comfortable that he was out of eyeline and earshot.

"Hey, it's me," Ely responded to the hello from the other end of the line.

"I had a feeling," Sera said as she made her way into the bedroom en-suite. Her bladder was notifying her it was time to make another type of call. "I mean, who else was it going to be? You are still the only one with this number."

Ely leaned against the side of the bus, smiling at the sound of his sister's voice. The comfort of her casualness. They spoke rarely, but it was always like no time had passed at all. She understood him and accepted his strangeness. "I need to see you."

"Bad?" That was a stupid question, Sera realized as she slid her pants from her waist and sat on the toilet seat. Ely never called at a good time.

"Pretty bad."

"I'm writing," Sera began, but that was a lie. She had spent several hours staring at a computer screen, thinking about writing. Okay, that was another lie; she wasn't thinking of it. She leaned forward with her elbows on her knees while holding the phone to her ear with one hand, she rubbed her head with the other, and released her bladder. The tension of the day, now Ely calling, her head felt clamped in a sudden vice grip. There was no sense directing the conversation to her lies about what she had not been doing. The reality is she had been obsessing. "Anyways, you know where I am. It's still off-season, so it's quiet. You stop at my place; you can get the other car."

Cradling the phone between her ear and shoulder, Sera wiped and pulled up her pants, collecting the phone in her grasp before it slipped. She stood up and flushed.

Hearing the strange noise in the background, Ely redirected the conversation. "Are you peeing right now?"

"No!" Sera said as she returned to her bedroom and flopped back onto her bed, legs dangling over the side. "I just finished."

"I'm sorry to be calling out of the blue like this," Ely said, looking side to side to ensure he was clear of any eavesdroppers.

"Don't apologize, it is how we roll," Sera said and sat up. Her tone changed to a more serious level. "Besides, your timing is impeccable as always. I've had weird stuff today."

Ely rounded the back of the bus to join the short line of people moving forward to enter the front doors. "Thanks, Sis, it sounds like we both have stories to share!"

The phone he carried was a pay-as-you-go, disposable model. Stepping out of line to a nearby garbage can, he twisted and snapped the phone so it would be unusable and buried it in the trash.

Inside the bus, it was only half populated, and it was easy to find a seat where he would be alone and could cozy up next to the window. He positioned the duffel bag on his lap and cradled it in his arms for security in case he dozed off.

Not paranoid, just cautious. That is what he told himself as the bus began to pull forward.

CHAPTER THREE

Night drew its blanket over the sleeping hours of daylight. The gibbous moon, free of any cloud interference, gave full illumination to cast long shadows from the large trees lining the property where Liz, the Olympic diver, as her father kept jesting, now fought off nightmares in her quest to find a decent night's sleep. Her blankets shifted and sheets twisted as she tossed and turned, her eyelids giving off the back-and-forth rhythm of REM sleep.

A Greyhound bus drove by. The headlights of the bus briefly captured the light of a figure hidden amongst the trees that watched the house in the distance where the girl slept.

Liz's eyes popped open. Every time she closed her eyes, she relived the moment at the bridge, diving from heights that terrified her, and now she was seeing a face in the water staring up at her just as she was breaching the surface.

Clutching her chest, she was panting as if gasping for air. Her lungs felt like they could burst. It was as if she had just reached the surface of those frigid waters again. Reminding herself that she was dry, almost, the sheets felt sweat soaked, Liz slowed her breathing to calm herself. These were only nightmares reliving her encounter. Exhaustion was redefining itself, and as she lay back down into the pillows, she was afraid she would go insane if she did not get some decent rest.

Outside, the hooded figure moved closer to the front of the house and stopped in the shadows along the side of the porch, standing frozen, waiting.

The figure moved along the front of the house along the concrete pathway that led around the left side to a gate leading into the backyard. There was a rustling sound of movement, followed by a deep bark of a dog. The intruder had been discovered, and its presence was being announced by the dog's alertness.

Liz had finally succumbed to sleep, and her exhaustion-induced slumber kept her from being disturbed by Barney's barking, the family dog.

The same could not be said for her father down the hall in the master bedroom. He was wrenched from his sleep, sitting up to regain his senses. To his right, his wife lay on her side facing him, and he could see by the light creeping through in slivers where the curtains didn't completely meet that her eyes were open.

"Damn dog!" Liz's Dad barked in frustration. This wasn't the first time the dog had woken him up in the middle of the night by barking at a bird, or squirrel, or nothing but the air itself.

"He is just doing his job," Mom commented as she reached out to pat her husband's arm.

Dad got out of bed and began putting on his robe. "I better see what's up."

Mom was half sitting, leaning back on her elbows. "Let him in, then. It's probably a deer or something."

"It better not be a skunk again," Dad chuffed as he stormed out of the room, rubbing sleep from his eyes.

The stranger reached through the hole in the fence, unlocked the gate, and slipped into the backyard. Closing it quickly but quietly, hoping for no rusted hinges, the stranger stood with its back to the closed gate, pressing into the shadow of the house eaves. The dog, no longer barking, inquisitive about who had entered its fenced domain, rounded the corner and stood at the path, huffing and staring. The stranger bent down, and the dog raised its hackles, a guttural growl of warning to be careful. The stranger held out a hand in offering, beckoning, and the dog padded closer. The other hand of the stranger was behind their back, holding a large knife, like a scorpion ready to sting. Once the dog was close enough, the stranger struck so quickly that the animal barely yelped.

Placing the bloodied knife onto the grass beside the walkway, the stranger lifted the limp head of the dead dog to gaze into its glassy, motionless eyes.

"Not the one," the stranger said, and laid the dog back down.

Liz's Dad trudged through the kitchen towards the back door. There was just enough moonlight to cast a glow of light through the large windows around the breakfast table. Aware of the room's surroundings, he didn't bother flicking on any light switches.

Barney was not barking anymore. It had probably been the squirrels again, or just the freaking air. Whatever it was, it had Barney make enough noise to wake him up. The dog was probably back asleep in its shelter, or causing a raucous so he would be let in.

Dad side-eyed the fridge. If he were up, he would steal a piece of the leftover cake hiding there. First, he would get Barney inside, then he would have cake. He would take sweet pleasure in having some revenge by not sharing it with the dog. There had to be some justice to being dragged out of bed...again.

He pushed open the screen door and held it open with one hand as he called out into the yard. "Barney! Barney, come on, boy!"

In the night, off to the side, standing flat against the house, was the stranger. The man of the household didn't bend forward to look for the dog or take one small step onto the porch, otherwise, he would have noticed the invader. But he didn't. Instead, Liz's Dad looked down in reaction to the explosion of pain in his gut as a knife plunged hilt deep into his stomach.

The Dad gasped as the blade was withdrawn, causing him to pitch forward. A soft 'thunk' sound punctuated the night as the knife was driven into his midsection again.

The knife was withdrawn a second time, and the Dad crumpled out the door onto the porch. The stranger was on him immediately, kneeling over him and driving the knife into the dad's neck.

As Liz's Dad bled out, the stranger leaned in close to his face and peeled the lids back from the left eye to stare into it.

"Not the one," the stranger whispered.

Liz's Mom was a deep sleeper. Sometimes, like tonight, she was aware of her husband getting up for whatever reason, the dog, an overactive bladder, an overactive gastrointestinal issue, or even an overactive imagination. On other nights, she was completely unaware. When her husband shared his reason for awakening, like tonight, she rolled over and was back in dreamland.

The stranger stood over her, watching her sleep and mimicking the pace of Liz's Mom's soft, slow breaths. Liz's Mom didn't awake as the knife slid across her throat, paring skin to release an arterial spray of blood to douse the covers, floor, and even the walls. As the last bits of blood gurgled out, the stranger used its thumb and index finger to pry open the left eye.

"Not the one," the stranger whispered.

Then, in frustration, the stranger stabbed the corpse violently several times.

With waning patience, the stranger moved briskly down the hall. A door on the left was open. Even in the dark, it was a bathroom and did not warrant investigation. The last door down the hall was pushed closed. The last possibility, the obvious destination, the stranger breathed deeply in anticipation.

Once she felt the presence beside the bed, Liz opened her eyes slowly. She reached over and clicked the bedside lamp on. Its yellow glow revealed the stranger.

"I knew you'd find me," Liz said. No fear or emotion was on the girl's face. The voice was of someone else hidden deep inside her. The other presence that drove her to save that girl. Liz, not Liz, repeated herself, with a little more spite this time. "I knew you'd find me."

"Then you should have stayed hidden!" The stranger replied.

The knife, bloodied by Liz's dog, Liz's dad, and Liz's mom, glinted in the lamplight. Now it was Liz at the surface. Now it was Liz realizing she was in danger, that something had happened to her family. Now it was Liz who screamed as the stranger drove the knife into her belly. All the screams that reverberated within the bedroom's walls were Liz's as the stranger stabbed her numerous times. It was Liz who screamed for her parents. She cried out several times for help until the blood choked her throat and gurgled from her mouth.

The stranger had found what it was looking for. A poor teenage girl and her family were the ones who suffered the repercussions of that discovery.

CHAPTER FOUR

"Are you laughing at me?"

Sera startled awake with those words reverberating in her head, echoing from the dreamscape she was just yanked from.

She must have dozed off at her desk. She leaned back to stretch out the kinks in her body.

"Are you laughing at me?"

Not a question. Just an angry statement, loud in her mind, sparking memories.

Another day, another morning, trying to keep up with his sister. It wasn't just because she was in her final year of high school and Ely was in the tenth grade, they were practically the same height. It was the fact that Sera couldn't go anywhere slowly. She just naturally speed walked. With her, it was never about the journey; it was about reaching the destination. Keeping up with her was one thing, but doing it against the swell of morning students filling the school halls was another.

Ely reached his locker, no longer needing to keep chasing, no longer feeling like a salmon swimming upstream, he called out. "Have a good one, sis!"

Her head snapped back over her shoulder to give him a wicked look. Once Sera entered the High School doors, she seemed to hate any public reference to being related, so Ely took every moment possible to irritate her with a public display.

"And don't leave me waiting at the car again," she shouted, obviously annoyed with him.

"That wasn't my fault yesterday," Ely shouted back, grinning ear to ear. He could see her slight smirk behind the evil stare she was attempting to throw. She wasn't mad at him. She never was or never had been, not even when they were little.

"Never is. Don't be late!" She waved him off.

Ely watched his big sister for a moment. Watched her disappear into the wave of students. He couldn't help smiling at their exchange. God, he loved her. As teenage brother and sister, they were supposed to be that cliché of hating each other and be at constant war. That cliché of Sera being a senior in school and pretending he didn't exist so her younger brother wouldn't ruin her reputation. Ely was supposed to hate her for getting everything first, being able to do everything first. They were not that cliché. They were best friends. A bond tethered from their life together that had these two siblings impervious to any stereotypical relationship.

There were only a few more moments before the bell rang and the mass of students filling the hall began to separate and head to their designated classrooms. Sera leaned back against her locker, laughing with her two friends. She had her books and required items in hand, prepared for the bell, but soaking up every minute to socialize. Her two friends were Marla and Misty. She referred to them as the M & M's, obviously because of the letter their names started with, but coincidentally enough, the two of them were addicted to the candy. Marla was the worst. Everything she had was an M&M licensed product, from her pens, pencil case, laptop *cover, and backpack. At their age, it would appear a little immature, but Marla pulled it off.*

Back against the locker, flanked by the M & M's, Sera had the bird's eye view of the students passing by. Her peripheral vision picked up on one student, and her laughter slowly faded.

Tommy, the school loner. The freak. The one that was ostracized. Not because anyone bullied him or picked on him, maybe in his earlier years, that may have happened, now most were a little afraid of him. He moved like a shark through the sea of morning students, predation in his eyes.

Trying not to look but keeping him in sight, Sera's eye accidentally locked on his. She quickly disengaged and returned her focus to the M&M's, reigniting her laughter, overcompensating a little.

He was there, pushing through Marla and Misty, into Sera's face as he yelled. "ARE YOU LAUGHING AT ME?"

Sitting there, Sera shook her head. She could almost smell Tommy's breath bursting into her face in that moment, so long ago.

Just as she saw the anger in the old man's face at the grocery store. And the spite on the woman's face at the checkout lane.

Sera bent down, grabbed the small trash can under her desk, and threw up into it.

Sitting up, wiping her mouth with the back of her hand, her breath felt rapid and out of control. She wasn't laughing.

<u>CHAPTER FIVE</u>

Lost, pulled, or just an insomniac, Ely often found himself wandering the streets. Finishing a shift at the restaurant he worked at, following the hustle and bustle of the kitchen after a busy weekend night, the walk late at night was a decompression. Quiet streets to stretch his legs compared to fighting traffic, where the roads always seemed busy with cars, no matter the time of day. So, he walked, and often wandered.

He turned abruptly and walked back down the block he had just traversed; almost unaware he was doing so until he caught himself. He must have been more preoccupied than he realized as he redirected himself. It was probably best to go home if he was so tired; he was automatically retracing steps.

Three apartment complexes filled the street he walked in, and Ely startled himself to realize he was on the wrong end again. He stopped and found himself staring at the complex in front of him. The one he had passed three times now in repetition. This was not a street he had walked before. This was not a building he had visited before. He had no friends or relatives here. Giving his head a shake, he moved on. He walked, watching his feet a few steps, one foot in front of the other, looked up, and in front of him was the same building. He had walked in a small circle.

Somehow, he had transitioned inside and stood in front of an apartment door on the first level. There was a dank smell filling the hallway to accentuate the dirty walls and stained carpeted flooring that was almost bare in parts from overuse. It was a complex to house those who ended up here. It was hard to imagine picking this piece of paradise of their own free will.

Ely rapped the back of his hand against the door before him. Free will? He wasn't even sure why he chose to be here in this moment.

The door opened slightly. The interior chain lock restricts its distance. Filling the small space beyond an angry face of a young man peered through. "I think you got the wrong address, buddy?"

There was no verbal response or hesitation from Ely. He kicked at the door hard, jarring the doorman beyond. It was enough to remove the weight when Ely threw his own against the door. The chain lock pulled from its mooring, and the door snapped into the doorman, sending him flying off his feet.

Inside now, standing over an unconscious doorman, what must have been a crash pad for druggies lay before Ely. Liquor bottles were strewn about. The sweet smell of smoke, with a flavor twist of puke and sweat had invaded his nostrils. One guy was spread-eagled eagle passed out on a recliner. The rubber band around his bicep added to the obviousness of his drug of choice, as a couple of needles were on the floor by his feet. To the side, the kitchen table was laden with other types of groceries, full ashtrays, bongs, and a woman. It was hard to tell her age as her head was buried in her arms, down on the table. Hopefully, just stoned out of her mind and still breathing, and she had difficulty discerning from where he stood. Plus, it was not a concern at the moment.

The concern was that the two men who were sitting before Ely were playing some sort of video game on the 80" flatscreen TV before them. At the sound of his break-in, they had dropped their controls and jumped up to face the intruder.

Only the couch acted as a barrier between Ely and the two. One of them was a smaller, lean guy who was shirtless and ripped with muscle veins that popped out of everywhere. His hair was greased back to better show that his eyes were dark with hate.

The second guy was worse.

A behemoth with meaty hands that looked like they could crush coconuts in those bare fists. Those fists that were curling and uncurling in anticipation of treating Ely's head like a watermelon.

"What the…?" The wiry one had jumped up in surprise at the intrusion. He quickly pulled a gun from the back of his pants and pointed it in Ely's direction. "Don't move, man!"

Ignoring the demand, Ely was already closing the distance between himself and the men.

"Oh, you picked the wrong day, dog!" The behemoth was traversing the couch barrier in pursuit of Ely.

Evading, Ely moved with swift motion, in the opposite direction, and rounded the kitchen table. The woman passed out against it, didn't even flinch at the commotion. In a flickering thought, Ely wondered if she was even still alive or had overdosed right there and nobody knew she had passed into oblivion. Not even the two losers sitting a couple of feet away from her. They were wrapped up in the video game they were playing to notice or care.

He only hoped that was not the case with his brother. That was the quick thought that snapped him because he did not have a brother.

A duffel bag was on the table. As Ely rounded the table, he grabbed it.

The wiry guy tracked Ely with the end of his gun, popped off a shot that shattered a bottle on the table. "I said, don't move!"

Ely kept moving. He quickly closed the distance, staring down the end of that pistol trained on him, swung the duffel bag to knock the aim away.

"Ugh!" The wiry guy was surprised as his shot went off wild.

Keeping the momentum, Ely swung the duffel bag around again. It was heavy and felt like a sledgehammer. He swung in a full arc, catching the wiry one full on in the face and chest, sending the guy flying back into the large TV and shelving unit amongst a shattering cascade of fractured glass, sparks, and video game cases.

"Son of a b…" The Behemoth was yelling.

Ely wheeled, steadying himself for the oncoming onslaught of those enormous mittens that sat at the end of repulsively large arms. But the Behemoth wasn't moving. The wild shot of the gun had caught him in the chest. The Behemoth was staring at himself in disbelief, mesmerized by the petals of blood blooming on his chest and the red covering those hands.

"Son of a Bitch!" Rage filled the Behemoth's face as he moved forward at Ely. One step. Two steps. And the Behemoth fell, tumbling over the couch to land at Ely's feet. A tough bastard, as he grabbed for Ely's leg, he gurgled out one more. "Son of a Bitch."

Ely moved deeper into the apartment, down the hall, and into the first bedroom. Another woman lay there, naked, half hanging off the bed in a deep, drug-induced sleep. He got close, crouched before her, and opened one eye.

"Not the one," Ely muttered in a barely audible whisper.

On the other side of the hallway was a second bedroom. He flicked on the light inside the door to reveal the room's emptiness.

Heavy breaths escaped his lips. Anxiousness? Anticipation? Fear?

Desperation. It was desperation. A desperation that was exhaled when he entered the bathroom.

In its depths, a young, black teenager was unconscious in the empty bathtub. Still fully clothed, but saliva ran out of his mouth. On the floor beside the tub was a spilled bottle of vodka and a needle.

"I've got you, little brother." Ely was at the boy's side, hefting the limp body up and into his arms. "You are not dying either. I promised to watch over you."

Moving to leave the bathroom and escape with the teenager in his arms, Ely caught his reflection in the bathroom mirror. It was not his reflection that stared back.

The moments after were gone. Ely found himself in the alleyway behind the apartment building. The young boy was still unconscious and cradled in his arms. The duffle bag was dangling off the crook of the inside of his right elbow. In the distance, police sirens could be heard as they converged at the front of the building.

Ely suddenly woke up. It was a dream. A very vivid dream. But there was too much clarity of detail, and as he saw that mirrored face, he realized it was a memory. He glared out the window of the bus and the world passing by.

It wasn't a dream.

He stared down at the duffel bag in his lap. The duffel bag stuffed with cash that he had been using to get by for the past few months. He twisted the handles in his hands.

Not a dream.

I saved that boy.

And stole a bag of money.

I saved that boy. I didn't even know him. I don't know how or why I did it. I don't know how I would have known he was in trouble, or why I didn't do anything for the other overdosed people.

The bus came to a stop, and other passengers began to get out of their seats to prepare to disembark. Ely sat there staring into his faint reflection in the window. He didn't know that boy; he had a vague memory of him being his brother. Ely thought to himself, not mine, someone else's brother, but it felt like his in those moments. Why the heck would I be having other people's memories?

The one thing he knew for sure was that it freaked him the hell out. And he prayed he was not having some psychotic break.

The taxi pulled to the side of the street, and Ely exited after paying the driver in cash he had discreetly secreted from the duffel bag. The cab pulled away, and Ely started up the walk at Sera's house. He could not determine how long since he had been here. At least he knew how he got here. And why was he here? No psychotic breaks this time. He also hoped the key was hidden where he remembered it to be. Assuming things had not changed. He had forgotten to ask Sera. If it wasn't where it was supposed to be, he may have pre-emptively thrown away the disposable phone he tossed before getting on the bus.

The flower bed lining the space under the living room window and the front sidewalk that led around to the side of the house once held an array of seasonal flowers meant to accentuate the large bay living room window just above. But the garden had not been manicured for a while and weeds had quickly invaded to show a lush green instead. The weeds did a better job of concealing the fake garden rock that Ely was looking for to retrieve the spare house key. It was still there.

Closing the door behind himself, a chill ran through Elys' body. It felt cold in here. He kicked off his shoes and headed towards the kitchen, where the car keys were. According to Sera's instructions, that's where they were supposed to be kept.

He didn't take a direct line down the hall to the kitchen. Instead, he found himself wandering into the living room. The sparsely furnished living room. The fireplace mantle did not hold any family photos, as most houses would, just a single vase. Ely ran his fingers along the mantle's base to draw a line in the dust. Sera was a single woman, so she didn't need much, but not only did the house feel cold, the room looked cold, desolate, and abandoned. The dust proved she had not been here for quite a while. Sera was spending most of her time at her cabin. And he couldn't blame her really for not wanting to be here.

Especially because of losing her daughter. Ely had moved deeper into the house and leaned against the doorframe, looking into a child's room. Inside the room were a crib, a changing table, a white dresser, and a rocking chair. It had been around five years since she lost her baby girl. The most precious thing in Sera's life was gone in a moment. It wasn't a cold emptiness that filled this house; it was a sorrow. A deep sadness of the loss, all the dreams for the future, the anticipation of first words, first steps, and the utter joy. He stepped inside the room and stood beside the empty crib. Now that he was standing there in the silent emptiness, he felt like a selfish jerk, only calling when he was in need, while his sister carried this loss, shouldering it on her own.

The room was painted in a light pink with a wallpaper border of circus images dominated by cute elephants. Ely smiled a little, grateful for the lack of clown images. As happy or juvenile an image of them could be, there was always a sinister sense about them. Even if the wallpaper border contained images of evil clowns, there would be no sinister feeling in here, he thought, as he looked down into the crib and a warmth spread over him.

Ely put his hands on the crib rail, closed his eyes, and took it in.

His eyes popped open as a sharp pain stabbed into his head. Suddenly, an inflicting headache, like the ones that pierce behind your eye in a migraine attack. But Ely wasn't prone to headaches and never mind migraines. This pain wasn't in his head. It was in his mind. He grabbed the sides of his head and let out a silent scream, mouth agape but no sound, as he dropped to his knees in blinding agony that dragged him down.

He lay beside the crib, eyes open wide, tears on his cheeks, staring off into something somewhere. He wasn't seeing cute little circus bears anymore.

CHAPTER SIX

The sun's setting rays speared through the tall pines outlining Sera's property. She referred to it as a cabin because of the exterior's log façade. The interior hosted a decent sized kitchen with a large two-door refrigerator containing much more cubic volume than she would need. She did enjoy cooking and was quite skilled in the culinary arts, but being one, the need for large-scale meals wasn't often necessary. And she rarely (never) hosted any large gatherings. Sera was in the kitchen now, leaning back against the counter with a glass of wine cradled in her hand that threatened to spill in her inattentive crossed arms. She was lost in thought, staring at the floor. Usually, she took joy out of this part of her home away from home (more her real home nowadays).

The main floor, which mostly hosted the modern kitchen, was open to the living room. The outside wall consisted of large windows giving bright views to the forest outside, and at night, an expanse of stars only visible here in the country, secluded from city lights. Sera sipped her wine and gazed at the living room windows. The sun was setting and filtering its glow through to accentuate the dust that floated like gravity-free snowflakes of miniature size. She half-smiled at the smudge on one of the windows that she refused to clean.

One night, curled up in the chair, reading against the single lamp over her shoulder, a deer had roamed close, pressing its cute little nose against the window to peer in. It had stood there awhile, gazing inside, eyes locked with hers until something outside startled it and the deer disappeared back into the darkness and supposed safety of the trees.

To Sera's left, a pot lid rattled to announce the contents within had started to boil. She swiveled slightly and switched off the burner. Her appetite was waning. Her thirst was not as much as she gulped instead of sipping from her glass. It had been one of those days.

Refilling her glass from the bottle to her side, Sera stared up at the ceiling, lost in thought. She was distracted, uneasy; it had not just been "one of those days." It had been a strange day. One of those days, something needling at the base of your skull, you can't put your finger on it, but begging for release, for understanding, just a vague shadow memory of ghosted familiarity. She took a long sip, another day of not getting any work done again.

She went to fill her glass again, but the bottle had already been emptied. Dropping it in the recycling bin under her sink, she was sure she could not count polishing off a bottle of wine in record time as an accomplishment.

Light blared in through the living room windows. Headlights from outside cast an announcing glow.

"Damn, I've been so distracted I forgot about my guest," Sera muttered to herself. She was disappointed in herself for forgetting. A little annoyed because she was not in the mood for company.

Pulling the front door open, Sera was greeted by an all-smiles Stacey. "Hey, wine delivery as promised!" She had exited her car and was bouncing forward, holding up the brown bags of the provisions she had brought. Stacey was on the front porch in front of Sera. "Something smells great."

Holding her space and not making way to invite Stacey in, it was obvious Sera's expression was dulled. She was not matching Stacey's excitement.

Sera's body language was off, half leaning into the door frame to block the entrance. "Hey. I'm so sorry but I am feeling like crap. I'm going to have to rain-check."

"Oh no, really?" Stacey stopped, her exuberance deflating.

"Yeah. I'm sorry. I would have called before you drove up here, but I've just been out of it! It's been one of those days, you know," Sera apologized. "I've been so bothered and stressed out. I haven't gotten any work done, and it's all cumulated into a developing migraine."

A little pouty and pointing towards the bag containing the wine, Stacey replied. "Alright. I'm dying of hunger and ready to get my drink on, but I understand.

"I am really sorry, I am, and for the record, the guilt trip is working."

"Good," Stacey said. "I do those well, and it has benefited me a lot over the years."

Stacey backed down the front steps and turned towards her car, waving over her shoulder. "And I'm keeping the wine. And I'm holding you to the rain-check!"

"Counting on it. Drive safely," Sera waved goodbye and closed the door behind her and retreated into the house.

Back in the kitchen, Sera went to the fridge to find another means of refilling her glass as an incentive to discern why she was feeling so off today and what was nagging at her so much. The headlights from Stacey's car cast their eerie glow into the living room again. Sera felt like a total douche for sending her off like that but the thought of entertaining just felt exhausting. That was the problem, she just felt exhausted. The wine wasn't helping. Maybe a good book would, if she couldn't get any writing done, perhaps reading could calm her mind.

She looked up, and the glow from Stacey's headlights was still invasive to Sera's sanctuary. It was weird she had not left yet. Maybe she was upset and plotting her revenge in the car.

But in all seriousness, she was taking her time leaving. Sera went to the living room window and peeked through the curtain. The headlights were blinding against the dark of night outside, making it impossible to see into the interior. Sera watched for a moment. This was too long. Something felt wrong.

Deciding she needed to go outside to check on Stacey, Sera stood on the front porch and called out. "Stacey?"

Of course, Stacey wouldn't hear her from inside the car. Stepping off the porch, Sera paused, the hairs on the nape of her neck tingling. She barely gave it any recognition, assuming it was the chill of the night air.

When she arrived at the driver's side door, Sera half-leaned over to peer into the murkiness beyond and tapped on the glass. "Stacey?"

The interior was ghostly illuminated by the green hues of the dashboard lights. It was enough to reveal that Stacey was not inside.

Sera stood to look around and was startled as Stacey was suddenly beside her. Sera had not heard her approach or felt any presence, but Stacey stood outside by the rear driver's side door. Her head was down, her hair draped over her features, with a little hunch in the shoulders in an awkward stance. It was a strange pose that looked unnatural and felt malicious. Sera was fully aware of those hairs on the back of her neck this time that stood straight with an electric charge.

"My god, you scared the hell out of me!" Sera said, catching her momentary loss of breath at being surprised. "What's wrong? Why haven't you left?"

Feeling a strange unease, Sera started slowly backing up. "Say something!"

Keeping in step with Sera's, Stacey paused and crooked her head up with a weird twist of the neck. "You rejected me!"

Everything happened so fast then. Sera was slammed back onto the car hood as Stacey pounced into her.

"What the hell?" Sera yelled out. If asked in another moment, she would realize she wasn't sure if she was calling out over being physically assaulted or for hearing those three words rasp from Stacey's lips.

The two women wrestled against the car for a moment. Sera managed to break out from under Stacey and half roll-slide off the side of the hood. Finding her feet, Sera bolted around the front, back towards her house, the beams of the headlights having a strobe effect as each of the women's forms sliced through them. One was running in desperate fear. The other in hateful pursuit.

Sera had a slight gain and bounded up the few steps to the front door. As she breached the threshold of the doorway into the house, Sera didn't stop; a deep fear propelled her, and in a fluid, swift motion, she reached out and threw the door shut behind herself. There was a bang as Stacey crashed into the door, throwing it back against the wall in her pursuit. It made Sera fully aware that crazy Stacey was just a few steps behind her, hot on her tail.

Stacey slammed into her from behind, sending Sera flailing into the counter. The wind flew from her lips in a grunt as her midsection slammed into the counter edge. Before she could react, strong hands, stronger than what little Stacey should have been capable of, grabbed at her and spun Sera around to be face to face.

"You won't laugh at me again," Stacey snarled with a fist poised to strike.

That fist slammed into Sera's face once, then again, dazing her. Sera struggled to hold the woman off, but it was all happening so fast, as she still gasped to catch her breath, and now white sparks danced behind her eyes. And now Stacey's hands were around her neck, squeezing.

Sera pulled against Stacey's arms, trying to break the grip, and then, in desperation, flailed, reaching out for something, anything...

The stove. Fingers crawling, searching, they found the handle of a pan she had placed there, intending to cook something.

Sera swung with what energy she had left and caught Stacey in the side of her head, a nice clang as she clocked her enough that the grip around her neck loosened and the woman stepped back disoriented.

Sera took advantage of the moment and swung again with both hands on the pan handle as if it were a baseball bat, and this was the bottom of the ninth with bases loaded. Stacey flew back into the counter and crumpled to the floor.

Sera shifted the handle of the frying pan and appreciated it briefly while she stood over the moaning body of someone who was supposed to be a friend. A strange day where the fate of her intentions to cook had left her the opportunity to save herself. Stacey was trying to get up. Sera stepped over her and hefted the pan, readying to deliver a conscious rending blow.

It had been a day of total weirdness, capped off with a supposed friend going bat-shit crazy!

One of those days, you are not sure you will see the end of.

Stacey grabbed at Sera's leg, trying to pull herself up. Was she trying to pull Sera down? Did it matter? She was still attacking.

The kind of day when your world turns upside down.

Sera swung down.

But you fight because, in the end, there must be some sense to it.

Unconscious, Stacey was splayed out on the kitchen floor. Suddenly exhausted, Sera slid down against the cupboards in a sitting position at the end of Stacey's legs.

Sera pushed Stacey's right foot with a shove, making sure there was no reaction.

CHAPTER SEVEN

The next morning, Sera sat on the edge of the unused bed in the spare room she had left made up for guests, but it had ended up more of a storage facility. She had barely slept. Partially, her mind was racing after the strange events of last night, and partially because her body hurt from being knocked around during the strange events of last night. She adjusted herself with a slight grunt and stared down at the high school yearbook she had looted in her pillage of the room's closet in some hour of the night.

Back then, those high school years, her thoughts kept running back to you. She wasn't focused on being attacked by a supposed friend who went suddenly crazy over a cancelled dinner. No, that would be normal. Sera knew she was not currently normal. Had she ever? Her high school experience was average. It was the earlier years of her life that were crazy. She had let them go. Well, she always told herself she had let them go when those particular demons came out to haunt. But this was something else. And she was sure she knew what that something was coming back to haunt her. As secrets often did.

Even though Sera commandeered the family minivan like a pro as she entered their high school parking lot, dodging oblivious students cutting through the drive or other impatient drivers, Ely still drove her nuts with his side-seat driving. He had just gotten his licence a couple of months ago and knocked over the garbage cans by the front drive at home every single time he backed out, but he thought he was a professional and constantly shared his perceptions of her driving misdemeanors.

"Go, go, we are going to be late," Ely pestered his sister.

"I can't you moron kids are walking in front of us," Sera retorted as she pointed to the kids crossing the parking lot beyond the hood of the car.

"Fine, then I am getting out of here," Ely's patience had reached its limit as he opened the passenger side door to exit the car. "I can't be late again!"

"You stress too much," Sera yelled out to him as the door closed after him. She shook her head as Ely crossed in front of her and gave a hurried wave. He stressed too much. And he was getting worse lately. She was able to inch forward again and was startled as a school bus honked its determination to have the right of way. It was good that Ely had jumped out early. He was ranting about her not seeing the big yellow tank and following standard school parking lot etiquette.

At least she could park in peace now.

Amongst the streaming thrum of the packed hallways and sea of students, Sera stowed her belongings away in her locker and grabbed the required textbooks. Ely worried too much; the second bell had not even rung yet. Closing her locker, she spun to be greeted by Marla and Misty, her two besties. Misty could barely contain herself to tell Sera how she had bumped into Ely on the way in and that he was all worked up because she had ruffled his hair.

"Why do you bug him, Misty?" Sera laughed. Knowing full well how much Ely would not have enjoyed that.

"I can't help myself," Misty replied. "Your brother is just too adorable."

"Yeah, and even cuter when he gets all flustered," Marla chimed.

Wrapped up in her conversation with her friends, Sera was inattentive to the shark swimming through the streams of students.

Suddenly, he was pushing through Marla and Misty, and was right in Sera's face, forcing her back to press into her locker so she had nowhere to retreat.

"ARE YOU LAUGHING AT ME!" Tommy, the school loner-freak, was yelling at her. He was suddenly just there, in her face.

Marla and Misty were to the side in shocked disbelief. But Marla, being Marla, the one in their trio that never took shit from anyone and was always quick to react, was already on Tommy pushing him back. "Leave her alone, you freak!"

The wave of students stopped flowing at the sound of the commotion, and a crowd gathered to watch the outburst and take in the spectacle.

Tommy stepped back and raised both hands to give the finger to the trio of girls. "I'm sick of you laughing at me, bitches!"

Misty moved in and wrapped an arm around Sera, who was still shocked at the verbal attack coming from out of left field.

Marla stepped in front of her friends in a defensive position. It didn't matter if Tommy was twice her size; in an antagonist stance, she stood to defend against the crazy boy and replied with two middle fingers thrown in his direction. "Self-centered much, Freak? We weren't even talking about you, Mr. Invisible!"

"Okay, that was a little much for first thing in the morning," Sera said, exasperated with hands on knees as she watched Tommy storm away into the crowd.

"That guy is seriously obsessed with you," Misty comforted with a hand on Sera's back.

"Hardly obsessed. Pissed is more like it. Why me, though I have no clue," Sera straightened herself to shake things off before turning to Marla. "Thanks for the intervention, but was it a little harsh?"

"Harsh? What, me? That freak was in your face!" Marla said.

"You worry too much about others' feelings, Sera. Don't worry about Tommy's feelings, if he even has any," Misty chimed. "He's scary. He deserved it. Plus, nobody would be surprised if he showed up one day to shoot the school up. Guy has serious issues."

The student crowd had quickly dispersed once the theatrics were over, as getting to class on time now took precedence in their minds.

"His issues are something we can all agree on," Marla pulled her two friends into the hall so they could also make their way to first class. "But the more important issue of the day is whether Sera has decided if she is going to come to the river today or not?"

Sera slowed her feet and tilted her head back in exasperation. Marla was horrible at taking no for an answer. "My dad will kill me if I go. He made me promise not to hang out there."

"Promises! Promises!" Marla gave Sera's arm a little tug. "What to do with promises?"

"Then lie, you little angel," Misty said. "You are old enough to make your own decisions. Let cute little Ely have the car. Tell your dad we are hitting the mall, and he will be none the wiser."

Sera stopped in front of the girls' washroom and pointed at her two friends as she backed towards the door. "Pit stop. But I will think about it."

"Promise?" Marla was coy.

"That means she is coming," Misty said. "I'm telling Ely at lunch that he gets the car. Don't let him down now."

"No promises," Sera laughed as she held her crossed fingers. "And quit flirting with my little brother."

"No promises!" Misty laughed as she and Marla, the M&M duo, locked arms and continued down the hall, now sparse with students as classes began.

Having finished the reason for her "pit-stop," Sera stepped out of the stall she was occupying, only to be taken completely by surprise by the person sitting on the counter of the row of girls' washroom sinks.

"Hey," Tommy said with a wave at her.

Shaking off the surprise, hiding her slight concern, Sera moved towards a sink, washing her hands. "This is the girls' washroom, you know?"

Tommy jumped down from his perch and moved closer, looking at her, their reflections in the long mirror. "I needed to see you alone. I needed to say sorry for earlier."

"Staking me out in the washroom, maybe, isn't the best venue," Sera stated, finished rinsing her hands, and moved towards the dryer. "This whole thing this morning, we were not even laughing at you."

He was not giving her space and moved beside her to plead his case. "I don't know what came over me. Everyone hates me. They all treat me like I'm a pariah and act like I'm a freak."

Having dried her hands, Sera turned to him, not buying into this self-pitying apology. "That outburst at my locker, picking this venue to apologize, it doesn't help your case."

"It's just that we used to be close. We used to be friends," he reached out to her with his words and physically.

His hand was suddenly on her arm, fingers sliding down in a weirdly seductive manner that made her pull away. "We weren't that close. It was middle school, and we hung out in the same group of friends!"

He kept closing the space, pressing closer, not endearingly, but with a growing frustration. "You keep rejecting me."

"I don't even know what this is that you think I am rejecting," Sera replied, confused, and made her way to move past him towards the bathroom exit.

He blocked her. A boiling emotion of anger came over his face as he was almost begging now. "I just want to talk to you."

Inside, her nerves let loose a kaleidoscope of butterflies, as she felt a deep unease being alone with this guy. Externally, she was suddenly confident and released an assertiveness as she pushed by him. "You don't get someone's attention by freaking out in the middle of the school and embarrassing them. And then stalking them in the bathroom!"

"Then stop rejecting me!" He had caught her arm as she moved by, forcing her to turn to him. "Be my date at the dance next week?"

Frustrated and losing her patience, Sera yanked her arm back. "You need to stop this! I've told you before I'm not looking for a boyfriend, I'm not doing the dating thing, my only focus is my studies right now."

"Oh really? Like at the river where everyone studies?" Anger and desperation made Tommy shake with his words. But then, seeing the look in Sera's eyes, that look everyone gave him, diffused the heat inside of him. "I'm sorry. I'm sorry. Just say yes, please say yes."

Sera was at the bathroom door to make her escape, stopped, and turned back to Tommy. "I'm late for class. Quit bothering me. Quit bugging me. I'm sorry, but no! It will always be no. So just stop."

The door was pushed inwards, and a couple of girls entered the bathroom. They were surprised to see a boy in there, which provided the opportunity for Sera to slip out.

Ignoring the giggles and stares from the two girls. Tommy's attention did not waver from Sera. The piercing of her words flared that heated desire again, turning it into instant rage as he pushed one of the girls out of the *way and yelled at Sera as she disappeared into the hall. "You want it to stop? Then stop rejecting me!"*

He spun and slammed his arm up into the mirror, cracking it. The two girls pressed deeper into the bathroom, a little frightened, but more disgusted by witnessing the freak's temper tantrum.

The next morning, as the student body entered the school, they were shepherded into the gymnasium. As they trickled in and filled the bleachers, a low rumbling thunder echoed against the walls. It was an orchestra of shoes padding along the floor, the tinny beats of steps against the metal bleachers, and the collective wonder buzzing of what the heck was going on.

At the podium, stood the principal, looking more serious than he normally tried to portray. His eyes were cast downwards, not giving recognition to the entering students, but waiting for the cacophonic symphony to end. To each side of the principal sat a line of teachers. Some solemnly watched their wards enter, others whispered to each other.

When Sera found a seat with the M &M duo, she looked down at the line of teachers and could feel the mood wafting up towards them. Something was wrong this morning, something was very wrong here.

Sera redirected her gaze down the rows of bleachers. Ely was a few rows down from her, but just as she saw him, as if he felt her eyes drift over him, her brother turned and looked back up at her. Their eyes locked, and Sera shrugged her shoulders in sync with Ely. Neither of them had gleaned any snippet of rumour to silently share.

In her peripheral Sera noticed Misty waving down at Ely. Misty was an ostentatious flirt. And she could flirt with whomever she wished, just not Sera's little brother. Sera shot an elbow into Misty's side as a sharp reminder he was off limits. Misty returned the jab with a scowl. It wasn't an angry exchange, just one of the expressions to tell Sera that she was having no fun.

Ely was glaring at her also. Sera slowly shook her head at him as a reminder to keep his place in the high school jungle hierarchy. There was no way of entertaining any form of relationship between her friends and brother, even if it was only innocent flirting.

Misty jabbed her again and leaned in to whisper. "Quit being a poor sport. It's all in fun."

"Fun for you," Sera turned to her. "But it will break my little brother's heart."

"I'd enjoy breaking more than just his adorable little heart," Misty jested.

Sera didn't enjoy Misty joking about wanting her brother, and she was just about to shut her down with a bit more seriousness when the principal started to make an address.

"I apologize for shepherding you all here first thing in the morning, but we have some incredibly sad news."

The principal paused, squeezing the sides of the podium, not sure what response to anticipate from the students.

"I know you will handle what I have to say with the utmost maturity," he said, in the hope of tempering any of the jokers lying in wait in the bleachers. Every assembly they had, serious or fun, had a heckler or two *looking for attention and reactions. He continued. "We need to bring you together to let you all know at once that Tommy Durant is no longer with us."*

Rustling and murmurs ignited a low buzz that the principal quieted by raising his hand. He was going to have to hit it straight on to quell any disruptive rumors. "He was found last night at the bottom of Voyager's Bluff. I know this place is more commonly referred to as the sadly, but aptly named suicide bluff, and in this case, it appears to have earned that moniker because the authorities have deemed the loss of Tommy as a suicide."

That collective buzz came to life again. It was louder this time as the students processed the shocking news. The principal lowered his head as he thought he might be getting by a heckler free, but was sure he caught a 'Loser' tossed out in a male voice, followed by a 'Surprise' from someone else. The principal was fully aware that Tommy Durant was a bit of a loner and not the most popular in this school, but the insensitivity of teens was baffling to him. Maybe insensitivity was their coping mechanism in this world that was horrendously difficult to navigate. He hushed the crowd to carry on and finish what was required. "I know this is horrible, shocking news. Counsellors are available if anyone needs, or if anyone knows anything to help explain this tragic event. Any information might help bring comfort and closure to the family."

The assembly adjourned, and students emptied the gymnasium to erupt into the hall in a cacophony of the news they had just been told.

Pushing their way through the younger students, Sera and her two friends walked in a tight pod to whisper amongst themselves.

Marla leaned in close. "Well, at least he won't be stalking you anymore, Sera."

"Oh my god! Have some compassion," Sera was shocked at Marla's insensitivity and looked over her shoulder to ensure nobody was listening to their conversation.

Marla stepped out of their little pod to walk backwards in front of Sera and Misty, her arms out to accentuate her point. "I do have compassion for us. Now we won't have to be tortured by his presence anymore."

Misty jumped forward and grabbed Marla's arms. "Zip that stuff! If anyone overhears, they'll think we are responsible, or that we pushed him to it or something."

Sera kept walking. She was upset with Marla's carelessness. It was just yesterday that Sera had the confrontation with Tommy in the girls' washroom. And those two girls had walked in as witnesses. She felt too close to this and wanted to be as far away as possible to anything involving Tommy Durant. The truth was she was feeling relieved she wouldn't have to deal with him anymore. But that thought also twinged a bit of guilt in her stomach.

Arriving at her locker, Sera waved off Marla and Misty. They were still going on about the suicide and barely even noticed Sera peeling off.

Sera opened her locker. A folded piece of paper, resting on the top pile of her binders and textbooks. Hesitatingly, she reached down to pick it up and leaned in deep to her locker to investigate what it was. It was a folded note with her name outside, so it was not here by accident. She leaned out to ensure no prying eyes were close. Ascertaining she was safe; she unfolded the paper.

You will never laugh at me again!
You will never reject me again!
T

A shocked breath escaped Sera's lips. She looked over her shoulder, slightly panicked that someone would see what she was holding. Her breathing became rapid, and she had to bring a hand to her chest to try to calm herself. The faculty had just announced to the entire school that Tommy had killed himself. Sera looked around to verify she was alone, and no other student was in her immediate vicinity to notice her panic attack. A few were wandering the hall and were too engrossed in their gossiping conversations that they were not paying attention to Sera. She slowly crumpled the notice into her palm. Squeezing the letter into her fist so tight it hurt, her breathing was rapid, and she was finding it hard to think. She needed to get control of herself.

Tommy had always been a little obsessed with her. She closed her locker door, slid the crumpled note into her pocket to keep it close, to keep it with her, then leaned back and rapped her head back into the metal door in a light tapping of emotional concern, or mental fracturing, she wasn't sure. The only thing she was sure of was that if anyone found out about this note, then, just like her friends said, they would think that she pushed him to it.

Memorabilia she had retrieved from the closet surrounded Sera as she came back to the present, kneeling amongst the yearbook that had been her inception down memory lane, along with photo albums and a couple of small boxes containing trinkets of the past. A certain piece of paper was clutched in her right hand.

Finding that note on the morning of the announcement of Tommy's suicide had weighed her down with a lot of guilt, to carry, to work through. She had never told anyone what she had found in her locker, a parting gift from her deranged suitor.

Sera picked up the yearbook again and drifted her fingers over the embossed lettering of the cover. There was still half a school year left to commandeer and try to survive without the stigma of Tommy Durant's suicide casting its shadow over her. By the time Sera had realized she should tell someone, it was too late. Keeping the secret past the initial few moments made it metastasize, and she couldn't bring herself to do it. Instead, she tried to forget about it.

Blaming herself for Tommy Durant's death. Blaming herself for her daughter Anne's death, blame and guilt. Mountains of guilt pressed harder as she jogged through these memories of the past.

Sera shoved the albums and boxes out of her way as she stood up. All the self-blame and guilt were probably why she was still single (not even probably — just was, she was sure).

The paper crinkled in her hand. She should have thrown it out, burned it, been rid of it, but she never could. Sera had kept it all these years. Maybe in case she needed it as evidence. Maybe as a reminder of the kind of person she was for keeping this secret.

Staring at those words and thinking about how Stacey attacked her last night, Sera suddenly realized that she could never escape the past, and in her case, the past had truly come back to haunt her.

Old, crumpled note in hand, Sera bolted out of her bedroom and hurriedly descended the stairs to the main floor. It was a miracle she did not slip or trip and break her neck. She flew past the kitchen to stand before a door that led to the basement. Hand on the doorknob, she inhaled deeply.

Now it was time for calm, to be collected, to have her wits about her as she opened the door to enter the basement and face her past.

The wooden stairs creaked under her feet as Sera made her way down into the basement, one assured, determined step after another. It was an unfinished and dingy place that she only really used for her laundry. Otherwise, it was a storage facility for a few forgotten items, holding boxes and board games, decorated with an adornment of dust and cobwebs.

Off to the left was the one small, rectangular window that let in enough daylight to chase shadows away and highlight the washer and dryer pair. She generally didn't need to turn on a light if she was down here during daylight hours. A basket of dirty laundry sat upon the washer waiting for her attention.

But she was not here to attend to the laundry.

In the middle of the open room, tied to a chair, mouth covered with duct tape, eyes wide in horror, screaming a silent scream, sat Stacey, confined. Blood caked on the one side of her head where she had been struck by Sera the night before, Stacey was a mess of confusion, fear, and sweat.

In a few quick steps, Sera was at Stacey's side, yelling at her and shoving the old note into her face. "What is this? Who are you?"

CHAPTER EIGHT

The secondary, two-lane highway was bereft of vehicles except for Sera's Audi sedan Ely was currently driving. And he was grateful for that, as he checked the rear-view mirror for the hundredth time. Maybe it was because he knew if he got pulled over by a highway patrol officer, they would think he was strung out on drugs. Heck, he felt like he was strung out on drugs. Or maybe his neurotic rear-view obsession was to ensure the past stayed behind him, knocking him over in that house. He had been confined to it and was not currently barrelling down this lonely road.

He could not explain what happened in Sera's house. He just knew his head would not stop pounding, and he would feel more at ease once he reached his sister. He would feel safe. He could shake this haunted feeling.

Ely squeezed his eyes against the thrumming in his head. He had probably taken six Tylenol already, but the pain had not subsided. He reached over to the passenger's seat to retrieve the bottle of pills he had picked up earlier at a gas station. While trying to maintain his lane, he fidgeted with the child-proof cap that was not conducive to opening while driving, but once he was successful, he popped a few more into his mouth and chased them with the remaining half bottle of water that had been resting in his lap.

Tossing the empty bottle onto the passenger seat, he rubbed his temples with one hand, partially obscuring his vision. Attempting to persuade the headache into a manageable dull roar, he moved his hand to the back of his neck.

"Oh my God!" Rushed from his lips as his eyes popped wide open, his face contorted into fear-filled surprise.

Just ahead, too close ahead for the speed he was travelling, in the middle of the road, a male deer with a few female does and a couple of their fawns in accompaniment. Just standing there, the buck staring as the bullet of a car bore down on him.

Ely stomped on the brake, and the tires screeched with black rubber trails. With pursed lips and clenched jaw, he thought he might break the steering wheel. He gripped it so hard, pushed against it to brace for the impact as he cranked it hard to dodge the live-action obstacles filling his windshield view. The momentum forced his head to smash into the side window. There was a moment, a glimpse of his reflection, where he caught himself in the rear-view mirror as the car slid to the side, but it wasn't his face. It was a flash of a baby's face, caught with a parade of stars as his head smashed into the side window.

In a fraction of a second, Ely pressed his eyes closed to blink away the ghostly reflection. He applied the brakes hard and twisted the steering wheel. It wasn't his driving skills, but the animals seemed to move as if guided by an invisible hand, avoiding the car and preventing it from becoming a metal-screeching mess.

The car skidded to a stop at the side of the highway, and Ely watched the deer continue its harrowing escape into the treeline just beyond the grassed pasture lining the roadway.

Then he quickly turned, popped open the driver's door, and leaned out to exorcise the contents of his stomach onto the asphalt. Ely breathed heavily and wiped the side of his mouth while holding his position. He looked over his shoulder at the forest but saw no deer. He survived the encounter unscathed.

73

CHAPTER NINE

Weary, tired, and sore from being held in place in this stupid chair for lord knows how long, Stacey pulled back in defense as her vision blurred with the drape of the white paper in front of her when Sera shoved it right into her face, yelling. Breathing heavily from her nostrils, Stacey cried a muffled help.

Acting in a desperate rage, Sera grabbed the edge of the tape and roughly ripped it off.

"Ow! Are you crazy! What the hell!" Stacey shook her head against the sting.

A little crazed, a little desperate, Stacey held the paper note in her hands and smothered it against her face as if it would evoke some exorcistic reaction. "Tell me! Tell me! How do you know of this? Why were you repeating the words from this?"

Stacey threw her head back to get that damned paper out of her face. She was tired, and her throat was dry from a night of drought. Her lips stung, and her body was past aching and was now just numb.

"What are you doing?" Stacey managed to rasp. "I don't know what you are talking about. I've never seen this before!"

Sera stepped back, still displaying the note. "No, listen, last night you attacked me. You sounded like... You acted like this boy from high school."

Stacey tossed her head back and forth in confusion. "Are you crazy? This is insane. I never attacked you. I woke up tied to this chair in your god-damn basement!"

"Then how do you know these words?" Sera flailed exasperated. She paced back and forth in front of Stacey. She knew her memory. She knew those words. She knew she wasn't crazy, but whatever was happening was crazy. Insane. Sera needed answers.

"Then how do you know these words?" She softened, reaching for an explanation.

Stacey strained forward against her bonds in a desperate plea. "Sera, you need to let me go. I have no clue what you are talking about. Just let me go, and we can talk. We can figure this out."

Sera ignored what Stacey was saying. She couldn't hear anything besides the past rumbling in her head. Hands on knees, she bent forward to look deep into Stacey's eyes. Sera was calmer now, more sympathetic in her reach for some understanding.

"There was only ever one person who ever said those things to me. And you show up saying them?" Sera said, still searching Stacey's eyes. "Now you show up saying that. You attacked me, so I need to know, who are you?"

Stacey slumped back in her chair, feeling defeated by the wall of crazy she was confronting. She looked up from under her brow at Sera, desperate to make her understand she is innocent. "I didn't attack you. I'm the one being held captive here. I didn't do anything. You have been cooped up here in this lonely place, hiding from everything, and I think you're depressed or something. It's made you a little crazy. You are acting crazy."

"Crazy? Crazy?" Sera was spitting into Stacey's face with rage. "In my last year of high school, I got this suicide note. And several people have repeated the words on this note to me in the last couple of days."

"There are just words. It's just a coincidence. Please let me go," Stacey begged.

Sera grabbed Stacey's chin between her right hand's thumb and forefinger, squeezing her head tight to look right into her eyes as she delivered her stone-cold words. "I don't know if you are possessed or crazy yourself, but you are not going anywhere until I figure this out."

***

Not sure how he had ended up there, Ely found himself on the grass on the side of the highway. Running maybe a 10-meter-wide strip along the shoulder of the road, creating a buffer before the forest line, created a deep barrier of tall trees and foliage. He was on his back, staring at the blue, cloud-speckled sky, blinking away the sunlight and trying to regain his senses. The near-death experience of almost plowing into the herd of deer must have hit him hard. Lifting himself to be braced on his elbows, he looked to the right towards the treeline. There was no sign of any deer. His car was still there, so he had not wandered far, but he needed to discern how long he had been out of it. He had no clue what time it was, but his cellphone was in the car. Ely rolled over to get to his feet, but once he was on one knee, a stabbing sensation exploded in the side of his forehead. A piercing thrum that paraded light behind his eyes. Clenching the side of his head, squeezing his eyes shut, he fell over to the ground again. And a series of those recent strange memories flashed again through his mind like a flickering movie reel.

Still on hands and knees, feeling an intense confusion of identity crisis, Ely's attention shot forward to the treeline when he was disturbed by the light crackle of a snapping branch, and the crinkle of dried leaves on the forest floor. It was one of the deer. A doe, gingerly stepping towards him, slow and methodical as if the space between the doe and him was a minefield, she was navigating through memory.

Silent and beautiful, it stepped closer until it stood right in front of him. Ely was amazed but stayed frozen in place, not wanting to spook the animal. It all seemed weird, a little creepy even, after everything that had just happened to him, but he did not want to break the tranquility of the moment.

The doe stared at him a moment, the depth of those black eyes casting back a funhouse mirror reflection of Ely back to himself. Then one more step and the doe bent its head to rest it against Ely's. Warm breath cascading in waves over his face. And he could feel something in him stir. A notion of urgency and pulsing adrenaline. But the doe stood still, head against his, its breath quickening even though it was not retreating in fear.

But it was a fear that emanated. Not of Ely. Something dark. The doe stood strong, but now shivered. Not cold, terror, and Ely could feel that he needed to escape, to run.

On his hands and knees, he scuttled back a few paces, then got to his feet and hurried to his car. Opening the driver's door, he looked once more, and the doe was still there, resolute, watching.

In the car, Ely shifted into drive and pulled back onto the highway, accelerating steadily to escape the dread that had wafted over him. He squeezed the steering wheel and gave his head a shake. The memories, the deer, and as his eyes flitted to the rear-view mirror, the doe was still there, getting smaller as the car increased its distance. Ely kept checking, watching the unmoving doe until its reflection disappeared.

Reunited with her companions, the doe danced through the forest as the herd moved as one fluid entity, amongst the trees and over small logs, leaping over tiny creeks with seamless effort.

The buck in front cleared with ease, a large log, with powerful hind legs propelling it over. The others followed and, upon landing, were spurred to running faster in startlement. The doe quickened by being suddenly left behind, and it made her attempt to leap over the barricade. Coming over the other side, something from the shadows grabbed her. Panicked bleating escaped her mouth in warning to the others to keep running, as her eyes popped wide in response to a sudden pain.

On the forest floor, eyes glazed open, the doe inhaled a few final gasps of air as blood spewed from the wound on her throat.

A human figure bent down on one knee and looked into the lifeless eyes of the animal it had just killed. "You should have stayed hidden."

CHAPTER TEN

Sitting halfway up the basement stairs, elbows resting on knees with her head cupped in her hands to rest, to think, and to try to find some sense or clarity, Sera felt more exhausted than anything. Her ass was numb from sitting in this spot. How many hours had it been? She had long given up interrogating the person tied up in the basement.

The one she thought was Stacey, but was convinced it was not Stacey at all. Stacey was just a shell housing a dark memory. Sera lifted her head to peer down at the figure in the basement. Tied to the chair, Stacey...it...whomever, was listless in a sleeping state.

Fed up with the charade, Sera stormed down the bottom half of the stairwell and kicked the chair. "Wake up!"

Startled awake, Stacey blinked her way back into the reality of her situation. Her body ached everywhere. Stacey could read the anger and frustration in Sera's face and was instantly scared of what was coming next as the woman stood in front of her, staring, assessing, contemplating. Stacey was not sure. The only thing she knew for sure was that her bladder was not going to hold out much longer. She was about to say as much when a bang from upstairs startled them.

It wasn't a bang. It was the successive beats of a knock. Someone was here, knocking at the front door.

"Shit!" Sera hissed under her breath and turned towards the stairs.

Not missing the opportunity to be rescued, Stacey yelled. "HELP!"

Sera spun instantly and pointed a warning finger. "You better shut up and keep quiet!"

The two women stared at each other as another round of rapping could be heard from upstairs. Sera rushed past Stacey to a laundry basket on top of the washer. It was not folded. Dirty clothes are waiting for their load. Sera grabbed a couple of used socks and rolled them together.

"On second thought," Sera said as she shoved the bundle into Stacey's mouth. "Better safe than sorry." And she bounded up the stairs, the door slamming shut in her wake.

Stacey attempted to yell, but it was only a muffled garbling as she choked on her saliva, trying to extricate the dampening wad of cotton from her mouth.

At the front door, Sera shook her head and inhaled a deep breath to compose herself. Looking through the peephole, she could see it was Ely, and the breath was released in relief that it was him.

She threw the door open and smiled at her brother on the doorstep. "You are such a welcome sight."

Ely stepped in and embraced his older sibling. "I was just about to say the same! I'm so glad I made it here. I have so much to tell you. So much I need your help with."

Sera released the hug and directed Ely towards the kitchen, pointing to the basement door. "You couldn't have come at a better time. There is a man in my basement!

"What? My god! What happened? Are you okay? Have you called the police?" Ely was taken aback as he let loose his barrage of questions.

Sera paced, unsure of how to explain the events that had transpired, but she knew she could trust her brother. She hoped. "No, I'm fine. It's not like that...it's...Remember Tommy? That kid in high school that was obsessed with me, the one who committed suicide." A deeper breath this time. "He's in my basement!"

Ely nodded, taking it in, a little confused as he moved towards the basement door. Protecting his sister was the forefront of his actions, but, with trepidation, he turned back to his sister. "Wait, Sera. Tommy's dead. You just said it yourself. He is dead. But he is in your basement?"

Sera stared at her brother, knowing what she was saying made zero sense, as he came close to her and placed his hands on her shoulders to be eye to eye.

"Sera," Ely asked for her undivided attention. "Part of the reason I am here is to tell you that Tommy didn't kill himself all those years ago."

Much to the chagrin of the school faculty and various parents who were aware of the extracurricular activity. Many students attended the river in the valley, which wasn't far from the school. It was a walkable distance for most, in a nicely treed park garnished with well-kept pathways that joggers, cyclists, and couples use on their daily stroll. And the park was visited by families on the weekends.

But directly after school hours, the students descended. At least they mostly held to one spot where the river was wider, its bank sandier, and the flow was quieter, all these conditions coming together to make a perfect swimming spot and an even better hangout.

Going down into the park valley during lunch hours was prohibited, but the principal could not enforce anything once the final school bell rang. After that, it was up to the parents' discretion. All through his tenure, he had sent notes home, sent emails, brought the issue forward during meet and greets, and on and on, a fruitless effort, but one he always made all the same. At a minimum he was covering his ass if anything serious ever did happen down there.

The park was a wonderful place for people to visit and enjoy. The concern was that when you had groups of teenagers congregating in any certain place, trouble was bound to ensue. Drinking, drugs, other things, and all-around rabble rousing. Plus, he constantly received complaints from park goers of the mess left in the students' wake, or music being played too loud, or they had gotten carried away with their language when a family had been on a stroll along a path within earshot of the swimming hole.

It was a constant headache. With it being close to summer, the school year ending getting closer, the frequency of the students descending on the swimming hole increased. The groups got bigger.

Today was one of those days. Dozens of students gathered on the sandy banks. Several waded in the water, boys splashing girls who acted like they didn't *want to get wet, while others passed a football back and forth.*

Down to the right, a rope had been fixed to a heavy branch from a tree that edged the riverbank. Students took turns doing their best Tarzan or Jane impressions, swinging over the water to let go and plummet into the slow-moving waters.

Deeper in the woods, a figure was nestled in the concealment of some brush and tight growth of trees that made a canopy of shadow to keep him hidden. This was not the first time he had used this spot. He had tried others, but this had become a certain favourite. Far enough away to be hidden, yet close enough to watch the others in their fun.

From this vantage point, he knew that the kids partying at the beach were just an illusion of innocence that painted the afternoon. They were all fakes, liars, and backstabbers. Their laughter and shouts of fun that echoed up towards him in his spying seclusion made his stomach churn. It wasn't a chorus of innocence. It was the innocent naivety of their indestructibility. He balled a fist and pounded it into his stomach. They were oblivious to how easy it could all be taken away, innocence shattered. They were not indestructible or impervious at all.

But what did he care? He scanned the area in search of the one person he had come here for.

A roaring cheer from the crowd below directed his attention to the water, a large splash was subsiding in the wake of some trick maneuver one of the guys had performed off the rope swing to show off his bravado. And they all played into the hands of the spectacle.

And there she was, knee-deep in the water in a tight group of her friends. She was unimpressed with the antics that everyone else was laughing and clapping about. She was strong, independent, and he could tell she was restless, not wanting to be there amongst the sheep.

"Sera," her name escaped his lips as his right hand slithered down into the waistband of his pants, then deeper.

Feeling the swelling hardness of his groin as he admired her from afar, he pulled his hand out abruptly. He needed to wait. Wait, so he could show her how they needed to be together, that they were meant to be together. Other times, he had to relieve himself of that pressure, right here on the spot, their spot. But not today. Even though the urge throbbed in his pants, he had to wait. Today would not be from afar.

Today it would be real.

She will not reject Tommy Durant again.

Sera was not sure how she had allowed her friends to convince her to come down to the river. Finals were around the corner, and she had promised she would not get ensorcelled with spending every afternoon goofing off down here. So far this week, she had been breaking the routine. That was what she had promised herself, but Marla and Misty together were an indomitable force. And now that she had let Ely take the car, she was stuck here until one of them decided to leave.

Tomorrow. Tomorrow would be different.

No more messing around. Straight home to her studies. Sera drove her hands deep into her pockets to ward off the slight chill as splashing water speckled her exposed arms and face. And shit. The car keys were in her pockets. Being rushed along by her "supposed" best friends, she had not given the keys to Ely after all. He was probably waiting for her by the car right now.

"I have to go," she told Misty. Marla was too busy laughing with another couple of friends. It was a good thing because she was the more persuasive one and wouldn't accept her taking off so soon.

"You stay," Misty gave her a quick, flirtatious smile. "I'll drive him and be right back."

"Absolutely not," Sera replied as she gave her a fun shove out of the way. "You are not driving my brother anywhere. Ever."

"You are a spoilsport, you know that?" Misty said.

"I know that. I'm comfortable knowing that. I'll sleep easier," Sera laughed as she made to exit the water.

Catching her about to leave, Marla grabbed her arm to keep her.

From his voyeur hideout, Tommy's breath quickened. He could see Sera was preparing to leave. Marla was holding her back, and they were laughing in a playful tug of war. Sera pulled free and waved a few goodbyes before making her way toward the path to exit the valley.

Alone.

As she walked up the path, Sera couldn't believe she had forgotten to give the car keys to Ely. It did make for the perfect excuse for her to get out of there early, though.

Having moved quickly to close the gap, Tommy stepped onto the path just down from Sera. He looked behind to ensure nobody else was coming along. The coast was clear. He smiled as he looked back at her to continue his silent pursuit.

Closing the space between them, Tommy's heart thumped wildly in his chest. Now overcome with unabashed lust. He was so close her scent was in his nostrils, so close he felt spittle drool off the corner of his lip as he salivated with anticipation of the moment to come. *Nobody else is on the trail.* They were alone, no interruptions to concern themselves with. The ruckus from the party below ensured any noise she made would be lost. *She would never laugh at him again, never reject him again.*

They would finally be together.

Not far, someone ran through the underbrush, running shoes tearing through the forested area in a relentless pursuit, as jean-clad legs whipped tall weeds and low branches.

The runner in the woods didn't stop as they bent and picked up a rock, larger than their palm, in one fluid motion.

Unbeknownst to Sera, her stalker edged close behind her. Tommy was sneaking up on Sera, but he had to move fast or risk being heard. Closer, he watched her hair bounce with each step and imagined what it would *feel like once those flowing locks were tangled in the grasp of his hands.*

Lost in his aggressive fantasy, too focused on his prey, Tommy was oblivious as something, someone, flew out of the forest shadow and slammed into him. He was tackled off the pathway into the brush. Once he hit the ground with a whoosh of air escaping his lungs, sharp pain erupted in his back. Worse was the explosion he felt in the side of his head.

Startled, Sera spun around. She was sure she heard something, felt something behind her, but the path was empty. No other classmates were coming up the trail. She shrugged, sloughing it off with the reasoning that it must have been a deer, or she had disturbed a small forest dweller. Being more worried about getting to her car, she turned and jogged the rest of the way. Well, if she was completely honest with herself, she was sure the sound had been from an animal, but the hairs on the back of her neck gave her enough of a tingle to quicken her step. She wasn't scared. She just wanted to hurry for Ely's sake. That is what she told herself.

Lying in the tall grass, a low moan rustled Tommy back from his quick blip of unconsciousness. He felt a weight holding him down. A person was on top of him, kneeling over him, his arms held under his knees, but between the Mariachi band of stars parading behind his eyes and the glare of the sun encasing the figure, all he could see was the outline of a shadow. He struggled to move, twisting and heaving to get the weight off himself.

The lighting shifted, and clarity was coming back to his vision.

"You? You are her little brother?" Tommy searched for reasoning. Blood coughed from behind his lips. "What did you do you little shit?" Tommy was enraged and shocked at being stopped from reaching his fantasy. He wiggled an arm free and felt the wetness on the side of his head. "You're dead. I'm going to kill you, you little shit, and then your sister is all mine." Tommy reached up to grab Ely. In reaction to the sudden movement, Ely's arm shot down like a viper and smacked the rock into the side of Tommy's head again, forcing it to snap to the side with its force.

"You can't have her," Ely whispered in a feather-soft voice.

Blurred vision again, Tommy went to swing his free arm in defence, but all he saw with any clarity was Ely's arm raised high with the rock in hand. Tommy's head exploded in pain again. Once, twice, three times, the wet smack crunched in his ear as the assailant rained the makeshift hammer down onto Tommy's head. Consciousness pulled the drapes closed, and the stars behind his eyes went instantly dark. The thumping of blood in his ears went silent.

CHAPTER ELEVEN

There is never a deeper breath that could be taken than the one Stacey had inhaled to see a man standing before her with Sera, knowing that someone had discovered her kidnapping. She was clueless as to how long she had been strapped to this chair and held prisoner. If she wiggled her hands or feet, she could not discern if it was the cold basement or the loss of feeling from being contorted into this position. The snot dribbling from her left nostril said cold, but that was most likely from the saliva-soaked sock in her mouth, making her wheeze. One nostril was plugged, and she could not inhale a decent breath through only the right until she calmed herself, slowed, and took the air in deeply.

She started to breathe heavy again, chest heaving, not in panic, but in excitement because here was someone else here and she was saved. Stacey still had no real understanding as to why Sera had kidnapped her. She didn't care. She just wanted to be free. And here was a saviour. Although the man before her was not in a police uniform, was not adorning a badge, and was not hurrying to untie her. But she did not let her hope wane. There was no room for it.

"This is a woman!" Ely shouted as he pointed towards the woman tied to the chair. "You told me you had a ghost of a teenage kid from high school down here, and somehow I found that palatable, but this person is a completely different gender."

Sera paced like a caged panther. "No! I know this sounds crazy, but it's Tommy from school, years ago. This woman is possessed!"

Stacey looked back and forth between the two of them. Stacey didn't give a fuck she just wanted to be let go. She jerked in her chair and let out a muffled cry for attention.

Ely turned to her and pulled out the sock from Stacey's mouth. "Possessed?"

Stacey coughed and gasped for air before looking up at Ely gratefully. "I'm not possessed." Her desperation kept her from fully catching her breath. "My name is Stacey. I work in the grocery store in town. This is kidnapping! You need to help me!"

"She's right," Ely shrugged at Sera while holding the balled-up sock as evidence. "This looks like kidnapping, Big Sister."

Big sister? Stacey deflated. The man before her was a family member.

Sera angrily held up a finger to Ely in a hold-on-a-minute motion. "Watch!" She leaned in to yell directly in Stacey's face. "I'm laughing at you! I'm rejecting you! You possessed freak!"

"Your sister is off her nut! She hit me with a frying pan!"

"Wouldn't be the first time," Ely mumbled under his breath.

Stacey shook her head. Did this guy make a joke? She was screwed!

Sera also heard Ely's joke and scowled at her brother for making light of the situation. She turned and shoved the note in Stacey's face to elicit a possessive response. "Is this not your handwriting?"

"No, because I'm freaking left-handed!"Stacey strained forward against her bonds and yelled as much as she could with her dry, raspy throat.

Frustrated, Sera roughly scrunched the paper into Stacey's face, forcing Stacey's head to snap back as if she had been punched. "That proves nothing!"

Seeing she was at a tipping point, Ely grabbed Sera's arm to push it away and moved in close to block the tied-up woman from Sera's rage. "Calm down!" Being closer, something invaded Ely's nostrils. He bent closer to the captive and sniffed. "What's that smell?"

"I'm sure it's me," Stacey said. I pissed myself about four hours ago, no thanks to your crazy sister."

"I swear to you, Ely," Sera pandered to Ely to plead her case. "Last night she sounded like that guy in high school who used to stalk me. You remember the guy who committed suicide?" She stepped back in revelation. "Although you were saying it wasn't suicide?"

Ely grabbed his sister by the arm to pull her away, partially because he needed to de-escalate the situation, but mostly because the conversation he needed to have with his sister was for her ears only. "Let's go upstairs. We need to talk."

Stacey panicked. "What about me?"

"Sit tight," Ely said as he shoved the balled-up, soggy sock back into Stacey's mouth. "And keep quiet."

As soon as she reached the top of the stairs and breached the basement doorway, Sera wheeled on her brother. "What?"

Ely motioned her forward, prodding her to sit at the kitchen table while he ensured the door was closed behind him. "We need to sit." Sera didn't heed him; she paced. "I need to sit," Ely demanded.

"That guy, Tommy, he didn't commit suicide," Ely told her.

Sera looked over her shoulder back at him. "What do you mean he didn't kill himself?"

She came to the table quickly and placed the high school note on the table in front of her brother, tapping it with her index finger to accentuate her point. "He did. I know she did because he left a note in my locker. This note!"

Ely leaned forward to bridge the distance with his sister and took her hand, drawing her to sit across from him.

"The note was his confession. He was obsessed with me, you remember. I never told anyone when I found the letter because I didn't want to be blamed for him committing suicide, but in a way, it was my fault." Tears welled in her eyes.

Letting go of her hand so she could wipe her eyes, Ely leaned back in his chair as revelation washed over him. "You've carried that guilt all these years?"

Sera nodded, then stared at the note before her.

"It wasn't your fault," Ely reached out to her with his words. "That wasn't a suicide note. That letter was a warning. He was coming to attack you that day. Maybe more. Maybe worse."

Sera shot up in her chair. "What are you talking about? How would you even know that? How could you know that?"

Dropping his elbows onto the table, Ely buried his head in his hands. He needed his sister to listen. She was desperate for answers, but he needed her to hear him.

"It doesn't matter right now!" Ely was muffled with his face cupped in his hands. He lifted his head to look his sister squarely in the face. "Listen, this is weird. I get here, and you have a captive in your basement. It's strangely convenient. And you say she is possessed? That she is that Tommy?"

"Yes!" Sera replied. "Unequivocally, and I know it sounds insane, but I am not out of my mind. I just need to know how you think he didn't commit suicide."

"I believe you, Sera, but let me explain," Ely said as he got out of his chair and began anxiously pacing. He understood the irony as he had just moments ago forced his sister to sit down and stop moving about like a caged tiger, but some things just required pacing. "Remember when I was young, and I was all impulsive and seemed to pick up on things quickly?"

Sera looked at him, unsure what this had to do with the possessed girl in the basement and her high school stalker, but she nodded.

Ely continued. "Like when I would tell mom to watch the grocery bag, and 2 seconds later it began to rip at the bottom. The time Dad was driving, I was bugging him to stop the car. He was mad at me because we were running late. He stopped, mostly to shut me up, and a second later, a dog came bolting out in front of the car. We would have killed that dog if Dad hadn't listened to me."

"Kind of...vaguely..." Sera shrugged. "But what does this have to do with Tommy?"

Ely got down on one knee to Sera and took her hand in his to secure her attention. "It has to do with Tommy because I believe you when you say that's him in that woman's body downstairs. I believe you because when I think about all these odd moments in my life, I've come to the conclusion I'm possessed!"

Sera's head was gliding back and forth. Not to mention no. Just a deference to comprehension.

Ely continued. "Not an evil-cursing, God-puking, bile, head-twisting kind of possessed. But my actions are not my own kind of possession. I feel it, and recently I've been remembering stuff. I know Tommy didn't kill himself that day because…because…" He inhaled a deep breath, not believing he was about to say the next sentence out loud. "Because I killed him."

Standing in reaction, Sera came back strongly at him. Her tone was disbelieving. "That's not funny! It's not possible!"

"I get that. I do," Ely tried to be persuasive and compassionate as he moved close to his sister. She looked dizzy, and he worried he might have to catch her at any moment.

She steadied herself. "How…how would you have kept that a secret? How were you not caught?"

"I don't know…I didn't even realize…I didn't know until I got here! It all came flooding back to me. Like it was blocked in my memory. So much is coming back to me suddenly, all at once, and I'm scared."

"You're scared? I can't even comprehend what you are saying."

"I don't understand things any more than you do right now. But maybe to make you believe, we can figure this out together, we can help each other understand. Can you answer me one question?"

She felt ready to run, the need to get away. There was no running, so she turned to Ely. "What!"

"Who is Wynnie?" Ely asked with a tilt of his head.

Surprised, her breath escaped her, leaving her so that she could barely make her words audible. "You are not supposed to know that name."

Ely just looked at her with his arms raised, his motion conveying the layered mystery he was trying to solve in figuring out how he knew. The next step was going to be explaining to his sister how he felt someone else in his mind. Sera thought she was going crazy, being haunted by her past through a woman she held captive in her basement.

Crazy? Ely knew he was already there.

CHAPTER TWELVE

Ely remained in his seat at the kitchen table, watching Sera pace back and forth, chewing her lip, stopping to lean against a counter, she chewed her cuticle of the index finger on her right hand, staring at Ely as she did so. Her mouth opened about to speak, slammed shut, and then she was pacing again. All in all, in a complete bundle that was about to self-combust. He watched her move back and forth, back and forth, not sure if the floor would wear out first or her nerves.

"Please stop pacing and talk to me," Ely reached out to her.

Sera stopped and stared at him. Then she started. "Wynnie was Mom and Dad's first child. Mom lost the child late in the pregnancy. They never talked about it and tried wiping the painful experience from the family history books. Trying to forget and avoid was their coping mechanism. I only know because mom reached out to me when Anne died." She breathed deeply, containing her emotions at the memory of that moment, then pointed at Ely. "But how do you know? How do you know we had a big sister?"

"Honestly," Ely said endearingly, needing his sister to hear and believe him. "The name just came to me. I think I've been possessed." The way Sera's left eyebrow raised, Ely realized he was not off to a good start, but he had to continue and get this out, get it off his chest. "When I went to your house, something hit me, and the flood gates opened." He paused, not sure what her reaction would be when he said that. Her house and the painful memory that lived inside were a very sensitive topic, and he did not want to lose her attention right now. "It was Wynnie who killed Tommy or drove me to kill Tommy. It was to protect you, save you." Ely breathed deeply and blurted out the last few words. "Technically, your unborn older sister is who saved you that day!"

Sera didn't start pacing again, she didn't yell, she just looked at him and said softly. "That's insane. How is this even possible?"

"I don't know," Ely shrugged. "You are the one who thinks a woman in your basement is your high school stalker. How is that possible?"

And down in that basement was the forgotten woman. Stacey refused to be a victim. The only one that was going to help her was herself. So do something. Even though she was exhausted, thirsty, and in pain, she was able to muster a dry scream of frustration that burned deep in her throat as she shook her head back and forth in unison to the outcry. A sad, barely audible from behind her sock gag, cry for help. What could she do? Tossing her head side to side in frustration, a glint of something reflected light. Stacey stopped, her nostrils flaring with heavy breath as she directed her attention to that glint. It was something metal. On top of the washing machine, beside a basket of clothes. Metal, and it was something sharp. Scissors. An access to freedom that could have been miles away for all it mattered because she was tied to this stupid chair. Stacey stared at the scissors with a longing desperation. They were right there. So close yet a world away, all at the same time.

Don't be a victim.

A grunt escaped her, and she began rocking her chair side to side, back and forth, making the effort to move closer to the washing machine. Even if it was only millimeter by millimeter, she would get there. It was working. The chair moved. She stopped and listened to the upstairs. Nothing. She worked with more diligence at the opportunity. Rocking, shaking, Stacey seemed to find a rhythm as the chair began to gain ground. Then she startled as the chair tipped too far to one side. Stacey quickly tried to adjust her weight, but it was too late; she was toppling over, landing on the concrete floor and banging her head into unconsciousness.

Upstairs, oblivious to the failed escape attempt, Ely left his chair and came around the counter towards his sister. "I just know I have done some weird things in my life. I know I've had blank moments. I keep coming back to the word impulsive. Because that is the best way to describe the feeling, to describe some of my actions." He inhaled deeply, knowing this was the kicker that might push Sera away. "But in your house, I went into Anne's room. Something happened. Every moment of my life flooded into me. Knowing it was Wynnie the day that Tommy died. Knowing all those other times it was my actions."

"But?" She beckoned him to continue.

"But, it wasn't me driving the ship," there, it was out. "It's not like I hear voices, but I feel it. I've been ripped open inside, and something is there, on the peripheral, a calling." Ely buried his head in his hands and mumbled through them as if he didn't want an answer. "I'm not insane, right?"

His big sister grabbed him by the shoulders to draw him close and then took his hands away from his face. She placed her own on his cheeks and lifted his downed head to look at her.

"I probably would have never believed you if I had not been experiencing my nightmare tonight," Sera comforted. "But are you telling me you can see the dead? Are you telling me you can see my daughter and talk to her? Are you telling me with all I've lost? She's here?"

Ely looked away, unable to meet her eyes. "No, I'm sorry, it's not like that!"

Sera removed her hands from his cheeks and crossed her arms over her chest in reservation, closing herself up, holding back the wave of tears welling in her eyes. "Of course, it couldn't be like that. Why wouldn't it be?"

Silence.

A knock at the front door stole the siblings' attention. Neither moved to answer; they froze, unsure of what they had heard, not wanting it to be what they knew they had just heard.

A second rapping jolted both brother and sister Ely was the first to speak. "A little late for visitors, isn't it?"

"I wasn't expecting anyone," Sera said as she stepped forward and grabbed the handle.

Before pulling the door open, she looked back over her shoulder at her brother, and their eyes locked. They were both thinking the same thing.

Amidst their day of revelations, there was now a surprise visitor to contend with.

Sera slowly opened the door and looked out to the porch where a blonde woman stood displaying a law enforcement badge.

"Good evening. I'm looking for Stacey Patterson. If I could come in and have a moment of your time," the lady on the porch said as soon as Sera's face appeared.

Amidst their day of revelations, there was now a surprise visitor to contend with.

A detective.

CHAPTER THIRTEEN

Earlier that day, deeper into the forested foothills of the area where Sera lived, was an area riddled with trails frequented by hikers and a horse trail for riding enthusiasts.

Much to the chagrin of Buck and Meryl, who resided in the area, the number of city folk who utilized the trails was getting bigger and bigger. Buck and Meryl had lived here for over two decades and knew the trails like the back of their hands. While this forest was just a fragment of the larger national park, it did host many visitors throughout the year due to its proximity to the neighbouring town, and it was only a little over an hour's drive from the city's limits. When they were younger, many trails were dirt trails, deer runs, or worn paths along creek and river edges. A lot had changed since those early days of bushwhacking on horseback, especially in the last five years. With civilization encroaching and the frequency of visitors growing, the trails were all built up, signed, and the parking lot enlarged to accommodate the increase. Buck and Meryl used to come out on weekends for their rides; the parking lot was always full. Buck's back no longer tolerated riding all day anyway, so they had resigned their riding to a couple of nights a week.

It was still common, even on a weeknight, to come across a small group of hikers on a trail. Over the past several years, more properties have been subdivided as people sought to set up their sanctuary away from the hustle and bustle of city life without being hours away from the amenities that city life provided.

Today wasn't one of those days. Higher on a ridge, as they rode their horses towards the trail bend that would lead them down, Buck and Meryl could see the parking area down in the distance, and it was practically empty. The temperature had dropped in the last half an hour, and now the tall, forest pines swayed in the wind that had metastasized from a slight breeze. And being exposed, they could feel the trickle of rain patter down on their hats and leather saddles.

"The parking lot is practically empty," Meryl shouted to her husband.

Buck turned in his saddle to look at his wife and point to the distant sky. "They were all smarter than us, getting out of dodge before the weather hit. Those dark clouds are coming in fast with that wind." Then he coughed a deep raspy cough.

"I think we will make it," Meryl smiled, trying to be positive. It was not because she was afraid of getting wet, it wouldn't be the first time they were caught in the rain, but because of that cough. The cough they didn't talk about that had shown up the last few months after Buck recovered from a bout of the flu. Meryl was beginning to hate the sound of that cough. She hated that he refused to go to the doctor even more. Turning down the slope, the married couple were side by side now on the wider berth of the trail down to the parking lot as they bantered in the trotted descent.

"We never should have taken that new loop; we lost too much time," Buck said as the rain started to get heavier.

"Oh, quit your complaining. Where's your sense of adventure?"

"It's going to be washed away in two minutes," her husband barked. Some thunder rumbled from high above as if to accentuate his point.

"We'll make it," Meryl said, encouraging her horse to pick up its pace.

The last few strides across the parking area, the skies opened, and a deluge ensued. The rain came so suddenly and so heavily that they were soaked before they could dismount.

Feet on the ground, holding tight to his horse, and not appreciating the sudden change in weather, Buck called over from the side of his horse. "We didn't make it!"

Meryl, fed up with his ornery grumbling, barked back. "It's not the first time you've gotten wet, so shut up and be quick about it."

Even over the heavy thrum of the rain, thunder could be heard rumbling overhead as the couple hurried to untack the saddles from the impatient horses. They wanted out of the rain, also. The rumbling sky ended with a big clap that spooked Meryl's horse, and he pulled back on his tie, rocking the trailer. She dropped her saddle and calmed him before moving to release his tie. That was all they needed for the halter to snap and the horses to take off in a panic.

Buck saw what transpired and rushed to her side. "They are losing their calm demeanour. Get them in the trailer and I'll load the saddles."

Meryl untied her horse and gave the lead to her husband. "Your damn back isn't loading any saddles. You load the horses. I'll get the gear." She loved her husband, but hated his stubbornness. He was fine taking the saddles off the rack and tossing them onto backs, and bending and lifting were no longer in the cards for his lower back. Last time he did it, he was on the couch for days. He knew it was a weakness; he hated to concede to it, so they continuously had to do this dance every damn time.

Having loaded the horses, they both got into the cab of the truck. Inside, shaking the wet from their hair, the rain took a sudden pause as if it was only heavy to torment them when they were outside. Now, in the sanctuary of their vehicle, it softened. In the driver's seat, Buck started the truck and leaned forward to flick on the heat to ward off the chill induced by their soaked clothes.

He looked up, the windshield was defending against an enraged storm as the rain started drumming again, making it hard to see anything beyond the front hood.

"It is coming down now," Buck said, looking at his wife before shifting the gear into drive and getting ready to pull away. "I don't want them fussing in the trailer, so we will just take it nice and slow."

"Wait," Meryl's hand slapped into his chest, signaling him to stop. "Do you hear that?"

Pushing his foot to the brake, Buck turned to his wife. "Hear what? I can't hear a damn thing over this rain drumming against the truck."

Meryl popped open her door and leaned out into the downpour. "Just hold on. I think it is coming from the bathroom."

"What is? How can you hear anything? I can barely hear you," Buck said and reached out to her. "Now close that door."

But she was gone, out of the truck and into the rain. He could see her race past the front of the vehicle and take off to the outhouses.

Dumbfounded by this woman that he called his wife, Buck just shook his head as she disappeared into the veil of the storm.

The truck rocked a bit. The horses were impatient and nervous about the weather. They were kicked out of fear of the storm in the trailer.

Drenched now and shivering, Meryl reached the doorway to the lady's washroom at the outhouse building. She grabbed the handle to pull the door open and stopped. She didn't feel like she needed to pee. There was a momentary pause where she second-guessed herself, standing there shivering in the downpour before she moved to the men's door, whipped it open, and disappeared inside.

The wipers swished back and forth at the highest setting, but it was still difficult to see out past the hood. The rain was not letting up, and Buck shook his head at his wife running back into the storm. When that woman had to pee, a tornado couldn't stop her. He rested his head back and closed his eyes, patiently waiting for her return.

A bang startled him forward. Not thunder. Meryl stood at his window, hitting it with her fist to get his attention. Buck pushed his door open. "Holy hell, woman, you scared the heck out of me. What is going on?"

"Call 9-1-1!" She yelled at him panic stricken, then disappeared again, running back towards the washroom building.

Bursting into the men's washroom in pursuit of his wife to see what all the fuss was about, Buck found Meryl kneeling at the pit toilet. The toilet lid was open, and she had an arm in, reaching. He could hear her muttering, 'please, please, please.'

Buck placed his hands on her shoulders. "I've called emergency services. They are on their way." He leaned forward to look over her into the depths of the toilet. "Now what the hell is going on?"

Nothing was more infuriating than moving on autopilot and being in the dark about what was happening, but after all these years, Buck trusted his wife. If she said move, he moved. And he did, but now he needed answers. "Oh my God!" Escaped his lips and whatever was in him. Fear for his wife. Frustration with the weather. The adrenaline of calling 9-1-1 and then chasing after Meryl, all drained from him as if a vampire had leached all the blood from his body in a single moment. The muscles in Buck's legs went soft, and he crumpled to his knees beside his wife.

A couple of feet down in the depths of the urine, feces, and toilet paper was a baby, crying and alive.

"They are coming. They are on their way," Buck repeated, almost more to reassure himself than to be concerned that his wife didn't hear him the first time.

The soft cry of the child echoed off the cylindrical concrete of the short tube leading into the holding tank. Buck looked down again into the pit of piss and shit, ribbons of used toilet paper streaming white banners against the murk of human waste. "How the hell did a baby get in there?"

They looked at each other. He knew the answer. Meryl knew the answer. Someone had abandoned the baby. Someone, desperate or just sick in the mind, had dropped the baby down there to get rid of it in a remote place. Maybe the expectation was that the infant would drown in the dark pool. Maybe, the person had not even thought that much in whatever desperation or evil had driven them to leave the baby here.

"Let me try," Buck said, and put his hand on Meryl's arm to get her attention. He was not much taller than his wife. His reach would not be much longer. His attempt would be as futile as Meryl's currently was, but he couldn't watch her struggling a moment longer.

Meryl relented in her attempt and sat back onto her heels. "Why?" That was all she said, and she was barely breathing when she looked at her husband.

He had no answer. He took his turn reaching into the toilet. There wasn't enough space to shove his arm into the hole and look down for the baby at the same time. Shoulder deep against the seat ring, Buck was fishing blind. There was no way his hand would even be close. The pit was too deep. It was a useless attempt, but he preferred making the desperate effort himself, watching his wife.

"How the hell did you hear the baby crying from inside the truck?" He asked Meryl. Even without the thundering storm and heavy rain, it would have been almost impossible to hear these soft cries. It was nothing short of a miracle she had heard.

"I don't know," she looked at him hard for a long moment as if she was trying to recollect or find a legitimate answer. "I don't know. I don't know if I heard anything, as so much just felt…I just felt the need to come here."

"Well, thank God you did," Buck said. How didn't matter. All that mattered was that, amongst a storm, a light could blaze a path and be a saving grace.

CHAPTER FOURTEEN

On the front porch, shadowed in the beckoning dark of the night, was the stark reality of the consequences of Sera's actions. Branches of the tall pines in the distance swayed in consort with a light wind that had picked up and made a soft hushing sound as if to whisper the secret that inside a captive was held in the basement of this place. And Sera held her breath, knowing she was the only barrier standing between those two things clashing together.

The looming detective standing on the porch pressed closer to look over Sera's shoulder to get a better view of the interior. She turned back to Sera with a stern look on her face to accentuate her impatience of having to repeat herself. "I said I'm looking for Stacey Patterson."

Even though she was surprised by this late-night visit, Sera stood resolute in her position, blocking the doorway. Well, maybe not resolute. Her lower lip caught between her teeth, her attention held by the whispering pines that she watched over the detective's shoulder, resolute was more frozen in place as she tried to compose herself and not look as flustered as she felt.

"I'm sorry, Stacey?" Sera shook her head. Was her panic showing? No, she was resolute. Be resolute. "No, I haven't seen her since the other morning at the store."

Or was that this morning? The panic inside was blending the timeline in her head. Too late to recant.

Don't panic.

The detective thumbed over her shoulder at the parked cars collected at the front of Sera's house. "Really? Because I'd beg to differ, considering that is Stacey's vehicle right there."

Sera craned her neck to over-emphasize that she couldn't understand what the detective was referring to. But there it undeniably was. Sera's jeep, the vehicle Ely came in, the assumed detective's car, and lastly, Stacey's.

Don't panic. Or don't let her see you panicking, Sera thought as she fumbled for words. "Oh, that? That is Stacey's car. I am pretty sure of it. Yes." Was the panic showing? Be resolute in the lie. She breathed. "I mean, she was supposed to come over for dinner, but she never showed...so..." See, that was a panic-free, reasonable explanation. Stacey was supposed to be here, and she never showed up. Somehow, between parking her car and walking the dozen-odd steps to the front door, and disappeared. And Sera had not left the house to notice the car was parked there. Nor did she call her supposed friend to find out why she had not shown up for dinner. Those were the things she would insinuate if she were in the detective's shoes.

The detective wasn't buying it and pushed her way past Sera. "Yeah, I think I'd better come inside so we can discuss this further, and I can have a look around." Those insinuating shoes fit perfectly. Shit.

As Sera slowly pushed the door to close, the wind rustled the surrounding trees again. Was it a final calling whisper? Sera felt a shiver run through her as the detective pushed past, or was that the hush of darkness walking into her house?

She turned to follow her visitor and caught Ely's eyes piercing into her, a silent conversation between brother and sister, they knew they were in trouble.

"And you are?" The detective questioned

"Ely, I'm Sera's brother," Ely responded with an outstretched hand that the detective reluctantly accepted.

Keeping hold of his hand longer than necessary for a common, introductory handshake, the detective drew in a little closer to Ely, looking him over. "Well, this is unexpected."

"It is," Ely responded in an attempt to pull his hand away. "We don't get visitors out here often."

"This isn't a visit, though, is it?" The detective let Ely's hand slide free but kept her attention on him as if she was trying to piece something together. "Do I know you?"

"I can't imagine how," Ely brushed her off.

"You both live here?" The detective directed her query at Sera.

"No, just me," Sera replied. "Ely is visiting."

"Well," the detective continued, not showing any care for the answer. "I'm here because there has been a missing person report filed for Stacy Patterson. She didn't show up for work today, and her co-workers said her last known whereabouts were that she had plans to come here for dinner yesterday."

"I don't know what to say," Sera shrugged in a vain attempt to lie. "She never made it."

"So just her car did?" The detective looked at both in turn, expecting an answer.

Sera stared back at the detective. Something seemed off. No, felt off. They were lying of course because they knew damn well where Stacey was. Irrelevant. Regardless of her gut feeling, they needed this detective gone. Sera's mind swam in circles. She was a writer, so write a story. Use your imagination, be convincing, and tell a tale that will get this woman out of your house.

Stacey's eyes fluttered her awake from the spell of unconsciousness. Getting her bearings, she found herself on the floor beside something metal. Arching, craning her neck, she realized it was the washer. The scissors were on the ground, they might as well have been on Mars. She froze. Her head was pounding, but had she heard? Yes! Voices upstairs. Stacey listened intently to discern what they were talking about or if they were on their way down to her. One Sera. Two, the brother. Three, another woman's voice. There was someone else up there.

She resisted the urge to scream. Every fiber in her being wanted to cry for help, but she could only release a muffled sound with the stupid sock wedged in her mouth. Soaked with her saliva, but her lips were dry. Even if she could scream, she had to play this right in case it was another family member. But just in case she was heard, they would blame it on a television in the basement. Stacey knew one thing; she needed those damn scissors to untie herself. She struggled, pushing back into the washer, trying to gently nudged it, hoping the scissors would fall off, but without making a huge racket. The right arm underneath her was on fire from being tied and the pressure of her weight rocking back and forth as the wood of the chair dug into her. A crack made her wince. Then a sudden panic, waiting for the flash of pain to announce she had broken something in her arm. Not bone. The crack must have been from the wood.

Stacey was crying now. Tears welling in her eyes and muffled moans from behind the sock in her mouth. She wasn't crying from fear. It wasn't from the pain. It was a quiet release of desperation at the glimmer of a teasing hope.

She rocked harder.

There was that sixth sense that pushed Ely to experience different and strange events in his life, but after shaking the hand of the detective, his stomach felt uneasy. Something was off; it felt strange. Watching her pace back and forth between Sera and him, the pieces did not fit. He caught Sera's eye; their eyes spoke the same message. They needed to keep the detective from discovering the possessed hostage in the basement. Ely took the lead, putting up a brave front to protect his sister, he stood smugly with his arms crossed.

"Who called in the missing person's report? I mean, isn't there a protocol or timeline for that? You are here asking about a grown woman who has only been missing for several hours. Isn't there a forty-eight-hour rule?"

The detective raised her eyebrow at Ely's questioning and got in his face to show she was not intimidated. "It's a little different when you are talking about a cabin in the woods, and the victim's car is in the driveway. So why don't we stick to me asking the questions!" She pushed past him. "I am going to have to look around."

It wouldn't be difficult to investigate the main floor with the open concept plan. One sweep and everything was there in plain sight, with the kitchen and large living room taking up the expanse of the main floor. There was the short hall leading down to her office and the main floor bathroom, otherwise, it was the stairwell leading upstairs and the door that led to the basement.

The basement door was where the detective directed her first steps.

"Be my guest," Sera said and directed the detective towards the stairwell that led upstairs. Write the story. Control the narrative. Be the character. She had not missed a beat, appearing welcoming with nothing to hide as she blocked the path to the basement door and beckoned the detective to follow her up the stairs. "The upstairs is this way."

There was thumping. All three of them stopped at once to listen to the rapid pounding. Footsteps on the stairs were all Sera could think of, and before she could say anything or react in any way, the basement door flew open, and Stacey came bursting through.

The woman was a horrific mess, dirt and grime on her face mixed with caked blood, duct tape streaming from her wrists and ankles. As soon as she saw the other person in the house, the detective, Stacey, was screaming for help.

Frantic, Stacey dropped to her knees and grabbed onto the surprised detective's legs, continuing her pleas for help. But now, dehydrated from her internment, it was in a dry raspy whisper from her parched, raw throat.

The detective quickly looked over at Sera and Ely in suspicion, then turned her attention to Stacey, looking down at the desperate woman clawing at her leg with a death grip.

"Are you Stacey Patterson?" The detective questioned.

"Yes! God, yes, please help me," Stacey begged for salvation.

"Or Tommy Durant?" The detective grabbed Stacey's hair and roughly yanked her head back to better look in her eyes.

A twitch. A piercing of the eye. Whatever it was, there was a confirmation in the way that body subtly moved. Sera saw it. Ely felt it. The detective had not been asking a question. She had been making an affirming statement.

In one swooping motion, the detective withdrew her sidearm from her hip holster. "Then you should have stayed hidden."

The firing of the gun reverberated off the walls, and Stacey's head snapped back, her body flailing backwards.

Sera let out a wail. There was the truth in that slight body jerk of Stacey...Sera gasped for air at the horror before her. A flash of an old memory, before dropping a plate of Spaghetti Bolognese. Pieces of Stacey's head reminded her of her dinner- the meaty shards of her skull, mixed with the sauce of blood and tendrils of brain matter. Sera gagged, grabbing onto the wall for support as she bent over with bile rising like lava in her throat.

The detective stood over the dead body. The pool of blood emanating from the crater in Stacey's head quickly grew in its radius. The detective slowly moved her left foot to keep her shoe from getting stained as she turned to Sera and Ely. Sera was already rushing at her, sliding to the ground and grabbing at the victim on the ground, a person, until all this craziness ensued; she had called a friend.

"Oh my god! What have you done?" Sera screamed at the detective.

"What have I done?" The detective looked down at Sera. "More important is what am I doing? And that's charging you with kidnapping, unlawful confinement, and murder."

Sera was shaking her head uncomprehending.

"But it was you!" Ely was startled at the incredulous accusation.

Before he could react, the detective spun on him, swinging her arm wide and whipping him across the face with the gun, sending him sprawling backwards into a kitchen counter where he slammed his side and slid to the ground.

"Was it?" The detective screamed. "Was it me? Is anything what we perceive it to be? It is the story I tell."

Skittering across the floor on all fours, Sera moved to comfort her brother, who was holding the side of his face from the sting of the blow and disoriented from the strike.

"Why?" She looked up at the detective, Sera's voice desperate for understanding.

"That is the mystery, isn't it?" The detective paced. "I mean, am I here to punish you for the kidnapping and murder of a young woman?" She stopped and looked at both of them hard. "Or am I here because you murdered that poor, young man, Tommy?"

There it was. Ely stopped rubbing the side of his face and, with the support of the countertop and assistance from his sister, managed to get to his feet. He leaned on the counter to steady himself as his head spun, but he needed to be on his feet. Something felt off about this whole situation. It was not a coincidence that he had come here to confess things to his sister. This detective wasn't a real detective. She wasn't in law enforcement at all. She was something else entirely. Maybe she was like him.

"You know...don't you?" Ely pressed for the truth.

The detective stopped pacing. Instead, she now wore a Cheshire grin. "I know."

"Know what?" Sera yelled. "What the hell is going on?"

The detective ignored Sera's questioning and continued. "I know what goes up must come down, and eventually all heavens fall." The off-kilter grin faded, and a stern darkness filled her gaze. "I know I was a moth, drawn to your flame." She pointed her gun at Ely's face to accentuate her point. "But you know what it is like, don't you, Ely? You know it's as simple as telling a father to stop the car, so he doesn't run over a dog bolting onto a street." She stepped closer, holding his attention.

"How sometimes the weight of a black hole pulls you right in, as if every ounce of heat is being bled from you. You know it. You feel it. Sometimes it's the hot thrum in your head of those voices that scratch at the inside boundary of your skull, electric impulses of red-hot crazy. A hunger's force that you cannot ignore, driving you, compelling you."

"You're like me, then?" Ely could barely form the words, eyes wide, trying to soak in an understanding from the strange woman before him.

"Everyone is like you," the detective started to explain as she pointed to Ely, then Sera. "And her. Everyone's the same, just on different levels. They all experience "those" moments.

"Like when a parent suddenly wakes up in the night and is drawn to check on their kid, only to find the child is gasping for air, choking on something unknown. How did that parent hear the silent plea from the deafness of sleep. How lucky was that family that the parent woke up in that moment to be able to save that child from choking to death?"

Sera shook her head, unsure if an actual answer was expected.

"Those moments when you are lost in your world, standing on a street corner, and your friend reacts to hold you back for that fraction of a second, so you just miss becoming a crimson-staining hood ornament on a passing car," the detective carried on her introspection.

A pair of twenty-something girlfriends, shopping bags dripping from their arms to mark a successful afternoon, laugh together without a care in the world as they meander down the sidewalk of a shopping district. It was a Saturday, and the shopping crowds, either out on a mission or just spending the day browsing, were like a fast-moving river that would sweep you along if you didn't stand strong against the current. The two friends were not swept away but immersed in the current as they made their way down the street, hurrying to make a lunchtime reservation and leaning on each other as they laughed through the reminiscence of a party the other night.

They stopped with the flow of people at a street corner. Inattentive to the crossing walk lights signalling "Don't Walk," the one friend instinctively stepped out as her peripheral vision caught others moving and assumed the light had changed. Her friend grabbed her by the back of the shirt and yanked her back just as a taxi went blaring by.

"When you make that miracle catch of a rogue ball at a baseball game."

Strolling through the park, this mom concluded that the carrier vest she wore was probably the best invention known to man. Her infant was pressed against her chest and held securely in the snuggle harness, little legs dangling, and head kept safe. Tiny little head that she stroked with her free hand, then kissed. She stopped and took a sip of coffee from the thermos-mug she was carrying. The little one was suffering from colic. Which meant she was suffering from a lack of sleep. Coffee and these strolls in the park were the only solace she could find lately. For whatever reason, the baby slept soundly out in the fresh air, resting against her chest, and although it didn't afford her any much-needed rest, the walk and quiet from crying were the best she seemed to hope for lately.

A community ball game was being played at the diamond that the path ran by. A crowd of families and kids. The mom closed her eyes and lifted her face to the sun. This colic phase was temporary; it felt like an eternity, but wouldn't last forever. She just needed to not lose her sanity in surviving the temporary.

She was jolted, at the same time hearing a soft thump. A teenage boy was next to her, his hand right in front of her baby's head, holding a baseball.

"Wow, that was close," he said with a bright smile and then ran off, tossing the baseball up and down in his hand. The one he caught just before it bulleted into her baby's head.

"It sure was," she mumbled to herself and kissed the soft skin of the sleeping child. Too close, shook her head as she began her walk again, sipping her coffee. She looked back at the game still in play and thought that, regardless of how utterly exhausted she was. She needed to be more attentive.

The detective continued. "Or those powerful moments when a child, living miles away, gets the sudden urge to call home. Only to find a parent has fallen gravely ill."

The clock on the conference room wall ticked its second hand in a monotonous circle. Jerry looked at the clock and flipped his cell phone over to check the time on the display. This meeting was running way over. His leg bounced up and down in a steady rhythm. He checked his phone again. The missed call log showed his parents had called ten minutes ago, and ever since, his stomach had been tightening, his leg demonstrating his impatience as it pulsed in movement. Clock. Phone.

His boss was asking him something. He answered, then checked his phone again.

Five minutes later, the meeting finally ended. He hurried back to his office and wasn't sure why he had the knot in his stomach. So, his parents called. They called sometimes. That is what parents do. There was no message, just the missed call notification. It meant nothing. His dad hated leaving voice messages. And they were not the kind of family that had scheduled visits or scheduled calls every Sunday. They were a random family. Visiting when they could. Calling when the impulse hit. And it had been a week or so since he talked to his parents. Getting to his office and sitting in his chair, he realized it had been more like a couple of weeks. And now they were calling to check in because he hadn't.

So why did this feel different? Why did he hit the callback button? Did he feel like vomiting all over his desk? As the phone rang, he swivelled in his chair and pulled the garbage can closer, just in case.

His father answered. Then his world fell apart.

Because of that knot in his stomach, his impatience in the meeting, the foreshadowing of what he was hearing from his father on the other end of that line. The words were ticking off like that second hand on the clock. The words pulsing like the rhythm of his shaking leg.

Routine appointment. Mom. Discover. Cancer. Stage four. Time. Months. Arrangements. Treatment. Home.

Then Jerry did vomit into his small wastebasket.

The detective spun in her spot, arms outstretched, then stopped and waved her gun at Ely as she pierced her eyes at him. "Somewhere. Some night. Sometimes." Smiling with a wide grin, her features expressing a wait until you hear this one message. "A man takes his dog for an evening stroll."

The residential street was a quiet one. It was an older neighbourhood with large trees lining the boulevard that created a myriad of shadows, cast by the streetlights emitting their soft glow. That is why this man loved living here: large boulevards, large trees, and large front yards. He walked this path every night with his dog, Goldie. She was a Golden Retriever, and yes, the name was a bit in the nose, but it fit. And not simply for the name of her breed, but because of the golden, yellow flecks she had in her brown eyes.

There were a few regulars that he came across, the familiars, but everyone pretty much kept to themselves nowadays. He wasn't chatty, so nods and a simple hello worked for him. The most he had to small talk was when he passed another dog walker, and their two canines engaged in their sniffing ritual.

He was out later than usual tonight, so the street was empty, just the soft breeze rustling the trees and making the shadows dance as he walked their usual path. Lately, their walks have been getting a little later each time. Goldie was fourteen and not as energetic to get up and out for the nighttime exercise. The only time she got energetic was when she came across her favourite fire hydrant, and lately, she wasn't listening when it was time to resume their walk. Old Goldie would sniff that thing for hours if he let her, and often, as she was getting deaf, or simply more stubborn in her old age, it was turning into a struggle to get her away from that darned fire hydrant. He didn't like having to get stern with her, so they stayed on the other side of the street to avoid it in their travels. She would eye it as they passed by, at least avoiding the tug of war.

On this night, with it being later than they were taking their walk, nobody was around to witness the man abruptly turn, stroll up a front lawn, and stand there, staring at the house before him.

Goldie felt the tug on her leash and reluctantly followed, but her attention was on the fire hydrant across the street. The one she never got to visit anymore. The tension on her neck released, and she took that as permission. Fire hydrant in her sights, she bolted down the lawn, leash dragging in her wake, and into the street. As she ran into the street, she looked back, but the man wasn't giving chase; the man was moving in the opposite direction towards the house.

The dog was oblivious to the car bearing down on her, caught in the glow of headlights, and the vehicle came to a screeching halt just before her. Goldie cowered a moment, her face just inches from the front grill of the car. Overcoming her fear, she was up again, moving out of the headlights and towards her fire hydrant.

Inside the house, the man stalked the halls as if he lived there, moving through the dark to slither up the stairwell to the upstairs bedrooms. He stood just inside the doorway of the master bedroom. Before him, a woman was fast asleep in bed.

The woman in that bed was named Julia. She was a single mom trying to make a life for herself and her eight-year-old son, who was just down the hall, asleep in his room. Lost in their slumbering depths, neither was aware of the man who had broken into their house and stalked the halls.

A weight on her, pain in her arms, pressure on her face, ripped from the sanctity of dreams, Julia's eyes popped open. Julia found it hard to move. Someone was on top of her, a man. Hot breath wafting onto her face, he pressed close. Instantly awake with fear induced adrenaline, she began to fight and struggled to get free. Her arms were held above her head. One of the man's hands held her wrists, crossed over tightly against each other. She was trying to scream, but the man's other hand covered her mouth so she could only elicit a muffled squeal. She tossed her head side to side. The hand clasped over her mouth also covered part of her nose, making it hard to catch a decent breath, and the more she tossed her head, the more weight he applied, the pressure forcing her deeper into the pillow. She could barely move. She could barely breathe. It was inciting panic in her. But her panic was for her son down the hall. Whatever was happening in this moment, his safety was paramount.

The weight of him straddling her kept her from being able to kick out, but she bucked her hips and squirmed to try to knock him loose. To get him off. She struggled for air, trying to bite the hand over her mouth. She wrenched, yanked, and pulled, trying to get an arm free.

In response to her fight, to silence her survival instinct, he bashed her in the side of her head. Once. Twice. Three times.

Stars paraded behind her eyes as she heard him chastise her with a Julia, Julia, Julia. Slurring her name in that drinker-drawl just like her alcoholic ex-husband used to do. Like he used to do when he would come to her at night, not accepting the rejection of his flirtations earlier in any given evening. Like he used to do before he committed suicide, because he had been such a loser and had failed in his mission to drink himself to death.

Her mouth was free. He had used that hand to smash her head in when she had tried to bite. She tried to call for help, but only elicited a moan because of the pain ringing in her head, a hard knee in the stomach forcing her air out.

Then another pain, sharp and fast. Her underwear being ripped from her body, the elastic band, not easily torn, bit into her skin.

That got a scream out of her.

That got another punch.

That got her hand around her neck. He had not been successful silencing her with a hand over a biting mouth, so he was pressing and squeezing her larynx shut instead, strangling her.

She was being choked as she felt him force his way into her. Eyes wide and adjusted to the dark, she could see more of this stranger's face. He was no one she recognized. But she recognized those slurring words. She recognized his movements against her as he moved in and out raping her.

That felt like her ex.

A noise. A Mommy. She turned her head and looked at the bedroom doorway where her son stood, confused, rubbing sleep from his eyes. Mommy.

That kicked something inside her. Fire-rage, a mother's fierceness to protect, she yanked an arm free and smacked the hand off her throat. Air. Breathe. The single gasp she took was exhaled in her yelling to her son to run. Get help, the Neighbours.

Then there were stars again, sharp pain in the side of her head, her throat closing again. A blackness was washing over her.

The boy was initially frozen as he watched the man hit his mom, but he remembered other nights like this with his dad from when he was younger. Those nights were burned into his memories. Those nights still gave him nightmares. So, when he heard his mom say run, the instinct was to do as he was told and not question.

He ran. down the hall, half slipping, almost falling down the stairs in his panic, and out the front door, across the lawn to the neighbour, he could see light from a television emanating from behind the curtains of the front room. He drummed on the door, yelling for help.

Only a few seconds passed until the door flew open, the boy was ushered inside to safety, and the neighbours called the police.

"When the authorities arrived, they found that man still straddling, kneeling over the now dead body of the mother," the detective said. "He still had his hands tight around her neck, and it took three police officers to unclench those hands and pull him off. He wasn't struggling or trying to fight them off, he was just frozen, muscles locked tight as if he was stricken by death and seized with rigor mortis.

"This stranger had broken into a house, raped and murdered a woman that as far as anyone could discern was a random attack.

"The man, the dog walker, sitting stunned in a squad car, had no idea what he had just done, or why he had done it. The woman was a stranger to him. He had never had rape or murder fantasies in his life. He had no recollection of the egregious act he had just committed; the only explanation he could give was that something must have come over him.

The detective shrugged and then, careful not to step in the surrounding pool of blood, squatted beside the lifeless body of Stacey. "And something had come over him, or like your friend here, someone had come into him."

Standing again, the detective moved closer to Ely and Sera to finish her explanation. "This all happened to change the direction of the boy's life."

"What? Why?" Ely questioned.

"For better or worse, for good or perceived evil, we will never truly know the why of it," the detective said with that sly grin that alluded to her knowing more than she was letting on. "It's for the higher beings to steer the flow of the universe."

"But the mom. That man's life," Sera was uncomprehending, disgust written on her face, especially for the way the detective was sauntering around in front of them, gun in hand, with no regard for Stacey.

"She was a catalyst. He was just a vessel."

Frustrated or angry, she wasn't sure which. Sera got in the detective's face and yelled. "Why are you telling us these things? What do you want from me?"

The barrel of the gun was pressing into Sera's forehead, forcing her back. "Don't you move. I'm not here for you. You are irrelevant. A candle that can be snuffed out with but a puff of air."

The detective kicked Stacey's body. "I thought it was her, but she had to be silenced." The detective looked around the gun, seductively twisting her neck to take Ely in. "But Ely, Ely has something I want. He's a little more special."

Somewhere deep in the surrounding forest, a distance from Sera's house, in a clearing illuminated by the light of the moon, several deer were grazing. Their ears twitched with alertness as they placed delicate steps, making selective bites from the small field.

A large buck oversaw the group, his pride of antlers seeming too heavy for his head that shot up, and he snorted a haze of breath into the coolness of the night air. There was no sound to cause his distraction, but the heads of the female doe around him looked up in response to his alertness.

The buck was running, bounding into the treeline with the herd in close pursuit.

The detective still had the muzzle of her gun pressed into Sera's head, but her attention was on Ely. "You are the special one. Even back then, weren't you? You didn't know it yet. The real quandary to that night, when a dog ran out into the street and you had a sudden urge to get your dad to stop the car a second before that dog would have been turned into a speed bump, or was your impulse to save that woman and maintain the boy's direction in life?"

Ely went back to his thoughts. His memories lately seemed muddled because of the blackout moments he used to have. Fugues were now brimming to the surface of his memory, his actions, but not necessarily his life. Sometimes.

But that night, he knew.

They were coming home from the movies. He and Sera were in the backseat. Dad was driving, and Mom was there. The mom he always wanted to remember from before that fateful night, but he couldn't think about that now. Mom was in the passenger seat, sitting sideways so she could see her kids better as they talked about the best beats of the movie. They laughed as they recalled certain lines and remarked on their favourite scenes. It was one of those special moments where the euphoria of happiness, of feeling that family bond, sits with you.

Then Ely was lurching forward in his seat, grabbing onto the back of the driver's seat and yelling

"STOP!" in his dad's ear so loud their father slammed on the brakes as a shadow bolted in front of the car.

Ely remembered that night well.

Not just because of the positive family moment. Because Sera had been thrown forward, their dad had yelled from being startled. Not due to them all laughing after the shock had dissipated when they saw the dog go traipsing off.

That night had stuck with him because when they pulled away, a piercing pain stabbed into his head, his stomach flipped, and he felt suddenly ill. Ely had not recalled ever feeling a pain like that one. Not until the explosion in his head when he went into the baby's bedroom at Sera's house the other day. That was different, though; this was worse, much worse. As his dad drove away Ely had sunk in the back seat feeling like he was about to lose his bowels and crap his pants as fire spread through his gut. Wrapping his arms around his midsection and looking out the window so his sister would not notice the grimace on his face or the glistening of building tears in his eyes. Too much candy and popcorn at the movie? That is what his young brain figured as the discomfort subsided. Now he realized it may have been a reaction to missing the signal.

The impulse may not have been for the dog.

Weird little Ely. They had joked over that story. Scaring the shit out of them all and saving a stray dog.

He had not thought about that night in forever, yelling at his dad to stop the car and save the dog. And now the idea was there, that maybe it wasn't for the dog. He had been yelling to stop at a man they had never noticed. The man proceeded to rape and murder a woman in front of her child's eyes.

Shaking his head, that didn't matter now. A gun pressed into his sister's forehead; Sera mattered now. Ely pushed himself between Sera and the detective, his arms raised to draw attention to himself and communicate his surrender. "If I'm the one who is so special, then you just talk to me. Sera has nothing to do with whatever it is you want. So, you keep that gun off her, and you tell me what it is you want. I'm right here."

"You don't get to dictate the terms here," the detective chided. "As far as what I want. You are coming with me, and we are taking a little trip."

The gun was off Sera now, that was a relief, but the detective now trained it on Ely, motioning him toward the door with it. Ely didn't move. He stood resolute in defiance of the orders being given to him. There was no way the detective was taking him and leaving Sera alone, alive. There had to be a resolution that guaranteed her safety. "You explain what it is you want from me. My sister comes with us. Then I cooperate."

A darkness crept over the detective's face, shaded with a burgeoning anger and impatience. "Fine!" She barked and grabbed Sera by the arm, roughly shoving her to the front door. "You two start moving towards that door, and I'll explain. I'll explain what you are feeling, what you have become aware of. I'll explain that this is the spirit world calling us. Using us."

Ely had caught Sera as she stumbled forward and directed her behind him so he could be a shield as the siblings walked backwards to always keep the detective in sight.

"But now, it is happening more often," the detective continued as she pressed towards them. "Just think of ultraviolet rays bombarding the thinning ozone layer. This is like the spirit world racing for a home, a vessel. The mystical barrier around us is just like the ozone layer. It weakens and has holes torn into it, allowing more ultraviolet rays through."

The detective stopped, tilted her head back, and flung her arms wide in proclamation. "The gates have flown wide open. The beacons have been set. People will do things, catastrophic things, there will be no rhyme or reason, or perceived accidents. People won't know. We are not talking about possession, where the churches of the world may be awakened. It is far more subtle, obsession, the slight pushes, the momentary lapses."

Now she was looking at them, Ely and Sera froze at the slight glint of a smile she proposed, revealing the full-on crazy. "The spirit world is bursting at the seams and needs to re-seed. Some, like you, Ely, the spiritually sensitive, are awakening. I am here to ensure none like you will delay our dominion. I am here to hunt your sons and daughters of light. To ensure darkness rises to bring a new dawn."

"The end of times?" Sera questioned.

"Think of it as a new beginning in time," the detective's grin widened. "This isn't a bad thing. It's an evolution thing."

Stepping back, Sera bumped into the door. There was nowhere left to retreat except into the night beyond. She reached behind herself and wrapped her hand around the doorknob, slowly twisting to release the latch bolt from the striker plate so they could move quickly if the opportunity to escape presented itself.

"Now, enough delaying," the detective said as she quickly moved closer and struck Ely in the side of the head with her gun, sending him reeling to the ground. "Him I need, but you are just a distraction…"

Wood exploded from the door beside Sera's left ear before she heard the shot go off. The splinters forced her forward, tripping over her feet, but at least her hand still held firm to the doorknob that swung open in her descent.

Sera did not miss the moment, as she struggled to find her feet and bolt out the door.

In pursuit, the detective filled the door frame, firing her gun into the night. "…a witness to be blinded, to be silenced."

Red-hot fire burst through Sera's shoulder, and she was sent flying forward, tumbling over the hood of the right edge of the detective's vehicle and disappearing down its side.

Sera swivelled to her butt and shimmied back until she was pressed into the driver's side door, hoping in the fleeting second that she was shielded from any further shots as she held her injured arm and inspected the wound. Blood was soaking her shirt, but as she pulled the fabric back to investigate, she could tell the bullet had only grazed her. Still, it hurt like a red-hot poker had been slapped against her shoulder, and her arm felt too heavy to lift.

Another gunshot panged against the metal of the car's hood. Then another into the windshield and continuing out the driver's door window to send fragments of shattered tempered glass raining down onto Sera's head. She had to move; it was dark outside.

Clouds covered the stars and moon to press in a deeper blackness of night. Fear-induced adrenaline, pain, and shock made the surrounding area look like a black hole as her head swivelled side to side to get some bearings and pick a route for escape.

"NO!" She heard Ely yell, followed by a thump and varying grunts.

Yelling in defiance, Ely charged at the detective, her back to him as she pursued Sera through the front door. He dove into her, wrapping his right arm around her neck, and the two of them struggled out into the night.

Again, that gun hand flew back and caught him square in the forehead. The detective thrust forward, and Ely was flipped over her shoulder. He flew onto the hood of the car, and the momentum took him sliding right over the side, where his vain rescue attempt left him painfully landing right alongside his sister.

"Fool," the detective called out as she rounded the front of the car, ready to fire again. "I need you. But not necessarily in one piece."

All three turned their heads as rustling and snaps came from the forest's edge. The detective's stern visage turned to surprised terror as a female deer, breached from the near treeline, was charging right at her. The detective barely had a chance to move as she slid to the side to dodge the deer, which hit her right on. Two others followed, then a male buck with his large antler rack snapping branches as the quartet of deer, blinded in their escape from whatever it was they were running from, drove them out of their sanctuary of the forest

The first doe disappeared over the top of the car with little bounding effort. The second veered at the last second to the left, rounding the front. They were each coming like arrows straight at the detective. The third leapt late, and it's back hoof clipped the side of the detective's head with bullet force, sending her reeling back stunned into the side of the car.

Ely and Sera were on the ground, shuffling on hands and butts towards the rear of the car, they were just as surprised as the detective.

The detective held the side of her head as she steadied herself against the car. Then the buck slammed into her, straight on as a missile, head down low, his antlers piercing her midsection and pinning her to the vehicle as he slumped with the impact.

The siblings on the ground shrank back in horror. The buck's hind legs still twitched in movement as it released short, shallow breaths. The detective didn't move.

"Oh my God!" Was all Sera could mutter. "Oh my God!"

"C'mon, get up," Ely enticed Sera to her feet. "We need to go."

Sera winced as he gently pulled on her arm. She was still bleeding out. He tore at the sleeve of his shirt to rip off a portion for a makeshift bandage that he tightened around Sera's arm.

"What was that? What just happened?"

"A miracle," Ely said matter-of-factly. "Now let's go."

"Where? Go where?" Panic was creeping up her spine, working its way to envelope her.

"I don't know. Anywhere. Just get in the car. We need to get you medical attention."

Off to the side was the detective's gun. Her grip had been released, when the buck killed her. Ely bent down to pick it up.

He turned, and Sera was moving around parked cars, inspecting each one. The tires on her jeep, Ely had driven over. Stacey's car was sporting a couple of flat tires

"How? She must have slashed all the tires," Sera informed Ely. "All of our cars have flats."

They both turned in unison to look at the detective's car. The tires were all inflated. The only problem was that the vehicle had a dead body pinned to it.

Ely looked at the carcasses before them, then up at Sera and shrugged.

Sera was shaking her head. "We are not unpinning her or going through a dead person's pockets to find keys."

"That buck is half on top of her, it's probably too heavy. You can't help with that arm," he agreed as he looked around. "We are going to have to hike out."

"Follow me," Sera said as she grabbed her brother's arm and directed him into the forest.

It was dark, the pines reaching high, creating a deeper black on the ground, and the two of them made a right pair of Hanzel and Gretel as they moved in panic mode through the trees. As her arm pulsed in pain, the only comfort Sera had was that they had already slain the witch.

In the clearing of Sera's cabin, the detective's eyes popped open with a gasped breath. She looked around to get her bearings, but her attention was drawn down to the weight on her body as the stag's head lay limp in her lap, its antlers pierced in her midsection, the piercing from her chest and midsection. She fingered the antlers, grabbing hold, and tried to force them out.

They barely budged. The movement only caused white-hot flashes of pain to erupt from her stomach area and more blood to ooze.

"Well, this complicates things," the detective murmured to herself. "Missed every major organ, didn't you, you big bastard." Her breathing was laboured and heavy. "My luck. Your fate!"

Impaled, bleeding, and currently stuck, the detective turned her head side to side, searching for the brother and sister. She saw them, barely shadowed by the scant moon as they disappeared into the trees.

"Your sister can run, but you can't hide," she couldn't help but smile a little as she pushed on the buck's head, trying to extract the horns from her torso. The parade of fire that erupted from her insides caused her to pass out again.

CHAPTER FIFTEEN

On a grassy knoll that crowned the bank of a small creek, Sera rolled over from her fitful sleep. Some time in the night, they had stopped to rest. As the warm sun on her face drew her awake, Sera realized they must have dozed off. The sun was coming up to introduce dawn.

"We have to move," she said, fear still directing her, and she ordered Ely without even looking for him.

"Good morning," he replied. He had been awake, standing behind her on top of the embankment.

"Why didn't you wake me?" Anxious, not fully having her bearings, but upset that Ely had not roused her to continue their escape.

"It's okay. Right now, we are okay. And I only just woke up a minute or two before you. I think once we stopped, the adrenaline wore off and we both passed out," Ely replied.

"You think," Sera retorted. She was not happy being in the middle of nowhere, being exposed. Then she winced from her wound.

"C'mon, let's check that out," Ely said, taking her arm and gently unwrapping the makeshift bandage. "Bleeding has stopped, probably going to scar, but you should live." He turned and walked to the edge of the creek and crouched down to wash the sleeve bandage.

"Should live. I'm sure. My sanity is where the biggest scar is going to reside, though," Sera retorted as she joined her brother at a nearby creek and began splashing water on her face and washing the blood from her arm.

With the rag, Ely retied it around Sera's wound. "You are going to need stitches," he commented after closer inspection of the wound.

"You are right, I do," Sera winced as Ely pulled the makeshift bandage tight. "This is crazy. We can't just keep running aimlessly through the woods."

"I know," Ely said, looking at her. "I was just trying to get us safe, get distance between us, and that crazy detective. Anywhere seemed better than there."

"Well, crazy detective is dead, so let's figure out what we are going to do," Sera said as she rubbed her forehead. A tension headache was clenching down. "First, how do you suggest we explain a gunshot wound and two dead bodies at my residence?"

Ely was shrugging. "Hunting accident! Or do you have a better idea?"

"I do," Sera walked backwards up the creek bank while hitching a thumb over her shoulder to motion a direction. "My neighbours. They are an older couple, but he used to be a large animal vet. He could probably patch me up. And they should have a car we can borrow."

"My legs like the sound of a car," Ely responded. "But wait. Speaking of cars, we need to go back. I left a duffle bag of cash in your car."

Sera turned to look at her brother with a raised eyebrow. "Why do you have a bag of cash in my car?"

"I don't know. It was from one of those episodes I have. We could use that money."

"I have money. And even if I didn't, we are not going back," Sera turned and began walking away, ending the discussion.

With his head hung low, Ely reluctantly fell in step. "But it was a lot of money."

They walked together along the creek, a little slower than when they escaped the night before. Their bodies were sore from sleeping on the ground.

"Yeah, a car would be great," Ely continued. "Even better will be if they have some ibuprofen."

Sera paused in mid-step and looked around. "We should have gone directly there last night. I didn't think in the moment because we were running in blind panic. We've come in the opposite direction, but we can loop around. We should be there in a couple of hours." She took a breath as she tried to get her bearings. "Just don't blame me if we get lost."

"Might get lost? You live here. How can you get lost?"

"Because I don't explore, and I am not a hiker."

Ely looked back at her. "Well, at this point, being lost is the least I would blame you for."

"How can you be joking?" Sera threw her arms up in exasperation.

"That's the only thing keeping my sanity from unravelling," Ely said as he turned his back to her to begin the long march ahead.

***

The horses could hear Buck coming down the short trail before they saw him, and he smiled at the soft nicker they delivered as a good morning.

"Good morning, boys," he returned, as he rounded the small storage barn and began loading the pushcart with square bales of hay.

He tossed their breakfast over the wood-railed fence and rested against the top rail to watch them a moment. The morning sun was reaching down through the tall trees that rustled their awakening with the gentle breeze that caused the higher, lighter branches to sway. Buck felt old this morning, heck, he felt old every morning lately. Meryl and he had been here many years. And while some things never changed, others marked their time here together. The short path from the house to the horse pen was wider and a bit deeper. The trees were taller. Buck loved every bit of it. He loved this little piece of heaven they had built together. The two of them had never had children, unless you counted the four-legged ones, their horses. Buck arched his back to work a kink out. Yes, he felt old, but these daily rituals made him feel alive, kept him alive. If a city dweller, he probably would have ended up in an old fart's home by now, and that darn well would have killed him. He needed the open, the space.

Everyone was too scrunched together in a city. That is why they had stayed here. More people had moved into the area over the years, but everyone was still far away, the forest still concealing enough that nobody even felt like neighbours. Not like a city had neighbours. A family lived across the south, on the other side of the river. They had a couple of teenagers who must have had friends visit because sometimes he was walking with Meryl, and they could hear them down by the river. They were good, respectful kids just having fun, not the raucous, trouble-making type. And to the West was that writer lady, but she was more of a recluse than they were.

A whistle came through the trees, the horses lifted their heads to listen. It was Meryl's bird call to let him know it was time to return.

"That means my breakfast is ready, boys," Buck tapped the top rail of the fence. "I'll be back later to open the gate."

The creaking of the back screen door gave notice of Buck's arrival.

"You better hurry and wash up, mister, I called for you twice, your breakfast will get cold," Meryl demanded.

"You only called once," Buck replied as he kicked off his boots and hung his coat.

"Twice," Meryl popped her head around the corner, holding two fingers.

"My hearing is fine, and it was once, don't you try to fool me," Buck chided as he sat at the kitchen table.

Meryl just smiled behind his back as she grabbed the pot of coffee. His hearing was not fine, but there was no sense arguing with Buck about it. It was more fun to tease him occasionally, anyway.

Just as Meryl set the coffee pot back onto the maker hot plate and prepared to sit with her husband, there was a knock at the front door.

"Are we expecting anyone?" She asked.

"Not that I'm aware of," Buck replied, motioning for her to sit. "I'll get it.

"Well, we don't get too many surprise visits out here."

"Probably somebody with car trouble again," Buck grumbled at the intrusion as he got up from his chair.

Pulling the front door open, Buck was a little surprised to see a woman standing on his porch. She was half leaning against the side of the door as if exhausted. Her coat was held tightly closed with one hand, and with the other, she lazily held up a badge to identify herself.

"Hello, can I help you?" Buck greeted, before considering the woman's posture. She was either tired or maybe hurt. But her stance was off.

"Are you the couple that found that baby?" The detective asked as she slid the badge into her coat pocket.

"My wife was, yes," Buck responded with a cocked eyebrow. They had already been through everything with the police after Meryl had found the baby in the outhouse the other week. It seemed strange that an officer would show up now, unannounced.

What made him more uncomfortable was the detective's mouth twisted into a half grin, and she stood tall.

"Who is it?" Meryl was in the living room, calling out to her husband.

Buck stepped back to answer his wife, giving her a view of the woman at the door. "A detective? She is asking about the baby you saved."

"Then come in, come in," Meryl waved the lady inside.

Buck gave way so the detective could enter the house. Then closed the door behind her. He rubbed his head, a little frustrated. His breakfast was going to be cold now that this woman had shown up.

"You are the one who found that baby," the Detective said as she reached out to shake Meryl's hand.

"Yes," Meryl said, but instantly felt unease as soon as the words escaped her lips.

The detective held Meryl's hand firmly as she looked back at the husband and then turned to press in close to the woman. "Then you should have stayed hidden."

***

On a stretch of a two-laned road, the detective's unmarked cruiser was parked on the side of what could barely be considered a shoulder. It was a small stretch of weedy earth of maybe five feet and then a wall of forest trees. Tall pines were so close to each other that their branches were interwoven in places. Passing traffic would have to angle out to the other lane to get by because there was not enough room for her to fully clear the roadway on either side. When the detective parked, she had glided over to the other side, so the front of her vehicle faced oncoming traffic. This way, the damage on her driver's side was mostly concealed.

That made her laugh. The cruiser couldn't be considered unmarked anymore, could it, with the denting and blood stains. The detective shimmied over to the passenger seat to exit the vehicle. Even if the driver's door were operational, she would not have been able to squeeze out with her tight parking job.

Leaning against the cruiser, the detective looked both ways for oncoming traffic before lifting her face to the mid-morning sun to feel its warmth. It was a bit of a wait for the help she needed to come by on this stretch of road, and the chances of someone stopping would have been slim in her previous state. Luckily, there were clothes at the old couple's place that she could borrow. She adjusted the zippered hoodie that covered the t-shirt she wore underneath. Maybe the hoodie and baggy jeans were not professional law enforcement attire, but at least she was somewhat presentable now that she was out of her dirty and bloodied clothes.

It was not as long as the detective anticipated before a vehicle could be seen off in the distance, coming down the highway. As it edged closer, the detective smiled to herself. It was a school bus. If it were full of students. Perfect! She needed hunters. Ely and his sister had escaped her, but they were on foot somewhere in these woods.

The detective stepped out into the middle of the road to block the path of the oncoming bus. She waved for the driver's attention, motioning for the bus to stop.

As the bus came to a halt and she moved to the door, students were already either leaning out the windows or pressing their faces to the glass to see what the holdup was about. They appeared older. The detective gauged that it must be high schoolers. She could not have wished for a better scenario. The doors parted, and an adult came to the bottom of the three-step entrance, leaning out the doors to address the woman standing on the side of the bus.

"I'm Coach Carter," he introduced himself. "Can we help you, car trouble?" Of course, he was a coach. The man was dressed for the track with shorts, knee-high white socks against the pristine black runners, and a whistle dangling around his neck like an Olympic medal.

The detective gave her a badge flash. "We have some fugitives in the area. I'm going to need everyone off the bus!"

"Really," Coach Carter was intrigued, but the woman on the side of the road was dressed informally, if not a little shabbily, for law enforcement. "We are on a deadline here. We are on our way to another school for a pre-season scrimmage. There isn't time for this."

"And I don't have time to go back and forth with you," the detective said sternly to him. "So, everyone needs to get off the bus."

The coach pursed his lips. "We didn't see any other blockades. How come there are no other cruisers out here?"

"There is a blockade a few miles up. Other officers are en route to join me at this location. I've been in pursuit of a couple of fugitives, and we are in the process of getting checkpoints set up." She knew this coach's type. It wasn't that he didn't believe her; this kind of guy just didn't like taking orders from a woman. If he had any inkling of what she could do to him, he would be on his knees in subservience. "If you want to miss those checkpoints before they are fully set up and even more delays, I suggest you get everyone off the bus and let me do my job."

The coach leaned out the door to look down the roadway as if he expected to see an armada of police cruisers barrelling down the highway, then looked her up and down. He was still skeptical. "Can I see your badge again?"

"Sure," the detective responded as she reached into her back pocket for the badge. Her preference was to deal with this with everyone off the bus, but it was enough with this guy. As she presented the badge a second time, she reached out to offer to shake his hand. He instinctively accepted, and that was all it took.

To the bus driver and the teens paying attention to what was transpiring at the front of the bus, it looked like the coach passed out as he went weak, buckling at the knees and tumbled off the stairs onto the pavement.

The detective quickly stepped over him and up into the bus, where she placed her hand on the bus driver's shoulder, and he too instantly slumped forward in his seat.

Some of the teens on the bus were getting out of their seats, wondering what the commotion was. The detective was moving past the first couple of rows, quickly reaching out and touching the kids with a slight graze as she went by. They went rigid for a brief second and then they were rising to fill the aisle behind her.

To the others, she was shouting against the increasing unease of the students. "It's okay. Remain seated. Everything is okay."

Everything was not okay. Some of the students picked up on it faster than the others and began pushing the other students out of the way to escape the woman who was approaching them. Something in this lady's eyes, and the students who were rising to follow her. It was that innate feeling to escape that got them desperately trying to get out of her way. But there was nowhere to go except into the crushing weight of their peers as they gathered at the back of the bus, yelling over each other as a couple of them struggled with the rear emergency door, but because they were being pressed against it, they could not get the leverage to get it open.

This is what she wanted to avoid, the pandemonium. With their panic, getting all of them under her dominance would take more effort. But that was okay, she didn't need all the students. Either way, nobody on that bus was going to make it home today.

CHAPTER SIXTEEN

"Might get us lost," Ely chuffed, swatting a mosquito from his neck as he followed his sister up the short hill from the river's edge they had been following for the last hour or so.

This supposed last leg of their journey had been the most exhausting. Sera was adamant it was a shortcut, but Ely was sure any other route would have been not only faster but easier. Coming this way forced them to push through thorny bushes that left tiny cuts on every part of their exposed skin. Then they had the excruciating effort of making it through a bog where their feet felt like they were encased in cement with every laboured step. They had briefly pondered turning back, but the wall of thorn-riddled bushes closed them in. Plus, bogs were never that big. Wrong. With quadriceps on fire and calf muscles threatening to seize up them they finally reached firmer ground. Reaching the flat ground along a riverbank had been a momentary relief until it was found to be uneasy ground with moss-slippery rocks and mud in certain places. Sera had slipped and gone down on one muddy patch, and they were both certain she had sprained her ankle. Resting her foot in the cold water alleviated the pain, and luckily, she had only twisted it. That would have been a whole other ordeal if he had to support his sister on a one-legged hike out of these god forsaken woods.

None of that compared to the bugs.

Ely was thirsty. Ely was hungry. The vampiric blood-sucking mosquitoes were tormenting them ever since they got close to the water.

"Might get us lost?" Ely repeated himself as he slapped the side of his face to end the life of another blood sucking bug.

"Well, just be glad this didn't happen in the wintertime," Sera quipped. "We would have frozen to death."

"I'd rather freeze to death..." Ely smacked another bug. "...Over slowly being eaten alive."

Sera stopped and looked back at him. "Quiet! Do you hear that?"

"I hear the river and buzzing. That's it," Ely was exhausted and could only manage sarcasm.

"Up this way," Sera pointed up the short hill and the animal trail ahead of them. "Horses. My neighbours, Buck and Meryl, are up this way."

"I can't believe we made it," Ely smacked himself for the umpteenth time. "I don't even care about borrowing a car now. I just want food." Smack. "And to wash myself in calamine lotion."

"Shut up, I know your vain attempts at humour are to try and keep me distracted from the nightmare we are in," Sera said as she led the way again.

"Not trying to be funny, I just really want to know what is in your pheromones that these bugs leave you alone, and treat me like I'm a drive-through."

At the front door of the house, Sera knocked. Ely leaned against the railing of the three steps of the front porch and looked around. It was an old place, unlike Sera's cabin, which was modern and quite fancy, but it was well-kept and had a welcoming feel. It was easy to imagine an old couple spending their evenings snuggling on the swing that was on the porch, watching the stars, and reminiscing.

Even better was seeing the truck on the gravelled drive. A horse trailer was still hitched to it, and heck, if the old couple were not willing to lend them their truck, maybe they could borrow the horses from the pen they had passed on their way up here.

"What are we even going to say to them?" Sera stole his attention as she waited for the door to be answered.

Ely moved up beside her. "As little as possible. No! A home invasion, that will explain a lot."

"It won't be lying. It was a home invasion." Sera knocked again. "Great, no answer. They don't seem to be home.

"Well, their truck is there. They can't be far."

Long, narrow frosted glass panes framed the front door, each about six inches wide and extending the full length of the door frame. Sera pressed her face close to the window. She could not get a clear look inside, but was hopeful she would see blurry movement of one of them coming to the door. The truck was here, neither Buck nor Meryl seemed to be outside, so maybe her and Ely's arrival was disturbing a nap, and they were slow to answer the door.

Sera knocked again. "I don't think they are home. We might have to wait out here on the porch."

"We have wasted enough time getting here. We don't have time to wait as two bodies are currently rotting at your place," Ely said. You know them, right? Maybe we can go in and borrow the keys, and leave a note."

"I'm sorry," Ely tried to console as he got to his feet, realizing his words had the opposite effect than intended.

She looked at him, eyes red and welling with tears. "How do you even know it's her?"

With an offered hand, Ely pulled his sister up into an embrace. "I'm sorry. I thought it would help. I thought you would want to know."

He paused. Sera had buried her head in his shoulder and was shaking it back and forth. He could hear her mumbling how crazy this all was.

"But now I realize...I just know..." Ely's head snapped to the side. There was a push from somewhere deep inside of him. "...We have to go...Now!"

Ankle be damned he grabbed his sister's arm by the wrist and bolted out of the alcove, down the hill and to the left around several boulders that had taken perch there a millennia ago.

Sera looked back up through the trees to see what the urgency was. A moment later, two boys, men really, and three girls in cheerleader skirts descended on the hiding spot.

Ely had directed his sister to move just in time. His stomach turned as he led her away from the relentless hunting pack because he knew in the briefest of moments, it had not been him. It was an aunt, some dead aunt he had never met, but had known Sera as a baby, that was in him, pushing him forward. Before, he just suffered blackouts and would find out later how much damage he had caused or was in. Now, the feeling takes over his mind and body, too strange to comprehend. This time it didn't make him feel physically ill. He felt sick knowing he was being used, even for something good. He had no control over himself, sometimes causing chaos like Mr. Hyde, other times acting as a saviour.

"I have to catch my breath," Ely stopped to hide behind some bushes. By choice. His choice. Heck, it was his ankle forcing him to stop. Even his body betrayed him and forced his decisions.

"I can't hear anything," Sera was listening for any sounds to mark that they were still being followed. "It's strange. They are not making any noise besides their footsteps, not a single word. And they are teenagers. Did you notice that?"

"They may be. The guy I hit with the branch was twice the size of me," Ely said.

"How are we going to escape them?"

"We keep moving. Wait!" A glimmer of something caught Ely's eye from the far distance. He moved from the cover of the bushes and into a clearing. "Sera."

Preoccupied with keeping an eye on the hill above them, Sera turned at her name, but it took her a moment to see where Ely had disappeared. A second louder whisper led her to him.

When she was at his side, Ely pointed to the town below. "That is your town, right?"

"Yes. I don't know if we should go there. The authorities may already be looking for us."

"Is there a church there?"

"Yeah, why?"

"That crazy detective was talking about possession. A horde of silent, zombie teenagers is chasing us. I figure a church seems like the next best option for us."

Sera didn't warm to the idea of heading into town. There were too many people she might bump into. Roaming the woods was not getting them anywhere. They did not have their stories or shit together to deal with the police yet. House of God, it was a hopeful respite and sanctuary.

"Sounds like the only option," Sera agreed.

<u>CHAPTER SEVENTEEN</u>

Getting down the hillside and into the valley had taken Ely and Sera much longer than they anticipated due to Ely's ankle and their growing anxiety that burgeoned into paranoia that the zombie teens, in their stealth, would jump out at any moment. Ely's ankle was better but weakened, and moving downslope on uneven terrain caused him to roll it a couple of more times. Coupled with Sera making them stop every few steps to listen for the football squad, it felt like they were barely making any progress.

This was the second day they had been on the move with nothing to eat and little water. By the time they made it to the church, they were haggard and dirty. The parking lot was empty, so there was no concern that the church was hosting what must be a late afternoon mass, wedding, or funeral. With one more look around to ensure they were not being followed, or anyone was watching them, they disappeared inside.

It was not a huge church, mid-size, befitting of a town, and old. It was kept well, but the architecture reflected its age. Once inside, Ely and Sera were in the front lobby, the narthex, because the church was not very big, gave them a clear view down the central aisle, lined by rows of pews on either side. At the end, behind the altar, was a large cross with a crucified Jesus statue, gazing solemnly at parishioners during a service.

"Do you see that?" Sera said as they moved down the aisle, stopping halfway to get a clear view of what she had seen.

Their eyes had not been playing tricks on them.

165

Stuck to the lower portion of the statue of Jesus was the assumed resident priest. Crucified against the legs of the statue in a mimicking pose of the crucifixion display, he was attached with various knives. Blood ran down from the punctures to drip off the priest onto the feet of the statue of Jesus.

Hand over mouth, Sera gasped. "Just like Buck." Then turned to Ely. "Is this real?"

"Everywhere we turn...death awaits us," Ely was more muttering to himself in disbelief than replying to his sister. The hope of finding a sanctuary and reprieve drained out of him.

There was a clapping of hands from behind. They turned together and from the last pew before the arch to the narthex, the Detective rose to a sitting position to reveal herself. Ely and Sera had been too distracted by the crucified body of the priest at the altar that neither of them had paid any heed to look down the rows of pews.

"Everywhere you turn," the Detective said with a wide grin as she slid from the pew to block their exit through the front. "There will be no sanctuary."

Ely and Sera pulled back in shock.

"Detective? How?" Ely verbalized his surprise.

She moved closer, opening her arms wide as if to expect a welcoming embrace. "Oh, I think by now our relationship is on a more personal level. The word Detective is so generic. My name is Tory, and it's time to face facts. I will always be steps ahead. There is no hiding. The light inside you is a beacon, a lighthouse that draws me, but we need the darkness."

Ever the protector, the big sister, Sera placed herself in front of Ely as they backed down the aisle in step with Tory to maintain a distance.

"How are you alive?" Sera asked in disbelief. "Why are you even doing this? Talking about snuffing out light, what reason is there to want to bring death, darkness, and all this misery?" Then she was yelled at in defiance. "Why us!"

"What single-mindedness," Tory half laughed as she replied. "In the animal world, to the nocturnes, darkness is their light. Kind of like the resurrection of Christ." She pointed at the oversized statue of Jesus. "Now is the time for a new dawning."

She was closer. Ely was frantically looking for an escape route, but they were running out of aisle and time.

Eyes on Ely, Tory pointed. "Give yourself up." Then twisted her lips into a sadistic smile. "Or that child of hers will suffer eternally."

"Are you talking about my daughter?" A sudden flame ignited in Sera, pushing away her current state of fear.

"I'm a lot closer to her than you," Tory taunted.

"Lies!" Sera yelled as she lunged forward in an overwhelming rage.

Ely grabbed her just in time to hold her back.

Unfazed at the aggression, Tory continued. "I was there. I was the one who took her from you while you slept. Not S.I.D.S. Not in your case, it was no such thing. Just a word to give a title to the unexplainable. It was easy to snuff out something that shines because you were like every inept parent. Oblivious in your sleep.

Taking the world for granted. Believing in the natural order of things. Not even protecting her, not able to save her. Your one role as a parent failed."

Now, Ely was the angry one. They had reached the end of the rows of pews, so he pushed his sister to the side and dived forward at Tory. "Bitch!"

"Yes, this is what I want," Tory smiled as they fell back into the aisle, tussling to the ground.

It was only for a moment that Ely felt like he had the upper hand, and then he found himself on the bottom as Tory managed to position herself on top of him and dropped several blows to Ely's face. She was fast and stronger than Ely could have anticipated, as the stars paraded behind his eyes.

Grabbing onto a pew, Sera got to her feet, unsure how to help as the two struggled on the ground.

Knees straddled over Ely to immobilize him; Tory caught Sera's movement with the corner of her eye. She delivered another punch into the side of Ely's head, grabbed his throat with her right hand to hold his attention as she pointed up at the sister with her free hand. "First, she dies." Now both hands were around Ely's neck to wrestle that last bit of consciousness from him. "Then we open you up for all those sweet bits inside."

His head was lifted and slammed down onto the floor. Although carpeted, it was hard underneath. A second time. Ely fought but couldn't get his arms free, and he was tapped out from the hiking, the lack of nourishment, the punches to his face he had accepted, and the cracking of his skull against the floor. A third slam and everything was blurring, going grey.

The body below her went limp into unconsciousness. Tory immediately got up and turned to attack Sera.

Sera was half full of rage at the lies this woman had spewed about her daughter. If she truly was at fault for Anne's death, then this Tory bitch was about to experience the truth behind a mother scorned. The other half of her was filled with terror that Ely may be dead. She couldn't get a clear view of him, just his legs. He was unmoving, but as the other woman stepped towards her, she heard him.

"Sera, move!" Not dead, but his voice was hoarse from the choking. "Move!"

There was a rumble from the right side of the building. Sera moved instinctively at her brother's instruction, and seconds later, the church wall exploded inwards as a travel bus came barrelling through.

Debris flew everywhere, pews being forced to the sides as if snow under a plow's shovel as the bus bulleted towards Ely and Tory, who was caught in mid-step, standing close. Directly in its path, Ely was on the ground, lying limp and flat as the bus drove right over him, leaving him untouched to pile drive into Tory.

The bus came to a crashing halt on the opposite wall, pinning the mangled body of Tory between its front grill and the rubble of the church wall.

Scrambling through the debris, Sera grabbed Ely by his armpits and dragged him away, closer into the lobby of the church, before she fell to her knees in shocked exhaustion. A beaten-up Ely cradled his head in his big sister's lap as they both tried to catch their breath and some comprehension.

"What the hell just happened?" Sera looked down at him, relieved he was awake and not dead.

"A miracle? Guardian Angels? You pick!" Ely coughed. His throat was still hoarse from the strangling.

Sera cradled her brother, looking down at him. "You think? What are we going to do now?"

"Find others."

"What? What others are there?" Sera replied.

Ely managed to get up to perch on one elbow and pointed at the wreckage before them. A couple of Tory's limbs could be seen sticking out from the side of the front end of the bus. "That woman keeps coming back to life and coming after us. She had said she was hunting us, sons and daughters of light. That's plural. This is a bigger thing than just me, and you. You felt it in the forest."

Sera helped Ely to his feet, where he doubled over for a moment in obvious pain from the beating he had been subjected to. But they needed to move.

Ely held up a hand to say he was okay and, with a groan, got himself upright to continue his perception. "Around the world, there are stories of people and bouts of possession, sixth sense, being able to communicate with the dead. I can't be the only spiritually sensitive, there must be some truth to some stories. Ones like me being used as a vessel, not just the ones moving on instinct under an obsession.

"And after the deer, I don't believe this is the last of Detective Tory." Sera shook her head.

"No, I doubt it," Ely agreed. "So, we need to find the others."

"But how?"

Ely looked at her sympathetically. "Maybe your daughter can help us."

***

In an ethereal, time-displaced elsewhere, of a nether place, a shadow of a young girl walked among a lush garden beaming with rays of light reflected off pools of crystal clear, blue-hued water, highlighting the thin iridescent wings of butterflies. The young girl twirled and twirled in bare feet on soft grass, leaped and skipped, then stopped abruptly. She came forward to an invisible edge and pressed her small hand forward against an invisible barrier, feeling the clearness of a window that wasn't there.

PART II

CHAPTER EIGHTEEN

The clear sky was only blemished with a few clouds, adding cushioning reflections of an orange, fiery haze as the sun travelled its westerly descent to settle in for the night. The brightness of that setting sun reflected off the Boeing 737, which was only a couple of hours away from delivering its cargo of passengers safe and sound.

The skies were clear, but the passenger jet suddenly bounced from turbulence, causing the pilot's stomach to rise as the plane dropped altitude.

"Whoa! I'm awake," The pilot quickly reasserted himself to the control panel, checking gauges to verify the jolt was not a mechanical error.

No alarms were going off besides the notification of the altitude drop. He was sure some of the passengers in the cabin were losing their lunches right now. He would check with the crew once he felt secure that they were not going to be impacted by further turbulence.

"Is the autopilot compensating?" He turned to his co-pilot.

The co-pilot checked the gauges and responded. "Speed is being reduced and reacquiring altitude."

"Okay. Let's get the seatbelt signal on."

The co-pilot was leaning in closer to the control panel. "Jesus, we lost almost 200 feet."

"It's a perfect day. We are not close to any mountains. There are no storms. Where did that come from?" The captain was feeling a bit unnerved. He had been flying for over twenty years and had experienced a lot in his aviation career, and he knew what Clear Air

Turbulence was. CAT, as they referred to Clear Air Turbulence, was the acronym for turbulence experienced at higher altitudes when there were no storms or mountain regions in the area, and they were flying inland, so there should not have been any atmospheric pressures to cause what they had just experienced. And what the plane just did was not CAT. That was not turbulence. The plane had just dropped. It was as if they were driving and went straight off a cliff.

"I don't know," the co-pilot responded. "But you can bet dollars to donuts that it gave the passengers a start."

"I'm sure it did. Notify the cabin, I am switching on the seatbelt sign, and I will call ahead to see if we should be expecting a rough last leg," the captain ordered. He would not mind the rough weather ahead, as he could plan and deal with it.

A flight attendant in the front of the cabin at the flight attendant service station found herself on the floor, dazed and confused. Passengers were screaming and yelping. Trying to regain her composure after hitting her head, she noticed the Inflight Supervisor beside her, using the interphone to communicate with the cabin.

Her supervisor hung up and then switched to provide an announcement to the cabin. "The seatbelt sign has been activated. The captain advised that we had just experienced a little turbulence, so please remain seated in case we experience more."

As the supervisor finished her announcement and returned the interphone to its cradle, she whirled and gave the stewardess on the floor a pessimistic look as she snapped her fingers at her for attention and motioned for the stewardess to get up as she quipped her name. The supervisor wasn't usually so abrupt, but in this case, she was not so concerned with whether her co-worker was okay, just that they needed to get into action.

Seated on the ground, rubbing her head and feeling the haze of confusion dissipate, Bes wasn't impressed with this woman towering over her. Whatever name the woman was barking at her didn't matter. It was the name of the body she had just inhabited, and she would have to respond as if it were her own. She was Bes and she was here for a reason, she needed to act the part until she got her shit together. Her true name was Beskah, but it remained a secret. She endured being called whatever they chose.

For the mission, she needed this body and had to play her role, enduring the person snapping fingers and barking orders at her. It was all for the mission

Brushing her jet-black hair from her eyes, Bes accepted the supervisor's hand as she got up. Time to play the role, act subordinate, but friendly. Who knew? Maybe they were best friends outside the workplace. The usual flashes of memory from being integrated were not happening yet to give her any insight, so Bes just had to feel things out. "A little turbulence? You liar!" Sly, playful grin. "That was the biggest drop I've experienced in my career." That was the truth.

"Shush, or you will scare the passengers," The supervisor gave her a playful smile.

So they were on friendly terms, not just boss and employee, which made things easier to work with. Bes almost felt a little bad for what happened; this poor woman was smiling, but Bes could see the worry behind her eyes. It had been the strangest bout of turbulence she had experienced; she wasn't admitting it to maintain her strength of character. A supervisor was trained not to show nervousness or panic. That didn't mean she couldn't feel nervous or panic, especially when what had just happened wasn't exactly the rumble and shake of turbulence.

The supervisor looked down the rows and saw that several passengers had their hands up to call for attention, and call buttons were being raised by others.

"Well, we better heed the call to action," Bes commented in response to the lit requests for service.

"Yes," The supervisor started to get prepared. "And get napkins, lots of napkins. I'm sensing several spilled drinks."

***

Somewhere else, in a place of hazy ethereal energy, two spirit-shadows rested against a fallen log on a mountain path, watching the blue sky and clouds rolling by on invisible winds.

"She needs help. She needs to be protected," The elder of the two said.

"How will I find her?" The other asked. His name was Sol. A son of light.

"You will know. Trust." The one who was Sol's guide advised.

"I thought you would say have faith."

"Believe in yourself. That is the only faith one needs."

"And the hardest faith to hold onto," Sol responded with a heavy heart as he stood up.

"Find others, they will strengthen you. She will be hunted. They may have already started. We lost her once. We lose her again...

"I understand. We lose her again, and it's all over," Sol expressed his understanding. He stepped forward and paused. A moment of reservation. It wasn't that he doubted the severity of the situation; it was just a blink of a heavy heart because he would not be back. He was embarking on a one-way trip.

A single step and he was gone.

***

The old lady in the window seat of row 56 fiddled with her fingers because she didn't have her sewing kit. She remembered when you could sew and smoke on a plane. Though she hadn't smoked in decades, sewing had been her way to keep busy and avoid smoking. The plane rocked and scared the passengers, but her hands fidgeted out of habit, not fear. She believed that keeping her hands active prevented arthritis, which was common among her peers.

In the three-seat row she occupied, the middle seat was empty, and the aisle seat was filled by a young man of east-Indian descent. He had been nice enough when they chatted earlier. As she watched him now, she couldn't help smiling. The turbulence had not scared her, nor worried her; she had experienced enough in her years of life that a few bumps in any proverbial road did not faze her, but the gentleman sitting in her row was completely unfazed. He had been napping when the turbulence hit. Instead of gazing out of her window, she was staring at him. He was still deeply asleep with a calm and peaceful expression on his face. She wasn't fazed by much at her age, but this young soul sitting beside her was in a deeper state of peace than she could ever imagine to not even being jostled awake.

Suddenly, the young man shot forward with his eyes snapping open, like a delayed reaction to the turbulence. Gasping as though he were at a loss for air. That gave her a momentary start because she had been staring at him so intently.

He was looking about as if lost, trying to get his bearings. The older woman thought it must have been some dream to hold him under like that.

"You're all right?" she leaned over the empty seat between them to pat his arm in comfort. "It gave me a bit of a start, too."

"What? Where?" The man was trying to get his bearings. He was disoriented, everything felt fuzzy, so he blinked hard twice and looked around himself, at himself, taking in the features of his hands before he felt his face.

He had arrived in this other existence. The race was on, he didn't know where the starting line was. Now he had to trust. He took a deep breath. Trust.

Now that his vision had cleared and the tingling cascaded throughout his body had dissipated, it was time to play the part.

"I'm Sol," he said to the old lady seated next to him as he reached out to offer his hand in greeting. "Do you know where we are?"

The old lady raised an eyebrow because she was certain that was not the name the man had introduced himself with when they had initially seated on the plane. The poor soul seemed quite disoriented. "Where we are is never a question. We are always where we are supposed to be." The older woman replied.

Sol sat up and gave the old lady a sidelong look, replying to her strange response. It was not the direct answer he had expected. She just smiled back at him and pointed upwards.

"Lights on. Better buckle up," she pointed again at the signal above their row of seats.

Moving down the aisle to check on the passengers, assist them with clean-up, answer their questions, and offer support, Bes noticed how much fear influenced these people. Her lips moved, and she smiled sincerely, but internally, she felt frustrated. She was searching for someone she could not yet identify.

She continued along the aisles, touching an arm or grazing a finger while passing a napkin. Her target might not even be on this plane. She was traveling to her next destination, yet questioning if the drop indicated otherwise. She always checked when possible, sending out a radar pulse to cast a wide net.

Down a few rows, she saw the east-Indian man wake up in a start, fear in his eyes. She watched him for a moment, talking to the older woman in his row. It wasn't like these others. It was a confusion.

Bes moved toward him and crouched beside him, placing a calming hand over his forearm. "Are you okay, Sir? The turbulence startled you awake."

"Must have been," he replied.

"But I am going to need you to buckle up," Bes said, moving her hand to his shoulder. "We don't expect any more bumps, but it is for your safety."

The old lady in the window seat leaned over. "That's what I was telling him."

Contented, the man buckled himself, and Bes moved off and down the aisle. A few steps away, she chanced a glance back over her shoulder. It was interesting how when she approached the man, crouching beside him, visibly spooked. Maybe she had caught him off guard. Maybe. And then he had slowly withdrawn his arm into his lap, pulling away from her touch. Interesting to say the least. A pulse of radar, perhaps. A vibration on a web. Not an intended prey, but maybe there was another player on board?

After entering the code on the pad outside the cockpit door and being granted access, Bes entered the cockpit and pulled the door closed behind herself. Having already identified her on the security screen, neither the pilot nor the co-pilot turned in their seats to greet her. They were busy monitoring the controls and ensuring they were prepared if another turbulent bump decided to pay a surprise visit to this flight. That was fine with her.

She was a hunter, using this form to follow a trail. It was by chance that an unseen one appeared, unless they were on the same path, or she was the one being hunted. It might have felt safe among the crowd, perfectly camouflaged, but it underestimated who it was dealing with, the lengths Bes would go. Chance, fate, it was irrelevant. To secure her position, she would kill them all. The entirety of the plane would be sacrificed.

Bes leaned in between the pilot and co-pilot's seats, making small talk by informing the two crew that the passengers were all safe and looked after. She inquired if they needed any refreshments themselves as the meals were to be presented shortly.

Those were the words of distraction. Her left hand had found its way to the pilot's shoulder, where she held it as she spoke. The touch, the thought, the opening and calling forth of someone else, something else to utilize the body for her bidding.

The pilot's head slumped forward a half-second, then snapped up again.

"There you are," Bes said as she stepped back behind the co-pilot's seat. "Do it now." She commanded.

The pilot grabbed the controls and forced the plane into a dive.

"What are you doing!" The co-pilot yelled, as internal alarms began going off.

He tried to react, but Bes had already reached around and grabbed hold of his tie and yanked it back to strangle him.

There was not even a second to defend himself against the attack before the pilot leaned over and punched him in the side of the face. Dazed, the co-pilot tried to reach back and smack away the hands that were pulling at his tie, trying to dig his fingers into the cinching around his neck to ease the pressure. But then the pilot was out of his seat, holding his arms, pushing his weight on him, delivering more punches to his face.

As he slipped from consciousness, the co-pilot could hear the stewardess' words delivered with a soft laugh. "What are we doing? What must be done."

"All of them just for one," the pilot smiled up at her. "It's like winning the lottery."

The cockpit blared emergency alerts with the dangerous pitch of the plane's nose as it shuddered to flatten out. The pilot jumped back into his seat and grabbed hold of the control stick, pushed as hard as he could forward, and locked his elbows to hold the plane in its dive. Veins on his forearms and biceps popped out with the strain it took to keep pushing the stick forward. The entity that inhabited the pilot was lost to the discomfort of the exertion, though. A wide grin and a tunnel vision stare into the sky beyond as he fought against the design measures of the plane.

The instant chaos of the passengers echoed up from within the cabin.

Passengers of the plane were thrown forward in their seats, and everything shook as if they were in the epicentre of an earthquake. Unsecured items of laptops, cellphones, and purses flew around, whipping people in the head and body. Air masks dropped, but the force of the pressure and shaking made it almost impossible for anyone to get hold of the masks as they danced above them in a swirling motion. After a few torturous seconds, the cabin area transitioned to a war zone as the overhead stowaway compartments began to pop open and baggage shot out as makeshift missiles.

Sol was reaching for the mask above him, stretching to get it in his grasp, when a blood curdling wail caught his attention. A steward had lost footing, unable to get herself seated, buckled in time, and braced against the pull of the descending plane. Unable to hold on more than a breath, she had been lifted into the air and slammed against the ceiling. Now she was in freefall, tumbling down the row of seats along the roofline in a firework of blood sprays as she slammed into others and went tumbling down the length of the cabin in a pained parade of injuries, bouncing like a limp ragdoll.

Even though the woman was spiralling over the rows toward Sol, everything slowed in his vision, and he saw with terrifying detail as a man a few rows ahead tried to grab the woman to save her and halt her descent. The man's waiting arms snapped back against the weight of her multiplied by the g-force dragging her, and his forearms burst open as they bent back against the seat, and his radius and ulna bones snapped out of his skin.

The man howled in agony and could be heard over the screeching metal, drumming of debris, and wailing passengers.

The stewardess was bulleting straight to them.

Forgetting the mask, Sol leaned over as far as he could, grabbed his row mate, and shoved her down into a crouch position as hard as he could. The thumping and whooshes of air were felt as the woman passed over them.

He released his grip over the old lady, but they both remained bent over as had been instructed in the safety procedure demonstration at the onset of this miserable flight.

Eye to eye, the plane was shaking as if every bolt would come loose, and the two were staring at each other in the unspoken knowledge they would probably be the last faces either of them would ever see.

Something hit the window at the lady's seat hard. Her head was turned towards the aisle, staring at Sol, her hand reaching out for his. Sol saw the crack. Sol saw the instant splintering like ice over a lake in spring. The window shattered. Then chaos ensued with an erupting thunder of the wind as the gap caused the plane to begin to peel apart.

"Oh my god!" That was all Sol could manage to yell. But over the noise, it just looked like he was mouthing the words to her.

The old lady sat up a little, her hair whipping about her face, her chair shaking as it threatened to be torn from its moorings. A soft smile and a calm expression of peace were on her face as she replied to him. "I don't think he is here right now, but you are right where you are supposed to be."

Then she was gone. Disappearing outside in the tidal wave of suctioning vacuum of air and debris being yanked outside in the depressurizing undertow of the plane tearing apart.

Sol held on for dear life. How was this right where he was supposed to be? This couldn't be it. This couldn't be what he was here for: to arrive and have it all be over in mere moments. This wasn't the mission. If he had lost already, then it was all over.

Closing his eyes in a deep breath, Sol told himself one thing. Trust.

When he opened his eyes, something was flying at him, bulleting for his head. There was a brief flash of sharp pain. Then nothingness.

CHAPTER NINETEEN

The airplane had crashed into the top of a hill in a cataclysmic mess of fire, torn metal, and scorched landscape. From a distance, the burning wreckage that lit up the night was like a volcanic glow of fire, smoke, and ash in its path of charred earth. To Bes, the lone survivor, as she sat away from the heat, taking in the scene, it was a pyre of flame against the night sky

A beacon.

A signal.

Amidst the glow, she could see the charred bodies of the passengers, and it brought a smile to her face. Ashes to ashes, and all that. The lives that were moving forward on a path, destiny, fate, or just the common, average, daily course of being. The beliefs of the cattle were humorous to her in the way they searched for reasoning, for purpose. Cast against the night in the blazing glow of the fires of devastation, she couldn't help but reflect on the things she had learned being with these others for those different moments.

A boxer circling in a ring as cheering crowds surround her and the opponent who delivered a series of blows before she was able to ascertain where she was. Who she was. But in that moment, she was impressed.

The human body was an amazing thing. It could be beaten, and it could persevere against exhaustion.

Memories of previous lives floated into her memory.

She was a cop in the middle of a shoot-out, bullets peppered her body in a rain of semi-automatic gunfire, sending her flying backwards against the squad car.

It can withstand all types of punishment.

As a nurse, Bes watched the police officer, who was previously recovering in a hospital.

Be taken to the brink of death.

In the crowd, as a fellow officer, she watched that policeman, standing on a stage, with the support of a cane, receive an award for his earlier sacrifice.

And come back to fight another day.

Bes had stayed close to that one. Directed to see him through his recovery. Putting his life on the line, the sacrifice he had made in the line of duty, made him a hero. With that perception, that protection of who he was seen to be, protected him in the years to come from prying eyes and investigation of the true work he would continue.

Bes was a nurse tending to a patient in a cancer ward, setting the I.V. for the woman's umpteenth chemotherapy treatment. She really couldn't recall the why of that one. Sometimes they blended, lost in the multitudes she had obsessed over for seconds, or possessed for days. The visage of that woman just stuck with her, haggard, balding, and drained from her fight. Bes remembered her kindness, her smile, the determination not to give up that blazed behind those eyes, showing how the body can be ravaged by disease and endure insufferable agony.

She was skydiving from a plane with three others. One person's chute opens in a tangled mess and does not deploy properly.

The body can be ravaged and can endure, or simply fall from grace.

From her soft glide position, Bes was witness to the other skydiver as they shrank away from her in a hurried descent.

On the ground, Bes unlatched her parachute harness and ran to the other in her group who had fallen to their death. Before she reaches them, Bes can see they are sitting up.

And rise like the proverbial phoenix to face another day.

A summer day in a park filled with people. A picturesque moment of happiness as couples walked hand in hand. Families at picnic tables laughed over lunch, others threw a frisbee for a dog, and children were playing with kites.

Resilient.

Standing in that park, Bes looked at her hands. Man hands.

"Throw it, Dad," a boy shouted from a short distance away.

This man's hands are holding a football. The boy in the distance was his son. The obvious target. She remembered thinking this man would never forgive himself, and that she didn't care. She was only using him for a moment. The emotional agony he would torture himself with over the coming years was not her concern.

Even with the miracles of evolution, as strong, resilient as the human body is...

The ball was thrown hard, it sailed high over the boy.

...It was such a fragile thing.

In the vain effort, the boy jumped up for a catch and missed, landed, and turned to chase the ball. The son ran, arms ready to catch the long bomb as the dad had taught him. Looking up, running, gauging its descent. Watching the ball. Not watching where he was going.

As the dad, Bes did not shout a warning. She just watched as the boy ran out into the parking lot.

Before she left the body of that moment, she enjoyed a little smile as the sounds of screeching tires, scraping metal, and shouts of people echoed across that afternoon like thunder clapping its hands to silence any happiness

Life. Resilient and glass tempered in unison. On one side, a strong, enduring thing that eludes death a million times a day. On the other hand, a fragile thing is lost in an accidental moment. With no explanation, no rhyme to the reason. Because maybe the explanation is not tangible enough and is discounted as by the grace of God. And for those who do not give spiritual belief merit, pure luck, or happenstance. Probably the explanation could not and would not be accepted or believed.

The things at work that are unseen, and not all our actions are our own. If they knew, that would be their prayer.

Enough reminiscence.

The hunt, the chase, was still on.

Reflected against the haze of the smoking horror of the forced massacre and the glow of burning wreckage, arms straight out to her sides, Bes performed one slow spin in sinister glee. She knew this was the right place to be. She could feel that what they were doing was the right thing.

Plus, it was a lot of fun.

There was a call to ring forth.

This wreckage was a pyre, a signal, but she needed more.

A sparkle caught her eye. Bes walked to the edge of the hill, and in the distance, city lights gleamed. She needed more. And there was the perfect place.

<u>**CHAPTER TWENTY**</u>

For reasons Father Perez could not put his finger on, this time of the day had become his favorite. Long after the final mass had been closed, sitting in his office finalizing preparations for his sermon the next day, he would tidy his notes and relax back into his chair with a calming breath. It was right here, right now, that he recently found that he was the most at peace and was enjoying himself the most. The utter calm and quiet of the church. He found it took longer moments to enjoy this solace each day before retiring to the rectory for the evening.

Tonight, he stayed longer than usual. He had received the news that Father Byrne had been murdered across town and had made a mockery by being hanged against the statue of the crucifixion. Then a bus crashed into the church. It had not been determined whether this was related or a strange coincidence. So, after the shock abated, Father Perez prayed and reflected on the loss of a brother. The crisis and suffering of the world could make one with lesser faith wonder what the world was coming to with the atrocities that the human race was capable of. But there was still a lot of good out there to balance the scales, hope was bred every day. Despite the horror that had happened to Father Byrne, Father Perez took comfort in the people of his church.

He had been leading this parish for almost ten years now. He performed two masses four times a week. The number of attendees had dwindled over the years, but he was proud that he had a strong enough congregation to maintain the double masses. He held love for all his parishioners, and there were the regulars of his parish who remained to pray after the sermon was done, or even because they desired a private conversation with him. Listening, sharing, and guiding are why he chose the vocation he had.

But, in the quiet, he felt closer to God.

Father Perez sat up in his chair and chuckled. It was just because he was getting older that he felt closer to God, and because he was older, he needed more time with himself.

He grabbed his coat from the rack beside the office door and slipped it on to prepare to make his rounds before heading over to the rectory for the night.

As Father Perez came from behind the main altar, he paused a moment to look across the nave. With two main aisles of pews, each 25 rows long, and another two aisles on each side with about half the rows, he was proud to shepherd a large congregation. It warmed his heart that most of those seats were full every Sunday for the main service, that the community of parishioners was strong and had not been dwindling, as was the norm for other congregations. After the tragic death of Father Byrne, his parishioners would need his strength in the services to come. With other churches needing extensive repairs, Father Perez was sure some of those who attended Father Byrne's service would be filling these seats.

A soft light drew his attention to the bye-altar of candles at the side of the west wing of pews. A woman was standing there with her back to him.

"Good evening," Father Perez announced his presence as he drew closer to the woman.

But she didn't hear him. Didn't acknowledge him.

Instead, she rambled in a whisper as she lit votive after votive. "Even in places of light, there will always be shadowed corners for darkness to breed. It is overcast. It is underneath. It is night."

Almost all the candles were lit now, their glow flickering against the walls. She continued. "Sun stars eventually extinguish and fade away, but the dark depths of the ocean are forever more, and the blackness of space is infinite."

She finished and stared at the bye-alter a moment before turning her head to look over her shoulder at the man just behind her.

Father Perez swallowed as he caught her eye. He didn't show it, but he was a little taken aback that she was aware he was there, and had been ignoring him. "You surprised me. I wasn't expecting any parishioners at this time. Are you just here to offer prayer?" He could see she was in a stewardess outfit, but was dirty with ash and smelled like fire smoke. "Do you need help, or is there something I can do for you?"

"Yes, I need to light a pyre. I need a signal to reach out into the darkness," Bes said as she waved her hand over the burning votives.

Father Perez thought it strange how some flocks wandered in before he replied. "Well, God is the light."

"Not exactly what I had in mind," Bes said.

"Then, how can I help?" Father Perez asked.

She fully turned to him, and Father Perez could see the faint quiver of a smile on her lips as she said. "By being the spark."

She grabbed Father Perez, yanking and pushing his face into the candles. Several snuffed out on impact, but they were still hot as the glass votives dug into his face and dozens of burning stings licked his skin. As she held him firm, other candles to his side grabbed onto his clothes and grew in power. "Burn for me!" The priest flailed, trying to escape as his hair and vestment caught on fire. "Burn for me and be my never-ending prayer."

Once he stopped struggling and succumbed to his death in the flames, the woman left him lying there smoldering on the bye-alter as she sat back on the nearest pew to watch the flames reach up along the wall.

"Not a prayer, a signal," she stated as the dead priest's charred flesh smoked and smoldered as the flames reached upwards to spread. "The light of fire. The darkness of ash. All light is eventually dimmed and snuffed out by what it consumes. Darkness exists to replace it, once it is gone."

The woman stood and reached forward to shove the priest to the ground. "The dark of night is ignited." She sniffed in the scent of his burnt flesh before reaching over him, grabbing a couple of the candles that still flickered.

Bes sat in a pew and pulled one of the hymn books from the bible rack on the backside of the pew row in front of her. The fire was not catching quickly enough, so she methodically ripped pages from the hymn book, lit them from the flame of the votive, and dropped them to the carpeted floor. It was slow work at first, but therapeutic. And once the carpet caught on fire, the flames spread like a plague.

Heat. The feeling of slow cooking in a cramped oven snapped Sol awake.

Fire blazed in parts a short distance from him. But not so distant. The flames were close enough that the heat sucked the breath from him.

Feeling like he was suffocating, trying to grasp a clean breath, Sol tried to move away but was stuck. He was still seat belted into his chair. Looking around, fumbling to find the latch, he was by a tree line, lying on his side. Somehow, the chair had been ripped from its moorings on the plane during the crash.

Finding the latch, he went to release the metal buckle. The coupling was hot to the touch, making him pull back with the sting to his fingers.

Slow down, he thought to himself, and pulled at his shirt to untuck it from his waist. Using a material as a cover for his hand, he unlatched the belt and rolled out from the chair.

On his feet, Sol covered his eyes from the brightness of the flames against the clack of night beyond. Other seats were scattered on the scorched ground, occupied with the charred remains of the passengers they had held.

There was no reason that he should have survived or been able to stand. He walked away unscathed, except for a throbbing headache, a hoarse throat, and a biting soreness around his waist where the seat belt had dug in.

How could this have happened?

His mind flashed to the raven-haired stewardess, touching his shoulder, her hand lingering a moment too long. It had been her. She had happened. An adversary on the same trajectory. Had all of this just been to stop him, or was it a coincidence that he was on that plane? Did it matter at this point?

As much as he could with the heat pressing against him, Sol searched amongst the dead. He was not surprised that he was not able to find her. He had miraculously survived. Why would the same not be for her?

Searching was pointless. He couldn't bear the heat or the sight of the burning bodies anymore. Sol moved away. He needed to continue his mission. It was very likely the stewardess who came to his mind's eye was hunting the one he was here to protect. Why else had their paths crossed?

Coming to the crest of a hilltop, Sol looked down at the cityscape in the valley, trying to get his bearings on the next steps he should take.

"You are a son of light," Sol said to himself.

In the distance, amongst the city lights, a bright star flared. A building was burning.

"So, follow the light."

Even though it was not the kind of light or type of sign he expected.

Sol looked back at the flames from the plane wreckage reaching into the night sky, then back to the valley and the burning building. Pyres in the night. Signals.

"No matter how tainted it may appear to be, a sign is a sign."

Sol felt a desperation wash over him as he looked up to the sky to question the nothingness before beginning the long descent down the hill and into the city.

CHAPTER TWENTY-ONE

The night was illuminated with the firework display of emergency vehicle lights as paramedics and police cluttered the area surrounding the church of the late Father Byrne. The area had been cordoned off and by some stroke of luck the news crews had not arrived yet because, although the bus crash and death of the bus driver was tragic, the autopsy would provide some reasoning as to what had caused the accident, the strange thing about the scenario was the crucified priest hanging on the wall. Crime Scene Investigators had just arrived to investigate the murder as the rescue crew dealt with the bus and its two victims. The bus driver and the woman were pinned between the grill and the south wall of the church.

A police officer came over to the two paramedics working to remove the deceased bus driver.

"What is it with churches tonight? "He commented. "This accident, and on the other side of town, a call just came through that another one is burning."

"We are going to have our hands full for sure," one of the paramedics responded as he collaborated with his partner to transfer the bus driver to a gurney. "Another crew should have been here by now."

Another ambulance drove slowly past the cordon and parked close to the bus crash. Bes exited the driver's side of the vehicle. Once a stewardess, she had abandoned that attire for the medical garments she now wore.

"What a mess," Bes muttered, as she released the gurney and pulled it from the back of the ambulance, taking in the scene around herself. It was a little funny that Tory and she had both made a scene at a church. Tory had not been so great at the execution, but she was never one for finesse like Bes was. Sure, causing some kind of cataclysm at a church was cliché, but the symbolism always had a great effect.

Making her way towards the crashed bus, two other paramedics gave her a nod as they wheeled their gurney, occupied with a body bag, towards Bes.

"Is that the bus driver?" Bes asked, pointing at the black body bag

"Yes," one of the paramedics responded.

"They are still extracting the priest, and investigators want that scene kept clear, but there is another deceased at the front of the bus. They already moved the bus back to extract the body. Just needs a bag and tag," the partner advised.

Great, the other deceased had to be Tory. Bess had her extraction operation to execute.

Another paramedic crouched down, finalizing the preparations for the deceased to be transported.

"I've got this," Bes said with a hand on the medic's shoulder. "They need help on the other rig."

The medic stood up in reply. "No problem. The deceased is ready to go. Are you sure you don't need a hand here?"

"Thanks, I'm good," Bes waved them off. I'll get one of the detectives to help me load."

Kneeling, Bes looked around to ensure nobody was nearby and unzipped the body bag a quarter of the way to inspect the body inside and mumbled to herself. "What a mess."

It was Tory. A bloody mess of a Tory, but at least Bes had found her.

She waved over an officer for assistance, and with his help, Bes got the gurney carrying Tory's corpse into the back of the ambulance. With the bus secured, Bes made her way to the driver's door, took a quick look around to check if anyone was watching, got in the driver's seat, and slowly pulled away. The slight grin reflecting at herself from the rearview mirror let her know she was impressed with herself at how smoothly the snatch and grab had gone.

After taking an erratic route through various side streets to ensure she had not been followed, Bes navigated the ambulance down an alleyway where she pulled to a stop and killed the engine. Retreating to the patient care compartment, she sat on the bench and leaned in to address the unmoving body bag. "He got away, didn't he?"

"Yes. Again!" Came the muffled response from within.

Bes unzipped the bag to release an alive, albeit bloody, mess of Tory.

"Again?" Bes asked, a bit of condemnation in her voice.

"Don't act so surprised," Tory responded as she sat up and swung herself around to face Bes, pushing some matted-bloody hair away from her face. "You know he is protected. Plus, that's why you are here, isn't it?"

"Yes, I was pulled from my Middle East sanction, where I was having so much fun. But someone had to come and look after your ass. Landing was a bit rough getting here. I had to crash a plane. A suspect was onboard," Bes shrugged her shoulders to be nonchalant. "That puts me up by a few hundred while you've botched the job and can't even nail down one." Bes leaned in and poked a finger at one of the holes in Tory's right breast, where she had been pierced by the stag antlers. "And you are a total mess." Touched her face where her left eye was puffy, and her cheek was scraped raw from the impact of the bus. "You have holes in you, and it looks like you have been through a meat grinder."

Tory slapped Bes's hand away like her injuries were no big deal. "I know. It takes a lot of energy to keep this flesh bag moving, but it is worth it. I like the face."

"I'm even surprised you are alive."

"Sheer force of will. It is that dominance of will that enables us in the ether place to obsess, or such as you and I, possess."

"I forced a plane crash and came away unscathed. You are hunting one and..."

"Get over yourself," Tory rebutted. "Anyone can cause a plane crash. And just so you know, I've accumulated a few belt notches along the way." If Bes wanted to be competitive, Tory was happy to oblige.

"I bet you have, opportunistic bitch," Bes smiled at her.

Bes led Tory to the front of the ambulance, where she took her place in the driver's seat. Tory moved to position herself in the passenger seat but paused.

"I thought there was a weird smell in here," Tory gave Bes a disgusted look as she pointed to a dead body of a naked female perched in the passenger seat. "You couldn't have done something with this?"

"That was the paramedic I had to steal this ambulance from, and I needed her uniform for my disguise," Bes explained. "I was coming to extract you. I didn't have time to do anything with the body."

Leaning across the body, Tory opened the passenger door and shoved the corpse from the seat. Ejected, the deceased woman crumbled to the dirty pavement like disregarded refuse.

Tory had an angry-pouty look on her mangled face as she settled into the passenger seat and pulled the door closed with a slam. "Great, now I get to sit in a wet seat the whole way."

"Quit your complaining," Bes retorted as she began to drive down the alleyway. "At least now you have a hunting partner."

Tory pulled down the sunshade and leaned forward to inspect herself in the mirror. "Then let the hunt resume. But first, I need to clean up. And alcohol, lots of alcohol, I hurt everywhere."

CHAPTER TWENTY-TWO

Cold, hurt, and feeling alone, the heavy weight of doubt shadowed Sol as he slowly made his way down the hill. The doubt was a fifty-pound sack on his shoulders, weighing him down. He was not sure if he even headed in the right direction. He had been sent on a mission with practically zero guidance.

The descent steepened and being lost in thought he was inattentive to the footing and slipped, landed hard on his butt, and slid a few inches.

He had braced himself with his hands, and now they hurt from the sting of the rough ground. Sitting there, he inspected them, just dirty, no cuts, and rubbed them together to knock the dust off. He stared at those hands again. The hands of someone else, a body he had stolen to use on this mission to find someone lost. Staring at the hands of a stranger, he drifted back into where he was before arriving on that airplane. In that displaced time, the other and himself, spirit shadows in an ethereal place of somewhere unseen, to where he was now.

"You have your mission. The girl is priority one," the other with Sol instructed, and Sol nodded, understanding. *"Faith has been weakening for years. These Sisters of Darkness, as we so eloquently chose to refer to them, have already taken a foothold. The embers of chaos have been blown upon, and things set in motion before we were aware or able to mobilize. This already sets us at a disadvantage."*

"The other side is already winning?" Sol questioned.

"I wouldn't go that far. They have a head start. A big head start. But we can still pull this together. There is much riding on your shoulders."

Here they were with no tangible identity, just the identity of self. And Sol of late, wondered how long that would last. His head hung solemnly. "My cross to bear."

"You don't have to carry it alone on that mortal plane. We already have players on the board. Find the Winemaker, for he will quench your army's thirst and douse the flames of chaos."

And now he was here on this hill, alone, but in reminiscing about where he was before all this, he felt some comfort. Maybe he was feeling directionless because he did not know specifically who he was looking for, but he knew one he had to find. The Winemaker.

So that was going to be his first step. Find the Winemaker.

***

Outside the two-floor motel, the sign that beckoned weary travellers from their long highway drives flashed "Vacancy" in neon red just below the larger lighted sign that shone the motel's name, "Lamplighter's Inn." For the past however many years, this motel has always had a vacancy. The flyover interchange that was built a decade ago drew traffic away. Now the motel was a victim of the less travelled secondary highway. And being victim to fewer patrons over the years showed its wear and lack of upkeep. A victim of circumstance.

The building was a straight rectangle shape and consisted of twenty rooms. Ten on the main floor and ten on the second. On this night, four vehicles adorned the parking lot. Outside of room eight, on the main floor, near the north end of the motel, was parked an ambulance. The owner & manager thought it was weird that a pair of paramedics were booking in for the night, but over the years of owning and running this place, it wasn't the first time strange bedfellows had booked in for the night. The prospects of selling disappeared once the interchange had been built. Retirement was a notion long forgotten as his wife and he held onto this motel to eke out what livelihood they could, so it got easier to look the other way, cash was cash, if they didn't wreck the place. It may have gotten rundown over the years, but they still cared for their Lamplighter Inn, their home, being older and less revenue coming in year over year just made it hard to maintain the upkeep.

Inside room eight, Bes sat naked on the toilet, her face buried in her hands with elbows perched on her knees. Her paramedic outfit was in a heap at her feet Beside them was the messy pile of Tory's bloody clothes.

Tory herself was in the shower. She popped her head out from behind the shower curtain. "Flush!"

"Not my fault," Bes removed her face from her cupped hands and looked up at Tory. "It's the disgusting weakness of these flesh bags."

Tory just chuffed and retreated behind the curtain. Bes finished on the toilet and stepped into the shower behind Tory. She circled her arms around Tory's waist and pulled her in close, pressing herself into Tory's back.

"Excuse me! A little forward," Tory feigned resistance.

"There is a weakness of this flesh, but there are pleasures of it also," Bes said, kissing Tory along the nape of her neck between words. "Don't deny yourself. It's a benefit of being on the front lines."

Tory turned, and the two women faced each other, kissing in a naked embrace amongst the rhythmic flow of the shower water.

***

Sol watched from a block away as the emergency crews battled the fire consuming the church. He had been drawn here because, from a distance, the glow of the flames against the night sky mirrored the smoke-red haze that adorned the sky above the plane crash.

Find the Winemaker to douse the flames of chaos.

The other man's voice echoed in his thoughts as Sol moved in closer to the chaos of the emergency crews and gathering crowd of onlookers. From the gossiping crowd, he overheard that the only person found inside by the rescue crews was the resident pastor, who had been found dead in the building. There was nothing, or nobody, for Sol here.

Sol realized he had been heading to where he thought he should be, not trusting his instincts to move where he needed to be. His eyes were drawn to the sign across the street that read "Pig & Sickle." It was a pub. From the outside, it looked like a nondescript place, small by the width of the street front, with no patio for summer night patrons. Through the main window, which had the pub's name etched into it along with a cartoonish picture of a pig holding a sickle, the dim lighting inside made it hard to see how busy the place was. Maybe it was not where he needed to be. He was exhausted, and if you wanted to find a winemaker, a small neighbourhood pub seemed as good a place as any.

Inside the pub was quiet this evening, and Sol found only one occupied seat at the long bar. Others were seated at the booths, but there only seemed to be maybe three tables occupied. After receiving the beer he ordered, Sol took a long sip and then pressed his forehead against the mug. The cold felt good inside and out after the heat he had borne from the crash and felt on his face from the church.

His solace was broken when he felt a jab into his shoulder, accompanied by a hey to get Sol's attention.

Parched and exhausted, Sol was not in the mood to be disturbed. He had come here to rest and gather his thoughts on his next move. But it seems like that had all been wishful thinking.

"Hey," the person who had come to stand beside him, poked Sol a second time.

Sol didn't raise his head in response, he just turned it slightly to look sidelong at the man who was so offensively introducing himself, jabbing at Sol to demand his attention. Sol wasn't sure what was ruder, the two-finger jabs into his shoulders, or the pulse of alcohol breath that accompanied the three-letter word the man had uttered twice. He was a big, burly man with full hair and a fuller beard. Sol quickly assumed this guy was probably used to getting his way, so manners, common civility, and introductions were not his best suit. Especially when you added, what Sol assumed by the breath was a decent volume of consumed alcohol.

"Excuse me?" Sol said

"You need to leave," the man demanded.

Sol tried to ignore the guy, did his best not to be confrontational as he turned to look, tending to his drink. "I'm just having a drink, friend, and looking for a place to rest my feet."

"Find one elsewhere," being ignored, sloughed off, angered the man, he pushed his face in close to Sol's to accentuate his point. "We don't want your kind here."

Sitting up, Sol spun on his stool to directly face his aggressor and fully take him in. Several other men were standing behind this supposed racist, and they were all wearing sneering, angry looks on their faces. Strength in numbers. Mob mentality. The invisible prod is charging the man's pointless rage. "Really, and what kind is that?" Sol took a long sip of his drink as he looked hard into the man's eyes to determine if there was a fuse to be cut. "The only kind I know myself to be is humankind."

"No!" The man leered into Sol's face again. Two fingers of the man acted like arrows piercing into the front of Sol's shoulder. This jab was the hardest yet, threatening to send Sol backwards off his bar stool. If there was a fuse to be cut on this man, red wire, green wire, Sol had picked the wrong one. "You are the terrorist kind!" He waved behind himself to present his group of friends. "We think you are the one who started the fires. Our kids went to Sunday school in that church. My wife baked cookies for that poor pastor that they found in there all crispy like a god-damn piece of overcooked bacon."

Sol tried to be sympathetic in a vain attempt to quell the escalating tension, leaning a bit forward with his hands open in offering. "I'm not your enemy."

"You look like one," the man sniffed hard at Sol. "You even smell burnt and like smoke."

"Your only enemies are the things that are silent in the darkness. The things you are blind to seeing."

"Are you mocking me?"

"No, I'm just trying to explain," Sol dropped his head a little in exasperation. "We all see what we want to believe and believe what we see when blinded by our emotions. So, we can open our eyes and see that we are all the same kind." The man's angered face did not change. Time for another tactic. "Why don't I buy all of you gentlemen a round?"

Before he could even offer a smile, the burly stranger grabbed Sol by his shirt, hoisted him off his chair in one swift motion, and pulled Sol in close to growl into his face with accent spittle. "Oh, we'll have a round. Maybe two or three."

Being used as a human battering ram, Sol was driven through the door of the Pig and Sickle Pub and tossed to the street, where he painfully skid-rolled against the asphalt. Expelling Sol wasn't enough for Burly

Man, and he was in hot pursuit, bearing down on Sol, clapping a fist in his other hand to foreshadow the beating he was about to bring forth. His buddies followed in his wake, spilling out onto the sidewalk, shouting violent encouragements

Sol rubbed the back of his head and grimaced. Partially anticipating what was supposed to happen, but if he had the time to be honest with himself, it was out of frustration. He was not supposed to be here. He should not have needed to be here and been drawn to this moment. The world was supposed to spin on its own. Without interruption, without interception. This phase of existence was never supposed to be the stage for the war that was to be fought, but the world had changed. Not changed, Sol thought as he made to get up and looked hard at the Burly Man's hate-filled face, evolved, or better yet, a devolution was more accurate. It was ironic. Faith had weakened, but beliefs had grown stronger.

Not quite on one knee, Burly Man was on him, half pulling Sol up by a handful of his shirt while he pummelled Sol's face with blows that illuminated Sol's vision with stars. The chorus of the Burly Man's friends jeers as they circle closer.

An eruption of new sparkles blurred his vision with the crunch of a subsequent fist square into his face.

Sol was trying to defend himself. He didn't try to fight back; he was too lost, thinking of this man's intolerable, blinding hate. Of how it had become rampant. And hate is the breaker of faith.

Another blow and Sol reeled backwards down onto the asphalt. His shirt was ripped, and blood ran from his nose down around his lips to cover-drip off his chin to makeshift a fluid, crimson beard.

Wavering, unsteady, Sol pushed up on one leg, pain making every effort desperate. He should not have had to be here, but he was. Hate was a breaker of faith, but so was doubt. He was here, and he must stand against that now. He had to stand strong. He had faith in what he needed to do, and that was there to help him stand strong in this moment.

Barely on his feet, Sol was doubled over, but he managed to extend his left arm out, splaying his hand in a stop motion, trying to hold off the Burly Man.

"You don't have to do this," Sol wheezed.

"Yeah, I do," Burly Man stepped forward, grinning. Sol could see he was enjoying this. "Somebody needs to show that your type won't tolerate things anymore."

Sol coughed, and blood spurted from his mouth. "Won't tolerate? You don't tolerate." He wiped his mouth with his wrist.

This enraged Burly Man, and he delivered a brutal kick to Sol, sending him crashing down to the ground again as he yelled. "Don't tell me what I do or don't do. I protect my own, that's all that matters." Another kick went to Sol's midsection. "You fit the profile; you look like the enemy." A stomp into Sol's chest. "You are the enemy."

As his head crunched into the unforgiving ground, he reflexively gasped for air before consciousness flittered. Sol's last thought was that it was a pity this man didn't understand that looks could be deceiving.

CHAPTER TWENTY-THREE

The highway patrol car cruised down the road. Daryl was the senior officer occupying the driver's seat as he always did, and his long-time partner, Jeff, stared lazily out the passenger window as they made their way to the next spot on their route to set up the speed camera. It was mid-week, so traffic was lighter. Sometimes that meant more speeders because the road was more open, but it also meant fewer vehicles to catch. That didn't bother Jeff. Working the day shift meant the probability of having to deal with drunk drivers was a lot lower. Almost non-existent. Almost, but in his years of service, he never knew to take anything for granted.

In the distance, the sign of the Lamplighter's Inn could be seen.

"I've made some good memories in that motel," Jeff said, watching the sign enlarge as they drew closer.

"You say that literally every time we pass by that motel," Daryl noted.

"I know because they are good memories," Jeff gave his partner a sly smile.

"Not ones you share with your wife, though, right?"

"Now, who is bringing something up every time we pass this motel, huh?" Jeff looked skeptically at his partner. "And what are you getting at anyway?"

Daryl tilted his head to his partner to snare his attention while maintaining focus on the road. "Maybe, I'm just saying that you tend to abuse your position. Maybe, but I'm not judging."

"I've abused many in there in many positions," Jeff replied with a devilish grin. "So, judge away if you like."

They had similar conversations each time they were on this road. It was part of the ritual. They cruised by, and Jeff turned to look closer at the parking lot.

"Stop," Jeff was abrupt.

Daryl did a quick mirror check and slowed the cruiser, stopping just off the road.

Jeff thumbed over his shoulder back towards the Lamplighter's Inn. "Wasn't there a report of a stolen ambulance?"

Putting the vehicle in park, Daryl turned to look back at the parking lot. There was an ambulance parked in front of one of the rooms. "You're right. Let's call it in to verify."

Jeff pulled the radio to his mouth. "Dispatch, this is unit 3095."

The dispatcher came back. "Go ahead, unit 3095."

"What was the unit number of that stolen bus that was put out a while ago?"

"Hold on, unit 3095," the dispatcher replied and went silent for a moment. "The ambulance unit number was 0513."

"Thanks, dispatch," Jeff said, twisting in his seat to look out the rear window of the patrol car. "We have an ambulance parked at the Lamplighter's Inn. The unit number is not visible from where we stopped. Have there been any ambulances dispatched to this location?"

There was a brief pause before dispatch came back with a response. "No other units have been dispatched to that area."

"Okay, we are going to take a closer look to confirm if this is our stolen bus," Jeff replied, then replaced the handset before turning to Daryl. "Should we check in for old time's sake?"

"You flirtatious bastard," Daryl smiled at him. "This better not start any rumours back at headquarters.

Exiting the cruiser, they both made their way towards the parking lot.

Daryl slapped his partner on the back. "This could be embarrassing if some paramedic using your old playbook uses this hideaway motel."

At the ambulance, Daryl confirmed the vehicle number was the missing unit. He inspected the vehicle by attempting to open each door, including the driver's side, passenger side, and rear, all of which were securely locked. He then peered through the windows to examine the interior for any signs of someone hiding inside. He awaited Jeff's return from the motel office, where Jeff was seeking information from the manager.

Returning, Jeff took up a position with Daryl at the back of the ambulance.

"Guy in the office said to check room number nine," Jeff reported. "He said they never registered, paid cash, and business has been slow, so he went with it. Two female paramedics, as far as he could tell."

"Okay. Bus looks clear," Daryl said and drew his service revolver. "Let's go make a housekeeping call."

Room nine was directly in front of the stall where the ambulance was parked. The two officers took up position on either side of the door.

"Take point. I will cover," Daryl directed from his position on the left.

With a nod to confirm the plan, Jeff knocked on the door with the announcement. "Open up. This is the Police."

A few seconds of nothing in response from inside. Jeff pressed his ear to the door to listen for movement. Nothing. He readied to knock a second time with the intent of being louder this time. Fair warning. The manager had provided a key. If there was no response this time, they were going in. He went to rap his knuckles against the door, before contact, the door popped open inwards. Jeff turned to lead the advance, but something, someone, had grabbed him and he disappeared inside as if he was sucked into a dark vortex. Gone, and the door slammed shut with his vanishment.

Responding immediately, Daryl banged on the door to demand entry. "Hey! Hey! Open this door! Open this door right now!"

Inside the motel room, Jeff tried to get his bearings. It was dark with drawn curtains, the sliver of light cutting in through the gap in the curtains highlighted a woman on the bed, lying on top of the covers. Blonde, naked, and a natural blonde, as she displayed herself seductively with open legs.

Mouth agape, totally taken aback by what was before his eyes, Officer Jeff, was barely able to utter, "Oh my God!"

"Not around here," the woman kissed and seemed to slither in her subtle movements of beckoning.

Banging from outside. His partner was still out there. The door closed, the heavy knocking jarring the door against the frame, snapped Jeff's attention. Fumbling with himself, he raised his gun and pointed it at the siren seductress on the bed. "Don't move."

"My name is Tory," the woman said. "Come and stop me."

Jeff went to step forward. From nowhere, as if bleeding out of the dark corners, Bes was beside the cop, grabbing his wrist to divert his aim as he reactively pulled the trigger in his startlement. The sound of the shot was loud in the enclosed space as it went wild, hitting the floor close to the bedside.

"Who the hell?" Jeff attempted to pull free.

With the element of surprise, Bes had the advantage, having him by the wrists and keeping the momentum, she swung the cop around to keep him off balance and slammed him into the adjoining wall. His breath was knocked out of him, and before he could gasp a breath, one of her hands was around his throat, squeezing, pressing, lifting. Practically off the floor, he struggled to find a perch for leverage as his heels were up, and he could only feel the tips of his toes against the carpeted floor. With her other hand, this second woman twisted the gun out of his grip. So fast. Had he even blinked yet?

"Me?.. the hell," Bes pierced him with bitter eyes, then turned to Tory. "I'm going to need you to open him up."

Tory rushed off the bed to Bes' side to hold this cop against the wall as he struggled against the two women. The door threatened to break open as his partner yelled and demanded entry, kicking it with force. Jeff wondered why Daryl just didn't use the key the manager had given him and get the hell in here to save him from these crazy bitches. Then he remembered he had the key.

"Sounds like the roles have reversed," Tory said as she put her hand on the cop's face. "We are the wolves. But another little pig outside wants in with his huffing and puffing."

So close, in the moment before she pressed into him, her breasts pressing into him, the light had captured her more fully. She had puncture wounds in her upper torso, shading of bruises in her chest and the side of her face. This seductress was beautiful. Yes, but in an indescribable way that appeared taboo, it felt unholy.

"Somewhere, sometime, there's someone," Bes looked intently at the man. And I bet in his line of work, there are just plenty of those waiting for their opportunity. There."

The pair of women let go and stepped back in unison. Jeff slumped, about to fall to the ground, but caught himself, leaning against the wall for leverage as he took long gasps of air to catch his breath. Then his posture changed as he stood strong.

"There we are," Bes said, satisfied. "That didn't take much effort at all."

"The weak-willed never do," Tory patted the man on the cheek. "Makes this subservience easy."

The motel room door split from its moorings, and the door flew inwards. Daryl burst into the room, illuminated by the morning sun. Before he could even decipher the inhabitants in the room, Jeff was charging past the women and tackled Daryl.

"You!" Jeff spat as if it were venom.

The surprise attack from his supposed partner caught Daryl completely off guard, and he was overwhelmed in an instant, falling to the floor with Jeff on top of him, the man's full weight on him as he punched with his fist and forearms down into Daryl's face in a kinetic frenzy.

As the first spray of blood vandalized the motel room carpet, Tory couldn't contain that bit of a smile, a malicious grin, as she watched the one cop beat the other. Who had they released inside and obsessed this man with? An ex, a lost sibling, a wronged criminal from his past, whoever, the beating assault they were delivering spoke to a rage that had been stifled for a very long time.

Bes came to the injured cop's side and placed a hand on his shoulder, signalling to stop. "Well done."

The man straddled over the body on the floor and stopped raining blows down into the face beneath him.

"Now burn it," Bes ordered. "Burn it all in effigy to me."

Splattered with the blood of the savage beating he had just delivered, Jeff looked up at the woman before him in submission. "Yes, Beskah."

Pulling away from the motel parking lot, Bes looked at the side view mirror from her position in the driver's seat. Smoke could be seen billowing in streamers from the room they had occupied. A smile crept across her face as she turned back to focus on the road.

She reached out with her right hand and caressed Tory's left thigh. "We make such a great team. Two parts of a gun. You load it. I fire."

Where she could, Tory preferred a more subtle approach compared to Bes' flash and noisy cataclysm. Neither approach seemed to matter. They could load and fire a barrage, but there was one target that eluded them. All those voices in the nether should have been easy to find the one they were searching for, but there was barely a whisper to benefit their search.

Tory had a needling at the base of her skull that something was back there, something they had missed because of the distraction of the two cops. They were drawing away, not moving towards. Bes was certain it was time to stop chasing; better to set a snare. So, the next step was setting the trap.

CHAPTER TWENTY-FOUR

The headlights preceded the lone car as the driver made the last turn onto the laneway that led towards home. It was a weeknight, late, so his was the only vehicle moving through the labyrinth of this quiet suburban neighbourhood. The street was lined with big yards, and huge overarching trees that held shadows against the soft yellow glow of the streetlights that held the darkness at bay.

The driver pulled into the front driveway of his house and put the car in park. He always parked outside the garage when he came home late so as not to disturb his family with the sound of the garage door rattling open. Plus, it was a tight squeeze. Over the years, the garage had been turning more into a storage facility than a carport.

He pushed the button to the left of the steering wheel to release the trunk of the car. Exiting, he went to the trunk and pulled out a hockey stick and a large duffel bag, made his way to the front door as he fumbled with his keys while juggling the heavy tote of gear.

Inside, he bent to drop his gear. His lower right side was twinging with a strained muscle, causing him to grimace and rub at the spot as he slowly straightened himself. He loved playing in his fun league once a week, but as he got older, the games were getting harder on his body. He wasn't sure what was worse in the morning, his back, or the bumps and bruises that would reveal themselves. It was supposed to be a fun way to stay active, be social, but nobody went easy on each other. Once they were on the ice, they all acted like teenagers, slamming each other into the boards, knocking into each other with jabbing elbows.

From the front landing, there were three steps into the front hall. On the second step, the lower left side protested again. It was a sign that it might be time to take up something else with less contact, like golf. With a yawn, he realized early morning tee times might be more enticing than these late-night ice times they were relegated to.

Moving into the house and down the hall leading to the bedrooms, the balance of their quartet family, son, daughter, and wife, should have all been asleep, but the glow that emanated from the end of the hall where the master bedroom was signaled that his wife was still awake.

Shoulders suddenly a little heavy, a quiet deep breath, he took a few reluctant steps down the hall. He just couldn't have been lucky enough that she'd be asleep already. The two of them had been experiencing some troubles lately, well, she had been having some mental health struggles, and that was causing the strain. It was hard because he didn't know what he was walking into. Tired, he was expecting the worst. Then he silently cursed himself for being an asshole. She was doing her best. The fact that the doctor had switched her meds again wasn't her fault. She was doing her part. He needed to do his part by being supportive and not going into every situation thinking he was about to trip a landmine.

Down the hall, he took a moment to stop at the first door on the right, peeking his head in, he could see his daughter Sera fast asleep.

"Munchkin one accounted for," he whispered to himself and blew her a quiet kiss.

The time out with the boys was great, but he also hated missing the end-of-day time with his kids. It just felt wrong missing out on the nightly ritual of teeth brushing, hugs, stories, requests for water, Sera's impromptu bedside chats where she came up with weird questions because she didn't want him to leave, and she thought she was tricking him into staying so she could be awake longer. So being out for some alone time was good for his mental health, it came with the kick when he got home, and he felt guilty for missing a night with the kids. There were only so many before they didn't need stories, didn't want hugs.

The next room was Ely's. All that could be made out were some unmoving lumps under the blanket, so Munchkin Two was also checked in for the night. Ely always slept buried, which was kind of cute, but the poor boy also experienced horrible nightmares. They used to think it was just a way to get attention and be able to sleep with mom and dad, but the six-month bout of night terrors he had a while ago evidenced, he was not faking. Luckily, he had not experienced those for a few months now, but he was still plagued with nightmares. It made Dad a little sad. Ely was a happy kid, but the interruption in sleep from these ongoing nightmares had been weighing on his cheerful nature for the past couple of months. They had been weighing on Dad. He just hoped beyond hope that the current strain in his relationship with his spouse was not the reason. The counsellor they started Ely with last month didn't think so, but so far, Dad wasn't convinced.

Under the blanket, eyes wide, Ely stared into the darkness. He heard Dad breathing and then heard him leave. Dad tried to be quiet, but he was not as stealthy as he thought. But Dad stopping by his bedroom isn't why Ely was awake. He had been lying here frozen for the last ten minutes. He kept his head buried under the blanket, too scared to peek over the edge of the covers. If you couldn't see the Boogeyman, the Boogeyman couldn't see you.

The words in his head said. Stay hidden.

"Who's there?" Ely asked in barely a breath, then held it, not wanting an answer. Hidden from sight didn't mean Ely couldn't hear. And something was whispering in the dark.

Captured in the door frame, Dad could see his wife was wide awake. She was curled up, sitting back against the headboard with her attention on the television, providing the light source.

"Hey," he said in a soft greeting when she didn't acknowledge his arrival.

She didn't turn to look at him, just maintained a stare at the television. "Didn't think you would be this late."

"Didn't think I would be," he responded while making way to her side of the bed. "The guys convinced me to stay for beers. I know I'm going to regret it in the morning." He leaned forward to kiss her on the forehead. "Sorry if I kept you up waiting." He pulled away to look at her closely, she had not even flinched with the kiss; she

had just maintained the same position, the same stare. "Is it the new prescription that's keeping you awake?"

"I'm awake," she waved him off. "Not everything is because of my depression."

Not everything he thought to himself. But this thing sure seems to be. She had never had an issue with him going out before. She had always encouraged it. But this infernal depression that was beating her down was changing her. And he hated it.

He had to be patient. He hated it, this depression, the drugs. But he didn't hate her. Her he loved. Not who she had been lately, but he loved her. They would see it through.

He moved to the bathroom suite and waved from the doorway. "Sorry, just making sure you are okay." He poked his head out of the doorway. "I'm just going to shower so I don't keep you up any longer with my sweaty stink."

Once he retreated into the bathroom and she heard the water run from the shower head, the wife pulled a pillow close to her face so only her eyes were looking over the edge to glare at the spot by the en-suite doorway where her husband had last shown his face.

Voice muffled behind the pillow she had pressed hard against her face. "Why wouldn't I be okay, stuck in this house?"

She pressed her face so hard into the pillow that her forearms and hands shook against the pressure.

"So, change it," a voice said to her.

The wife stopped and looked around for the origin of the voice. The television was on mute. No kids in the doorway. Husband is in the shower.

"So, change it!"

The wife was startled to catch her reflection in the bathroom mirror. Standing in the doorframe, staring at the shower, her peripheral vision startled her. She had no recollection of getting out of bed.

In mid-lather, the husband thought he heard his wife in the bathroom and peeked his head out from behind the shower curtain. She wasn't there.

"Did you say something, Honey?" he called out.

No response. He stood there baffled for a second. He had been hit by that unexplainable feeling of being watched that people get. Maybe she had come in for a tissue or something and had already returned to the bed.

In a zombie state, the wife shuffled down the hallway. She stopped at the open door of the boy's bedroom, blankly staring inside the room at the bed.

So, change it.

In his hideaway under the covers, Ely began to tremble in frozen fear. "Go away! Leave her alone!" He mumbled between chattering teeth.

He had to risk it. Peeling back his comforter ever so slowly, gently, he stole a look from the edge of his covers. Nobody was there. Just the lingering scent of his mom's perfume that usually brought him comfort, but on this night, it felt invasive.

Mom moved past her daughter's room, unaware she was passing it, she shuffled in step to that echoing mantra in her head.

So, change it!

Into the kitchen where she stopped at the counter, head cocked, staring at the knife block.

So, change it!

Ely was back to his reclusive spot under the protection of his covers, eyes squeezed shut; he did not want to look again but responded to something unseen. "I am awake."

Run! Hide!

Fear blazed from his eyes when they popped open to those two words ringing in his head like a bell. But he didn't trust them. His nightmares had been so real, they felt so real. He awoke from dreams with dirt on his bare feet that he had hidden from Mom and Dad, or the scratches, the scuffs on his knees. He had to suffer through the burn and sting so none of them would ask what was bugging him.

Maybe he was a sleepwalker.

But it always felt like something else.

I can't. I can't. That was all he repeated in his mind, too scared to move.

Run.

I can't. Please stop. Why? He was going to ask. Why are you doing this, but one word rang back to him after the why.

Sister!

The mom no longer shuffled in a zombie state. Now she was an arrow hurrying down the hallway with purpose, directed at a target, a large kitchen knife held so tightly in her hand the knuckles burned white.

With a towel wrapped around his waist, the husband went to his dresser to find pajamas. The television was still on, but the bed was empty.

"Hey, where'd you go?" he called out to his wife, then turned at the sounds of heavy footsteps behind him. "Jesus!"

In silent answer, his wife barrelled into the room with predator swiftness, one step, two, onto the bed, she launched at her spouse in a stabbing attack. The couple tumbled backwards into the dresser in a melee. Searing hot flashes across the husband's forearms as he tried to block her slicing at him with the chef's knife. The husband did not allow himself to cry out in pain, scared that it would awaken the kids. He kept half an eye trained on the door, hoping their slumber was deep enough that the few bangs and bumps hadn't disturbed them. It had stolen too much of his attention while trying to keep his wife at bay. There was a piercing sensation as the blade drove deep into him, and they both disappeared in a tumble beside the bed. He could no longer see the door.

Some rustling and grunts, and the wife popped up, using the side of the bed as leverage to pull herself to her feet. Because of the blood on them, her hands printed the sheets, her hair was matted, and dark stains were on her nightgown. A wild look was in her eyes, not of fury and rage in her attack but of enjoyment and fulfilment. With the dripping knife, she stepped onto the bed to cross over the mattress, oblivious that the obstacle was in her direct path to the bedroom door.

Quick step down the hallway and into the boy's room. At his bedside, posing to strike, she lifted the knife into the air, and with her other hand, whipped back the blankets.

Only to discover the bed was empty.

Head tilted to the side, she stared at the empty bed for a moment with her tongue glazing back and forth over her top lip as if she had to process discovering his absence.

A creak from another room snaps her head back straight in attention. The mom moved with rapid steps into the girl's room. Without pause, she was at the bedside again, pulling the covers away with magician swiftness.

Empty.

Pushing themselves as deep into the corner of her closet as they could, Sera held her brother tight. She was behind him with one arm around his chest to pull him close and keep him still, the other around his mouth to keep the slightest breath silent.

He struggled momentarily, and she realized she was also covering his nose and had to adjust her grip.

She had no clue and wasn't sure if she was confused or frightened. Ely had come into her room, shaking her awake and yanking on her arm to pull her into the closet.

He hadn't even been calling her to wake up, all he kept whispering was Mom...Mom...Mom.

Sera wasn't sure what was going on, but only half-awake, she heard some thumping from somewhere in the house and instinctively trusted Ely.

Maybe something was wrong with Mom. Why it was scaring Ely, she had no clue. Dad had talked to them both several times to explain that Mom was going through some stuff and wasn't always feeling herself. She was seeing a doctor, but they needed to be patient because some days she might be more tired than others.

And when she thought about it, this wasn't the first time Mom Sera's room. She had sloughed it off before, but her skin prickled up her arms, as Sera realized she had awoken to Mom standing in her doorway or at her bedside a few times before. Sometimes when she stirred awake and would say "Mom," Mom smiled, hugged her, and told Sera to go back to sleep. The other times, Mom had just silently left, and Sera had fallen back to sleep, thinking her parents were weird.

A couple of times when passing Sera in the hall or coming into the kitchen, her Mom had knocked into her or pushed her. She always quickly apologized like it was an accident. The fear emanating from her little brother, shaking in her arms, made her question those moments. Maybe something more was wrong with Mom besides just being sad. She didn't act sad, just weird or angry.

There was that one time when she was brushing her teeth and Mom stormed into the bathroom, pushed Sera against the wall, and put her hands around Sera's throat. And for the times Dad said Mom was not feeling herself, this time she saw it; something flashed in Mom's eyes. After a second, Mom had let go, caught their reflection in the mirror, and barked at Sera to hurry up and get to bed. That night, Sera cried herself to sleep. In the morning, she woke up to find Ely sleeping on the floor beside her. Maybe Mom had scared him, too.

Sera was old enough to know she should have told someone about it, but couldn't bring herself to. Those strange incidents, because Mom wasn't feeling well, didn't compare to the rest of the time when she was a wonderful mom.

There were heavy footfalls of someone rushing into the room. Sera listened. All she could hear were deep, heavy breaths.

If this even were Mom. Maybe someone had broken into the house. Why weren't Mom and Dad waking up to help them? Should she call out for help?

Sweat beaded on her brow because there was something with those breaths; it wasn't a snore, but a low growling.

That swept the sleepy fog from her brain entirely, and now she felt it, and Ely was frightened. She squeezed Ely tighter as the low guttural, growly breaths and creak of the flooring announced the intruder was moving towards their closet hiding space.

A moment of silence.

Wide-eyed, Sera and Ely stared at the closet doors, silently praying they wouldn't open.

But it did, whipping open in a blink with a thudding force. The kids screamed in unison as their mom leered down at them with an angry face they had not seen before.

Then her demeanor changed, and Mom dropped to her knees, pulling her children to herself with a reassuring embrace.

"It's okay. It's okay. It wasn't me. It wasn't me. That was not me. I didn't do it," Mom kept saying to them.

The room was dark except for the amber glow of the nightlight. Being held close to her mom, Sera could feel a wetness and saw dark blotches in her mom's hair. Worse, looking over her mom's shoulder, on the floor behind her mom, glinting off the soft hue of her nightlight, Sera saw a knife.

Sera pulled back then to look into her mom's eyes. "Didn't do what?"

Her back to the door, Mom didn't see, but before she could answer, the kids yelped in surprise as Dad stumbled into the bedroom, cut and bleeding, and struck their mom in the back of the head with a hockey stick.

The kids tumbled out of her arms onto the floor, watching as Dad moved in closer and kicked her away.

"DAD!" Sera screamed at him to stop as they witnessed the violence before them.

Dad stopped and looked at his two kids on the floor. "Your mom has gone crazy. She tried to kill me."

With Dad distracted, Mom hissed and lunged for him, hands held out like claws and teeth bared as if she were some feral animal. He swung the hockey stick hard, catching her in the side of the head. It splintered and snapped with the blow, knocking her into unconsciousness.

On his knees, he pulled his kids close, quickly checking them over. "Are you alright? She went nuts." There were no signs of physical injury to his two children. "She didn't get you. Thank God, she didn't get you."

He was taking the scene in, kids in his arms, crazed wife unconscious on the floor. On the left side of his chest, just above his heart, and below the shoulder area, it burned and bled from the large gash of being cut. "You were both fast asleep. How did you know to hide?"

Sera put her arm around Ely. "It was Ely. He woke me. He knew something was wrong."

CHAPTER TWENTY-FIVE

Ely, dripping wet with a towel around his waist, leaned against the bathroom doorframe and surveyed the motel room. The dim bathroom light revealed two double beds, a long dresser holding the TV and two lamps, and a small table with chairs by the window. It was not fancy, but it was secluded and safe enough for them to take a break and gather their thoughts. Ely was about to call out to Sera that the shower was free.

After their ordeals and tramping through the woods, they both stank. Ely was half surprised the motel attendant had even granted them a room. His big sister could be convincing when needed to be.

Instead, he paused a moment. Staring at her back as she lay on her side, facing away from him, Sera had fallen asleep while waiting her turn. Still dressed and on top of the covers, she must have been exhausted to pass out so quickly.

But then he could see her shoulders gently rise and fall as she tried to contain the muffled sobs. She wasn't sleeping. She was crying.

He decided not to disturb her and moved toward his bed to get dressed. One step forward, and warmth emerged inside of him from somewhere deep. In that fraction of a second, Ely thought the feeling was as if he was passing out, and in the next instant, that sensation cascaded up from a well to blanket him.

Fingers on her back, feathered touches up to her shoulder with the slightest graze, before a hand caressed her hair. Sera froze. She was about to lose all composure because the touch felt like...a disturbed look washed over her face.

Sera rolled over, and Ely was standing at her bedside.

"Stop!" She barked and slapped his hand away. Sera then grabbed his forearm to shake him out of the trance he seemed to be in. "Ely! Ely!"

Her brother was shaking his head, back to himself, pulling his arm away in startlement. "What!"

Sera moved to a sitting position on the inside edge of her bed, facing her brother. "It was her, wasn't it? Anne? It was Anne, wasn't it?"

Ely could only nod as he flopped down to sit on his bed, facing his sister, but hanging his head as he could not look into her eyes.

"It needs to stop," Sera demanded, grabbing Ely's chin to lift his head and face her. "Do you hear me? It needs to stop. This is too hard for me to take."

"I'm sorry. It's like she swims to the surface and reaches out to you. I can't control it," Ely dropped his head again. He could hear his sister's strained words, could feel her pain, the way she had gripped his chin so tightly, barely able to contain herself.

Sera made him look at her again. "You need to try. I can't take this anymore. Everything that is happening, with everything going on, this thought, this knowledge, that my daughter, my dead daughter...that she..." She leaned in close to Ely. "I can't believe it, and it is breaking my heart all at the same time, wanting it to be true." She pulled back and pushed Ely in the chest, unable to contain her frustration. "And why not me. Why can't she be with me? I carried her. She is my child. If she is here, I want her back. These little bits rip into me."

Ely stared at her. He had no words to say. He couldn't imagine how his sister was feeling.

"Plus, it is freaking creepy. You were stroking my hair, and you are not even fucking dressed!" Sera turned away and resumed her position on her side, trying to calm herself, wishing for sleep. But the gaping maw in her chest was a blackhole trying to suck her in.

She had never let Anne go. Sera thought about her every day, but she was coping. She had gotten to a place where she could live a normal life now and not feel the crushing guilt every single moment of every day. Okay, somewhat live, she had turned into a recluse, but whatever. She was doing better than she was. The thought of her daughter being right there on the other side of some veil, it wasn't that it was just hard to take in and comprehend, reality is she hated that she couldn't just touch her and be with her again. She couldn't define her feelings, lying there, Sera knew she was angry, and jealous that her daughter wasn't with her instead of obsessing over Ely.

***

Shivering, aching, Sol lay on his side in the middle of the street, surrounded by a puddle of his blood after the beating he had been subjected to. He tried to pull himself into consciousness, but his vision was blurry from the raindrops pattering down around him, blending into the pooled blood that began to run in small rivulets.

A pair of black, high-laced boots stepped into his eye line as they stopped near his head. He was too weak to object as a figure, shadowed by the night and concealed by the hood pulled over their head to ward off the drumming rain, bent down over Sol to roll him onto his back. He felt his legs elevated, the figure anchoring its grip on his ankles under its armpits. Then, with a huff and a tug, he was slowly dragged away, disappearing into the dark maw of an adjoining alleyway.

***

After a fitful sleep of tormented nightmares filled with experiences of the past he had never lived, Ely awakened to the brightness of the morning sun. Shielding his eyes so they could adjust to the light, he could see it was bursting in from the open door of their room. He looked over to his sister's bed, and it was empty.

Worried, Ely got out of bed and instead of wasting time dressing, pulled the blanket from his bed and wrapped it around his shoulders as he shuffled out of the room.

And there was Sera, sitting on the curb of the parking lot just outside their door. She was taking a long gulp from a bottle of wine.

"Drinking this early?" Ely announced his presence.

Not even startled by her brother's surprise arrival, Sera swivelled to look up at Ely, staring out into the parking area. "I've decided the best coping mechanism might be to turn myself into a raging alcoholic." She turned into a backward-looking position and took another sip from the bottle. "Besides, I deserve some leeway under the circumstances, don't you?"

Ely took a position next to his sister on the curb edge and extended his legs out for a stretch as he leaned into her to bump her shoulder with his shoulder. She was hurting. He felt too much, he was part of the problem, but desperately wanted to be part of the solution. "I'm sorry I wasn't there when you lost Anne."

Sera bumped her shoulder back. "You reached out. I wasn't in a place to let you be there. Or anyone else for that matter."

"I could've tried harder," Ely grabbed the bottle from his sister and took a long gulp. "We are pretty screwed up people, aren't we."

"We take after our parents," Sera's eyes went hard. Her words were not meant to be sarcastic. "But if there was ever any doubt before, these last few days solidify we are crazy, screwed up, take your pick."

The blanket slid haphazardly off Ely's right shoulder as he tilted back to chug on the bottle of wine. He grabbed the corner of the blanket to wipe the side of his mouth before passing the bottle back to his sister. As Sera talked, his eye caught a vehicle in the distance coming down the road.

"Stacey was my friend," Sera said. "Not my best friend, or a remarkably close one, because let's admit it, I haven't allowed anyone to be close to me in a very long time." There was a pause as Sera held a full emotion back. "But she was a friend, and her brains were blown out of her head before my eyes. The Jeffersons were my friends, brutally slaughtered and gutted like animals."

She drank more wine than took a deep breath, a realizing, submitting breath. "And none of it matters. I'm sick to my stomach over it, but it doesn't matter as much to me as knowing my daughter is close, she exists. It is on the other side of some unseen veil, so I can't touch her, but she is there." Sera looked at Ely. "That is the worst of this. That hurts the most and makes this impossible to cope with."

He thought he would have seen tears welling in those eyes, but they were dry, hard, and it almost made Ely burst into tears himself at the thought of what all this craziness was doing to them. His attention was stolen again by the vehicle coming closer from a way down the road. Ely could swear it looked like there were lights on the top of the car, the emergency lights, one that would adorn a police vehicle.

***

The ten-floor apartment complex was large enough that it filled a city block. A homeless man pushed a shopping cart, laden with his life's possessions of a few scrounged belongings, down the sidewalk that lined the front of the building, covered with boards to barricade any entrance. The building once housed a first-floor kaleidoscope of amenities from a liquor store to a small grocery, a dry cleaner, and several other stores. The balance of the building holding rental residences, but hardships through economic downturn in the area had left the building abandoned several years ago. Although it had been locked and boarded up, other residents had eventually moved in to find refuge; the homeless, squatters, and addicts were some of the building's current tenants.

Somewhere, in the bowels of that building, Sol, half lying in the grime of the hard concrete floor with part of his back resting against a wall, painfully fluttered to consciousness.

He blinked hard several times, getting his eyes to adjust and trying to get his bearings. What looked like a teenage girl hovered over him. She was wearing ripped jeans, tall, mid-calf black boots, and a hoodie. Sol vaguely remembered the hoodie from out in the street, where he had been beaten and abandoned.

Upon closer inspection, the young woman was dirty, and her clothes were lightly stained. Seeing he was awake, the girl bent down to check on Sol. "Look at the sunshine in those eyes."

With some effort, Sol adjusted himself to sit upright. "Who are you? Where am I?"

"I'm Claire," the young woman reached out a hand to introduce herself. "I brought you here to my...palace...to get you out of the rain." She stood again, pulled her hood off her head, and placed her hand on her hips. "But I think you need a hospital."

Feeling more alert, Sol looked around. Then assessed the girl. She was petite, but mid-height, must have been sixteen or seventeen with dark-brown hair that was probably straight with proper care, but was now a bit scraggly and fizzed at parts.

"I'm fine," Sol responded. "A palace? Where are we, really?"

"You got me," Claire chuffed, waving an arm at him. "It's not a palace, just your run-of-the-mill abandoned apartment complex. It's better to have that positive perspective, though, right?" She didn't stop for a breath, just continued. "You are safe here, though. Only the homeless and addicted fill these halls, and everyone mostly stays to themselves. So, if you are not going to seek medical attention, there are lots of choices here, like if you need a new body."

That got Sol's undivided attention as he pulled back in surprise. "I'm sorry, what did you just say?"

Claire crouched down to whisper in Sol's ear. "I said you are safe here. And I know what you are."

***

Taking in the morning sun from their perch on the curb outside the door of their motel room, Sera and Ely had been sitting in silence for the last few minutes. Ely was watching the vehicle approach with growing unease, but it finally caught Sera's attention also as they watched a police car come to a halt on the shoulder of the highway, the passenger side tires resting on the grassy berm that buffered the road and the parking lot of the Lamplighter Inn.

"What is this now?" Ely sat up, half ready to bolt. "They must be here for us. We'd better get back into our room."

Two officers were exiting the cruiser.

Ely was about to get up. Sera reached over and put a hand on his arm in a signal for him not to move.

"Wait! Stay cool. We don't know they are here for us. And we don't want to draw attention to ourselves."

"We are drawing attention to ourselves by sitting here," Ely whispered back behind gritted teeth.

They held their perch and watched as the two policemen crossed into the parking lot and then split up. One headed towards the farther end of the row towards an ambulance that was parked in front of one of the end rooms.

The second officer, on the other hand, veered towards them.

Everything in Ely's body vibrated with the urge to bolt. "We are sitting ducks here. He is coming right towards us." He tried his best to be a ventriloquist to hide his mouth movements.

Sera still had her hand around his forearm and squeezed it hard. "Just stay. Calm Down. Like I said, be casual. I think he is headed towards the motel office. If you act like something is wrong, he will think something is wrong."

Something was wrong in Ely's mind. They were probably being hunted by the police. Accused of Stacey's murder, involved with the old couple's murder, the detective's (not a detective) death via a bus accident (that was maybe not an accident), and Ely could not forget the priest who was in that church hanging out in a crucifixion.

"Natural and calm, sure, because casual is sitting in a parking lot in the early morning, downing a bottle of wine!" His sarcasm heavily draped his paranoia.

Much to Sera's credit and calmer head, the policeman did rush by them without a second glance and disappeared into the office. Before they could take the opportunity to retreat into their room, he was rushing out of the office and across the parking lot again.

Speed walking by Sera and Ely, he pointed at them. "You two need to return to your room right now. This parking lot needs to be cleared."

Adjusting the blanket around his shoulders, Ely didn't need to be told twice, wanting to be out of eyesight from the officer, he quickly went back into their room where he took up position by the window so he could look out and keep a watchful eye.

Sera followed him in and secured the door behind herself. "See, not for us."

"Not for us so far," Ely pressed into the window for a better vantage. "They seem concerned with that ambulance parked further down. Maybe there is an injured person in the room or something? It's hard to see from this angle."

"Will you stop being paranoid?" Sera reprimanded him.

"After everything, how can you not be paranoid?" Ely looked over his shoulder at his sister. "I live my life paranoid. Plus, how do you know we are not on a wanted list?"

Two loud cracks could be heard from somewhere else.

The sudden, sharp bangs made Ely startle back from his watchmen's position. "Did you hear that?"

"That sounded like gunshots," Sera replied, feeling a little nervous herself.

"You think," Ely said, then went back to stick his face through the curtains.

It was only a moment after the supposed shots that Ely saw two figures emerge from the room and move to the ambulance. Something was wrong. Pressing his face against the glass, angling his body for a better perspective, he could see the pair were not the police officers.

It was two women...and the one closest, getting in the passenger side of the ambulance...practically naked...blonde...

Ely turned from the window, white as a ghost. "Throw me my shirt."

Sera grabbed it off his bed and tossed it to him. "What is going on?"

"I just saw her," he said, letting the blanket drop to the floor and wrestling to get his shirt over his head.

"Who?" Sera felt the blood drain from her head. She knew who. She couldn't believe it or didn't want to believe it.

"My God! I just saw that detective, Tory, the fake detective. She was dead. But I just saw her walk out of that room. She's alive and right here. She must have killed those two cops!"

"What?" Sera pushed past Ely to look out the window for herself. All she could see was the ambulance driving away.

"The woman who killed Stacey and your neighbours. The woman that was killed by the deer, and then killed again by that freaking bus. She is alive!" Ely was in full panic mode, pacing back and forth desperately searching for his shoes.

"Do you smell that?" Sera turned to Ely.

Ely stopped, one shoe halfway on, and sniffed. "Yeah! Yeah, I do."

Sera whipped the motel room door open, and Ely followed her outside. Several doors down, black smoke could be seen seeping out in streamers from one of the rooms.

"You go to the office," Sera ordered Ely, pointing in the direction he should go.

Ely took a few quick steps, then turned back to his sister. "And what about you?"

"I'm going to check on the officers."

"Are you kidding me?" Sera was already moving away from Ely, ignoring him, so he followed her direction and turned for the motel office.

As Sera ran down the line of rooms, she knocked on the doors as she went by, shouting for anyone inside to get out or simply yelling fire. There were not many guests at this hotel, or incredibly deep sleepers, as only two other doors opened where the residents popped their heads out to see what was going on.

Flames could now be seen escaping the one room. Drawing closer, Sera saw the door was open, letting in more air to feed the flames.

Just outside the room, Sera stopped dead in her tracks. One police officer was lying dead just inside the room. But to her absolute horror, the other officer was sitting on the edge of the bed, staring out at her, as if he were on fire and burning alive.

"What the devil?" Was all that escaped her lips because the man looked like a charred demon, sitting there encased in flames that birthed from the bed.

"Devil?" The burning cop smiled and cocked his head at her which set Sera back. He should have been screaming in agony. "Devil is just a general term for those trying to claim dominion over earth." He raised his sissling arms to the sky. "And God is the name for those already in power. It's all perception."

The burning cop flopped back hard on the bed, kicking his legs and flailing his arms. "Oh my God! Oh my God! Oh my God!"

He stopped. Burnt with charred and overcooked, blackened skin, his features now barely recognizable, the man raised himself back to his seated position and brought his hands together in prayer and directed them at Sera. "See? Nothing!" He opened them and held them out to display their emptiness. "In my moment of need, nothing. Nothing from God!" Only the whites of his eyes against the charring skin accented by flickering flames, revealing his white teeth as his peeling lips pulled back to display a grotesque, twisted, sadistic grin. "Who's the devil now?"

Sera turned to run, took a few steps, and collided with the hood of a parked car. She paused for a moment to regain her breath and composure after what she had witnessed.

"Sera! Sera!" That snapped her attention. Ely was running towards her from across the parking lot, pointing and yelling. "Behind you!"

Instinctively, Sera turned to look, and the burning cop was right there, flickering and sizzling like a vampire caught in direct sunlight.

He was reaching for her, hissing through his scorched throat. "Who's the devil now?"

Sera rolled away, narrowly missing his grasp, and ran towards Ely. Brother and sister ran across the parking lot towards each other. The enlarging fire in the motel, a chorus cheering them on. Burning cop was in hot pursuit behind Sera and gaining, reaching.

In full sprint, Ely grabbed Sera and pulled her past him. "Keep going. Don't stop!" He yelled at her as he kicked out at the burning figure that just missed grabbing and potentially igniting her hair.

The burning cop was flailing on the ground, trying to get up to continue his pursuit. Ely kicked him again, hard this time, not just trying to knock him away from his fleeing sister. That seemed to take the life out of the burning cop as he stopped moving unless he had finally succumbed totally to the flames. There was a spasmodic twitch from the body on the ground, then nothing.

Turning to follow his sister, Ely saw Sera sprinting towards the police car on the side of the road.

Knowing full well her intention, he called out to her. "We can't steal a cop car."

"Is there any other choice? We can't stay here," Sera shouted back at him, already getting into the driver's side.

Ely ran after her. She was right. It just wasn't the best idea. It was the only one, though.

Getting into the passenger seat, Ely tried to catch his breath as he looked at Sera. There was one problem. "We don't have any keys, and I am not going back to check that guy's pockets."

Sera did not reply, just gave her brother a half smile and turned the key in the ignition to fire up the engine. At least one thing had gone right.

Before pulling away, the two of them looked back at the burning motel and the smoldering body in the parking lot.

"That guy was chasing you while burning alive," Ely sounded exasperated.

"I think he was possessed," Sera said bluntly, and they both stared at each other for a moment.

"You think?" Ely couldn't help the sarcasm. "I think I burned the rubber on my shoe when I kicked him."

Finding sanctuary in the police car, a moment for the adrenaline to lower, Sera lifted her hand to her mouth. "I think I am going to throw up."

"Throw up later," Ely said, pointing to the rearview mirror. Firetrucks could be seen approaching from a distance. "The motel manager listened when I told him to call for help. Those firetrucks are getting close. We need to decide what we are going to do here."

"We drive," having composed herself and her stomach no longer threatening to eject any of its contents, Sera moved the gear shift to the drive position. "We do what we have been doing. We keep moving."

She accelerated steadily, hoping they were far enough away before the emergency brigade arrived at the Lamplighter Motel and saw their police car leaving. She kept checking the mirrors to ensure they weren't being followed.

They didn't drive far. Once they were in the city limits, Sera found an alleyway within a commercial district that provided some cover for her to park.

Killing the engine, they both felt like they could finally breathe and sat with their heads back against the rests, exhausted and trying to comprehend what they had just witnessed.

"She was close. She is still alive, and she was so close to us," Ely broke the silence.

"Too close," Sera replied. "Maybe those cops threw her off, or maybe the fire was supposed to be for us?"

Ely still stared at the ceiling of the car, looking beyond as if he were watching the stars. "That cop was chasing you full sprint while burning alive. He didn't even feel anything. Detective Tory was impaled by a deer, crushed by a bus, but when in the glimpse I caught of her, she was moving around just fine. Plus, now it looks like she has a partner!"

Too scared they could be tracked in the police car they had "borrowed," Sera sat up and looked at Ely in revelation. "We can't stay in this car. We need help. How about, what was her name, your girlfriend, Sharon?"

Ely rolled his head to its side to look at his sister, then went back to staring at the ceiling. He had not thought about Sharon in a long time. Probably because she was adamant when she had told him in no uncertain terms to never call her again, to never think about her again, and that she was going to wipe the memory of their relationship from her mind.

***

Driving down the highway on a hot August day, windows rolled down, music playing loud, Ely rested his arm on the door and rested his other hand on the bottom of the steering wheel. Cruising position. It was a straight stretch of road. He looked over at Sharon in the passenger seat. She was relaxed with the seat reclined a bit. She was wearing those short-cut-off jeans that Ely liked so much. With having kicked off her running shoes Sharon had stretched her legs out with bare feet on the dashboard. All Ely saw were painted red toenails and long, tanned legs up to the frayed edge of those shorts that drove him crazy. He knew it, and Sharon knew it.

She could feel him looking and popped one eye open to catch him in the act. "Eyes on the road, sport."

"I'm watching the road," Ely laughed a little and reseated himself to make a point of looking directly out of the windshield.

"You better be. Don't forget I need the bathroom at the next gas station."

Ely reached over and patted her on the thigh. "Just rest. I'll wake you when we stop."

Sharon sloughed off his hand. "And both hands on the wheel."

It wasn't long before Sharon was sitting up, unable to rest, with her need to go to the bathroom becoming more urgent. Looking out of the window, she saw a gas station, Ely was blowing by.

"What the hell! I told you to stop at the next place so I could pee!"

Ely did a double-take. He had not even noticed any signs for an upcoming rest stop, nor had he noticed a turn off, nor the gas station itself. He blinked hard twice and looked at himself in the rearview mirror. A black panel van, the windowless cargo type, could be seen pulling off into the station.

He didn't want to admit that he had zoned out while driving, so he made an excuse. "That one just didn't feel right."

"It's not going to feel right if I pee my pants," Sharon quipped back, a little angry. Ely had been insensitive to her needs.

Unbeknownst to the couple bombing down the highway, back at the gas station, the black van came to a hard stop in front of the double glass doors of the storefront. Four masked men erupted from the vehicle, pistols and shotguns in hand, and charged inside the store. Two employees were behind the till, and a family of four was grabbing snacks and drinks for the next leg of their road trip. Before making any demands, the masked men opened fire on the employees and patrons, shooting them down on the spot.

***

The sense of urgency that ripped Ely from his sleep sent electric currents along his body that made every hair on his arm stand up in static erection.

He immediately reached over to Sharon to rouse her. "Sharon! Sharon! Wake up!"

She rolled in response to Ely's forceful shaking. "What? What is going on?"

"Turn on your light!"

She did and then half sat up to look at Ely, rubbing sleep from her eyes. "What is it this time?"

It wasn't a question. It was frustration. They had been living together for three months now, and this wasn't the first time Ely had woken her up from a dead sleep for no reason at all, or because of some damn nightmare. A couple of times, she had bolted out of bed because the house alarm had gone off, only to find that Ely, who had been sleepwalking, was outside.

"I think I heard something outside," he whispered.

Tired, exhausted, from too many nights of broken sleep, Sharon's frustration boiled over. "Then go check it out. You are a man. You don't need to wake me up for this shit. I don't care what you think you heard. I don't care about your damn nightmares, just deal with it, and let me sleep."

Before he could respond, she was out of bed and at the window, pulling back the curtains to look out into the night beyond. "Nothing. Nothing out there."

The figure in the yard shrank back at the sign of the light from inside the house and pressed itself against the house to be hidden from prying eyes in the window.

***

Opening his eyes, Ely recalled the blowout that ended their relationship shortly after that evening when Sharon had reached the end of her rope.

"Sharon," Ely commented to Sera. "Sharon is a lost cause."

He paused. Would she help if he reached out and explained things to her? Then he thought of how crazy their predicament would sound, followed by the memory of the venom in Sharon's words when she broke up with him. There was no way she would tolerate any form of craziness coming from him.

"Sharon is a closed door," Ely reiterated. "She couldn't stand my erratic behaviour."

Sera looked out the window in deep thought, then twisted in her seat to face Ely with the utmost seriousness. "Then that only leaves us with one choice."

Desperate or not, real or not, Sharon would never believe it was real and happening. But Sera was right, there was only one person who might help them, one person who would help them and believe them.

One choice, Sera had looked at Ely. It was their only choice. What were they risking bringing this to their father's doorstep?

CHAPTER TWENTY-SIX

The girl pulled away from him. All that echoed in Sol's mind were the words she had just spoken to him.

I know what you are!

What exactly did she mean by that? He tried to get to his feet, to be prepared to move if need be, because suddenly he wasn't sure if he had been rescued from the street or taken as a captive. Sol tried to placate himself. There was no reason to panic, he was sure he had just misheard her as he came back into consciousness. He slipped back down the wall to a sitting position. As he attempted to stand up, it was not merely specific parts of his body that were in pain; it felt like every part was protesting against any movement.

"You know who I am?" Sol clarified.

"Not who, what!" She gave him a Cheshire grin, revealing a secret she had held for too long. "I know what you are. I know you are something that has been sent here and is just inhabiting that shell of a body." She gave him a bit of a poke.

Pushing up to his feet, Sol teetered with a slight dizzy spell. Claire moved in quickly to present herself to lean on and brace himself from falling.

So, she knew his secret. That was a danger, but she was helping him, so the girl herself was not presenting as a threat. How did she know so much, though? "You are the same?"

"No, I'm a different breed. I was just one of the innocent vessels being used in this ageless war, but you see, I welcomed them." The feeling had balanced now, so Claire stepped back and extended her arms in a presentation. "And in that I have control."

Sol raised an eyebrow. "You welcomed...them."

"Well, that is kind of a funny story," Claire said with a quick smile, but Sol caught the flash of pain behind her eyes. She took his hand and began to lead him forward. "C'mon. You are going to need to take a load off for this one. I don't need you passing out on me again."

She led him down a hall and into a larger room where she closed the door. It was pitch black for a moment until the flick of a lighter illuminated the girl's hand. Claire lit several candles and pointed to a mattress on the floor. Sol took a seat, and Claire sat cross-legged in front of him.

"For context, I think it best if we go back. You see, I was a weird little kid," she explained to Sol. Initially, she seemed to be searching for words, unprepared, probably never expecting to be sharing her story with anyone. "When I was young, I was constantly getting into trouble for lashing out, at home, at school, anywhere. Did I have anger issues? I don't know. There wasn't a label then. Later, I was diagnosed with Oppositional Defiant Disorder. I don't think it was anything because it would come and go. Maybe I was vulnerable to intrusion, as young kids can be."

Claire exhaled slowly and closed her eyes. She recalled various incidents from her vivid past as if they were film reels that she was watching on repeat.

She opened her eyes to share the memories with Sol. "Like in first grade, while the teacher was addressing the students, I suddenly stood up and spun around in the aisle, my outstretched arms hitting her classmates on the head. I continued spinning, a marionette on strings, ignoring the teacher's instructions to stop and sit down, until the teacher physically had to force me back into my seat. And then I was screaming, a high-pitched howl of red rage. And all around me, stared in fear, with hands clasped over their ears.

"I was a few years older, playing tag in the schoolyard, a boy pushed me, and I was designated "it." Instead of continuing the game, I lunged at him with fingers shaped like claws, knocked him to the ground, and scratched at his face. The other kids in the playground circled but were taken aback by the sudden aggression.

"Another time, while watching television with my parents, Dad was flipping through channels, and I snapped with impatience, grabbed the remote from his hand, and threw it at the television. After being sent to my room for misbehaving, that red rage again, being confined. I was a hurricane and created a mess by tearing books, ripping pictures, breaking toys, and messing up my entire room.

"My parents would often lock me in my room because of my outbursts, or temper tantrums," Claire continued explaining. She was surprised she didn't blow bubbles if she burped from the amount of soap she had been forced to swallow as a kid.

Mom wasn't a suck on a soap bar kind of believer, she preferred to hold Claire by the scruff of her hair at the back neckline and force a shot of dish liquid soap down her throat to cleanse her of the stuff that would spew from her mouth. She had to admit for an eight-year-old she came up with some vulgar shit.

"But I could never remember the why, what incited it. I remember the temper tantrums themselves." Claire just remembered the carnage of her room being destroyed, dolls dismembered, angry crayon markings on the wall, and her parents' frustrated looks of disappointment.

"Then everything would be quiet. My mind was still. My parents were at peace. Our home was filled with the happy calm of contentment. I had grown out of my emotional outbursts and misbehaviour. I finally felt like my parents loved me instead of resenting me. I had friends, school grades were good, and I helped around the house without a tantrum.

"The volcano inside me had gone dormant."

For a while, as Claire would learn, it was always only for a while until an underground tectonic shift.

Sol did not offer any words, only an ear; he sat and listened, and was patient through the long, silent pauses as Claire recollected the pieces of her story. He could tell by her facial expressions, the crinkling of her brow, chewing of her lips to hold back her emotions that each piece she shared was getting harder.

She continued her story by digesting those past experiences and mustering the courage and trust. "I was a little older now, maybe twelve or thirteen, and I was washing the dishes after dinner. The dishwasher was broken, and the repairman was not coming until the end of the week, so I had to do it by hand. I lost it. But not because of the chore itself, but the coincidence of timing.

That dormant volcano had been awakened.

My mom had walked by, saying something about hurrying up and coming to the basement to help with laundry. I'm beginning to feel like a real Cinderella being punished for being myself.

There was that marionette feeling again. Once alone, even though the dishes had to be washed, I reached into the sink to pull the plug and release the soaped water. Then I began smashing and breaking the dishes against the sink, grabbing the clean ones from the drying rack on the counter, and adding them to the collection. The sink now filled with jarred pieces of ceramic plates and glass shards, mixed with the dinner's used cutlery.

And this is the foggy part, but Mom responded to the sound of the smashing plates. And I guess she just froze. It wasn't like she tried to stop me. She was frozen there in mute witness. I had my sleeves rolled up in preparation for washing the dishes. Claire lifted her. I lifted my elbows high and then drove my arms down into the jagged mess of the sink, slicing my hands and forearms. I extracted my forearms in a swift motion, then pushed them down into the sink a second, and third time, and then collapsed in what was an assumed suicide attempt."

Claire opened her eyes to return from nightmare lane. "I have no memory of this. But that is what the doctors and counsellors told me it was. Told my parents it was a suicide attempt. Maybe it was, but I will tell you I was not making plans to kill myself."

"I remembered lying in the hospital bed, my hands and arms were bandaged, a counsellor was in the room, droning on, and the nurses fussing.

"Recovering in the hospital, I became an emotional wreck. I went crazy in there. I felt captive, constrained, almost claustrophobic. I was just this being of pure rage, spitting at the counsellor, kicking out at the nurses. My parents were distraught. They were almost left with no choice but to have me committed.

But something switched in me, like I knew I was about to be trapped, and things changed instantly. The chaos inside me went quiet, the volcano dormant. With my recovery proceeding, working with the counsellor, acting like a normal person, my parents were allowed to bring me home."

My parents flanked me on both sides as they walked me to the front door. Inside, my parents were warm, cordial, glad to have me home, and proud of my progress. But I could see the distrust in their eyes. This last ordeal had left them drained. I was better. Things were better. From that day forward, I felt my parents didn't believe it."

"You had recovered, gotten help, you were home, so how did you end up here?" Sol asked.

Claire's smile was a sad one. "The struggles with me over the years, and then the last outburst that was deemed a suicide attempt, it was the final straw for my mother. My family was never devout followers; they had faith, but that last incident drove my mother to the church. She started to attend mass regularly. My father joined her on Sundays, and I did occasionally, but I was never pressured. It was a good thing. She stopped resenting me, began being more caring, and it was healing for our family."

That sad smile dropped into the vortex of the past. Time heals. Things were better. Claire felt better in herself. She had just turned fourteen, and the rumblings of that volcano from deep inside began again. Things were better until the onset of those small, sporadic eruptions here and there.

Sparks that ignited the nightmare.

Claire looked at Sol, and he could see the well of tears building in her eyes. "The distrust from the past had not gone away. Sitting on my bed, I could hear my mom and dad arguing. Mom and I had fought just that morning. Mom was no longer content with my attendance at church being my choice, she had demanded I attend with her regularly. It had been a yelling match. And now that they were back, Mom was going on about my aggression elevating again and that it was time for drastic measures."

Claire continued her story, but was not attentive to the words she expressed as her mind flitted back to that fateful moment and the days that ensued.

Drastic measures were needed.

Sitting there on her bed, rocking back and forth, pulling at her hair, Claire had never anticipated that her mom had already set wheels in motion.

The doorbell rang. A pause of silence, then her parents' voices and a third, a man's, wafted up the stairs.

Claire went to the hall and pressed herself against the wall at the top of the stairs to eavesdrop.

The guest who had arrived was Father Bracken, the pastor at the family's church, he was Mother's new bestie. But why was he here? They had never invited him over before.

Claire listened. They were talking about her. Mother had been way ahead of the game this time. A trickle of fear perspired at Claire's brow.

Father Bracken spoke about reviewing their information and that Claire was a special case. He was explaining that generally with this kind of practice, there would be two of them, but there wasn't time to make a formal request to his superiors, and in the effort of time, he was concerned with the delay if he had to present full justification. He went on about caring for them and what they were going through; he cared about what was happening to Claire. He was confident in his ability to handle the situation by himself. To see them through this trial. It wasn't his first time.

What the hell were they talking about?

Footsteps on the stairs.

Claire rushed back to her bedroom, silent as a cat, and back to sitting on the edge of her bed. There were whispers from the stairwell, the adults continued their conversation. A foreboding of dread prickled along the hairs of Claire's forearms as the three adults came to her doorway.

Mother, Dad, and Father Bracken. He leaned against the doorframe with a weird grin on his face, not a sympathetic or endearing smile, a cocky, wanting smile, like he was holding a secret.

"What is he doing here?" Claire asked skeptically.

"He is just here to talk to you. You refused to come with me to church, so Father Bracken agreed to come here to see you. We think if it's important, you speak with Father Bracken about what is going on." Mother said.

"And if I don't want to?"

Dad pushed into the room and pointed a stern finger at Claire's face. "You will, or we are taking you back to the hospital!"

Father Bracken leaned in towards Claire. "It's going to be okay. This will be an evaluation." He put a hand on her thigh, giving a little squeeze.

It gave Claire a shiver. And it was weird, too endearing when she barely knew him, the jingling of alarm bells gnawed at her. The touch had felt erotically tender, not reassuring, or consoling.

"Please don't do this," Claire pleaded with her parents as they pulled away from her room. "I'm sorry. I will be good. I'm sorry, I don't know why I get like I do."

Dad had his hand on the door handle, pulling it closed behind their retreat. "Don't worry, Honey, it's just an evaluation. I'm sure we won't need to go to the effort of a full-blown exorcism."

And her parents were gone, disappeared behind the closed door. The soft click of the latch bolt sliding into the strike plate reverberated in her ears like the clanging thud of a jail cell door.

Exorcism?

Claire didn't think she had been acting that badly, had she?

Father Bracken went to the door and engaged the lock. Claire's eyes widened as she watched him place a black leather bag on her dresser, where he removed his toolkit. He set up a camera on Claire's dresser, and she heard him say something about needing to record for his superiors' review. His voice was becoming muffled as Claire was fading away, drowning under the weight of some anchor in a heavy fog.

Father Bracken turned to her, looked her up and down, and said something about the sedative kicking in. Claire was trying to shake her head to sharpen her senses and ward off the descent into a veiled fog she was being pulled into. When was she given a sedative? At dinner, even before her outburst. How long had they been planning this? Then a blackness blanketed her under heavy eyelids.

Claire came to, regaining consciousness against the splash of something wet on her face. Father Bracken stood at the end of her bed, reading from a bible he held in one hand while he shook the aspergillum in his other hand to disperse holy water across her body. Why were the sprinkles from the metal thing in his hand cold against her skin? She looked down at herself. Her body was exposed, naked, except for her bra and panties.

"Stop!" Claire yelled.

"Awake now, huh? Come to your senses, have you, Demon?" That smile from Father Bracken again. "You are going to need them."

"What the fuck are you talking about?" Claire yelled at him. Not anger. Fear. She could barely move. She tossed her head side to side. Her wrists were tied tightly against her headboard. Claire twisted and strained to feel the extent of her mobility. Her legs could barely bend at the knee as she felt the burning of rope on her bare ankles.

Her legs were also restrained.

Before she could even finish, Father Bracken was at her side, clacking the bible shut in his hand with one swift motion then he swung it like a bat at Claire's head, clapping her on the left side of the face and making her head snap to the side with a stinging bite of a thousand wasps.

She was awake now, eyes wide with fear as her heart thudded with adrenaline.

Claire didn't even have the chance to capture her senses, and a weight was on her. Father Bracken had jumped onto the bed, straddling her, a hand over her mouth to stifle any scream.

"Let's cut the charade shall we, you spoiled little bitch," he hissed down at her. The weight of him, sitting just below her stomach, made it hard to breathe, or that was just the panic closing around her throat. Pain in her side. He punched her in the ribs, once, twice. "You will learn to respect your parents now." Another fist into her midsection. That one whooshed the air from her, and she gasped to catch a breath. "You will learn to bow in the face of God and your elders." A slap on the face. Pain to submission.

Each time she grunted or let out a whoosh of air in response to the suddenness and the pain, but then his knee was between her thighs, wedging, pressing, pushing her legs apart. She felt his hand down there. He wasn't punching. He was caressing her inner thigh. That sensation was almost worse than a pain response.

Head to the side of the pillow after the slap, Claire couldn't bear to look at him, and squeezed her eyes shut. His hand worked upwards of her thigh, circling over her panties, and the desperation of the situation hit her. Her body tightened, rigid, as inside her synapses fired in a rapid panic, shredding nerves into a fray.

He wasn't just an angry man being violent. He was a hungry man.

"Don't," she whimpered softly, hoping for the innocent desperation, the plea would stop the inevitable next.

"Who will believe a little liar like you over a respected man like me? You are all mine now. So, scream if you want."

Disbelieving his words, she slowly turned her head to look at him. That slightest moment of catching ripped fear in her as she looked into his eyes, his predator smile.

Then she did scream. A desperate howl erupted from her as he wrenched her panties from her body, the fabric biting into her waist before it tore away.

There was a pause then. She panted in desperate fear. He froze, just his head moving to look over his shoulder at the bedroom door. The locked bedroom door. No noise came from beyond in response to her screams. No parents bursting through the door to save her.

He just smiled down at her. "All mine!"

"Scream as much as you want," the man was euphoric in power as he moved against her, his spit flecking against her face as if his mouth was the aspergillum and saliva holy water. "Make as much noise as you want. Plea for help and salvation. They are just

the sounds of the possessed and the spring song to hell, the cries of the wolf. You have lost all credibility. Your parents will never believe you when I've made sure any word from you is a lie. You are a wolf in sheep's skin, fangs to bite and howls of deceit."

The utter helplessness washed everything from Claire in that moment of no belief, hope, or trust.

As he increased his rhythm, Father Bracken called out to mask his pleasure. "The power of Christ compels you! The power of Christ compels you!" His lips curled back in a devilish grin as he leaned forward to chime in Claire's ear with a seductive whisper. "The power of Christ compels me. The power of Christ compels me."

There was a wolf amongst them, but it was not her. The wolf had convinced her sheep parents that she was possessed and required an exorcism.

This vanguard of God's word was a liar.

Sitting across from her, Sol's features were drained with shock at hearing the young woman's story. For the last while, Claire had been speaking, but without eye contact as if she was in a faraway place, with her arms wrapped around drawn-up knees where her head was buried. It had not muffled her voice, though. Every word seemed to thunder and reverberate off the walls to Sol, their echo filling him with such sadness. He wanted to reach out and pull her close, hold her, but he fought against the instinct.He was sure this moment, the unforeseen future, the touch of an adult man would not be a comfort to Claire, a spark igniting the nightmare she had experienced.

"And your parents..." he asked.

Claire looked up at him now. He thought there would be tears in her eyes, but they were dry. "My parents? What did they do? They were lambs to the true deceiver. I heard him once outside my bedroom door explaining to my mom that he knew it was hard to hear, but they were doing the right thing letting him perform the lord's service and that I was one of the worst cases of possession he had seen. He kept them at bay by saying their presence would not only put them in jeopardy but could be a crack that would undermine any progress he had made. They had to be strong and take comfort in knowing that any cries for help or anguish, which there were a lot of, were just the demon's manipulations as it fought to keep hold. He filled them with assurance that he was winning.

"My mom would come in at night to clean me up. One particular day, he had hit me in the stomach several times, so hard I had puked everywhere. The bile of the demon he told my parents. That day, he had introduced me more personally to the aspergillum, making me soil myself. It only gave credence to the tales. But his magic was strong. Every night, I pleaded to my parents. That night, I told my mom he was hurting me; I begged her to hear me. And do you know what she said?"

Sol slowly shook his head, not wanting an answer.

"After she called me a liar, she said it was the demon talking. My mother just stroked my sweat-drenched hair away from my forehead and told me it was for my good, and through God, Father Bracken was here to rescue me and make me whole again. That is what the faith-blind bitch said." Claire got to her feet and began pacing. "I hurt everywhere. My bound wrists. My bound ankles. My private parts where he was torturing me. I had shit and pissed myself. But her ignoring me, not hearing me, my mother, that is what hurt the deepest. Those are the scars I carry, not these."

Claire moved close to Sol and pulled back the sleeve of her hoodie to show her wrists where the skin was puckered and scarred from the nights of the rope biting into her, burning wrist and ankle as she twisted and turned to get away from what was happening in her bedroom. "For several days, he had free rein to indulge himself, and under the guise of redeeming me, saving my soul, Father Bracken was breaking it by torturing me. He had stayed at our house, and all that time, my parents were just a floor away, breaking bread with that bastard. My cries of pain and anguish, desperately, incessantly, calling out for my parents to rescue me, were ignored because of his deceit, making him believe that these were all the rants of a demon fighting against expulsion."

Time had been lost to Claire in the dissipation of hope of those tormented hours. But there was that moment that was clear. Her eyes had popped open in response to hearing the door click shut to announce she was alone. She caught her reflection in the mirror, and something, someone strange, stared back at her from the vanity mirror. Even constrained by her ropes, her body was twisted and arched in an unnatural pose, unobtainable, even for the most proficient circus contortionist.

"In the end, that priest achieved the opposite result." Telling her story, Claire had not made eye contact with Sol. Now she looked at him hard. "He didn't expel anything from me. He awakened me. Awakened me to the true evil of this world."

CHAPTER TWENTY-SEVEN

It was late afternoon on a sunny day. Even if it were overcast, it would only add to the gloomy hue. The Bar, which served as a local restaurant during the day, was set deep in its oversized parking lot that remained sparse, even on busy days. Surrounded by tall pine trees, the place felt like it was dusk. It was barely noticeable except for a large sign at the parking lot entrance and a billboard further up the road, outlining weekly specials and happy hour times. Locals visited during the week for slot machines and meals at decent prices. They knew the weekly deals and realized happy hour lasted all day, with hour restrictions applying only on weekends.

Today was not a weekend; only a handful of cars peppered the lot. A Few tall lights worked overtime, emitting a soft yellow haze to ward off the shadows from the surrounding trees.

Bes parked the ambulance and turned it off. It was backed into a stall on the west side of the lot, away from any other vehicles. The walls of trees were too close, unable to exit the rear of the vehicle, without forcing the door against the resistance of branches. Ground keeping had never been a priority for the owners of this establishment, and the reaching branches of the growing trees extended past their boundaries.

"I feel like we missed something at the motel," Bes turned to Tory.

"I feel like we should leave the motor running, it's a little cold, and I need a drink," Tory remarked from her passenger seat. She was still only in her underwear.

"And something to wear. It isn't very covert to be running around half naked. You can't just waltz into a bar looking like that." Bes began chastising Tory. "We are not here to inherit the earth. This is a claim via subterfuge. A refuge from the eternal death, where we bleed out of the nether places. We must slither and be silent like snakes in a garden, slowly devouring the rodents to take claim."

"I hate being constricted. I want to let loose the hordes and ravage." Tory replied.

"We can ravage," Bes said. "We just need to maintain a semblance of covertness until we finish our direct mission."

Tory was shaking her head. "Then we better stop lighting pyres everywhere."

"Hey," Bes stopped her. "I didn't say there was nothing to do. We need to be stealthy. There will be no victory in an open war. A little slaughter here, a little depravity there, sprinkles to slow bake fear and create the fissures to break spirits. That is what draws them in."

"Looks like a little depravity is rolling in right now," Tory drew Bes's attention to a car pulling into the parking lot.

The vehicle was brought to a stop close to their position, parking in a stall in front of them. A woman was exiting the driver's position. She seemed oblivious, or uncaring, of the ambulance's presence. The woman was dressed in black yoga pants and a long top.

Bes leaned forward to better see out of the front windshield and pointed at the woman across from them, swinging her car door shut. "Look at what she is wearing. She seems about your size, Tory.

"That could work," Tory replied as she slid out from the passenger side.

Tory jogged across the space towards the woman for her attention. "Excuse me. Can you help me?"

The woman was surprised at the sight of the approaching stranger in her underwear. "You startled me!" She reached out to put a consoling hand on Tory's arm. "Are you okay? Has something happened?"

"So much has happened," Tory looked at her sympathetically.

"You must be freezing. What do you need? I can call for help," the woman began fumbling in her purse for her phone.

"To be honest, I just need your outfit."

The woman looked up, confused. And Tory was on her, grabbing her by the back of the head with a fistful of hair and smashing the woman's face down onto the top of the car.

"My friend thinks mine is inappropriate," Tory smiled as she whiplashed the woman, driving her face first into the glass of the driver's side door. She tugged on the hair for attention. "Can you believe it?"

Dazed, the woman half slumped against the vehicle. Tory bent in close to inspect the woman's face. It was bloody and mashed with a crushed nose and split skin over the left cheekbone that Tory was sure was broken. Good.

Blood was dribbling off the woman's broken and cut face in a steady array of plops.

"Tut-Tut! Careful now. We don't want bloodstains on them. They are a bitch to remove," Tory chastised as she released the woman, her body falling forward to slide to the pavement below and crack her head into unconsciousness. Tory stood over the body to finish her chastising. "Trust me, I know from experience."

Just as Bes came over, Tory stood in her newly acquired outfit, outstretched her arms to display the ensemble. "You were right, it fits."

Bes just shook her head. "That's great." And thumbed towards the bar. "Now, let's get you that drink and have some fun."

Tory clasped her arm around Bes' as the pair began traversing the parking lot. "Good because I'm sick of this subterfuge. It's time to throw the gates open. I miss the chaos of the old world."

"I'm with you," Bes said. "Keeping in mind that everything's been happening all these years has been about shifting chess pieces."

The double doors at the main entrance of the bar flew open, and a mountain of a man came bursting out.

Tory let go of Bes' arm. "Bouncer, you think?"

"There must be cameras, and someone saw the attack," Bes looked high at the various light posts. "Four of six inefficient lights work, but they have a security system to monitor. Who knew?"

Big and tough, the bouncer was charging at them like a rhino. To most, just the sight of him would be daunting. He was not lean and ripped with steroid-assisted muscles; this was a big, heavier set man. That didn't mean he was slow; he was coming in fast.

Once on them, he reached out to grab Tory with meaty paws. Tory side-stepped and drove her fist into his stomach, as he doubled over, she grabbed the back of his head to push it down and drove her knee up in unison so the two opposing forces could collide in blunt impact.

Bes stepped out of Tory's way, continuing her lecture. "We are not raising alarms. This isn't to be another Sodom and Gomorrah. It didn't work. There is a road map and rules."

Big bouncer arms flailed out to smack Tory away. The man-mountain was shaking off the stars, pulsing behind his eyes.

He had watched the unwarranted attack on the woman by her car and acted. That was what he was trained to do: react, subdue.

Circling him, predators with hungry eyes, these two ladies were different. A chill escalated up his spine in rapid pulses.

He reached for the one who had hit him and only caught air. Then she was close to him, snarling, lightning erupted in his groin, white flashes of pain blurring his vision, he didn't register the hit to his throat, just the gasp for air, taking in two large gulps of nothing. The flashes behind his eyes turned dark, obscuring any light.

The irony did not escape Tory. There was no bounce when the security bouncer hit the pavement, just a flat, motionless thud. She stomped on his head in disappointment to deliver a couple of consciousness-rending blows.

"Don't kill him," Bes said as she bent down to the unconscious body. "We can use this one."

"A little goblin to join our party?" Tory nodded to Bes. "I like it. But can he hunt?"

"Let's see," Bes looked up at her.

The man-mountain arose to his feet and was off, a juggernaut charging for the front doors of the bar.

Bes laughed as Tory clapped her hands in glee. Tory wanted to ravage, and sometimes there was a need to shake the trees; besides, there was nothing wrong with a little mass murder. It wasn't like a quaint little town bar off the beaten path, secluded, where the security guard had gone off his rails and massacred a group of regulars and co-workers, wouldn't send off any flares. There would be little reason for the authorities to question it. Plus, sometimes you had to cast a net to see what you could draw.

The bar was dimly lit with rustic wood paneling and wall sconces. The pool tables in the corner and slot machines with their bright lights were the most illuminated spots. At the center of the bar was a large rectangular main bar, accessible from all sides.

Bes sat on the top of the counter, a bottle of Don Julio tequila, already a quarter consumed in her hand. Behind her, collapsed on the floor in a pool of his blood, was the bartender; he had twitched and kicked a few seconds longer than Bes expected after driving a broken bottle into his neck; she had been momentarily impressed by his stubbornness and his will to live. It was nice to be surprised sometimes.

She couldn't say the same about the rest of the sheep inside.

Chaos erupted in the bar quickly. The darkness inside the bouncer unleashed a raging barbarian, surprising everyone. Tory entered and set emotions ablaze; her touch and kiss ignited frenzy among the patrons, who turned on each other.

The dinnertime rush had not yet arrived, so there were only maybe a dozen people, along with the bartender, waitress, couple of cooks, and a busboy. All of them were dead now, strewn about the wreckage and carnage that had ensued. There had been one sole waitress on duty holding down the fort. A few feet away from Bes, that woman was now on her back amidst pushed over tables and scattered chairs, gurgling incomprehensible pleas as she choked on blood filling her throat that she tried to cough out. It was a pointless effort as Bes' savage soldier lifted one of the wooden chairs above his head and brought it down, impaling the women with two of the four legs with vampire stake accuracy. The arterial spray shot up with firework elegance, marking his face in barbarian war paint.

Tory emerged from the short hallway that led to the washroom facilities, dragging a man by the scruff of his shirt; his pants were down around his ankles.

"What do you have there?" Bes called out to Tory.

"I found this one hiding in the laboratory pissing himself," Tory answered.

Bes breathed in deep, taking in the surroundings. "That smell! Copper blood, screaming bowels, the adrenaline of fear. That is the cocktail scent of death." She took a long sip from the tequila bottle, then wiped her mouth with the side of her free hand. "It's intoxicating."

"That it is," Tory agreed as she bent back the head of the man she was holding so Bes could see his face. His left eye had popped out of its orbit and dangled just outside the socket by extraocular muscles and nerves anchoring it. "I made him see the error of his ways." She dropped him face-first onto the floor. "He was not the one. None of them were. But at least I was able to get a bead on where we hunt next."

"That's great," Bes said as she jumped down from her seat on the bar.

The man on the floor before Tory moaned and stirred. Tory stomped her foot down on his back. The killing sound of snapping spine fluttered in the air on broken wings.

"Well now, you have blood on your shirt again," Bes pointed out as she led her soldier towards the exit. Tory inspected her shirt as she followed suit, and a single word of frustration escaped her composure. "Fuck!"

***

In the house on the street where he had lived for most of his adult life, the man sat in his recliner looking at the pictures on the wall. He used to be married and had two children, but they were no longer there. Within the walls of the house, many memories, encompassing both positive and negative experiences, contributed to his decision to continue residing there. His wife was not present, and his grown-up children rarely contacted him. He picked up a novel from a stack of books on the side table. All the books were by the same author—his daughter. Holding one of her books and seeing her picture on the inside flap of the cover jacket was the closest connection he had to her.

The author's picture had the same serious pose. In this book, though, it was different. In this picture, she had a hint of a smile. A shine in her eye. He liked this picture the most. In this picture, she was pregnant. Not visible yet, so the common reader would not have known, but he knew. She had already been feeling good about finishing this manuscript. After she had found out she was pregnant, she was beaming. She was floating on the proverbial cloud nine.

The picture used in her previous novels was professional and serious, but in this one, the girl he remembered, his angel.

And growing inside her belly, the granddaughter he would end up only meeting twice. The first time was shortly after her birth. And too soon after that, upon his granddaughter's death at the small funeral. Granddaughter gone. And Sera, his oldest child, lost to grief.

Never mind Ely, whom he had not seen in forever. It had been an eternity since he had even heard from him. And as such, the nightmares of the past had left him alone. He desired to reach out to his kids, but the fear of rejection over the large chasm that shifted their lives apart was too daunting. That feeling just made him bitter with himself for being a coward. He spent a lot of nights staring at the wall, reflecting on the past. What could he have done differently? How could he mend the relationship with his kids?

Sometimes he just wished the good times of the past could echo off the walls again.

The doorbell rang.

The sudden break of silence in the house startled him. He hurried to answer it, wondering who it could be. He was not expecting any deliveries. It had to be a solicitor. It was the only type of visitor he received anymore.

He pulled the front door inwards. A striking young woman was on the front step, smiling at him.

"Hello. Can I help you?" He said. Before the woman could answer, the man pointed subjectively at her, enticing a memory. "Wait-a-minute! You look familiar. I've seen you before. Yes. With my wife."

"Maybe," the woman gave a sly smile. "My name is Bes."

The man didn't acknowledge her introduction. He was still lost in thought, he replied with confusion. "But that was years ago."

From his vantage point, he had been unable to see to the side of his front porchway, but Tory came around the corner, moving past Bes, leering close to the man, malice in her eyes. "You smell funny. It is old and faint, but you carry the scent of someone we have been looking for." She pushed her way inside.

Turning to object, Bes shoved the man into the door as she followed. He was about to call out in objection to their intrusion, but the air erupted from his lungs as a blow was delivered to his midsection, and he fell to the floor. Looking up to the doorframe, stood this mountain of a man blocking out the remains of the sun.

Before he could catch a breath, the man picked him up and tossed him deeper into the house, where he landed at the feet of the two women.

Bes and Tory leered at the estranged father of Sera and Ely. It was time to play and set the bait, to flush them out. Take down their house, and they would have no sanctuary.

With the ensuing sounds of the home invasion, muffled thuds, cries for help, and shrieks of desperation, the man had gotten his wish. Although tainted in its fulfilment, the house was not silent anymore.

CHAPTER TWENTY-EIGHT

There was a long moment of silence that draped between Sol and Claire. When Claire finished sharing her nightmare experience of being tortured under the guise of an exorcism. The odd pair found themselves walking together down the long halls of the building. It was as if they felt together the need to move from the spot was littered with Claire's memories.

Not that the rest of the building was any better. The years of dereliction left the wallpaper peeling and stained from water leaks from the pipes that had not been heated through the winters. For unknown years, the abandoned building served as a tenement for the lost, helpless, and victims of society's vices. The carpets were dirty from squatters, and others used the place as a drug den. Most rooms no longer had doors. In some apartments, there were glimpses of several bodies lounging around in drug-induced hazes, from others, sounds could be heard of something living deeper in the bowels of that specific suite. There was a heavy weight of dread in the air, but oddly enough to Sol, not fear, just the desperation of the living barely holding on to any semblance of their humanity.

He could not bear that this young woman had suffered and was now existing here with no other refuge.

"I am so sorry," Sol said to Claire. His heart was aching for her, and he had to give her something, even if it was only words. "I am so sorry this happened to you. Men of the cloth abusing power has been a sordid tale throughout history. And it saddens me that you were a victim of it."

As they took their slow steps together, she leaned into him, acknowledging his caring words without showing weakness.

Sol stopped and turned to her. "You don't have to share more, but how did it all end? Did you escape? Because somehow you have ended up here."

Claire stopped and leaned back against the wall with her arms crossed. "He was done with me." She stated matter-of-factly. "To my parents, I was healed." She looked up at the ceiling, taking a moment of recollection, then looked at Sol hard.

Sol realized she had not been looking up in recollection for that brief moment, she was making a final decision on whether she should trust him to take him down the full road of her story.

"He told them I was cleansed and left. I was abandoned in my room until my mother came up to untie me, clean me up, and nurse me back to normal after the ordeal. That is what she called it 'the ordeal,' so grateful that 'the ordeal' was over. I was saved, now having suffered through 'the ordeal.' She had no idea. She was oblivious. But that wasn't the end of it. Like I said, the whole experience, the ordeal, awakened me."

Claire continued. "Everything was fine for a while. Then a couple of months later, we were at service, and I went to receive the sacrament, and when Father Bracken placed it in my hand, I looked up at him, and his tongue crept out of his mouth and seductively slithered over his top lip. Then he reached out, giving my shoulder a gentle squeeze and saying something about being glad to see me there, but his touch had sent my heart pounding, my blood pulsing with a loud drum in my ears that washed away any words. I'd been having nightmares of him, but I was trying to survive and move on for my own sanity's sake, and God forbid have my parents bring him back, but that tongue, that touch..."

Claire's breath was heavy as she slid down to the floor.

She looked up at Sol with tears welling in her eyes. "I'm here because I am wanted for murder. I killed that priest. But it wasn't me. It was something else, someone else..."

After the service that day, Claire was in the back seat of the car, and she kept panting, then hyperventilating.

"What is going on with you?" Mother swiveled in the front passenger seat to bark back at Claire.

"Hot...hot," Claire had pushed out through her gasps. It was a nice day out, but by no means a heat stroke kind of day. Behaving like a dog locked in a car with the windows up. Panting, chest heaving, eyes rolling into the back of her head.

"Just roll down the window," her dad said, and then did it for her from the set of buttons on the side of the driver's door.

Her dad didn't believe in air conditioning, he said it wasted an extra ten percent of fuel. The line of cars exiting the church parking lot had them at a practical standstill. There was no breeze, and the dead air did nothing to help her condition.

Suddenly in control of her breathing, Claire sat up in her seat and leaned forward to address her parents. "Can I get out and walk? I need the fresh air."

"Suit yourself," her father said, unlocking the door so she could get out.

"And no dawdling," Mother shouted. "It's about a twenty-minute walk, so go straight home. You still have chores to do, young lady."

She ignored her mother as she swung the door shut a little too hard, stuffed her hands in her pockets, and began crossing the parking lot.

The clergy house where the priest resided alone was only a block away from his parish, and it was always a nice stroll home after performing the day's services.

After he entered the house, Father Bracken hung his coat in the side closet and went into his office just down the hall on the main floor to drop his briefcase.

As he sat at his desk, it was strange that the laptop was open. He habitually closed it. He had been in a rush this morning, but it seemed strange to miss a step in his perfect routine. Life was chaos without strict routines.

He turned and was startled that somebody was standing in the doorway of his office.

"Claire!" he said, with a hand on his chest to calm his heart back to its natural rhythm after skipping a beat. "What are you doing in my house?"

She stepped into the room, closing the space between them. "I saw the way you looked at me during service today."

"I did no such thing," he barked. "Now get out of my house."

She edged closer. "Felt your touch." Closer. "I need to confess." Pouty lips, seductive lips. "I missed that touch."

"Are you here to entrap me?" Anger drew across him. He grabbed her and pushed Claire back against a bookcase and forcefully felt through her pockets searching for a phone or recording device.

Claire grabbed at his crotch, speaking in a dark tongue. "I think you failed your exorcism, Father." The words are barely illegible, sending a cold chill down the priest's spine.

He smacked her hand away, stepped back to straighten his resolve. He wasn't going to be played, wasn't going to be scared by this little girl.

"How dare you. I am a man of God. This is a house of God!" Father Bracken spat at her, reached out, and slapped her hard across the face, making her head spin.

Her head immediately snapped back to stare at him from under her brow.

"This is a house of God, and you dared," Claire said in a low guttural voice. She looked at him with a sinister sideways glare as she made an upside-down V shape with her hands and held it over her genitals to accentuate the area. "Even Jesus took Mary Magdalene with some gentleness," she jabbed two pointed fingers into the area of her jeans over her vagina. "This is the house of God, Defiler. This is the golden gate to the pathway of creation. And you entered without a welcome. Without invite."

The priest stepped back in horror at what was before him. This was not a young teenage girl, a victim.

This was something else.

Claire pulled an aspergillum from the back pocket of her jeans, rubbed her hand over the perforated ball at the top of the short handle, then tapped it against her other palm to assess its weight, as if preparing a baseball bat.

A flash in her mind's eye. So much of the time under those days being held captive for the exorcism were pushed into the dark recesses of her memory, locked away to protect her sanity, but holding the metal instrument she recalled in vivid detail the feeling of wetness seeping between her legs from the blood, the pain of being torn inside because he had forcefully used the aspergillum to violate her anus. The soreness was secondary, the true hurt was hearing his viper tongue tell his mother that Claire had broken her bonds and, under the force of the demon, had grabbed the utensil and defiled herself before he could stop her.

"You liked this tool, didn't you, Father?" Claire rasped in a burnt voice, seductively licking the head of the tool in her hand. "Liked using this on a young girl, pushing it into her private bits." She made a jabbing motion with it. "Thought you were cleansing her from the inside out, is that it?" Stepped forward. "Going to use it on you, let's wash away your sins with blood."

Father Bracken swung out in fear, widely missing the girl. "Out, you demon!"

The girl smiled at his fear. A demon, yes, Claire wasn't here anymore.

Father Bracken had wanted demons. So, she had brought him this demon.

Palms to temples, Claire rubbed vigorously as if trying to scrub the memory from her mind. "I could see what was happening. I could feel what was happening. I couldn't control it. And after what he had done to me; I didn't want to. Something reached down deep inside of me, past thought and down through memory, reaching into a dark corner of an unknown self. Somewhere I could hide and give way to that other thing from beyond the veil, a locked door of a bedroom that was opened to let one through.

That thing had slumbered and lay silent to allow me to pretend to my parents, but with Father Bracken's touch, when I received the sacrament that day, something dark bled from my heart, filling me with a haze and fury from what he did to me in the disguise of an exorcism. It cracked a fissure deep inside of me, and it had the opposite effect. It beckoned forth that which should be exorcised."

He wanted demons, so I brought him demons.

Sol stayed silent to let her get it out of her. She trusted him, and he didn't want to break the fragility through interruption.

"My parents had agreed to let him work and perform the ritual as he saw fit," Claire continued. "They blindly believed him when he said he was recording for reports and verification to send to his superiors. That day, in his house, I never found his camera, but on his laptop, I found that he was storing, keeping the videos for his personal use, or sharing, I don't know, but there was evidence that I was not the only one he had "exorcised." And what took hold of me. Took me over. The residue was there. Someone who had experienced what I had, only worse. Now dark and twisted. It didn't matter. It was my body that killed Father Bracken, savaged that body. It was me. My fingerprints, my DNA, are to be found as evidence. So, I ran. And I've been hiding here ever since."

Claire got to her feet and crossed the small space of the hall to put her hand on Sol's arm. "Until I was called out.. and sent...to you."

"You were called to me?" Sol raised an eyebrow as Claire led him down the hall into the doorless apartment. They stopped at the large window of the main living room.

The night encroached on the emptiness beyond.

"Yup! That is why I found you in that moment, why I dragged you here," Claire waved her arm in a presentation to the apartment. "I was called to you and sent to find you, but I don't think for the right reasons, considering you and I are at the opposite ends of the spectrum. Playing on opposing teams, so to speak."

Sol stiffened and pulled back. Had he been played, captured, and now hostage under the guise of being rescued?

Claire reached out to reassure him. "No, it's okay. Like I said before, I'm just another vessel that's being used in this ageless war."

"But you know? You are aware?" Sol looked down at her.

"Yeah, that's what I've been telling you. The whole fake exorcism wasn't just my runaway sob story. Why so surprised? You knew there would be others. I'm just a different breed."

"What do you mean?" Sol sought clarification.

"I was just a teenage girl. And with what happened to me, I welcomed them. I opened myself up, and we killed that priest. Now, I am revered, and no longer just being used like some vessel," she smiled and winked at Sol. "Now, I'm in control. I can hold them at bay. Use them to my benefit. And better yet, it has kept me safe. I've been safe here amongst this building's riffraff. Nobody messes with me. They stay clear. It's as if they can see what's inside."

Claire paced toward the door of the apartment and then back to the window where she rested her forehead against the glass to feel the coolness against her skin and to look beyond her reflection into the night that was seeping across the city. "Since I found you, I hear this chattering," Claire continued and tapped her forehead against the glass. Something is happening in this world. Something is boiling, coming to a head. I felt safe here, but now I am a little scared."

Sol reached out slowly and put a hand on her shoulder to show her some comfort and reassurance. "There is evil in this world. Often it is masked. You have embraced its reality, but I can see in your eyes that you are not that evil." He turned to look out the window himself. "You are right. Things are brewing. It is a darkness. I'm here to do my part to hold it at bay."

In Claire's reflection, tears were welling in her eyes that he could see. "I never asked for this."

"I know," Sol replied. "But you have shown your true self when you helped me. Help me still! We can be scared together."

Claire wiped her eyes; she had been on the verge of losing it.

"What do we need to do?" Claire asked.

With Sol's request, she found that survivor strength that had kept her going so far. Regaining her composure, Claire turned to Sol, resolute. He did not flinch in surprise when she placed her hand in his.

"I need to find the Winemaker, but the world is a big place, and time seems to be my biggest enemy," Sol answered.

"Well, you found me, so fate must be your biggest ally," Claire said.

And now she was wrapping her arms around him in a big hug. He did not reject it.

CHAPTER TWENTY-NINE

Ely and Sera plodded along the quiet streets of their old neighborhood. They had been on a long walk, assuming it was safer to continue to their destination on foot. Street Lights lining the laneways of cookie cutter houses began to pop on, not just illuminating the sidewalks and roadways, but a signal they had been on the move for several hours trying to reach their childhood home.

"Should just be another couple of blocks, right?" Ely said, a few steps behind his sister.

"It better be," Sera replied. "My feet are killing me, and my head is pounding."

"I know, mine too, but it was a good idea to ditch that patrol car."

"Agreed. The more distance between us and that motel fire, the better. It's just my feet that have disagreed."

Turning down a street corner was the final stretch towards their old residence. On one side was the row of houses. The other side was the west side of the park. It was a huge urban park that covered an impressive 6.2 square miles. The park was large enough that it divided three city communities. One on the West side, one on the East, and a third to the North. Its valley center ran down to the South end, where the park eventually sloped down to the river. The area was popular for hiking, biking, picnicking, observing wildlife, and fishing along the creek pools or down the wide river. Sera was sure high school kids still frequented the beach area of that river.

The sun was dropping behind the tree line, which didn't help the apprehension wrapping its tendrils around Ely's neck. From across the street, shadows beckoned amongst the trees, teasing his growing anxiety. He had never gone into the park since that day he awoke, lost. The day Tommy Durant was found dead.

Ely chanced a glance over his shoulder at the park. A white heat seared behind his eyes, shot down through his body, and flared inside his stomach, making him double over and drop to his knees onto the concrete sidewalk.

A few steps ahead, Sera heard the grunt from her brother and spun around.

Ely, holding an arm across his stomach while the other braced himself for balance. Sera could barely make out his muttering.

"That day in the woods, it just flashed in my mind's eye. I saved you from that boy, Tommy." With strain, he looked up at his sister. Sera grabbed his arm to assist. "But not me. It was Wynnie. It was our older sister, I didn't even know existed until you told me about her the other night at your cabin." Upright now, the flash of pain subsiding, Ely looked at Sera in revelation. "Our older sister used me to save you from that boy."

"Our older sibling, whom we never met, was watching over me?"

"Yeah, but that's not it entirely. It is the memory of that day that smacked me like a bolt of lightning. The understanding, the realization that I'm a murderer!"

Sera stepped back, confused.

Ely held up his hand for her to listen. "This Wynnie, our older sibling, driving me or not, I murdered that boy. We've been running and surviving, caught in this chaos, and I didn't even think of it like that. I've been too wrapped up in discovering what was happening to me, and how I've been used all these years...I didn't process...I didn't put it together..."

Sera cut him off. "You saved me."

"Did I? Do we know that for sure?" Doubt dirtied Ely's face.

Without missing a beat, the big sister grabbed her little brother and pulled him close into a tight hug, her right hand cradling the back of his head to hold him close, and whispered in his ear. "I know it. Understanding that a note was left for me, Tommy coming back through Stacey to hurt me, I knew in my heart of hearts that he was out for me that day. I'd be dead if it weren't for Wynnie. If it wasn't for you."

"Doesn't justify what I did," Ely's voice was muffled in Sera's shoulder.

"No, it probably doesn't," Sera released Ely from the hug, took hold of his face with her palms on his cheeks to hold his gaze. "But I believe it wasn't you.I believe it was not malicious. What was done was for me, for my life."

They walked down the block in silence. Then they both stopped, having arrived at their destination. They turned together to see the house of their childhood up the path from where they stood on the sidewalk.

Sera grabbed Ely's hand and squeezed it. "And we justify that day now, and everything since. We will get help. We will figure this out and we stop that crazy bitch from hunting us, and from hurting anyone else.”

Up the sidewalk, both took slow steps. They were not scared to meet their father, he was not a bad man, there was just a rift that would be hard to cross. The past had been a current, causing them to drift apart. Coming to their father, facing him, seeking his help, he wouldn't reject them, it was having to look that past in the eyes, that was the hardest. Sera was in the neglected patch of dirt beside the front steps, looking through the weeds.

“You think there is still a key under here?” She asked Ely, as she lifted the hide-a-key fake rock, turned it over, and opened the secret cover.

“Doesn’t matter,” Ely said as he checked the doorknob. “It’s unlocked.”

About to push the door inwards, Sera grabbed Ely’s arm to stop him, stepping to him to partially block the entrance. “I don’t want to go in there,” Sera said. “I don’t know if I can see him. He let her rot in that hospital.”

Ely pushed her hand away and went to turn the knob. “We let him rot in this house.”

Sera slid in front of her brother to block the entrance and held a hand to his chest to communicate a stop motion. “We have all been rotting in our prisons. I can barely let myself think straight to save my sanity most days, so let’s not play guilty over our father now.”

“You’re right, we are adults, there is nothing to be afraid of in there,” Ely tried gently to move past Sera.

Was he so sure that was a true statement? Once upon a time, there was a lot to be afraid of behind these doors. Those were the tendrils trying to pull Sera away now.

"Couldn't we have just called? We are just going to barge in there?" Sera didn't budge from her spot blocking the door.

Ely let his shoulders drop and let out a long sigh. They had been through too much, travelled too far, to sit out here on the front porch arguing, fighting against their apprehension. "Too much risk, he wouldn't answer. We need help. Where else can we turn? You know this. We already decided that this was the best option. It's the only option," Ely gave her a sympathetic smile.

Nervous, but defeated with nowhere to turn, Sera gave way, and they both entered the house, stepping into the past.

Once inside, the door closed behind them, and neither called out in greeting to announce their arrival. They just took a moment to take it in. Inside was quiet, dark as most curtains were probably drawn, but it was quick to tell the house had not changed a bit from the last time they had been here. Now that they were older, looking through more mature eyes, it seemed smaller. The front landing was smaller, and the hallway leading past the living room to the T intersection—kitchen on the right and bedrooms on the left—was shorter.

Ely was the first to break the silence as he called out. "Dad! Dad!"

Soft light. The glow of table lamps pushed the shadows out into the halls. Two steps in from the landing to inspect the living room, Sera expected to see her dad sitting in a lounge chair reading a book. One of hers, for the umpteenth time. He had always loved her books. Not just because they were his daughter's mindful creations, he genuinely loved them.

But then, why no response to their call out in greeting?

Empty chair. Because he wasn't there.

Sera gasped. The chair was on its side. The room was a mess. And on the far wall, spotlighted by the lamp, in large painted letters.

Welcome Home

She stepped deeper into the room, mesmerized, trying to comprehend the message. Ely was right with her. Pointing in silence, stepping ahead of his sister, he noticed it first. The words were large, sloppily written.

Welcome Home

Running at the bottom as if too much paint had been used. Red paint.

Not paint...Blood!

Realization was kicking in as he looked back at his sister, the concerned horror creasing his face, taking it in. There was blood splattered on the carpet, across the couch, the coffee table upturned, and cushions in disarray.

Without further hesitation, Ely hurried down the hall shouting into the depths of the house. "Dad! Dad!"

Sera was frozen, staring at the wall, muttering as she tried to comprehend. "Oh my God! What the hell?"

She turned to grab Ely, but he was rushing down the hall. She ran after him.In a stumbling rush, they burst into the master bedroom. The horrific scene on display before them slammed into them, holding them in place as if they had run into an invisible barrier. On the bed, a lifeless body, naked, positioned in the middle of the bed with arms out to the sides in a crucifixion pose. The bed was a sodden mess of blood and guts as the body had been cut and ripped open from sternum to waist, exposing all the insides. The scene before them held them in shock, it took a moment to identify the man.

Ely stepped in cautiously, went to the left side of the bed, and looked at the face with a wide-eyed death stare focused on the ceiling. "Dad?" He barely managed to whisper, having to force air out.

The other side of the bed, Sera was frantic, making erratic movements of indecision in wanting to touch her dad to check if he would still be alive, but knowing the absurdity of that thought, to grab him, but unable to have her body muscles respond. "Oh my God! Oh my God! What could have done this?"

Ely bent over, his hand on the nightstand for support, as his body writhed in dry heaves. "Not what, who?" Trying to stand up, he answered his sister.

In response, she was pointing at him, shouting his name.

Behind Ely was the walk-in-sized bedroom closet. Emerging from the closet's dark, shadowed cavern was the Boogeyman. That was all that clicked in Sera's mind. All those horror movies from when she was younger were becoming reality at this moment.

The Bouncer-soldier, now Boogeyman, was silent and swift as he lunged out, catching Ely from behind, unaware of Sera's warning.

The tackle drives them forward, tumbling onto the bed, the force rolling them over the father's body to hurtle over the opposite side onto Sera.

The mass of bodies, slide-crash to the floor, the men a mess of blood and guts of the corpse they had just rolled over. Sera was suffering the brunt of the landing as she was pushed back into a dresser, the two men landing on top of her.

At the bottom of the fighting pile, struggling to get out from beneath the wedge of her brother, Sera reached for the bed frame to grab as an anchor to pull herself up. Something metal caught her eye. Not the black matte metal of the frame, but brighter, shinier, silver.

Good old predictable dad.

Pinned in the cramped space between bed and dresser, Sera reached, stretched, ignoring the pressure on her body. The man-monster continued to rain blows down on her brother, who was losing because he was preoccupied with doing his best to hold off and block any of those punches from hitting his sister, who was trapped underneath him.

Ignore. Reach. A fist grazed off Ely and caught her cheek, sending a white flash past her eyes. Sera didn't blink. Focus. Reach. A foot and a half above her, the massacred body of her dad. Her estranged dad, whom she had abandoned because she had always felt he had failed them, had not been strong enough, had let them down.

But for any failing he had been, he had been predictable in his paranoia about things. He had let her down in certain ways throughout the years, but at this moment, he had left something for her, good old dad, predictable dad. In this moment, he was here for her and

Ely because that predictability still had him hiding a gun under his bed.

Each push or hit Ely sustained pushed the air out of her.

Reach.

Her fingers crawled on the underside of the bed, tips grazing the handle of the pistol that was held in a holster taped to the frame.

Dad didn't let them down today.

The pressure was released from her a bit. Ely forced the Boogeyman up a bit, trying vainly to push the man off or hold off another punch. It didn't matter; it was enough.

Enough for Sera to swing her arm out, pistol in hand, she pointed it past Ely's head and pulled the trigger.

The assailant flew off to the side with his brains blowing out the back of his head.

Ely and Sera lay there, trying to catch their breath, letting the thunder in their eardrums from the shot subside.

They struggled out from the dead weight of the body and got to their knees facing each other.

"Are you okay? Are you okay?" Sera kept repeating.

"I think. Are you?"

Sera was frantically shaking her head. "No! No! No, I'm not. This was her. This was her. Dad, we should have known." Now her whole body was beginning to shake. She was breaking down. "They've killed everyone we know...love."

Ely reached out with palms on either side of her face to hold her steady. "Not everyone."

***

Once upon a time, the woman that lay in the twin-framed bed of her cell had been a mother to a son, and a daughter. How long she had been locked up for, it didn't even register, days had blended long ago. On the wall opposite her bed, she could lie on her side and stare at the frozen memory of the past, which was a picture of her two children. The frame was off-centre as it had been placed where it would receive the most sunlight, resulting in the photo's color fading over time. The light came through a high-walled window equipped with metal webbing to prevent breakage, designed to let in light rather than provide a view of the outside. Currently, it is dark outside. The incarcerated patients in the Regional Psychiatric Centre had been locked down for the night. As lights were automatically turned off, the cacophony of the other patients rose with the nightly serenade of a twisted lullaby made up of torturous wails and crazed repetitious mumblings, declining to a dull white noise. The medications take effect, draping the patients' minds and lulling them into quiet rest, then eventual sleep.

Tonight, she was not lulled, or eyelids heavy with sleep. Tonight, she stared at the picture in the darkness. The picture was outlined, but her memory held every detail. When she was coherent enough and had a sense of self, she would remember a better time, a different time. She would whisper their names with apologetic love, over and over, the pair of names coupled with the two rhythmic beats of her heart.

Sera.

Ely.

When she had a sense of herself. A mother's inextinguishable love.

But that wasn't tonight. In the dark, she just stared.

Waiting.

The prison hospital was quiet in the depths of the night. A wraith, moving in blend with the shadows bleeding from darkened corners, Tory drifted down the hall of the psychiatric facility that Bes and she had infiltrated. Wearing a guard's outfit, she finally had clothes that weren't stained with blood. How long would that last? Another question, but she appreciated the moment.

Tory stopped at one of the doors along the hall, fiddled with the key ring on her belt until she had the right key, unlocked the door, and entered.

Before her, a woman lay on her side on the single bed, staring at the opposite wall, giving no recognition to the entrance of the guard. Tory tracked the woman's eyeline to the picture of the two children.

"You can wake up now," Tory said, putting her hand on the woman's shoulder to rouse her attention. "We found you."

Two blinks from the woman, but her gaze didn't shift. "I wasn't hiding."

"I know," Tory replied. "You have been waiting and biding your time." She bent at the knee to bring herself level with the patient, Tory had a wicked grin as she took one of the mom's hands in between her own. "Somebody is coming to see you soon. We need to be ready."

The mom sat up with her head hung low, curtained with greasy hair that had not been washed in several days. She slowly raised her gaze to the picture of the two children. How old would they be now? The pit in her stomach tightened, a gnawing deep inside, a feeling of loss and pain.

Once upon a time, something strange happened to her, and she attacked her children. Maybe that piercing inside was love. A love betrayed. It didn't matter. She side-eyed the woman who had come to her and was now leaning against the door, watching.

Her mind was not her own. She was not in control of herself.

It had not been for a very long, long time. Hence her residency in this god-forsaken place.

But her hibernation was over.

CHAPTER THIRTY

Down the laneway they trudged. Leaving the sanctuary of the abandoned building where she had taken residence since running away and hiding felt strange for Claire. Being out in broad daylight, she felt exposed and vulnerable. Assuming she had been identified as Father Bracken's killer, were the police hunting her? Had her parents been searching for her? As they traversed block by block without incident, she felt more secure. And sadder. Maybe her parents had not been looking for her at all. Claire figured they were probably glad she had disappeared. Not their problem anymore. Their love had probably drained from them with the disgrace of their daughter being called out as a murderer.

She was alone. Except for the voices. And Sol. He was a few steps ahead of her. Would he leave her also, abandon her?

The Winemaker was one of the first on his mental list. Claire's concern was that he had not recovered from the beating he had suffered the other night. He had promised her he was healed enough because he needed to get moving. Time was of the essence.

At a crosswalk, he looked back at her and reached out a hand so they could securely cross together. She was almost 15 and didn't need someone to hold her hand to cross the street, but she accepted the gesture. Her hand in his, Claire could feel in his grip that he was grabbing hold of her, not because he thought she was incapable. He knew she was scared and could feel her reluctance. Sol had taken her hand to physically say they were in this together, and would face the dangers ahead of them, big or as minuscule as crossing the street.

Feeling the embrace of Sol's hand with hers, Claire smiled at him. She wasn't alone. This was someone who cared. As they crossed together, hand in hand, side by side, Claire felt his warmth. Love. Not the romantic love, it was the familial love of a brother she never had, or a father, whom she hadn't felt any form of love for, ever. Her father had always been cold. Never endearing. When she was older, and she had suffered from her episodes, he had never done anything to comfort her or make her feel things would be okay. He always seemed let down, disappointed. He was questioning why he had been burdened with having to deal with a child.

So, how she felt, feeling this with Sol was foreign to her.

Across the street and down another avenue, he directed her into the alcove of a restaurant entrance, blocking her from being visible from the street as a police car drove by.

Sol checked to ensure the coast was clear, adjusted the hood of her pullover, and squeezed her shoulders before they were on the march again. They had a long journey ahead of them, and he listened when she directed him on which way to go next. He didn't doubt. He didn't mistrust. He just smiled at her. She was leading the way, but he was protecting her.

The sun on her face, Sol beside her, Claire realized that just a little bit of her wasn't scared anymore. And regardless of age and the fact that Sol was older, she was going to take care of him.

The taxi driver asked them three times if they were sure they wanted to be dropped off in the middle of nowhere. It was the country road they were on, and as the cab pulled away, Sol gave Claire that look, questioning her resolve.

"Trust me," Claire tapped him in the shoulder with a half-fist and turned to lead the way.

They stood at a high-tensile three-wire fence staring down the rows of a vineyard that the fence bordered.

"A vineyard to find the Winemaker!" Sol quipped as he followed Claire through the fence and down one of the rows. "Why am I not surprised?"

"Hey, it's what they told me," Claire walked backwards, beckoning Sol to follow.

A quizzical look was on Sol's face. "They?"

"The voices in my soul," Claire said, and made a swirly motion around her head to signify she was crazy.

"But still, it's a little on the nose, isn't it?" Sol smiled at her.

Claire's face changed; a scowl took over her features. She ripped a grape from its mooring and rushed into Sol, pressing the piece of fruit into his face in the spot between his upper lip and nostrils.

"Smell the scent," she hissed, not sounding like herself. She pierced her eyes at him, lifted her nose to the air, and sniffed twice in quick succession. "Smells like debauchery."

"You okay?" Sol was taken aback at the sudden change and the aggressiveness she had smeared the grape into his face.

They stared at each other for a moment. Sol wiped the chunks and juices from his face with the back of his hand.

Then Claire, shaking her head as if trying to get a spider out of her hair, turned and kept walking without another word. Sol figured she was okay. Battling the demons inside her, but for now, she was okay. He had to trust in that.

They came to the top of a small hill to look down at the rolling lines of the vineyard. Sol could not estimate the size of the acreage, but the vastness of the operation did not lessen the impact of the imposing and picturesque mansion visible in the distance.

A better choice to approach from as far away as possible. To sneak into the property from the farthest end of the mansion complex, but now, with the sun beating down on them and the apparent distance to the house, he second-guessed that choice.

As they marched down a never-ending line of bushes, Claire kept picking grapes and popping them into her mouth. Sol couldn't be bothered; he was being pestered, sweat beading on his forehead and dripping into his eyes with tiny salt stings, and the wetness down his back, his shirt sticking to himself.

Another incline up a small knoll, and they realized they were close enough now to better inspect the mansion. To keep out of sight, Sol guided Claire down to their stomachs. They crawled forward the last few feet to take refuge under the canopy of grape bushes.

Vehicles were parked in front of the building. To the side were a couple of delivery trucks. A few people could be seen milling around the trucks. Potential gardeners are working around the area in front. Enough eyes to catch two random strangers walking out to the vineyard.

"Looks busy," Sol whispered to Claire, even though they were far enough away not to be heard. "Let's rest here, and we can wait for the cover of night. At least there should be fewer delivery vehicles and people milling about outside."

Claire didn't respond. She just rolled onto her back and snuggled into Sol. Here she felt secure, safe, something that she had not felt in a long time, and the fires that raged inside her dwindled to embers.

CHAPTER THIRTY-ONE

The bedroom was dark except for the glow from the en-suite bathroom that radiated from the open door, and the steam from the shower. Sera was just outside the bathroom, basking in that soft light as she slumped on the floor, her back against the dresser. She and Ely had draped a blanket to cover their father's savaged body, done the same with the dead man on the floor, then she had quickly showered to get the blood off herself. Now she sat here waiting for Ely to finish doing the same. Sera couldn't stop herself from shaking, not from being cold; she was in shock, feeling crushed by hopeless despair.

She was oblivious to the water shutting off and the sounds of the glass shower door opening and then closing. Ely had finished washing the gore from himself. With a towel wrapped around his waist, he poked his head out of the bathroom door to look down at his sister. Seeing Sera's face, she was an understandable mess. Eyes puffy and nose red with wet cheeks from crying.

"I'm going to have to steal some of Dad's clothes," Ely tried to get her attention. "Skin may be clean, but we can't go traipsing around with our clothes covered in blood." He stepped past her and moved towards the closet. "Were you able to find anything?" It felt like a dumb question because she was sitting on a towel. She had just sat in that spot once he had gotten into the shower and not moved.

"Like what? Is there anything of Mom's still here? Is there any choice?" Sera kicked out a leg in frustration. Her words were coming out between sobs. "There is no choice. All of this. None of this. We are just puppets. She killed friends! She killed my neighbours. She killed our father!"

Ely could see Sera was spiraling. He was barely holding onto his sanity himself, especially with his father's corpse on the bed, the blanket outlining the body, that ravaged body, the blood on the floor...

"I'm sure she was involved here in some way, but the Boogeyman from the closet is the one that killed our father," Ely tried to keep her attention.

Sera was shaking her head back and forth. "Nope! No! Your back was turned, and you didn't see him emerge from the closet. This guy..." Sera pointed to the covered body on the floor. "He didn't have a speck of blood on him. He was just here to do her dirty work. It was her. It's all been her!" Her voice escalated in volume, wavering on the edge of hysterics. "She killed my daughter!" Sera breathed in deep, holding herself back from the tipping point. "So why from then until now?"

"What?" Ely asked as he shimmied into a top and a pair of jeans he had pulled from the closet.

"I was thinking about it while you were in the shower, running through the sordid events, and trying to piece things together. She said it was her, not a case of S.I.D.S. that stole Anne from me. Remember in the church? That she-devil said it was all her doing. I hate myself for not protecting my daughter. And I always will because I can't...I don't know how to move past it."

Her sobbing devolved.

Ely raced to her and lifted his sister to her feet, even though she gave no effort to stand and was a listless weight. He pulled her tight into his arms to hold her in this moment of crumpling despair and whispered into her ear. "You have to forgive yourself."

"Just let me fall apart," Sera cried as she tried helplessly to pull away from him, but he held her tight.

"You can. You will. And when you do, I will hold you as long as it takes to pick yourself up, but not now. You can't. You just can't. I need my big sister right now. You have to hold it together."

Sera leaned her head back, taking in air, trying to get together, hearing her brother's words, but still on the precipice. "How do we make it through this, past this?"

"Just how we got through those years with Mom. How we got through those years after Mom when Dad was lost," Ely loosened his hug on her to look at her face. "We do it by standing together."

"Not going to happen," Sera pulled away, rejecting his sympathy and condolences. She was about to spiral again.

"You didn't just let her die!"

Ely still had a hand on her arm to partially comfort her, but mostly to catch her in case she might collapse in her fragile state. Maybe mentioning Mom had not been the sibling bonding tactic to keep Sera from falling apart that Ely had hoped for.

Since that woman had said what happened, they had been running, or Sera had been doing her best not to feel the full weight of that confession. The weight was bearing down on her now, threatening to suffocate her. "Why? WHY?"

Ely pulled her close again and leaned his forehead against Sera's to whisper. "I don't know."

He had no answer, just the overwhelming desire to quell the raging despair inside his sister. He hated that he was powerless to take the pain away.

"Just tell me!" Her fists started to beat a rhythm against Ely's chest. "Explain this horrible pain away."

"I can't! I don't have the answers," Ely gently grabbed her wrists to stop her fists and pulled her tight into a hug again. He found himself staring over her shoulder at the covered corpse of their estranged father. "And none of those answers are here. We need to leave. We can't be here anymore."

She nodded against his chest. Being here was exacerbating their emotions. Staying here was dangerous.

They had hurriedly dressed in fresh clothes and met at the internal door to the attached garage, expecting to see the same old car their dad had. Parked inside was their dad's newer Chrysler sedan. It was a symbol of how time had passed and how things had changed.

Once Sera pulled the door closed on the passenger side, she looked to her brother as he was investigating the console to get comfortable with the vehicle's functions. "I can't believe we are just leaving our father like that."

"Our choices are being forced on us. What else are we to do?" Ely fired up the ignition. "After I found the keys, I called the paramedics to report a death. They should be on their way. Once they discover the other body, they will alert the police. Hopefully giving us enough of a head start."

Ely pushed a button on the garage door opener that was attached to the sun visor above his seat and began to reverse the car out of the garage.

"I hate this," Sera said.

Ely was already looking over his right shoulder to navigate the car out of the garage and down the driveway, so he caught his sister's eye. "She could have been lying about Anne, trying to throw us off?"

Sera shook her head. "The fact that she even knew about her, knew her name, makes me believe she wasn't lying."

Onto the street, Ely swivelled to resume the forward position and change the gear to drive, but paused when he caught sight of the item in Sera's lap.

"Dad's gun," she stated matter-of-factly.

Ely shrugged and began driving. "Good idea."

"We need to stay alive, to solve this, to prove our innocence when the authorities do catch up with us."

"To do that, we are supposed to be finding others."

"We can't focus on that. We are going to have to hope that any supposed others find us. Right now, we need to save Mom. This bitch is always two steps ahead of us luring us into traps."

Ely navigated through the residential streets of their childhood neighbourhood with pursed lips. Sera was watching the past flit by but was able to read Ely's thoughts. "So, let's go spring one more trap. Mom is all that matters now."

And then there was silence. Going to visit their incarcerated mother was something neither of them had planned on doing ever again.

This was one of those life lessons, plans change.

Sera had spent a good part of her life avoiding the repercussions of that word, change.

Ely had always run from it.

Yet, there they were, brought together by it.

CHAPTER THIRTY-TWO

The thunder jolted Sol from his sleeping spell. The journey to the vineyard mixed with the stress, they were exhausted, they hid to perform their stakeout and watched the comings and goings, the day waned, and eventually they had both fallen asleep under the enticement of the sun.

It was darker now, but a strange glow emanated from the sky, and the thunder kept booming, and booming.

Claire started to rouse beside him. Sol put a hand on her shoulder and signaled with a finger to his lips to keep quiet.

Once she had her wits about her and had rubbed the sleep from her eyes, Claire gave Sol a questioning look in response to the repetitive booming sound that echoed into the night sky. Together, they crawled to the top of the embankment to investigate.

It was not thunder. The thrum and thumping that burst from the mansion was loud music. The glow lighting the sky was from spotlights that swayed back and forth with smaller colored lights that illuminated the front of the mansion and marked the entrance to bid the guests to the party within.

The field adjacent to the mansion was converted into an improvised parking area, occupied by numerous vehicles. The presence of headlights indicated a continuous arrival of more cars, proceeding along the lengthy driveway towards the front entrance of the property.

Sol grimaced at Claire. They had been waiting for the cover of night to sneak into the mansion. Now it was a bustling nightclub with people everywhere, making it impossible to sneak in unnoticed.

"Maybe the crowd will help us," Claire patted Sol on the back optimistically, then jumped to her feet.

The oncoming swarm of guests had made it easy for the pair of them to slip into the fortress. The castle overlooking the vineyard dropped its refined mask, a chameleon shifting from day into the night. Sol and Clair easily slipped into the stream of people and were picked up in the swell, being funnelled through the wide double doors of the front entrance. No tickets were needed, and no cover charge was requested. Claire had not even been questioned about her age.

People could barely move as they were pressed together, packing into the room. In the epicenter, guests could be seen moving in synchronicity or popping up and down as they danced amongst the hypnosis of kaleidoscope lights. The ceiling in the main room had to be three stories high, and on the far wall was a large DJ stage, on either side were black towers of speakers where the music pulsed to serenade the euphoria.

"It is chaos in here," Sol yelled at Claire against the booming music and cheering crowd that threatened to wash away any intelligible word. "I think my ears are bleeding. Did we stumble on a special event?"

Claire's eyes were as big as saucers, and she could only respond with a shrug. She had lived a sheltered life. Her parents were strict, and she never had many friends. Either because of her behaviour (condition) growing up, or because her parents didn't let her out much. She didn't consider herself completely naive. She had watched videos or heard about parties at school, but this shit was next level. Mind-blowing!

Sol held tight to her hand, leading as he pressed their way along the wall. Claire had her other hand clasped around his forearm in a vice grip, worried about being ripped away downstream as they fought the current of the undertow of people.

They had made their way inside, and even though from the outside, the façade of the castle made the building look massive, like a building lost in time. Inside, flash to the present, everything was modernized. Edging to the side of the ballroom, Sol could see another doorway. They needed to get out of this crowd and blast music to get their bearings. He was pulling Claire along; he had no idea where he was going. Even though they had only just gotten inside a few minutes ago, the interior was enormous, it felt larger in scope than what the outside alluded to. Sol felt a crushing claustrophobia wash over him. He needed to get out of this pressurized crowd.

Sol leaned in close to Claire to yell. "Where?" He was hoping her voice would guide them.

Claire just shook her head. Even with Sol yelling into her ear, she could barely understand him. Her ears were ringing against the cacophony of music, whoops, and hollers from the crowds. But she caught the gist, Sol was looking for guidance. She was listening for further direction, but beyond barely being able to hear Sol yelling in her ear, if there was a voice inside her head, she could not hear it. She could barely hear her thoughts.

The voices were either being silenced or drowned out.

She was shaking her head at him. Either she didn't know, or was overwhelmed by the spectacle around them.

Escaping the ocean of people in the large dance hall, Sol and Claire found themselves enraptured at the entrance of another room of robust size. This room was more of a bar or lounge by design. Furnished in refined luxury with rounded dark oak tables accompanied by high-backed, plush red chairs with curved shoulders. If a person sat deep into a chair, they would be almost invisible to a passerby. On the far side of the entrance, a long bar filled the expanse of the wall. Adjoining sides of the room housed at least ten oval-shaped booths, also adorned with red, high-backed benches that wrapped around the tables to provide their patrons views of the bar but provided concealment from neighbours at the same time. Even though they were in an adjacent room just a short way down from the dance hall, sound dampeners or something had kept the music confined. Only a dull thumping of bass could be felt sporadically. The bar lounge here had its background music, but it was not so loud to deafen a conversation with your table mates.

Compared to the craze of the party room next door, to Sol, this seemed refined. Discreet luxury. But as he directed Claire towards an open table, on closer inspection, as they passed other tables, it was not that discreet. It was an indulgence in decadence. Some were smoking and drinking, but then others had their heads bent low to the table to fill their nostrils with drugs. Another had a platter with an outlay of needles.

"This is better, at least my heart isn't trying to drum out of my chest," Sol said, as they were taking a seat at an empty table. This place made him uncomfortable.

"I think it is a telltale sign we are in the right place," Claire said and pointed. "Look closer at that bar."

The ambience of the room presented huge pipes, accented with copper to fit, lining the bar's back wall. The pipe bent and led to the side where another room could be seen behind its glass wall. Several vats were on display, feeding into the pipes. The liquid inside is red, deep red, white, and rose in color. A brewhouse, but here they were distilling their wine. Not typical vats of craft beer. Sol looked around at the other guests. The majority were drinking from wine glasses. Only an odd few had a tumbler for a spirit or a pint glass for a draft.

Several bartenders worked the concourse of the bar. At the opposite end of the glass room, two women were lying, draped over the counter, with their shirts open as one of the bartenders poured wine over them. A few of their assumed friends were laughing or licking the spillage that covered the exposed chests, the color of crimson.

"I have to go to the bathroom," Claire said as she got up and looked around for a sign to signal where the restrooms were.

"Just be careful," Sol advised.

He watched Claire as she crossed the room, weaving amongst the tables, ensuring nobody stopped or bothered her. Then she went down into the alcove with the restroom sign above its entrance. Scanning the room as he waited for her to reappear, in a corner booth, a pair of couples were making out. The splash zone at the end of the bar was still in session, but now a couple of guys were removing their shirts to take a turn. Further down, a man and a woman at the bar, Sol watched intently. They were not receiving drinks, paying a bill, maybe. No, they were buying something. The bartender looked to be explaining and then passed them something, a card. Back at the booth where the two couples had been voraciously kissing and fondling their partners, a waitress was presenting something to them also. Back to tracking the couple from the bar. They walked together, close, intimate, the woman pressed into her partner. They were stopped by a man in a dark suit, security, Sol assumed, then he motioned them forward into the hallway he was supervising.

"Can I help you?"

The sudden appearance of a waitress startled Sol. "No, thank you."

She passed him a thin menu. "I'll give you a minute, then?"

"Actually," Sol kept her attention before she turned away to tend to another table. "Where are those people going?" He pointed to the guarded hallway close to the bathrooms.

The waitress bent down close to him and winked. "Special access to the elevators. You want to go deeper, you have to pay. I can set you up, though."

Sol smiled back. "I'll think about it. I'm just waiting for my partner to come back."

"You just let me know," she patted his forearm before moving off to serve another patron.

Claire came back and flopped into her chair, then thumbed over her shoulder towards the bathroom as she said, a bit exasperated. "There were two women having sex in there. Right on the counter."

"I saw a similar thing in one of the booths over there," Sol nodded in that direction.

"Two were having sex," Claire almost ignored him in her excitement at never having witnessed such things, or such a place before, as she rattled on. "A few others were doing some drugs, and one woman was hanging onto a toilet for dear life. I've never seen so much puke in my life. This place is nuts."

Sol stared at her for a moment. Where had they ended up, exactly? The journey had washed him up here in this festival of sin and rioting debauchery, a modern Gomorrah.

"Do you think the Winemaker you are looking for runs this place? Seems that way," Claire brought his attention back.

"No, not this place," Sol shook his head. That was something he didn't even consider. It was unfathomable. "If he is here, it is for a different reason."

"So why do we need to find him then?"

Sol leaned out to watch that hallway as another small group was showing evidence of their accessibility to the security guard.

He turned his attention back to Claire. "To help with this mission."

"And what exactly is this mission?"

"We are looking for something, someone. I'm not sure exactly."

"What? "

"Kind of flying blind. The Winemaker is the first step. After that, the mission is...it's faith."

Claire was shaking her head vehemently. "Like believe in God and trust his path, faith? I have been under the house of God's umbrella, and for me, there is no faith there." She started to get up. "Maybe it was wrong for me to come with you."

Sol could feel her instant rage at those words, faith, God, being used together.

"No, not like that," he consoled. "Faith that we are doing the right thing. Even if it feels wrong, like being in this place. Faith that you found me was a step. Faith that the path will be laid out for us as we take another step. And the next to follow is finding the Winemaker."

Claire was sitting again. "I trust you." She smiled at Sol.

"I trust you too. I think we need to go deeper to search. And the only access seems to be through that hallway. We need a card to get in. I'm just not sure how much it costs, or if I will even be able to afford it."

"You mean one of these cards?" Claire lit up as she pulled a card from her back pocket and flashed it in front of his face.

It was the size of an average playing card. But it wasn't a typical playing card made of thin cardboard and coated in plastic. The card she held looked metal. Blank shiny-gloss, deep red on one side, the other side a holographic etched picture that shimmied in color with the slightest movement of Claire's hand. The image was that of a Cheshire cat with its wide-grinning smile, and its tongue was snaking out, forked like a snake's would be. Strange, ominous, or just weird, Sol thought.

"Should I even ask where you got that from?" Sol was slightly concerned, but that did not override his relief that she had a means to progress their investigation.

"Puke woman in the bathroom. I was trying to help her and maybe pinched this. I heard some of the other women talking about these cards to get access to the other floors. Seemed like one might be handy."

"Clever girl," Sol praised her as he got up and took Claire's hand to lead her through the room.

A small group of two couples was before them, chatting up the security guard as he scanned their card. Sol could see past them that it was not just a hallway. The entrance was to an elevator bank. As the couple moved in and the security guard waved them forward, Sol felt nervous. They were not sure if the card Claire stole was the right kind; they were flying blind, and this could be a sudden end of the road.

He felt Claire squeeze his hand. "Faith. Every step." She whispered.

Here was this fifteen-year-old girl assuring him. Giving him courage. A young woman who should be broken but wasn't, and he felt a parental pride as she stepped forward confidently, presenting the card to the security.

"First time?" He looked them both over.

"Does it show?" Claire bounced with a bit of excitement. Her movement drew the guard's attention, so he didn't catch Sol's apparent nervousness.

"It always shows," the guard nodded towards Sol, then asked Claire. "What's your flavour?"

"Magic. I like magic," Claire didn't miss a beat.

"I recommend starting with floor four, then," the guard said as he passed the card back. He had a quick look at his watch. "The show started a few minutes ago." And bid them to proceed into the elevator. "Welcome to Wonderland."

Neither of them breathed a word during the short elevator ride.

Once it stopped and the doors began to slide open, strange atmospheric music bled into their space before they could see anything. Claire was the one with apprehension now. Sol wasn't sure if she was making a statement to him or assuring herself, as he heard her whisper under her breath. "Just a magic show."

It wasn't a magic show.

The elevator had not opened to a hallway where they had to choose their destination, like they were in a hotel; it opened directly into a large room.

The pair exited the confines of the elevator a few steps and stopped to get their bearings.

A man in a suit, same look as the security officer manning the elevator bay down below, tapped Sol on the shoulder and made a motion with his hand as if asking for something. Sol was a bit confused.

"Card," the doorman leaned in to be heard over the music, motioning to be shown something again.

Claire pulled out the card for the man to inspect. Satisfied, he motioned them forward.

It was a large room, sparsely lit so it was a moment for Sol and Claire's eyes to adjust. The focus and lighting were on a stage in the middle of the room, guests were seated at small tables, occupied by up to four.

To the left, another bar. Sol led Claire in that direction so they could get a better view of the stage, but were able to stand outside of the sea of tables that surrounded the stage's circumference like a castle's moat.

A couple of waitresses floated by them, ferrying drinks from the bar to the seated guests who were enthralled with the entertainment before them.

Sol had been looking around, taking in the room, gauging next steps, before he actually paid attention to the stage. Soft clapping from the surrounding tables drew his attention there, and he was suddenly horrified.

The entertainers on display were dressed in leather outfits of elaborate kink designs that left more skin exposed than they covered. Their faces were hidden behind the black masks they wore, but based on their physique, it was easy to determine that it was two men and a woman who were moving about on the stage. The first man wore tight leather shorts and a black leather cross harness that made an X symbol across his torso and was connected by metal rings at the center. The second man, besides the mask and leather pants he wore, was exposed from the waist up. The woman who looked to also be assisting wore thigh-high black boots and a black dress that barely topped her breasts and upper thigh.

From their vantage point, Sol has been unable to see the base of the stage. Now, on one side of the platform, one of the men was pulling on a rope that hoisted a woman three feet into the air. Naked, parts of her exposed, the rest of her bound in a complicated rope configuration as she floated above the stage in suspension as if a live piece of art. The other leather-bound man, assisted by the female presenter on stage, was clamping another naked woman into a large metal circle so she was held in an X-style pose, legs spread below, arms outstretched above her head to each side. The metal ring frame was also hoisted, maybe a foot from the stage floor. The woman assistant spun around a large black case that was set on wheels and opened the double doors to display a myriad of whipping instruments from small paddles to handled items with leather straps hanging in differing lengths of varying plumage.

The motions the presenters made, the way they moved, gave the appearance of a magic show, the lighting changes gave the illusion of the entangled woman free floating in the air as her presenter moved his hand above and below her to show the hoisting rope was no longer there. But Sol felt guilty for Claire being exposed to these adult displays.

"I should not have brought you here," he said to Claire, looking for an exit to get out of the room and investigate more of this floor. "Let's keep moving."

He could see the wide-eyed expression on her face as she slowly moved her side to side as if to say no, he should not have. Then up and down in agreement as she followed his lead.

There was an exit. Once in a hallway behind the closing doors of the magic room, Claire grabbed Sol's hand to make him stop momentarily. "Is that what adults find entertaining?"

What she had seen in the bathroom had been kind of exciting, but the magic room had suppressed that feeling.

Sol just shook his head in a no motion. "Sorry. I'm sorry I brought you here."

"No, it was me. Not your fault. But what if the voices," she made the circle motion with a pointed index finger by her temple again, to allude that her mental state was questionable. "What if the voices lied to me. What if leading us here was a joke, and the Winemaker isn't here?"

"The signs seem to point to this being the place," Sol said and squeezed her hand in reassurance. "Faith. Every step."

"That was my thing." Claire gently pulled her hand away and began walking down the hall. "You can't do my thing."

Sol smiled and began to follow her.

A few others came out of the door behind them. A quick look over his shoulder verified they were not security, and Sol was relieved.

The group that had exited the magic room. Quickly passing without giving Sol and Claire any attention. They took a joyful, quick step to get to their next destination.

The pair followed the group through a set of double doors into another ballroom type setting.

But this was more thematic than a simple dancehall. The walls were painted, accented with fake trees that looked to be growing out into the room from their painted origins, and the ceiling was covered in deep green foliage. The air even felt heavier in here. It was beautiful, giving the illusion of stepping into a dense rainforest. Except for the flooring. It was a dark grey, hard, stark with drains set, as if it were a dried pool bottom. On the far side of the wall, on a second level, behind a glass wall that was bordered by the foliage, large leaves could be seen, the Disc Jockey commanding the music that pumped through hidden speakers. Behind him looked to be a control booth of other electronics, and several others accompanied the space with the DJ.

On the main floor was a strange assembly of patrons.

Part of the crowd danced in the epicenter of the room, pumping to the beat of the music in a silent motion of a unified physical wave of worship.

Some were naked, while others walked around garbed in rain gear or with umbrellas. The small group they had followed were pulling out thin rain ponchos to slip over their expensive suits and dresses and protect the women's hair and make-up from what, Sol wasn't sure.

Pointing to the different people in the crowd, Sol leaned close to Claire, so she was the only one to hear him. "As we move deeper, each new room appears to have a different theme. I mean, what is this?"

"Club fetish," Claire responded, her head bouncing up and down to the beat of the music.

It relieved Sol somewhat that, besides the naked people, this seemed tamer than what they had witnessed in the other room. "I don't even know what that is."

"Me neither. Heard it once. Sounds like it fits," her head still bopped.

"It's like, each new room we find is an immersion in gluttony."

Mid-beat, the music stopped for a breath, a buzzer filled the void of silence, and the crowd erupted in cheers. Their raucousness was only drowned out by the music thumping back to life.

Attention was drawn upwards; the ceiling panels were retracting. Sol watched the crowd in the room, some had their arms raised to the ceiling, others tilted their heads back with wide open mouths and tongues out as if they were ready to catch snowflakes. Others had raised their hands or were holding empty wine glasses.

A soft mist hissed from sprinkler mounts set back deep in the ceiling recesses that were barely visible when the panels slid back. It added to the rainforest ambience just for a moment. Then the deluge started. A heavy rain was pouring from the ceiling. The pattering drowned out the music and cheering, playful, excited screams, as people were being drenched.

The pooling on the ground, as excess ran to the drains in the flooring, looked to be dark, not water translucent. Maybe it was the lighting. Sol could see the people around them, swallowing, raising glasses and goblets to their mouths to chug down the contents while some began licking the fallen liquid from the bodies of naked partners. Their bodies, their clothes, were getting wet, but he could tell by those close that it was not a clear liquid. It was red.

Claire leaned in with cupped hands and lifted them to her mouth to sip. "Wow, it's good. Really, good." She quickly did it a second time before turning to Sol with a smile. "It's raining freaking wine! No more doubts here. We are definitely in the right place."

For Sol, there never was a doubt. A tickling at the nape of his neck had him concerned about Claire. She was starting to enjoy herself, uncharacteristically. Maybe it was the wine, but she only had a few sips. Maybe it affected her because she was acting a little uninhibited, free, not as quiet, and scared. He had to get Claire out of here. This place was hurting her and beckoning something deeper to come to the surface.

He led them back out into the hall. Now that he had Claire out of the rainforest and was sure he wasn't allowing a minor to get stupid drunk on the raining red wine, Sol was relieved. He had not doubted Claire leading them to this castle. But from what he was seeing, if the Winemaker had manufactured this place of over-indulgence, should he even look any further? This was not the kind of place he imagined he would find himself.

Benefit of the doubt. Doubt was the mental virus that led to inaction. Doubt he could squash. Part of the problem was that they had to look everywhere. The biggest part of the problem was that Sol did not know what the Winemaker looked like. He knew the target was male. Based on Claire's internal intel, and because all the signs were blaring radiant neon, but the amount of people in here, the size of the place, it was a proverbial needle in a haystack, as they delved deeper into this sea of sin, a "Where's Waldo" without knowing what Waldo looked like.

Lost in thought, it wasn't until he heard voices behind him that Sol realized Claire was not beside him. He turned to see her back down the hall by the doors to the rainforest room. Some others had come out and were talking to her. Briskly closing the distance to them, he overheard one of them asking Claire if she was okay.

"It's okay, she is with me," Sol kindly dismissed the small group.

"She better pace herself," one of the women in the trio of couples seemed a bit concerned as they made to leave. "She looks like she is past the part of fun."

The woman was not wrong. Claire didn't seem okay, leaning back against the wall, head hanging low, breathing heavily.

"Claire," Sol tried to get her attention.

"I want to play," she mumbled back without looking at him.

"What?" He could barely hear her.

"I want to play!" She was a bit louder now. A petulant child, but the voice wasn't childish. It wasn't Claire's either.

Sol grabbed her shoulders. "Claire."

"Brought me here to fuck me, you selfish prick."

Sol stepped back. The venomous words and blank stare of her eyes gave him a start.

"But, I want to play," she said with a snarl and bared teeth.

Sol placed his hands on her cheeks to hold her gaze steady. She tried to bite him. He felt bad when he had to use some strength to keep her head still.

"Claire! I need you here," he spoke softly, trying to reason, draw her back, a little panicked. If he lost her now, they were both lost. "I need you to show me the way. I need you. You need to lead me to the Winemaker."

Claire went rigid. Sol reflexively let her go and stepped back. Her neck kinked hard to the right in chiropractic swiftness, her eyelids were fluttering butterfly wings of flashing chaos behind a lost gaze. She twitched, once, twice, and then her knees went weak, as she slid to the floor. Sol grabbed her in time to keep her from falling, steadied her as life came back into her eyes.

"Claire?"

"This isn't right," she said, grabbing his hand and pulling him to lead him down towards another elevator bank.

Once inside, the doors sliding shut, Claire pushed one of the buttons to select a lower floor. The button did not light up.

"Are you okay?" Sol asked from behind her.

She pushed again. Nothing. There was an LED screen with red lights below the row of buttons for the desired floor destination. Claire reached into her pocket to retrieve the metal access card and placed it against the small screen below. There was a small beep, and the lights within pulsed. When she pushed her selected floor button, it lit up this time, and the elevator began moving.

"Claire?"

"I'm fine," she said without looking at Sol. "And I'm sorry."

"You don't have to apologize to me. I'm just glad you are here. What was that?"

"We need to go deeper," she said, ignoring his question.

Then she looked back at him. A sadness in her eyes. But also fear, as if to say she had seen something, and it was just the tip of the iceberg.

CHAPTER THIRTY-THREE

Initially, the elevator had taken them up, Sol assumed. Now they were descending. In the elevator bank, they had found themselves, the buttons for floor selection no longer held numbers. Now they were defined by colors: Green, Blue, Red, Silver, Gold, and a barely discernible black. The access card Claire had stolen had red on one side. She tried it against the Silver, Gold, and Black sensors, but nothing happened. When she touched it to the green, blue, and red sensors, the boundaries of those lit up, and the elevator started to move.

Sol found it concerning that the card they had only granted them access to some floors. It was hard to imagine they would just randomly bump into the Winemaker, and he questioned himself if they even wanted to know what transpired in the excluded parts of the castle, but he was certain that was where they would need to go, deeper.

They quickly scouted through the green floor.

Then the blue floor with its kaleidoscope decadence of voyeurism. They saw small groups watching increasingly disturbing things. Once Claire started to ask Sol questions, he hurried her back to the elevator. He would have ordered her to wait in the main dance hall, but was too scared to let her out of sight.

The further they moved into this place, the further they plunged deeper into darkening themes of greed and lust. It was like the nine circles of hell they were descending through, bearing witness to others satiating their desires. Claire had already been through her version of hell and had managed to claw her way out, even though it kept trying to drag her back. Sol hoped this was not straining her emotional sanity to a breaking point.

The elevator stopped, and the doors opened to reveal the red floor. The hallway before them was dark. Deep maroon walls with soft candelabras three-quarters of the way up the walls at eight-foot intervals to light the way. On closer inspection, it was easy to see that each fixture held three fake candles of electric light, but they were designed in varying lengths with melted sides to give the illusion of real, flaming wax candles. The ambience was elevated by soft organ music wafting down the hall in a beckoning enchantment. Intended to be inviting, it was accented by moans that echoed from rooms beyond. Ribbons of LED lights lined the interface of the wall and floor, pulsing in the red glow that made the floor appear to be a slow flowing water, lava with the red, or blood.

Claire led with the first step. Sol followed, wavering a little as the motion of the LED made him unsteady at first, like they were stepping onto the moving walkways at an airport, but he felt more unease as he could hear Claire chuffing in a voice not her own in words about the River Styx and fare for the Ferryman. Pay your dues, the current beckoned.

The floor wasn't water, but it did feel like they were flowing in a strong current, unable to turn back.

The pair of them wandered through the maze of halls. They had descended to a place of being subject to seeing others give free rein to cast off inhibitions to feed their cravings: depravity. The past rooms of orgies, rooms of voyeurs watching, Claire wasn't sure because Sol had covered her eyes and shuffled her on so quickly.

They tried to investigate as much as they could. Some doors were wide open, allowing people to enter who had access to the floor; others were closed, and heads turned when it was opened. Others were locked. The door they were passing now was ajar. Sol could hear the soft screams of a woman, and peered in.

Claire was a few steps ahead, and Sol called to her to wait. He caught up to her and grabbed her hand to pull her back towards the room they had just passed.

"Those sounds," he whispered.

What he had glimpsed wasn't a situation of pleasure like the other rooms. No matter how perverse, macabre, or twisted they had been. This was a sinister thing.

Claire was scared this time. "No. Keep moving."

Sol held up a hand for her to wait as he backstepped to the door to get a second look at what was transpiring inside. The woman, whose features were young, was tied to a table in bondage. Her arms were pulled tight above her head. There was a snap, a whip, biting into her upper, naked thigh, splitting the skin with its force. Her head rolled to the side, looking out in the direction of the door. Her face flushed, tears, she was looking directly at Sol, the only inhabitant of the room to notice him there, no recognition of his presence; she was staring lifelessly, soullessly, into nothing.

Sol edged the door open a little to better survey the room. His eyes opened wide in horror to discover they had been going down the river Styx to lead into a sea of sin. The wider perspective of the captive woman. At the other end of the table-frame, she was strapped to her legs, bound tight at the ankles, elevated in stirrups that kept her legs spread as if she were in a doctor's office for a gynecological visit. Four men occupied the room in addition to the woman. Behind spotlights, a film camera on a tripod, one of the men was commanding the camera. Behind him, an older man sat as a voyeur, crossed legged in his relaxation as he smoked a cigar and called out directions to the other two men. Those were two muscular guys, dressed only in tight black leather briefs, their faces covered in leather bondage masks. One of them was standing in-between the captive's legs, gyrating hips moving in and out of her. The other circled the woman like a shark, holding a whip that he cracked across the bare belly of the woman in response to the seated man's orders.

"Again." *Crack.*

"Again." *Crack.*

The masked man dropped the whip and flashed a held scalpel towards the camera that he drew from a metal tray beside the bed, then he drew it down one of the woman's exposed breasts, causing a rivulet of blood to trickle down in its wake.

And those lifeless eyes that stared out at Sol. Lost in some world of despair.

Claire saw Sol about to push the door open further. She didn't know what he was looking at, but she grabbed his hand to pull him away, whispering. "Leave it, Sol. She is there by choice. They all are."

They silently retreated down the hall a few steps. Claire held tight to Sol's hand as she led him on to resume their search.

Crack.

The sound of the whip echoed out from the room. Claire felt the tug of Sol's hand as he stopped and removed himself from her grasp.

"She didn't look much older than you," he said.

"Her choice. Their choice. Stick to the mission," Claire said sternly, reaching for his hand again.

"I can't," Sol was resolute.

Claire watched Sol turn back towards the room and dropped her head. "Shit!"

Like a rampaging elephant, Sol charged into the room, ignoring the fact that he was outnumbered, attempting to catch the men off guard and seize an advantageous moment of surprise. The cameraman was closest. Sol drove into him, shoulder tackle, barreling the equipment and themselves into the man in the chair, creating an avalanche of camera, bodies, and lights that sent shadows pirouetting along the walls.

Landing on top of the cameraman, Sol drove his fist down into his face, once, twice, a third time, and the body went limp underneath. Sol snapped his head to see where the two masked men were, but his eyes caught the flash of Claire bursting into the room, sliding across the floor between one of the muscle-bondage guy's legs, where she drove her fist up into his groin.

"Fuck with that, fucker!" Her face was red with rage. Claire, but not Claire.

The older man, having extricated himself from the fallen lights, grabbed at Sol. The other bandit was racing towards them. Sol struggled to get free, but the director had a firm grip. Sol flung his head backward. Hard skull against the director's soft, accordion nose that burst in a stream of blood, the director loosened his grip and tumbled backwards to the hard floor, which rendered him unconscious.

Free, on his feet, the bondage-guy was almost on him. Sol grabbed the camera tripod by the leg-stand and swung the makeshift bat, knocking the bondage monster back into the wall. Sol flipped his grip on the tripod and charged forward, using the legs of the stand as if it were a three-pronged spear; he plunged the stand into the sadist's chest.

Across the room, Claire was straddling the chest of the other bondage man, raining a fury of blows down upon him. She looked tiny against the large, muscular frame, but it was apparent she had the upper hand by an uncontrollable rage, a possessed rage of silence. The only sounds were the wet smacking into the leather mask that was losing shape as the face underneath was being pulverized into mushy bits.

Claire may not have ever stopped the rage if not for the alarms that began blaring.

Standing over her unconscious assailant, Claire shook her head with her hands over her ears. The possessed craze washed from her face as she shouted at Sol. "What now?"

Sol moved to the woman on the table, pointing in response to Claire's question to a small, glass circle, barely visible, high in the crux of one of the corners of the wall and ceiling. "Camera? Security?"

It seemed nothing was taboo in this place, except for killing.

Claire went to the door. The alarm was louder in the hall, and the lights had transitioned from the moody red to a bright white, searing away the ambience.

Turning back to Sol, she said. "We need to go!"

He was at the captive's side; a needle was stuck in her arm. The men must have administered a dose of drugs before they charged in. He pulled it out and worked to undo her bonds.

"What are you doing? We need to go!" She was yelling for his attention.

"Everyone has a choice. Just not always a true choice," Sol looked at Claire as he hurried to free the woman. Her eyes were glassy, her mouth foamed with saliva. Drugs.

Claire rushed to his side to help him. "We don't have time for this. We can't take her with us."

"We can at least release her. She had chosen to be here now because there had been no other choice. Addiction, something else, her road left her here at a dead end. Nobody should be abandoned to this kind of end." Sol pointed to the woman's unconscious, two potentially dead abusers. "Their road drove them here with what they know. Violence. A narrow view of their purpose. Opportunity is their drug of choice."

In the distance, a raucous noise was heard outside the room. Claire went to check, and to the right, several security personnel were rushing down the hall in their direction.

"Great! We've got company!" She shouted over her shoulder. "Leaving now is a good idea."

Only the right arm of the captive woman needed to be released now, but as Sol fumbled with the strap, she heaved, her body bucking twice. There was more foaming at the mouth with a gurgling choking sound. Then she was limp.

"Now!" Claire yelled at him.

It must have been a reaction or overdose to drugs, but the woman lay there, exposed, violated, and now dead. Sol was filled with regret at being hesitant when they had first passed the room. It may have made a difference. It may not have mattered.

"Fucking, now, Sol!"

That time Claire's voice got his attention, and he ran into the hall.

Security contingents were coming from the right, they hurried down the left, pushing past others that had come out of adjacent rooms in response to the alarm and yelling of the security force.

The passageway ran to an end into a T-section of the hallway. hey ducked around the corner where Claire stopped and pulled Sol to her side, backs tight against the wall.

Sol gave her a quizzical look as running seemed like the best option.

"Hold on," she whispered, squeezing Sol's hand.

One of the security officers, faster than the others, was solo as he came racing around the corner in pursuit. Claire's outstretched left leg tripped the man and sent him flailing to the ground, where his gun spun out of his hand, twirling away.

The security guard had the wind knocked from him, but still scrambled forward to reach his gun. Claire pounced on him as she leapt forward for the gun.

In swift motion, she moved past the downed guard, casually shot a bullet into his back before turning back down the hall, and from her perched position, emptied the clip in a barrage of bullets at the other encroaching guards.

She leaned back against the wall, momentarily weak as she grabbed Sol for support.

"Sorry," Claire panted to catch her breath. "I don't know what came over me. It's like a bloodlust."

"Are you okay?" Sol asked, then chanced a look around the corner. All the security officers were down. Some were still, presumably dead, others with less fatal wounds were moaning in pained movements on the ground.

Claire leaned back, looking up at Sol from under her brow. "No...yes...I'm not sure how I did that." Her tongue glided slowly over her top lip. "Something was inside me there."

"So, with your demons, wasn't shooting those guys kind of like killing your kind?"

"I think my demons are more the kill-anything type. But I can tell you that a disturbing euphoria washed over me. And trust me, I wouldn't be remiss to never feel that again."

They pushed on. The alarm had stopped blaring, but they were certain that was not the end. There were cameras everywhere, concealed for the illusion of privacy, but everything everywhere was being watched.

The facilitators of this castle probably needed to ensure the guests were not upset or given concern about whatever emergency the alarm would have been announcing. Things were to be cleaned up efficiently. A room of dead patrons and several security guards littering a hall would take more effort, but this would not be the first time a place like this had to manage hiding an engagement gone sideways and keep the violence a secret, swept under a rug with the utmost discretion. People got carried away.People got hurt, so much alcohol or drugs. But wave a magic wand and make it all disappear, so the image of uninhibited paradise would not be stained.

Sol and Claire were barely looking into the rooms they passed. They hurried to get off the floor, but had difficulty finding another elevator. Claire pointed to a sign attached to the ceiling that directed them towards an elevator bank. Finally, around a corner, the elevator could be seen.

The doors slid open as Sol and Claire quickened their pace. More guests did not emerge. It was more secure. Pointing and yelling at Sol and Claire to stop. They were giving chase.

A stairwell was to the left Sol grabbed Claire and led her to the doorway.

Locked.

Sol yanked the access card out of his pocket and placed it on the wall sensor. It flashed red.

"The card isn't working," he panicked as he tried it again. In his peripheral vision, he was all too aware that the security force was getting closer. "Did you keep that gun?"

"Yeah," Claire responded. "But it's out of bullets."

He tried the card again. Red flashes. They had assumed their card was all-access considering how far they got into the castle, but even if it was, the security measures must have locked everything down.

"But I have this," Claire pushed past him and flashed another card. "I pinched this card off the security guy I tripped."

The sensor flashed green. They pushed into the stairwell, disappearing from the encroaching pack of security.

Calves tightened, and thighs burned, as Claire and Sol spiralled down the stairs flight by flight. It wasn't long until the door above slammed open and footfalls could be heard descending in pursuit.

They were almost dizzy, trusting in their feet as they went down. Shortly after, they rushed by a door to one of the floors, they heard it bang open. More security had entered the stairwell to give chase closer than the others in hot pursuit, as Sol and Claire were beginning to lag.

At the bottom of the stairwell before them was a large metal door. The only exit, an unknown on the other side. They either had to go through it or go back up the way they had just come.

Facing the guards was not a survivable option.

"Gun," Sol held out his hand.

"I told you there are no more bullets," Claire said as she handed it to him.

"Get the door open."

Claire flashed the card and pulled hard on the door handle. As Claire worked the door, Sol took the butt of the gun and used it as a hammer to smash the sensor screen.

Footfalls above were only a floor away.

Disappearing inside, they yanked the door closed behind themselves. Sol prayed the door was inaccessible because he broke the sensor plate outside, but he held onto the door handle just in case.

Banging. Thumping. Yelling from the other side.

"We're here," Claire was tapping his shoulder.

"Sol, we're here. I was right. The voices were right."

The door didn't budge. No electronic locks disengaged. Sol felt comfortable letting go and turning to see what Claire was going on about.

Then he saw for himself. It had not been a wild goose chase. The voices had not led them astray.

Before them was the Winemaker.

CHAPTER THIRTY-FOUR

Finally, they had found the Winemaker. In the basement room, Claire and Sol found themselves in, had the appearance of a medical facility. And before them, partially submerged, from the chest down, in a metal pool or vat, was a long-haired, gaunt man. His head hung limp to the side, but an air mask could be seen covering his mouth and nostrils with a thick tube running down to an attachment in the wall. Cables from the wall looked to keep him imprisoned, but were monitoring lines that attached to screens above. Intravenous tubes were attached to his arms along with other feeding lines that floated in the water below. There was a hissing sound from the pumps feeding several pipes that attached to the side of the vat, draining converted liquid, and sending it up the walls to feed other parts of the mansion.

The Winemaker had not been the mastermind behind the goings-on of this castle.

He was its prisoner. In the bowels of this mansion, in a grotesque scene of a horrific science experiment, the Winemaker was being held captive, drugged, fed intravenously, and oxygen provided by a respirator, to be used to produce his magic concoctions.

A man and a woman were off to the side at a large console that housed computers, more monitor screens, along with what looked like medical equipment. Dressed in long, white lab coats, they seemed just as surprised to see Sol and Claire as Sol and Claire were to see them.

"Who are you?" Sol questioned.

"I'm the doctor and this is my assistant," the man answered. "Who the hell are you! Nobody is supposed to be down here."

"Well, we are here for him," Sol pointed at the Winemaker.

The doctor turned back to his console.

"Hey, hey, hey!" Sol shouted. "Don't you move!" And brought the gun to bear.

Sol tossed the pistol to Claire.

"Stay right where you are," Claire demanded, pointing the gun.

Sol jumped into the vat to check for any life in the Winemaker.

"Who are you guys?" The nurse asked. "Because you are about to be in a shitstorm of trouble."

"Fuck you! And stay still," Claire barked back, waving the gun. "We are the shitstorm, lady." She was secretly enjoying this power position. To Sol, "Is he alive?"

Sol was working to remove the various tubes and cables and free the limp form. "He's alive. They've been draining every ounce of spirit out of him, but he's alive, barely. We need to get him out of here."

"Do that, and you are going to kill him," the doctor sternly advised.

"Then get over there and help him," Claire's order was accentuated with her directing them with the gun. "We'll take the risk. One way or another, we are leaving with him. A better chance than the slow death you mad scientists are doling out."

The doctor spun for the console.

"And I swear, if you try to touch that console one more time, I am going to break your hands," Claire shrieked.

That got his attention. The man froze, raised his hands, and backed away. He opted to help out with the extraction of their captive from the pool.

It took some effort to disconnect the Winemaker from the myriads of wires and tubes, but Sol worked quickly, pulling and ripping things out with no care. He didn't believe the threat that it would kill the Winemaker, and he was all too aware that the thumping, bumping, and yelling of security from the other side of the door they had entered from had subsided.

The limp body felt weightless in the water. The struggle was lifting him out of the tub when the dead weight was realized, regardless of himself, the doctor, and the nurse who were supposed to be helping. They didn't seem to be putting in full effort lifting the body. They were stalling.

There seemed to be some stirring from the Winemaker as Sol held him up with an arm and around and under the shoulder. Claire came to support the other side.

"How do we get out of here?" Sol asked the nurse.

"Elevator," she pointed.

That was a relief. Now that they had the Winemaker in hand, Sol had not anticipated having to carry him out of wherever they found him, and the thought of having to scale the multiple flights of stairs seemed impossible.

The yelling was back on the other side of the door. A loud bang. Another. They were trying to break it down.

"Here comes the shitstorm," the nurse smiled.

"On the floor," Claire ordered. "Flat on your stomach. Hands over your heads."

The pair of white coats complied.

Holding the cadaverous, naked man between them, Sol and Claire shuffled as they dragged the unconscious frame forward. Claire swiped her card, and the seconds before the doors slid open felt like an eternity, as they were counted off by the security force trying to breach the door across the room.

Once in the sanctuary of the elevator, as the doors were sliding shut, the doctor jumped up. With one hand, the doctor hit a button at the console, and the alarm started blaring again. With his other hand, he was holding up the middle finger as he tossed a sly smile at Claire.

"Son of a bitch!" She barked as the doors sealed shut. If she had a bullet, she would have taken a shot and blown away the glum look on that man's face.

CHAPTER THIRTY-FIVE

Inside the ascending elevator.

Sol leaned against the back wall of the enclosed compartment, supporting the Winemaker, who seemed to be stirring, slowly awakening from his faux coma delirium and bearing some weight on his own feet. Not much yet, but enough that Sol wasn't going to have to drag him through their escape attempt.

"That was close," Claire said. "More security is going to be hunting us, if not waiting for us on the other side of these doors. You know that, right?"

"I get that, Claire," Sol answered. He didn't have any delusions about how hopeless the situation seemed.

"We are going to be in for a fight," she continued. "Are you prepared to jump bodies?"

"It doesn't work that way," Sol gave her an apologetic look. "I'm stuck with this body. I had to undergo a full insertion for this mission."

"Great! We are fucked!"

The Winemaker was slipping, so Sol hitched him up and secured his grip, scowling at Claire. She wasn't helping his hopeless delusion.

"Look at us, Claire. The two of us and a semi-conscious corpse. Outside those doors, an army will be waiting," Sol took a deep, defeatist breath. "We made it. We found the Winemaker. But we are not going to make it out of here."

"Now you are one of little faith," Claire looked coyly over her shoulder. "When these doors open, you run, you go, get the Winemaker out."

The highlighted floor counter advised that they were almost to the main floor.

"And what about you, Claire? Claire!"

One more floor.

"Claire!"

Her back was to Sol. Claire faced the elevator doors, arms braced against the wall. She held up her left index finger to signal. Hold on one minute.

The elevator was coming to a stop.

"CLAIRE!" Sol screamed at the top of his lungs.

She didn't respond.

Inducing a possession, Claire's head snapped around before her, left, right, forward, whiplash backwards. A snarling pant took over her breathing.

Full stop. The elevator doors were about to slide open.

Claire looked back over her shoulder. Her facial features were contorted, eyes puffy and bloodshot red with yellow pus at the rims. "Claire isn't here right now." The smile across her lips wasn't a pleasant one. Pure malice as her voice erupted with a deep, sinister rumble. "This is my playground. My dominion!"

The elevator bay opened into a small alcove to an entrance on the main floor of the dance party that Sol and Claire had originally experienced upon their arrival.

Music thumped. Erratic lights beamed their hypnosis and illuminated the several guards that filled the alcove just outside the elevator doors, waiting to catch the occupants inside unaware upon their arrival.

The surprise was theirs. The doors slid open, and a possessed Claire flew out at them, a human bowling ball that crashed into the group of security, sending them reeling back, tumbling in a mass back into the crowd in a chaotic mess.

With the alcove somewhat clear, Sol took advantage of the situation and slipped out, moving off to the side and disappearing into the crowd with his cargo braced at his side.

Demon-Claire had landed squarely on top of one of the guards. Left hand grabbed his shirt by the neckline, and her right pointed fingers into his eyes. Blood shot out in response in two quick spurts. Left eye. Right eye.

She rolled off and lunged at another guard who was struggling off his back to get up, hit him back flat, and ripped his throat out with a clawed strength a 15-year-old girl should not possess.

The partiers closest to the outer edge of the rage scene were knocked back or disturbed by the sudden ruckus. Some pulled away. Others, unsure of what was transpiring, circled to watch.

Claire crouched in a predatory stance, arms out, fingers arched to form claws, as several guards surrounded her.

The onlookers of the crowd were suddenly more interested in the bloody brawl than dancing to the beat, pulled back in astonishment as a possessed Claire rose vertically off the floor, appearing to levitate as she lifted higher than the average person would be able to jump from a standstill.

Two guards flew back, having been hit by some invisible force.

The spectating crowd, believing it was part of the show, cheered in excitement. Others, closer to the bleeding security, realized something else was happening and pulled back in fear.

It was hard for Sol to navigate through the crowd. Security seemed to be focused on Claire, but it was still like swimming upstream of a raging river, being pulled by an ocean's undertow, and he was half-dragging the Winemaker along. He looked back. Did he catch sight of Claire rising into the air? As the crowd's attention was stolen, the pressure seemed to ease, and he was able to make better headway.

It also lifted his veil of cover, moving through the mass of bodies, and a guard, who was talking into a radio, caught sight of him, and raced at Sol.

Arms occupied with keeping the Winemaker up, as the guard was moving in for a tackle, Sol kicked him in the mid-section, dropping the man like a sack of potatoes, and pushed his way forward to press on with their escape.

Floating just out of reach of the mass below, two guards jumped to grab at Claire. Opening wide her mouth, expelling an abnormal volume of puke and bile down into their faces to sting and blind their eyes.

The splatter caught some of the onlookers.

The realization that this was not a part of the evening's festivities, masses of hands grabbed Claire and pulled her down as if she were caught in a single wave of an organism. All that was visible were her arms reaching out to grab onto something, anything, to pull herself free of the crushing weight as other guards moved in and part of the crowd were on her in a swarm, suffocating, kicking, and beating her into submission.

There was a pulsing moment of the crowd and thrumming music getting sucked into a void of quiet as a half-breath pause of silence seemed to still the room. Then it clashed together again. Signalled by the screams as the mass of bodies and limbs on Claire flew backwards, pushed away violently by some invisible, telekinetic force. Some bystanders and the guards that were on her were tossed high into the crowd, hurting others as their deadweight came back down.

In the epicenter, Claire was on the ground. Clothes torn and bloody. Still crazed in her possession, snarling and spitting.

She floated up to her feet, arms wide in invitation, seemingly weightless as she stood on her toes in ballerina fashion. "Lambs dare to bite a wolf!"

The music stopped. The lights came on to illuminate the room, and everything stopped.

A moment.

Then the screaming started. Then the red flowed. Not the wine the patrons were used to in this establishment. The red of blood.

The castle was in the distance as Sol struggled through the vineyard, trudging his way through with the Winemaker fully conscious now and moving on his own volition, but still needed Sol's support.

With the adrenaline purging from his system, Sol realized how tired he was, and half tripped onto the ground where he found himself sitting. "Sorry, I guess I need to take a moment."

"No apologies needed," the Winemaker joined him in taking a seat in an area that was depressed along the rows of grape trees that gave them refuge from any visibility from the castle. "Thank you for rescuing me."

"We are not in the clear yet, brother. Just a quick moment to catch our breath, but we need to keep moving and get out of here. We have a bigger war to fight." Sol was up and offered a hand to assist the Winemaker.

An explosion erupted. Both men hurried up to the crest of the small knoll. In a crouch, they could see that part of the mansion was on fire.

And Claire, running down the laneway of grape trees in their direction. She ran as if being pursued, but there was no one following.

Once she caught up to them, Sol grabbed her and hugged her hard. Then, seeing her condition, clothes ripped, bloody, covered in gore, he verified she was okay, then pointed to the fires. "Did you do that?"

"I don't know. It must have been me. But I don't know," Claire couldn't remember what had transpired. The trio stood together in the night watching the mansion's pyres grow and burn, and Claire whispered a guilt. "There were innocent people in there!"

"No, there wasn't," The Winemaker tried to assuage her feelings. "That is why, Sol, any war you may think there is, has already been lost."

"Nothing is lost if there is hope," Sol said. "If we stay resolute and believe.

"I'm sorry, but with what I've been subjected to, what transpired in there, for however long I've been a captive...the depravity...there is no hope for this forsaken world."

Claire turned to the two men and placed a hand on their shoulders to bind them in a trinity. "Then we bring it back. We light the flame."

"It looks like we have already done that," Sol nodded towards the burning mansion. "But this isn't the one. There is already a beacon. We need to find this flame of hope. And help carry it."

Sol made them leave, but the Winemaker stood to watch the castle a few seconds longer. He wanted to stay and watch it burn, hear the echoes of the screams from inside waft up the hill towards them. But this wasn't who he was supposed to be, filled with hate, resentment, and anger over being used and held prisoner. He stared after Claire for a moment. Besides Sol, she was the other person he needed to thank for liberating him. The poor girl, bruised and hurt in their fight to save him. A darkness pulsed inside her, constantly wanting out, tempting her, pressing her. He could sense it, felt it when she touched him. It was terrifying. But she kept going and was ready to keep fighting.

The Winemaker turned away from the burning castle to follow the other two. If she could keep on, so could he.

CHAPTER THIRTY-SIX

Rain pattered against the windshield as the wipers thumped back and forth on the fastest setting, trying to provide a microsecond of visibility that was hindered further by headlights reflecting the wet asphalt at night, and it amplified it, making it look like black glass.

The storm clouds were as dark as Sera's mood. Blocked out by any hint of the moon. Ely commandeered their father's 'borrowed' car down the highway. He half watched the road but was more concerned with Sera, who had not spoken a word since they had left their childhood home. For the past couple of hours, she had just sat there with her forehead resting against the passenger side window, appearing to watch the outside world blur by, but it was obvious she was somewhere else, staring back into the past.

They were both lost in the dread of their intended destination. It had been a long drive of silence, but Ely had the act of being the driver to distract him. He squeezed the steering wheel, twisting his grip back and forth. It would not be long now, and the drive of silence would be at journey's end, to the Regional Forensic Psychiatric Hospital.

The hole where their mother had been rotting.

Ely had lost count of how many years their mother had been incarcerated there. Before they were teens, he started to work the math in his head, then realized he didn't want to figure it out, didn't want to count. All he had ever tried to do, same as his sister, was to forget.

Ely reached out to touch his sister's shoulder, to let her know they were close, but stopped himself and reasserted himself back to the wheel, leaving Sera undisturbed in her thoughts.In the cabin of that car, they were both haunted as they raced to face that past.

Raced to beat an inevitable future and try to save their mom.

Ely looked over at Sera again. Worry creased his brow. When they were about to start this drive, Sera asked, "Why?"

The single word.

That was all she needed to say. Ely knew she was asking why they were risking their necks for somebody they had both written out of their lives.

Ely stared at her until she nodded and then put the car in drive. Nothing needed to be said.

They had abandoned her years ago.

They could not abandon her now.

Ely's thoughts travelled back to when they were young. The perception of their life in his memories was through those youthful, misunderstanding eyes. But now he could see it differently as he filtered through the past. In those years after mother had been incarcerated, father had been a broken man, living his life trying to pick up the pieces. To put a puzzle sense together to bring himself some comfort, some understanding as to why his picture-perfect family had become a nightmare. Sitting with Mom and Sera on the couch watching television, Dad comes home and leans over the back of the couch, ruffling Ely's hair. Sera jumped up for a hug and a hello kiss for Mom. But she just sat stoic, with no physical response in recognition of the endearment.

Those signs were when Ely would go to the kitchen for a drink while Mom was preparing dinner. She didn't notice him as he stopped in the entranceway, but he saw her, arms braced against the sides of the sink, head dropped down, crying. The sounds of her sobs were masked by the running faucet.

All Dad's energy went to holding it together.

All of Mom's energy went to holding on.

Which she did for many years. When he was young, Ely would catch her watching at his bedroom door from down the hall. At the patio doors, when they played in the backyard. Standing, watching, almost frozen. He was too young then to give the behaviour any recognition. Now older, it seemed like she was always holding something back.

Finally arriving in the early morning hours, Ely brought the car to a stop in front of the main gate to the Forensic Psychiatric Hospital.

He wanted to say, 'Welcome to the nuthouse,' or 'the crazy pen for the criminally insane.' But that would probably trigger Sera, so he kept his thoughts to himself.

The last time they had visited this place, it was not that long after Mom had been arrested for attacking her family. Regardless, it was thought it would be good for them to visit as she awaited trial, maybe help bring some closure to the family, or have the kids see their mother for the woman who raised them, not the crazy person that snapped one night.

But in that visiting room, she had affirmed the crazy-snapped person. Sera, Dad, and Ely had only been with Mom two minutes in the supervised visiting room when Mom lunged across the room, grabbed Sera, and tried to choke her to death. Dad knocked her away, but it still took three guards to subdue Mom and stop her from trying to kill his sister. That incident was emblazoned in Ely's mind. He was sure, just like Sera. Ely remembered hurrying after his dad as he carried a terrified Sera in his arms back to the car. They left that day. Never came back. Never saw their Mom again.

A few days after that incident, Dad received news that Mom had attacked and killed another inmate. Hurt a guard in the incident. He had only told them of this when they were older, when Sera had questioned how Mom had been imprisoned for so long.

A multiple offender, the proverbial key was thrown away.

Turning off the ignition, Ely leaned over the steering wheel to look past the rain-fogged windshield and reached over to get Sera's attention. She was still staring out her window into her miserable memories. "Ready?"

"No, I'm not ready," startled from being lost in thought, Sera pushed Ely's hand away angrily. "I can't do it. I can't go in there. I have worked so hard at leaving the past, and all this is forcing me to face it." She leaned forward to look past the windshield herself. "I went from living a normal life..."

"No, you were hiding," Ely cut her off and leaned over to take her hand in his. "And I am not disparaging you. You were being reclusive so you could lick an unhealed wound."

Ely got out of the car, hoping his initiating the exit would entice her to follow. With his door still open, he bent into the car to check on Sera. She wasn't moving a muscle.

"Your strength has carried you every day since your daughter's death, and that tells me you can do this. Everything we have survived and witnessed, the past few days, tells me you can do this."

She looked at him. "But this is the last straw. Being here now, I am on the verge of unravelling." Sera slowly got out of the car and looked at Ely from across the roof. "Here...now...I hate her. That woman in there..." Sera pointed towards the prison. "...That woman failed our family!"

"Maybe, or maybe we failed each other," Ely shrugged. "Regardless, she is still our mother. Blood."

On the right side of the gate was a ten-foot concrete wall with reamed barbed wire lining the top to add a splash of containment. To the left was the guardhouse that monitored the gated entrance before the concrete barrier continued its line around the perimeter of the property. Ely was a little surprised nobody had come out of the small building, so he began walking backwards towards it, thumbing over his shoulders to direct Sera. "So, we stick to the plan. Ensure mom is safe, catch the crazy murderess-woman, then go to the police and clear our names."

Sera followed, making a magic motion with her hands. "And presto! Everything goes back to normal."

"Well, now you are just being ridiculous," Ely chided. There was his sister, a spark in her eye with that quip. There was the strong woman he needed right now because he didn't want to admit it to her, but he was faking his bravado. He was terrified of seeing the woman they used to call Mom.

At the guardhouse, Ely pressed his face into the window that looked out to the gate and banged on the glass. "Hello? Hello, is anyone there?"

Sera had the more direct approach and opened the door to look inside the control room. It was empty.

"Nobody is manning the gate," Sera said, surprised. "That's a little weird."

A strange noise pulled their attention to the gate. They could hear laughing. A strange noise for the environment they were in.

Not too far beyond the metal bars, there came a cackling to precede four men that ran freely by. They were all dressed in gray pants and short sleeved shirts. Patients. Ely shook his head. Inmates. He had to remember where they were. Inmates in the front area of the building. Two of them held the legs of a fifth man they were dragging behind them. It was a prison guard, lifeless, a thin trail of blood painted the cement in his wake.

Shaking off the horrific sight, Sera grabbed Ely before they could be noticed and pulled him back into the sanctuary of the gate house.

"What the hell is going on?" She said to Ely.

"Is it a riot? Or just a few escaped patients?"

Sera counted off on her fingers. "The gate is unmanned. No other guards around. No alarms. Where is everyone else?"

Ely paced back and forth. "She beat us here. She beat us here. How the fuck did she know to come here. How?"

"Keep your voice down!" Sera snapped.

"We figured this could be a trap," Ely stopped and looked at his sister sincerely.

"Are we still going in?" Sera asked with trepidation.

"Do we have a choice?"

Her staring back at him was enough of an answer.

"Still got that gun?" He asked.

"You bet I've got the god-damned gun," Sera drew the gun holstered in her waistband.

Inspecting the panel of controls, they decided it was not prudent to open the main gate and drive in, giving a means of escape to all the inmates if a full-on riot or prison break was in progress. They had only seen the four escapees, but had to anticipate that things inside the prison were chaotic. Besides, all the systems seemed to be down, the computer terminal and phone system, so it was likely that the electric gate would not work.

There was another door in the guardhouse that opened onto the inside of the yard. Sera pushed it open slowly. All was quiet. She was horrible at gauging distances, but it was a good stretch, a hundred-yard dash to the main entrance. Straight shot.

She closed her eyes. It was not long ago that she was living her somewhat agoraphobic life. And now this.

All of this. She was about to run across a prison yard to the mother who hated her and had tried to kill her, not once, but twice.

And right into the epicenter of whatever spiderweb of a trap lay on the other side of those doors.

Good times.

Ely's hand on her back. Little brother. Not pushing her forward, a soft touch. A compassionate signal that they were about to be in the shit.

"It's just us," Ely whispered to her at that moment. "It was always just us. Me and you."

"Me and you," Sera whispered back, eyes steeled on the front access of the prison.

"And we stick together to see this through."

Sera reached around to hold on to her brother's hand and pulled him forward, bursting from the sanctuary of the guardhouse into the open.

CHAPTER THIRTY-SEVEN

In the main lobby, they stopped to catch their breath. Sera and Ely had not encountered anyone from their sprint from the guardhouse into the building. Nobody chased them. Once inside, nobody greeted them. The only welcome was the inhuman screams echoing from somewhere, everywhere, in the bowels of the building.

The waiting room was devoid of life, but there were splashes of blood on chairs and the walls. The plastic dividers at the reception area cracked, garbage cans were tipped over, and their contents strewn about. Down a long hall to the left, caught in the halo of the emergency lighting that pulsed, was a small group of inmates. Far enough away, they were unaware of the new visitors. Ely held a quieting finger to his lips and pointed Sera's attention down the hall. From their position, it looked like the inmates' backs were turned, and they were focused on something at their feet.

Just ahead, off to the side of the main reception booth, a security officer breached through a set of double doors, startling Ely and Sera. The man was frightened, sweaty, and his eyes were full of panic.

"My god!" He was surprised to discover two civilians before him as he leaned back against the door to brace it. "What are you doing here?"

Before a response could be offered, the man was jostled, lurching against the force from behind as someone slammed into the other side of the door. Once, twice, and the guard stumbled forward, unable to resist the pressure.

Several pairs of hands reached out from the depths behind to grab the man, by the hair, around the chest, on the arm, violently yanking on him to pull him back.

"Run! They're free!" He yelled wide eyed in warning to Sera and Ely. "They're all free!" And in an instant, he was sucked back from behind the door. "Get out! Get help!"

The officer was gone. The doors swung shut to give a breath of silence, as if the security guard had never emerged. Ely took a hesitating step towards the door, reached out a hand.

The doors flew open. Ely anticipated the return of the abducted security guard, instead, it was two male inmates, crazy-eyed with spittle flinging from hungry lips that dove out at him. Ely tumbled backwards as one of the enraged inmates drove into him. As he fell back in the tackle, Ely caught a glimpse of more inmates rushing down the corridor beyond.

"Door!" He managed to choke out before the back of his head cracked against the floor with the full weight of the inmate on him.

Sera raced past and slammed the doors closed with her body.

Pinned to the ground, the inmate on top of him, Ely struggled to get out from under the weight. His attacker raised a fist high to deliver a crushing blow. There was something in the man's eyes. A voided craziness.

The fist came down. Ely moved his head to the side just in time to dodge the strike. He had somehow dodged without realizing it. His head had shifted right at the exact moment, so the fist missed, but just barely. Ely heard the bones in the inmate's fisted hand snap and crack against the hard flooring when the man lifted his hand to punch again, oblivious that it must have hurt. Ely knew what to do. He had to give in and trust his instinct, to whatever pushed from inside. It was not him dodging the strikes, but someone else taking over. And that was okay. A fist shot down. Ely dodged again. Another shot, ignorant of the pain, his attacker was lightning fast. Ely let that inside of him be faster. React, just react. Ely's head snapped to the side, the fist missing, the air whooshing in his ear and teasing his hair, the crackle-pop of bones against the hard floor again. When the inmate lifted his arm and drew back for a fist, his fingers dangled like mangled, limp spaghetti noodles. He still drove another punch down, although no longer able to form a fist.

The epiphany hit. The man on top of him was acting the same as the burning man at the motel.

These were not just escaped prisoners. These were rage-possessed escaped prisoners. He and Sera had entered hell.

Not having success with the mangled-flesh fist, the inmate drove his head down to butt Ely's skull.

Move.

An impulsive shift, causing the inmate to miss again and sledgehammer his head into the floor, sprinkling sprays of blood from a shattered nose and cutting his forehead. Ely knew it was not him moving, and was grateful that he would have been knocked out. He was conscious of what was happening, not like the other times. He had to just give in and be a passenger. Let whoever was controlling drive him.

Oblivious to his injuries, the possessed man drove his head down in a second strike and missed. After the second meeting with the concrete, the man's face was a mess of blood, split lips, and crumpled nasal cartilage. On the third blow, the facial bone structure, already weakened, crushed into the ground, the neck snapping to the side as the inmate inadvertently killed himself. Ely went to roll the dead weight off himself and caught Sera bracing the door against the banging and thrusts from the other side. The other inmate was almost upon her, but she had the gun out, pointed straight at the charging elephant of a man.

"No!" Ely reached out to Sera in a yelled warning. "Don't!"

Sera fired a shot as the man was almost upon her. A bullet to the head at almost point-blank range that sent the inmate flying backwards to match the trajectory of the brain and skull pieces that blew out the back of his head.

"What?" The commotion quieted, and pressure relented from behind the door. She leaned forward to offer Ely a hand up. "I had to shoot."

"I know. I know, but the noise from the gunshot," Ely looked around. "I was worried about the noise. That it would be like ringing an alarm."

From down that other hall, the shadow mass of other inmates could be seen turning, moving forward, rushing forward in Sera and Ely's direction. Then caught unaware, Sera was almost tossed forward as the group behind the door surged against the barricade, renewed in strength, a tsunami wave against the doorway that Sera and Ely barely held back.

"We can't stay here," Sera said behind gritted teeth. Seeing the ones down the hall drawing closer, bouncing against the rhythmic slamming of the door. "I can't hold this."

"We run!" Ely looked at her. "Ready?"

They took off at a sprint, running in the opposite direction from the ones coming down the corridor. Instantly, the doors burst open behind them, and several crazed inmates tumbled through, stumbling and falling over each other. The only saving grace to Sera and Ely's predicament was that the two groups collided in a mass of bodies and limbs, gifting them a few seconds.

The two of them were running quickly, with the noise of the group chasing them echoing off the walls. Ely and Sera entered a room to take shelter. They slid under a counter desk inside what appeared to be a large administrative or security office. computer terminals lined the long counter they were crouched under; it was barricaded from the hall and small waiting area on the other side by protective glass that ran from the desk to the ceiling.

"Close," Ely tried to catch his breath.

"Too close," Sera nodded. "What the hell is going on? And where in god's name are we?"

In the corner of the room, two female bodies were crumpled in the corner, unmoving, wide-eyed in death. Their clothes were torn and bloody. Close to them was a female guard. Having been ravaged by a pack of crazed inmates, her neck was twisted, face already discoloring in lifelessness.

Ely pointed to the trio of bodies and whispered, "I think this must have been an admittance desk or security point. But in a different context, I think where we are is hell."

Banging against the glass, faces pressed to peer in, unaware that just beyond the glass partition, their prey was hiding, several inmates spied in then moved on, yelling in a unified chant. "Elysium. Elysium. Elysium."

Sera was knocked back as her brother fell into her with the sudden onset of an uncharacteristic seizure. Frothing at the mouth, his back arched, and arms kinked in violent contortions. Sera tried to constrain him. Partially to keep him from injuring himself. Partially to ensure his flailing didn't cause a noise to bring attention to their hiding spot.

"Ely! Ely!" Sera panicked. Her brother had never been known to have a seizure before.

Then, just as quickly as it began, it stopped. And Ely rolled out of her arms to his side, curling up in a fetal position, and wrapped his arms around his stomach. Gently rocking on his side, he moaned in pain.

Sera kneeled at his side, confused at what was happening. "Are you okay? What was that? You scared me half to death."

"No!" He grunted from behind gritted teeth. "It hurts. I feel so full."

"So full of what?" Sera felt helpless.

Ely popped up to a sitting position and clasped his hands to his head, struggling to speak. "I don't know. Just feels like I am going to burst at the seams." He said and fell onto his side again, mouth wide in a silent agony.

On her knees, Sera tried to keep low at desk level and shuffled down its length to find a phone. It was dark, but their eyes were adjusting to the low-level glow given off by the emergency lights that were on. She found a hardline phone, picked up the receiver, and held it to her ear. No dial tone. She let it go and left it hanging from its cord as she slid over to try one of the computer terminals. Screens were blank. There was nothing to call to the outside world for help.

"Computers are down. Phones are down. I have no clue what is going on with you suddenly, but you are obviously sick and need help. We have no way of finding Mom. We need to get out of here." Now they were trapped here, and her brother collapsed in a seizure with no guarantee this random onset would hit again. Sera's nerves were fraying.

"We will find her," Ely appeared to be regaining his senses.

"Impossible!" Sera crawled back to him and got in his face. "We can't just go running around blindly in a prison for the mentally insane when all the insane are not imprisoned!"

The pain from his episode had passed. The fire in his gut subsided. Ely crawled over to the door and stood with his back against it to peer sidelong through the glass partition.

"I can feel…a…pull. I think I have an idea where to go," Ely said once he finished verifying the immediate coast was clear.

Sera shook her head in denial. "You are going to have to face facts. We have been too late every time. This is no different. I hate to say it, but Mom is probably dead."

Ely stared down at her. "She's not."

"How do you know that for sure?"

"I just know it. I can feel it," he softened his plea. "Please trust me."

Sera scrambled over to the dead security guard and fiddled with the corpse's belt, giving off a few grunts of disgust. After a few seconds, she turned back to Ely and waved a set of keys at him. "Fine! I have the keys. You need to show me the doors."

Ely reached down with an offered hand to pull Sera up.

"And don't have any more seizures, okay?" She said as she joined him with her back to the door. "Scared the shit out of me."

Ely didn't respond in words, just hugged her in an embrace of trust and unity as brother and sister prepared to breach the sanctity of their hiding spot.

They slithered down a darkened hall, backs to the wall, wary and on high alert. At a crossroads, Ely stopped them to peer around the corner and check the adjoining hallway shadows beyond in the afterglow of the radiance of the emergency lights. No motion could be seen down in the hall's depths.

"So far so good," pressed in close, Sera whispered.

"It looks clear," Ely affirmed.

Then Sera gave a squeaked yelp. An inmate had snuck up from behind, grabbed a fistful of her hair, and yanked her back, whiplashing her neck and snapping her off her feet back into him, where he wrapped her tight in his arms.

"Pretty! Pretty!" His mouth was on Sera's ear with saliva dripping into it.

"Let go!" Ely spun at his sister's yelp and punched over Sera's shoulder into the inmate's face. Blood spurted as part of Sera's lobe tore when the man's head went back from the force of the blow.

Sera came forward, grabbing her ear in pain as Ely moved past her and struck the inmate a second time, sending him reeling to the ground. Ely stood over him, preparing to deliver another blow to incapacitate the man, but he didn't try to get up, and wasn't preparing to fight back.

Instead, he started to freak out, writhing on the ground and screeching as he shouted. "Beskah! Beskah! Beskah!" As if calling to someone.

"Shut up!" Ely delivered a conscious rendering kick.

Towering over the unconscious body, Ely looked up to ensure the noise had not caused any other inmates to come their way. Ely saw that his wish was not going to be fulfilled. A woman came around the corner, flanked by an entourage of possessed inmates.

"C'mon," Ely turned, grabbed Sera, and pulled her behind him as they ran in the opposite direction of the encroaching horde.

"Was that her?" Sera tried to look back over her shoulder but almost tripped in the effort. "The blonde bitch?"

"I don't think so. It might have been her motel buddy, but we are not hanging around to find out."

Down another corridor, they pushed through a heavy set of double doors and found themselves in the dining hall of the psychiatric facility. It was a huge room with rows of tables and benches. The tables and chairs were all bolted to the ground, so there was nothing to barricade the doors with. They felt a momentary panic of being trapped because their pursuers were about to fly through the doors at any second.

At the far end was the serving line concourse. Ely pointed towards it. "There has to be another exit through the kitchen."

They ran.

Seconds later, the doors behind them banged open, and the team of possessed feral prisoners was trailing them as they continued the chase, climbing over tables, benches, and pushing tray carts over. A gated door was the only entrance to the other side. Sera fiddled with the key ring for half a second before Ely pulled her to climb through the small gap in the counter. Sliding over something, someone grabbed her ankle and yanked her back, but she held onto the counter edge and kicked back hard with her free leg, pulling herself forward in desperation at the same time. The grip released, and she shot forward, sliding over the edge with the extra exertion onto the floor.

Ely had her and was helping her up as the prisoners slammed into the gated door and serving line barrier, crushing into each other in their rage-blind pursuit. Through the kitchen, another set of double doors that were open wide, offering a way out of the confines of the serving hall, and passage down another corridor.

Sera pulled away and retreated to the doors. She pushed them close together and fumbled with the guard keyset she withdrew from her pocket.

Ely stopped mid-step and spun around. "What are you doing? We need to keep moving!"

"I grabbed those keys. If I can manually lock these, it will buy us some time," Sera called back as she tried key after key with shaking hands. On the fourth selection, the key submerged into the lock. "Got it!"

Feeling secure behind the locked barricade, Sera chanced a look through the metal-webbed window. Bes and her entourage were drawing closer.

Now it was Sera reacting to Ely crying out. Sera turned, and a couple of possessed inmates came barrelling out of a room to tackle Ely back against the wall.

Then, to her shocked surprise, Tory emerged. And Sera was frozen, watching in stunned silence as Tory pressed into Ely, wrapped her hand around his neck while the possessed soldiers held his arms.

"Finally! Welcome to my playground," Tory smiled and kissed Ely softly on the cheek. "My trap drew you in." An evil smile was born across her face. "And you came like a rat sniffing for cheese. You should have stayed hidden, but you couldn't, and I knew you couldn't resist." She directed that smile at Sera. "And yes, I see you."

Sera drew her gun and aimed it at Tory. "Let him go!"

The she-devil squeezed Ely's neck tighter in objection to the order. "Big sister. Protector of the realm! Warrior! Trying to order me around. I'd say, color me impressed, but we know you are a failure at your duties. Daughter, strike one! Mother, strike two!"

Falling back a step in horror, Sera's arm lowered the aim of the pistol as her resolve suffered a slap in the face. "What did you do to our mother?"

Tory's expression changed from a sadistic grin to an apologetic, pouty face. "I didn't do anything. Mommy is just gone." She shrugged. "She ran away. All because of a broken heart."

The crushing pressure on his throat and arms held firm, made any escaping struggle of Ely's futile, but with the taunting, Sera was enraged and drew closer with quick, determined steps. She raised the gun and fired. One of the possessed lackeys holding Ely was hit and fell away.

"No!" Sera yelled in defiance over the sound of the gunfire.

A few steps more, the second inmate was blown away. Ely's arms were now free, so he could fight against the grip the crazy woman had on him. She just increased the pressure on his throat with inhuman strength. Ely's feet dangled a couple of inches from the floor as she drew him up the wall. Otherwise, she was paying no heed to him.

"Oh yes, you little Valkyrie, come!" Tory stared down at Sera without budging her position.

The other woman and her army had arrived but were for the moment held at bay. And that moment would be short by the sound of the doors behind her rattling against their locks and the banging pressure of their moorings.

Sera was deaf to it. Blind to it.

Her brother was being choked to death. Exhaustion. Frustration. The futility of being here, all Sera felt was rage. All she saw was red.

Closer still, Sera fired two more bullets. One caught Tory in the shoulder of the arm holding Ely, forcing her to release her grip. Ely slid to the ground, choking for air.

The other bullet hit the devil-woman somewhere in the head as she snapped back with the force of the impact, dropping to the ground.

Sera reached their side and kicked at the downed Tory. "Be careful what you wish for!"

The security doors burst open, and the horde of possessed inmates began squeezing through to press inwards, falling over each other in a hunter's rage for their targets that were now in sight.

Supporting her harrowed brother, Sera moved to escape but was surprised when Tory popped up, reaching for them. Bitch wasn't dead, but she was holding her left hand over her eyes, blood seeping between fingers. At least Sera had done some damage with that last shot.

"Touche," Tory called out when she missed grabbing one of their legs. "I've barely gotten over the hole in my chest from that deer episode, and now you shoot my eye out." On her feet, she was screaming now in the wake of Sera and Ely's running away. "You will pay for this! I'm going to open you so wide that demons will violate you for an unprecedented eternity of torment."

The horde gave chase, streaming around Tory in pursuit.

"Are you okay?" Sera could feel Ely lagging. "Your throat?"

"I'm fine," Ely's voice was rough. "Hard to catch my breath, just keep moving."

"I shot that woman twice. Once through her god-damned eyes, she got up and just shook it off."

"I know. And from the sounds of it, you pissed her off more than you hurt her."

"Which way now?" Sera asked in advance about the crossroads of halls they were coming up to.

"I don't know."

Sera looked over her shoulder in response to the thunderous sound rumbling down the hall. "They're coming!"

"I know," Ely looked side to side, trying to decide the best path.

A couple of inmates, faster than the others, ahead of the pack, came around the corner and into view.

"That's not good enough. Which way!"

"I…don't…know!" Ely's head snapped to the right as if unseen hands twisted it in a chiropractic move. He grabbed Sera's arm roughly and dragged her after him as the entire mass of the horde filled the corridor behind them, bearing down on them.

The early morning sun breached the horizon and was a welcome sight as Sera and Ely pushed through the front doors to escape. They kept charging forward towards the car to finalize their getaway.

Once they were through the guardhouse, opening the car doors to jump in, they both stopped, expecting bodies to be slamming against the main gate, climbing, reaching for them, but nobody was coming over the front concourse. The horde of prisoners was back at the main entrance. At the breach of the doors, Bes and Tory stood with their army pulsing behind them, swaying in a wave of bodies ready to shoot forward at the slightest signal, but holding at bay.

And Tory. That she-devil of a woman, was standing in front, smiling, totally unaffected, and ignoring the fact that she was bleeding from the hole in her head where her eye should have been.

Ely was frozen. Mystified. "Why aren't they still chasing us? They're just standing there?"

"Who cares!" Sera snapped at him to get his attention. "Just get in the car and drive."

They disappeared into the car. Ely threw the gear shift into reverse and peeled out, leaving rubber tire marks in their wake.

"She will ensnare them," Bes said, as the two women stood on the front steps unconcerned that their targets were escaping.

"A more fitting trap could not have been fantasized," Tory agreed. "Down the rabbit hole they go."

Bes raised her arms, and the possessed army rushed past them into the daylight to pursue the fleeing vehicle.

CHAPTER THIRTY-EIGHT

After the struggle to escape the castle, the condition of the Winemaker making progress on foot was slow, and the haggard feeling of both Sol and Claire after the whole ordeal, seeing the gas station in the distance was an oasis of nearing sanctuary.

Coming across a field facing the rear of the establishment. The trio collapsed in a grove of trees that provided shelter from the morning sun and the wandering eyes of passing vehicles.

A restaurant was attached to the convenience store that served the gas pumps. It did not look too busy. On the left, a few semi-trucks with trailers were parked. Breakfast scents coasted in on the slight breeze, not enough to discern anything, just enough to tease the nostrils.

"Ugh, my stomach is growling. I'm so hungry." Claire announced what the other two were feeling.

"We all are," Sol replied. "But you stink and look horrible with your puke and blood-stained shirt. There is most likely a no shirt, no shoes, no service policy, and the Winemaker doesn't even have pants. Never mind the shoes and shirt. I'll go down there. It looks like they probably have some tourist gifts. Hopefully, that includes clothes."

Claire and the Winemaker remained quietly concealed, observing Sol move across the field in search of something to make their appearance more conventional. Within minutes, both succumbed to exhaustion due to the overwhelming seduction of the warmth from the sun.

***

Under Sera's repetitive demand to drive...drive...drive, Ely backed away from the main gate. He shifted the gear to drive and was about to stomp on the gas pedal when he quickly looked up to check the rearview, afraid to let those two women out of sight. The mirror was filled with the face of an older woman, dressed in patient attire, an asylum escapee. Ely spun in his seat.

Sera, catching his reaction, turned to look, expecting to see the army chasing after them.

"MOM!" Sera squeaked.

Ely had not recognized her instantly, having been younger, but Sera did. Both were frozen in shock.

"So good to see you, Sera junior," Mom gave a hint of a smile, motioning Ely forward. "I suggest you do what your sister said and drive. Get us the hell out of here!"

Dumbfounded, he did what he was told, spun around, and punched it; the car lurched forward under squealing tires.

Sera leaned out the passenger window. She needed a moment; she needed the air. She felt the blood drain from her, oxygen leave, at the sight of her mother. Here. In the car. Alive.

Looking behind, Sera saw the dark-haired woman raise her hands, and the frenzied horde rushed forward, chasing on foot. They were inhumanly fast, a horde infused with distemper being pushed by a blinded, inexhaustible rage.

"Don't stop," Sera reasserted herself in her seat and warned Ely.

From the side mirror, she could see the compelled ones in the distance. Closer, a glimpse of her mom in the backseat. Sera began chewing her fingernails.

***

Once Sol had returned, he startled Claire and the Winemaker awake, and they all made their way stealthily back to the station. Sneaking in through the back into the washrooms, they had all cleaned up as best they could, wiping away the dirt, grime, and blood stains, and changed into the fresh clothes Sol had gotten for them.

Now they sat in a booth by the window of the restaurant diner.

Impatiently waiting for her food, Claire, newly adorned in an oversized sweatshirt, filled one side of the booth. She held the window seat, and Sol sat next to her. Across the table was the Winemaker, looking a little ridiculous, in Claire's opinion, wearing a t-shirt silk-screened with the image of a pack of wolves howling at the moon, and sweatpants. At least he was wearing clothes, and they all smelled better.

Either it was off-season, the wrong time of the week, or a stretch of road no one visited often, as only a few patrons sat at tables eating breakfast when the trio came in to find a seat.

Staring out the window, the conversation Sol and the Winemaker were engaged in was muffled background noise. Claire was lost in reflection on everything she had been through. Sitting next to Sol, there was an ease, a comfort. For once, she almost felt safe. Or this was what having an uncle, or big brother, was like. It was a comfort compared to the rest of her life. Where she had felt like a Magdalene seeking approval, but offered no feet to wash, a pariah in an ocean of hypocritical acceptance.

Claire, leaned forward to address the Winemaker. "So really, what is your real name? Winemaker is so long. And a little pretentious, don't you think? I should call you 'Cab,' like the wine!"

The Winemaker looked slightly offended as he lowered a cup of coffee from his lips. "No."

Claire smiled against the serious face before her. "Too on the nose? How about something with a little more panache, like 'Pinot'?"

"Not happening," shaking his head, the Winemaker rested his coffee on the table, leaned across to make his point heard, and shut down this ridiculous conversation. "Plus, why would you want to change, or better yet, disrespect a name that was given birth by the most sacred book in the world? I carry my name with pride."

"Wait a minute," Claire held up her hand. "Are you alluding to the bible stories of the miracles of Jesus? Are you telling me those are real?"

"Real enough," Sol joined in. "But could it be possible that at that time in history, a front man was needed to lead and bring people together? Maybe, others behind the scenes worked miracles."

"Wait! Wait! Claire leaned back; her arms spread out to accentuate her exuberance. "All of it is true. God! Jesus! All completely true?"

"Don't look at it as something concrete that must be true or false," the Winemaker said. "Belief is the true god."

They paused as the waitress, deaf to their conversation, stopped to refill their coffee cups. Claire was too frozen, her mouth agape at the revelations being tabled, to even be disappointed that the waitress was not delivering their food.

Once the waitress moved on to tend to other tables, Sol continued. "Belief creates a truth for anyone who carries it. How many gods have there been through the expanse of time? Everyone, even today, believes in different gods. But that isn't why we are here. That isn't what matters. What matters is that a dam has been broken. Those who have left this mortal plane, the essence of us, souls as we like to call them, are lost everywhere. Everything holds space, and in those other planes, room is getting tight."

"Often the best place, the only place to go, is back," the Winemaker interjected.

Sol nodded. "The population of Earth has exploded. There are lots of places to hide here now. Over time, some have done that. Some have just popped in to check on a loved one, and help them to take the right turn to avoid an accident." He held up a finger in warning. "But others want, need, a permanent residency. The other places, the heavens, and the hells, the everywhere, are overflowing and can't sustain them. A race for a new place has commenced. And that place is here. But having 'souls' inhabit bodies, suppressing the existing souls, all leads to a cataclysmic event.

"Cataclysmic," concern painted Claire's face as she tried to grasp it. "Are you alluding to Armageddon? The voices in me, the things inside me that want out, they want to bring it and force this change." She pointed at both men. "You guys, you are here to stop Armageddon, aren't you?"

"Stop? I don't think it is something to be stopped. We are just here to mitigate chaos," the Winemaker said.

"So, we're the good guys. Even though the things that take over me do bad things, we are the good guys."

The smile Sol gave her was a sympathetic one. "I don't know what defines good or bad. We all serve a certain purpose. There are the things we know are right, and what is wrong. Those things that express love, versus those that incite hate. Actions that cause happiness and actions that cause pain. Those who do wrong, incite hate, and purposefully act to hurt. Those are the bad guys.

"So, we're the good guys," Sera smiled.

This time, the smile Sol returned was genuine because he knew she needed that reassurance. She had felt hated by her parents all her life for the behaviours she had exhibited that were out of her control. Hating oneself, not forgiving oneself, was a deeper cut.

The waitress arrived and began doling out the plates to the three patrons in the booth. Claire started to eat immediately. Sol looked over her, out the window, hoping her belief was true. Knowing that they would be tested, he hoped he would not let her down.

***

Ely eased the pressure on the gas pedal now that he felt a safe distance. There wasn't much traffic on the road this early in the morning, but the last thing they needed was to be pulled over by the police, especially with their mother in the back seat.

As if reading Ely's mind, Mom leaned forward and placed her hands on her children's shoulders. "You came. All this time, I waited, and I knew. I knew you'd come for me." She sat back and looked out to the side, through the passing landscape, down into memory lane. "My children. My beautiful children. He, and I do mean your father, left me to rot in there, in that prison. He kept me from you, but I knew you'd come one day. That was my saving grace, the salvation I held onto."

The words leaking from her mother's mouth were a poison seeping into Sera's ears that crept down her spine with spider tendrils. She couldn't stand the twisting words, about to wretch, Sera swivelled in her seat and looked at her mother in disgust at her victim-spun perception of the past. "Dad didn't leave you to rot in there! You were there because you tried to murder us!"

Ely focused on driving but reached out and placed his right hand on Sera's shoulder to calm her.

Sera ignored the gesture. "More than once, I might add!"

"Sera, she was being used. We can't blame her," Ely reasoned.

"You just drive," Sera sloughed his hand off her.

385

"I fought every day for you two," crossing her arms over her chest in resolution. Mom looked her cynical daughter square in the eye. "Did you know that?"

"You were our mother. That was your job," Sera retorted.

"Were?" Mom swiftly pulled herself forward, Sera flinched back in her seat. Mom's torso was wedged in between the driver and passenger seat. She twisted to Sera, right in her face, getting close so her words were felt. "Sera, you were the light of my life. There was a spark in you so bright." She twisted around to face the driver's side. "And you, Ely, my strong little boy, always carried so much. It's like everything good in the world was…is…bundled up inside of you, it's a magical thing. But it's also a hardship to carry. I see it in your eyes. It was always there."

Ely gave a placating half-grin. "I need to drive."

Mom sat back exasperated. "I fought to protect that. That is a mother's sacrifice."

A mother's sacrifice. A mother's sacrifice. A mother's sacrifice. The words reverberated through Sera's skull. Those words were smug, contrite, from a woman who tried to kill the children she says she fought to protect. And her kids were still here. They were the ones rescuing her. Sera felt a hot rage well up in her chest, a lava boil ready to explode, and a crushing weight around her heart. She hated the woman in the back seat, wearing the name of mom like it was a badge of honor with no inkling of an apology on her lips for what she did to her family, how she scarred her and Ely. Sera had fought to exist with the hole inside of her, the loss of her daughter.

Sera looked over at Ely, focused on the road like he was driving to get away from the woman in the back seat, unknowingly of how to deal with that.

She stared at him. Sera's eyes squinted, a little resentment maybe, she thought there was a comfort in knowing Ely had felt her daughter's presence, but in this moment, it just made her heart fracture.

Moving as a flowing shadow in an erratic path, like a flock of starlings in murmuration, the horde tirelessly pursued from deep in the distance, racing on a trajectory through trees and over hills, chasing their target down winding paved roads.

***

The arrival of food had gratefully stemmed the flow of Claire's questioning, as she immediately dug in.

The Winemaker, on the other hand, felt ravished, but cherished his first bite. "I have no recollection of how long it has been since I've had real food. Held captive, kept in a coma-like state and fed intravenously..." He paused to place another forkful of hashbrowns into his mouth and nodded to the waitress who stopped to ensure everything was fine with their order and refill their coffee cups.

Something is coming.

Not the words, the feeling spiked inside Claire's head like a lightning strike. She choked on the scrambled eggs she had been shoveling, dropped her cutlery, and braced her hands on the table, pushing back. With the sudden onset of pain in her head, her mouth opened wide in a silent scream. Sol and the Winemaker turned to her in concern.

Behind gritted teeth, hands clamped on the table edge, Claire barely got out the words. "Something is coming. Something wants out...being called...I don't know if I can hold it in."

And wham, she threw her head forward down to bang against the table, caught the edge of her plate, making the array of eggs, sausage, and pancakes flop and scatter.

It was hard enough that the few other tables of patrons leaned out of their booths or turned at their tables to check where the commotion originated from.

"You are alright," Sol leaned in close with a comforting hand, a stabilizing hand, on her shoulder. His words came across more as a command than an assurance.

"Okay...okay," Claire leaned forward, eyes squeezed shut, taking deep breaths. "I'm okay...subsiding...I'm okay now." She sat up and smiled weakly at Sol. "That felt close."

The waitress was at their table again. Swift at her job, she reappeared out of nowhere to check that everything was okay. Luckily, Sol was able to convince her that Claire was prone to seizures, that she had her medication, and everything was fine.

"Liar," Claire hit Sol in the shoulder, trying to normalize things and show she had regained her composure. "So, this evil inside me, be it a genesis or an apocalypse, is coming to a head. Things are screaming inside of me, and the three of us have found each other, here together. Do we not need to seek help through the religions? Through a church? Is that not the true vestige of power to save us?"

"No, it is the greatest deceit," Sol said, pulling his coffee cup to his lips. "Organized religion can be a breeding ground for intolerance. Bringing people together under the auspices of community and faith."

The Winemaker raised a hand to pause Sol so he could weigh in. "That is a somewhat skewed view of someone who has watched and experienced through the annals of time. There has been so much good that has been done through faith-based communities."

"Beyond any positive it has done in its name, in the name of gods, look at the wrong. Over time, certain churches have been created to draw in darkness under the guise of light. To do wolven wrongs while drawing in the sheep for good," Sol retorted. "The insurmountable evil, the gluttony of modern day, the falseness of the dark ages. The wars in the name of God. Need I go on? Just look at what happened to you, Claire, by a representative of organized religion. The pit of debauchery we found the Winemaker in."

"True faith is trust in each other. Resolution. Kindness. Love. These are the real religions. This world and those in it are the only church."

Claire held up her hands in defeat. "So, what do we do?"

"We find the true practitioners of those religions," the Winemaker said.

"We cannot involve the world churches and those who would only take the opportunity for power. We maintain a small strike force," Sol added and nodded to the man across the table. "We find the Winemaker who stands strong when he bled dry. We find those who will stand against the mountains of hate, just like you, Claire. You have every reason to give in, but you are sitting with us here right now. There are those coming that want dominion over this plane…"

Sol's words dropped off as his attention was pulled to the road and a car in the distance, coming down the slight incline to the intersection that met at the gas station. Several cars had come down that road since they had been sitting here for breakfast. Several others had driven by on the crossroad. This one held his attention because of the erratic way it moved, swaying back and forth into the other lane of the two-lane road. It drew his attention because some wanted dominion of this plane of existence, and the pit of his stomach wondered if they were barreling towards them right now.

***

They had no real idea where they were going. Ely just kept driving. There was no current destination. It wasn't asked, nor discussed by the passengers in the vehicle. Putting as much distance from the woman, Tory, and her army of prisoners, the only goal.

Figuring out where and what they were going to do with their mother would have to come later. If they had a moment of silence, he could think, and Ely could feel the stress and anxiety emanating from Sera every time Mom opened her mouth.

A quick glimpse in the rearview mirror at Mom, looking like a petulant child as she sat in the middle of the backseat with her arms crossed over her chest.

Sera was squeezing the top bridge of her nose between thumb and index finger, squeezing and rubbing in a futile effort to hold an oncoming migraine.

"I fought so hard," Mom couldn't keep silent. Ely couldn't remember her being such a talker. Years in a mental hospital probably changed a person. "I did everything to protect you. I wasn't just your mother. I had to be your guardian angel. Do you know how draining that was?" Mom slumped forward, perched her elbows on her knees, and buried her head in her hands. "It wore me down. It broke me."

That hit Sera with a sparked nerve. She was disgusted at hearing the pity party of excuses from the back. She lurched forward so fast to spin in her seat that her seatbelt engaged and kept her from moving more than an inch. Frustrated, she sat back, then jolt-twisted again. The seatbelt maintained its locked position, making Sera grunt in frustration as she searched for the clip and angrily pressed the button on the clip to release it.

Free of the encumbrance, she whipped around to face the woman in the backseat. "You have a warped memory in your self-righteousness. I don't remember anything like that!"

When Mom raised her head from cupped hands, her eyes were red, and her cheeks were wet with tears. "I fought every day. The depression was winning, though. It was a crack in the door to somewhere dark."

"And you were weak!" Sera pointed a finger at her mom, not falling for the emotional guilt the woman seemed to be spinning. Sera's life had been too tainted to suddenly feel empathy. You let that darkness in."

Jabbed that indicting finger. "You gave up and turned into something evil." Accusatory arrow jab of the index. "An evil something that stole our childhoods from us." Jab. Stick her on a cross, nail her in, and never let her down.

Sera's face was red with rage. Her throat pulsed at the memory of her mom's hands around it. No, Sera had put her mom up on a cross a long-long time ago.

And Mom seemed to drink in that rage as emotion drained from her face.

"Come now. There is no such thing as evil. Good, evil, is only a perception. Which is right?" Mom shrugged her shoulders. "Depends on how you see things. Two sides of a coin, you can only see one at a time, and one is always on top, but neither side changes its value." Mom looked past Sera into the rearview mirror, and the face that reflected was painted with an evil malice. "Unless you hold it up to a mirror."

Mom pulled herself up between the seats, craned her neck to look at her sidelong self in the rearview mirror. Both Ely and Sera reacted in defense, pressing their bodies away and into their respective doors, shocked at the sudden change from their mother. Soft and sorry to rage and venom.

"You let me rot," Mom got increasingly louder, turning to son, then daughter, and back to son. "You let me rot! All these years, I waited. And now, like predictable, fleeting children, lost in the forest, licking at candy houses, you came running into my arms. I was promised things, and now, I can deliver you."

Mom shot an elbow into Sera's face, then reached for the steering wheel and, in a tug of war Ely was not prepared for, yanked it towards herself.

The car lurched to the side of the road.

Ely pulled back, and the tires screeched against asphalt as it came back hard to the left.

Sera reached forward to grab her mom, but instead her face met that lightning-fast elbow again, and she was sent sprawling deep into her seat, the back of her head cracking into the window, erupting stars behind her eyes.

Ely struggled to maintain control of the car as they fought against their wild-eyed and crazy mom. And for half a moment, Mom sounded like she wasn't crazy anymore. Repentant. That maybe, just maybe, they could stop running from their past.

Fighting over the steering wheel, trying to keep the car from careening off the road, he quickly realized how fleetingly ridiculous those thoughts had been. Amidst the chaos inside the vehicle, Ely had the epiphany that the farther you ran from things, the closer they got.

"That is a mother's sacrifice, losing yourself!" Mom was screaming as she pulled herself over the middle console of the car into the front and squeezed herself between Ely and the steering wheel, blocking his view of the road. "Sera never made it. Your worthless sister failed in her task."

Then she was grabbing him, biting at his ear, the vehicle swayed as Ely was completely blinded.

Head still ringing, Sera flinched. Worthless. She failed.

Why hadn't Ely hit the brakes? It was hard for Sera to stabilize herself as she was pitched to and fro. They all were. The car was not slowing because they had run off the road and were barrelling down a hill. And closing the distance to a gas station.

"Hit the brakes! Hit the brakes!" Sera called out in warning.

But Ely didn't hear, couldn't hear, as Mom slammed her forehead into his brow. They jostled around in the cabin as the car careened down the uneven ground of the hill, picking up momentum.

"You carry it now, don't you, Ely. You carry that light! Let me see it. I need to see it," Mom was rambling amidst the struggle, then bit at Ely's ear.

Sera reached forward to grab her mother, only to catch a fistful of hair. It was enough to reel her in, and she yanked. Mom's head snapped back, and Sera lurched forward, grabbing onto her mom around the chest, ensnaring and using her body weight and all the strength in her arms to pull her mother into her. "Hit the brakes!"

Dazed, the weight of his mom off him, Ely shook his head to regain his senses and grabbed for the wheel, desperately trying to regain control of the car. His eyes widened as the car bounced over a curb into the gas station parking lot. He heard Sera yelling the word, brakes, and was about to react when his mother's foot kicked out at him, catching him square in the jaw. A second kick snapped his head to the left window of the driver's side door. As consciousness slipped from Ely, all he saw was the building looming close in the frame of the windshield.

CHAPTER THIRTY-NINE

The waitress returned to begin clearing dishes, drawing Sol's attention away from the window. The normal hum of the restaurant, dishes being delivered, the underlying current of radio music being pumped through overhead speakers, and the low volume buzz of others in conversation increased; other patrons were getting louder, yelling in warning. The waitress, standing at the edge of their table, dropped her handful of plates, which fell to the ground in a clamour. Sol looked up at her, and she was frozen in place, her face painted with stricken horror, oblivious to the dishes she had just dropped.

"Move, move, move," Claire was demanding as she pushed Sol to escape the booth.

Sol looked back at her in reaction to the urgency as the car from the hill, flying over the curb, and torpedoed toward the diner.

That horrendous noise of screeching metal, blended with screams, and shattering glass, erupted as the car was a wrecking ball into the front of the diner. Bodies flew amidst the flurry of chairs, tables, concrete, wall plaster, glass, in a tornado of food fragments and broken kitchenware. The vehicle cannonballed halfway into the room before it came to a halt, half crashed through the counter and row of stools that had lined it.

As the dust settled, there was an aftershock moment of silence. Then the cries of those injured could be heard. Some in pain, some calling out for whomever they had been seated with.

Sol, Claire, and the Winemaker were amongst the rubble, unconscious.

Having been ejected from his seat and tossed forward through the windshield with the impact and sudden lurching stop, Ely's body was a few feet from the hood of the car in the kitchen area, where he lay face down, unmoving.

Sera was listless in her seat. Mom somehow ended up in the backseat again. Unconscious.

Far away, at the top of the hill where the car had begun its roller-coaster descent, the marching horde arrived and gave pause in their pursuit. Tory and Bes pushed to the front of the flood of possessed, insane inmates and surveyed the catastrophe below.

Spreadeagled on the floor not far from where she had been sitting, Claire motioned awake, rousing back to consciousness. She looked around through the dust and smoke. The Winemaker was unmoving, body limp and slung over the front counter. She could not see Sol. Shaking off the dizziness, Claire got to her knees and began looking around, wanting to find Sol to make sure he was okay. And there was the car. Her head tossed involuntarily twice, and her upper torso convulsed in several uncontrollable waves as if she were experiencing a seizure. Her movements became jerky, she sniffed the air twice, and began shuffling toward the vehicle in jerky, unnatural movements.

Slithering onto the crumpled hood of the car, Claire reached in through the broken windshield and grabbed at the woman in the front seat, and began dragging the unconscious woman out of the vehicle. On the hood, Claire flipped Sera onto her back, grabbed her shirtfront, and lifted her close to smell her and inspect the one in her grasp. Claire's face contorted as her mouth was opened wide, saliva running in a steady stream from her bottom lip as if starved, holding this incredible morsel in her hands.

Kill the guardian.

A voiceless command seemed to enter her lost mind.

Claire peeled her lips back, exposing teeth like a predator, and bent down to bite at the body in her arms.

"Claire! Stop!" Sol cried out, holding onto the edge of the counter row for balance and his other hand in a stop motion.

When he awoke, he found himself on the other side of the counter, at the opposite end of where the car was. He pulled himself up to check on the others. He saw Claire moving on the car hood. She wasn't trying to help someone, she wasn't herself.

On the precipice of sinking her teeth into Sera, Claire snapped her neck to the side at the sound of the man's voice shouting her human name.

"Stop, Claire. Come back. Hear my voice," Sol pleaded as he crept forward. The Winemaker lay just before him. Sol shook him while focusing his attention on keeping Claire at bay from killing the woman she held by her shirt.

Demon-Claire dropped the body and stood tall on the hood, pointing with open arms towards the gaping hole in the diner's wall and the world beyond. "My brethren."

Sol looked outside and felt a sudden panic. Dozens of men, dressed in similar garb, were charging down the hill at them.

While eating, Claire had a small episode, banging her head on the table while saying something was coming. Sol had thought it was the car. Now he knew she had meant something else. Something bigger. Something worse. War Bringers were raging towards them in thunderous sounds of screeches and wails.

But why?

"Help us," a man pleaded from his perch, leaning for support against what was left of the door frame between the kitchen and the counter serving area. His face was cut, blood from the side of his head by his ear. Barely able to stand.

Aroused by the commotion and Sol's prodding, the Winemaker came to his senses.

"Help us," the man pleaded again, now to the two of them. "My name is Ely. There is a woman out there driving that mass. She has been chasing us for days and is hell itself."

A realization waved through Sol. "You didn't crash her on accident, did you?"

"No," Ely was shaking his head. Sera was in his eyeline, but he was cautious making any movement for her with the teenager acting all crazy and hovering above his sister. "No, I don't think I did. I was drawn here, but I can't explain. Not all my actions are my own. I know that probably makes zero sense."

"I understand, son," Sol nodded.

Ely haggardly pointed towards his sister. He felt like he had no strength left. "I need to get my sister and get out of here. I don't know why exactly, but there is a she-devil of a woman commanding that group out there, and she wants us. A burning inside says that can't happen. A burning inside says you can help me."

In his peripheral vision, he could see the first wave of several men racing across the highway, almost at the parking lot, a soft smile of assurance crossed Sol's face. "I can feel what is inside you, what drew you here."

Sol popped up on the counter and swivelled off to the other side beside the Winemaker. This was why he was here.

Moving close to the caved-in front of the diner, the Winemaker at his side, to face off against men who were coming, Sol looked over his shoulder towards Ely. "You run. We will hold them."

"But there are so many," Ely felt guilty asking for help and potentially serving these men up to slaughter.

"You run! We probably can't stop them. But we will hold them!"

In the parking area, a truck driver who had been eating in the diner stumbled out, dazed and confused, holding his head as blood seeped through his fingers. His other arm dangled limply from a dislocated shoulder. Two gas bar attendants had come out in response to the crash and were rushing to the injured man's aid. They were the first to fall as the first wave of possessed horde stormed across the parking lot, tackling the men, ripping them apart, pounding fists and screeching in victorious pleasure.

Sol touched the Winemaker's arm in signal as they moved towards the front of the diner to face off against the horde.

"Claire," he called back. She was there, taking a crouched position on the roof of the car. "The three of us make a trinity, the strength of an arrow, and we hit them hard. We hold this madness here. I hate to ask this of you, but we need you, Claire."

The two men ran, charging towards the hole in the diner.

From her perch on the hood of the car, Claire's head twisted back and forth as she opened herself to allow a demon to flow into her. Entities from a void she could not see vying for position, pillaging her mind for placement. She flopped onto her back. It hurt, mentally and physically, as her body writhed and contorted, but she held back those at the forefront. And from the pitch of a void, hands clambered out of a nothingness, reaching, pulling, pinching, and prodding. Claire heaved at the ethereal touches as the psychic imprints haunted her from Father Bracken's violating touch. About to mentally drown and be lost in unfathomable depths, Claire pushed back, ripped fistfuls of hair from her scalp as her sanity spiralled on the verge of loss. But she held on. Held strong against the whitewater torrent that threatened to overwhelm her, and gave in. Sol needed her, needed something stronger. Something dark, born of incomprehensible evil.

Claire's body floated up two feet from the car roof, spun, and dropped. She landed in a crouch, the roof denting under her sudden weight. Sol needed help, but he also needed a monster. Claire was possessed but had managed an alliance. All that hurting was washed away by a blackness. The price to be paid did not matter.

Crouched there with her head cocked and eyes dark, Claire's arms were out, fingers arched in claws. She exhaled a drawn hiss then leapt from her perch, sprinting after Sol and the Winemaker, on all fours like a feral animal.

"It all begins now," Bes stated from her perch beside Tory, up on the hill with the main contingent of their horde, as they watched the first wave encroaching on the diner.

Tory was pointing. "Well, well, do you see at the forefront? A true son of light races into the fray."

Sol charged out of the diner and dive-tackled into the group that was still in the throes of murdering the truck driver and two station attendants. Falling into a mass of limbs, he kicked out blindly, had one by the hair, and bashed the back of its head twice down into the pavement. His elbow crushed another's nose. He had to be fast, brutal, and unrelenting. He cursed himself for not grabbing a knife from the kitchen or anything to form a makeshift weapon.

Four more went racing by. They were ignoring him.

The Winemaker tripped a man and wrestled with another.

And Claire, sweet Claire that he had asked so much of again, came raging out into the parking lot, ripping into one's throat with an inhuman strength, spun, and her makeshift claws disemboweled another.

Incapacitating the prisoners around him, Sol got up to continue the fight. The next wave, another five men, were already upon them. Again, ignoring them, unless forced into confrontation. These war bringers were the offensive line sent first to breach the inside of the diner. And the three of them were too few to stop them all.

"We can only buy them a few moments," Sol said.

"Any moment is a miracle with this mass," the Winemaker replied as more were racing down the hill.

Sol grabbed hold of another racer blindly and, with the momentum, swung the prisoner around to throw him to the ground. The possessed was already scrambling to its feet, trying to scurry past. Sol drove his heel into the man's back, snapping the spine.

"Up there," The Winemaker pointed at the two women, who made their way toward the diner.

"The young man we are trying to protect said a woman was hunting them. Looks like two sisters of the night. I'm going for the head of the snake. Maybe we take them down, and this army will halt," Sol called out as he began running.

Without needing to ask, the Winemaker took up pursuit behind him. Claire came to his side. She was floating two inches off the ground, hands dripping with blood, lips painted in a crimson grin.

Pushing forward, they fought and delayed those they could. The three of them, an arrow piercing their way through to the root of this horde.

Hurrying to the car, Ely's only wish was that Sera was not dead. He did not know the extent of her injuries because of the accident, nor what that weird teenager had done to her. Only precious seconds had passed since he had regained consciousness, but once he made it to Sera's side, he was relieved she was breathing.

Noises off to the side. A couple of the possessed inmates clambered over rubble, making awkward movements into the diner.

There wasn't much time to attempt an escape.

"Sera, Sera, wake up," Ely tried to rouse her. Sera moaned in response. He was going to have to drag her out of here.

The inmates caught sight of their prey and quickened their pace.

There was no time.

He had her, one arm around her shoulders, the other cradling her under bent knees. She was so limp, moaning in stunned reaction or pain. Ely hefted. He had to run. Try to put any distance between himself and the soon-to-be attackers. He turned, and a few more were breaching the hole of the diner.

Too late. It was a wasted effort. The first two were there, diving into him.

Ely was slammed into the side of the car. He twisted in time to take the brunt but reflexively dropped Sera to the ground.

He punched one. The possessed inmate was unfazed. The second one was grabbing at him, trying to pin him.

Below, Sera was rolling from her back. The fall had jolted her awake. She was on her stomach, trying to crawl away.

A prisoner kicked her.

And Ely felt possessed himself. Enraged, he wrestled his arm free and struck out at the one that kicked his sister, trying to keep their attention on him.

Pinned again. Air whooshed from his lungs as a sledgehammer blow hit his midsection. A third inmate came running by, going after Sera.

Ely heaved forward, too much weight. The possessed were too strong. Ignorant of any pain.

Let go! He needed to let go. Open the door!

Ely's eyes went wide. Lids fluttered.

Don't feel. Just react.

His attempt to escape frantically resurged. Ely grabbed the one going for Sera around the neck and yanked him away from his sister. Squeezing with all his might to crush the larynx. Maybe they could not feel pain. But they needed to breathe.

In a pre-reaction, his head flew back. The hard part of the back of his skull smashing into another's face.

Ely swung the body in his arms, the movement snapping the neck. The crushed face had fallen, stunned, on the ground, so Ely kicked down with his heel. Once. Twice. A third.

Let it in. Let them in.

For Sera. For her daughter inside me.

He dodged. Then moved faster than he knew possible, twisted, and savagely punched at the last inmate.

For Sera. For her daughter inside me.

Anne is inside of me.

He looked up. More were coming.

Outside in the chaos.

It had been a slog. A tiresome charge up the hill, even though the incline wasn't steep, it was longer than it looked. And in the essence of time, more prisoners than Sol had hoped for had gotten by.

But once Sol saw Bes, he sprinted towards her. She grabbed him and, using his momentum, flipped him over her head. Sol came to a jarring stop with his back against a tree.

"Valiant effort," Bes moved in close and pressed her hands on Sol's shoulder, locking arms, holding him tight. "You Sons of Light aren't so tough! Being so pure without sin makes you soft."

The other woman, the blonde one, came to the side of the one holding him, and without missing a beat, plunged a knife into Sol's belly.

"Well, the greatest sin is failure," Tory smiled. And plunged the knife a second time. "Sinner!"

Ely had been moving on impulse, a puppet not caring what puppeteers handled his strings if it meant he could hold the inmates at bay, keep them from Sera. Two more lay unconscious at his feet.

Three swarmed by, targeting and charging at Sera.

Ely spun in warning. "Sera!"

She had been on all fours now, moving at a slow crawl, but at hearing her name dropped to her butt and twisted around with her gun out. Sera shot three times in exemplary marksmanship, hitting all three men with fatal shots.

Her brother moved quickly to her side to comfort and get her up. Keep moving.

"I'm okay. I'm okay," Sera said while checking the cartridge of the gun. "That's it, I only have one bullet left." She held up her hand to her brother. "Help me up. We need to get out of here."

They were only a couple of feet from the side of the car. They were getting ready to run, but they had forgotten someone. Sera's scream was too late as Mom came bursting out of the back door and tackled Ely to the ground.

Lost to whatever had taken control of her body, which was using her to wantonly commit violence and revel in the blood it spilled, Claire was still able to see the two women crowding around Sol. Stabbing him.

She raced to his rescue. The dark-haired one turned, and Claire, caught in Bes' command, dropped to her knees. With the forward momentum of her charging trajectory, she slid to a stop, leaning back limply on bent knees before Bes.

"Bow to me," Bes demanded of the vessel inside Claire.

Try as she might, Claire was held motionless. Her body under the thrall of Bes' power.

Tory leaned into the semi-conscious Sol. "Your sacrifice was for naught! We are here to raze the earth. Scorched earth, it isn't something to be afraid of; it is only a rebirth." She patted his cheek seductively. "Don't look at the oncoming darkness as something bad. It is just the sweeping change of a different dawn."

Sol may be dead. Claire down. The Winemaker fought his way past a few of the prisoners, raced the last few steps, and slammed his body into the blonde woman, stabbing Sol, sending her flying. In one swift motion as he passed Sol, he grabbed the handle of the knife sheathed in Sol's stomach, pulled it free among a wet noise and spray of blood, and whipped around.

"Never underestimate the power of sacrifice," the Winemaker said as he drove the knife into Tory's chest.

Letting her drop as she clung to the handle of the blade, the Winemaker turned to a shocked Bes and grabbed her right shoulder.

"The host you possess, did you know that more than half the human body consists of water?" He squeezed hard. "What happens if it is turned to wine!"

Not a question. A preluding statement.

Bes arched back in screaming agony as the inside of her body erupted in fire as if blood was now lava coursing through the frame.

They had fallen to the ground, Mom underneath Ely as her arms snaked up from behind, under his armpits to hold his chest in a vice, pressing his back into herself. With inhuman strength, the possessed mom held her struggling son tight as she skitter-kicked her feet to drag him back with her.

Sera had her gun drawn, trained on her mother as she stepped forward. She wanted to shoot, to save her brother, but it was their mom. Even though she was snarling with a contorted face and yellowed eyes, she was still their mom.

Sera was unable to pull the trigger.

Mom was pulling him and trying to drag him away. Ely had the realization that the possessed inmates had been holding him down, pinning him. Holding him captive. Just like Detective Tory in the prison hospital. She could have snapped his neck in a blink. They weren't trying to kill him.

They were taking him prisoner.

Old gods may wither and die, but as she yanked the knife out of her chest, Tory was glad that someone out there still had a little faith in her. If she had a moment, she would have been impressed with the abuse her body had been able to sustain and keep on going. But there wasn't that moment. Tory grabbed a rock and swung wildly at the man who held Bes, clocking him on the side of the head to send him reeling to the ground, where he rolled away down the hill.

Tory helped a recovering Bes steady her feet.

Sol was unconscious at their feet, bleeding from his gut wound.

"The idiots have forgotten the prize and now race back to us," Bes quipped. Their army withdrew from the campaign on the Diner and now charged back up the hill in response to their masters being in supposed peril.

Tory smiled at the response because those same soldiers had piled onto the Winemaker to subdue him and were now beating him.

And her new little subordinate toy, the girl, was immobile, frozen in stasis on her knees, staring up at Bes and Tory in subservience.

"Fear not, Bes," Tory pointed to the Diner wreckage below. "See, we have it. She is bringing him."

There was a glimpse of the mother, the tainted one, dragging her son back towards the hole in the wall. This would all be over before it had a chance to begin.

It was hard for Ely to breathe with his mom's arm around his neck, squeezing, as she kept yanking him back towards the opening in the Diner wall. He almost felt more scared of what was to come. Ely fully understood now, Mom was not trying to choke the life out of him. She was pulling him away from Sera to deliver him. Since that first moment in Sera's cabin, the she-devil outside had been trying to take him captive, not kill him.

But why?

He struggled against his mother, but her strength was surprising. If he could get his feet under him, but Ely couldn't get a perch, they kept sliding back inch by inch as Mom kicked against the carpeted floor, heaving, pulling.

Sera matched their every step to close the distance to reach her brother, keeping the gun trained forward but still unable to fire against her mom, possessed or not, trying to kill them again or not. Even if she could bring herself to pull the trigger, the risk was too high because Mom was using Ely as a human shield.

"You let him go! Let him go right now, or I swear," Sera vainly tried to give warning. "You've been dead to me for years, Mom. Don't force me to make it official. This last bullet is on you!"

She reached out to grab Ely's extended hand.

Mom hissed from over his shoulder and pulled back hard. Ely and Sera's fingers grazed each other but were unable to grab hold.

Slowly sliding by a row of diner booths, Ely reached out and grabbed hold of the edge of one of the padded bench seats to stop himself, holding on to an anchor from being dragged any further.

"Sera, it's me," Ely's words were filled with compassion and an understanding he was trying to convey. "Not mom. For this to end...it's me...shoot me."

Mom raged, releasing her stranglehold around his neck to bash down at his arm, trying to force Ely's grip to release. He held strong, fingers straining in the exertion of his grip.

Sera's gun arm wavered slightly. "What are you talking about?" Ely was not making any sense.

The realization flooded through him, and in that moment, Ely's mind flashed through all those past moments experienced as others. Impulse moments in the blink of an eye, events where he had blacked out for periods. An hour lost, a day lost, all these paths he had stepped on, footsteps that he made that were not his own. He experienced things in Sera's house when he was drawn to the vacant bedroom of Anne, all those paths diverging to this moment.

All this time, he thought it was himself. "Listen to me, Sera," Ely cried out.

Mom struck at him, yanked at him, in a stream of vomit, she belched black bile mixed with blood concocted from the black pit of her stomach, over him to disrupt his senses.

Ely shook it off. His only focus was reaching Sera with his words, to make her understand before it was too late. "I understand now. It's me they want."

Sera was listening but not paying attention. She moved in to grab her brother, but Demon-Mom made a motion to tear his throat, keeping Sera at bay.

From behind, Mom slammed her head into Ely. Unable to get him to let go, she was trying to crack his skull into unconsciousness.

"Sera! Sera!" Ely yelled to have her focus on him. "She's the beacon. I'm just the harbour. Listen to me, Sera." He begged. "Anne is the beacon."

That snapped Sera's attention, and she looked at Ely in her eyes.

"All this time I thought it was me," Ely was talking as fast as he could against the onslaught from his mother. "I realize now. I can feel it now. I'm just the harbour. Anne is the beacon. You have to shoot me. I'm the one, not Mom, to save us all."

More inmates, the possessed, were scrambling towards the diner, coming in fast at the command of Bes and Tory. A barrage of human missiles slammed into the side of the building, rattling the walls.

It startled Sera from her mesmerized confusion at what her brother was rambling about, and she brought the gun up, pointed it toward the hole, ready to defend. A hopeless single bullet.

Ely was yelling at her again, yelling for her attention and for her to do something inconceivable, nonsensical.

"Everything inside me," Ely strained against his mom, straining harder to reach Sera amidst the chaos of the situation. "Her inside me. Anne. Sera! Sera! Look at me.

Mom was biting at him. Screeching in glee as she ripped bits of flesh in quick bites from his neck, shoulders, and head. A weird triumphant calling erupted as she spat out a clump of his scalp when the rest of the possessed were heard drawing close.

"You have to shoot me, now, before it's too late," Ely was pleading. "For Anne. I'm just the harbour. She is the beacon. Shoot me. Release her. We need to release it. Release them all."

And even though he still held on, fighting against the creature that was once a mother to him, fighting for his sister's attention and understanding, that was when the real pain reverberated through his body. A pulsing wave of fullness like he had felt before, as if his mind would burst from his skull from the volcanic pressure.

"Are you insane?" Sera shook her head to dismiss what she was hearing while keeping her gun trained on Mom. "What are you even saying? You can't expect me to..."

"Sera, you need to understand. You were the light of Mom's life because of what you carried deep inside you. Just as Anne was the light of your life, they used Mom. They tried to snuff it out, that light, that fateful night. Mom lost. We almost lost. You can still fight. All of this I have experienced, I've been used through my life, this weird, insane life, was a gathering. These souls inside of me that have been coming to the forefront. It is all because of her. They have been trying to capture me. They want me. They need to keep me closed. You need to do this, shoot me. Kill Me. I have to die so we can open the harbour."

"I don't understand," Sera cried and pleaded, the gun wavered in her hand. "You are my little brother. I can't. This makes no sense. I can't do this. We can make it. We can make a run for it. You are my little brother."

"Then be my big sister and do what needs to be done!"

"Little Bitch can't," Mom snarled up to get Sera's attention.

Inmates were inside, racing to Mom's aid to grab Ely.

This was the final moment of opportunity. Ely stopped struggling for a moment to be resolute in his words. "If you kill her and not me, we are all dead. It is over."

"Little Bitch can't do what needs to be done. Kill me. Shoot me," Mom teased.

A couple of prisoners were on Ely, breaking his grip, dragging him away with Mom's assistance.

A last desperate, pleading attempt, Ely shouted at her. "Trust me!"

"I do," Sera said and stepped forward. "But I can't. I can't lose you. My daughter. I can't."

"She couldn't then. She can't, now. You lost your daughter once. Kill him now, and she is lost forever, ever, and ever," Mom had a wide, evil, taunting grin.

"Stop! Stop teasing me, tempting me with lies. Anne is gone. She is dead," Sera's emotions were about to snap as she banged her head in quick succession with the flat of her palm.

More inmates entered. Some are adding strength to pull the captive. A few are preparing to attack Sera.

Ely looked at her deeply, trying to speak as fast as he could amidst the grabbing hands. "I love you, sister. You were always there for me. Let me be there for you now. Let me protect you now as you always protected me," Ely begged.

"By shooting you!" Sera was dumbfounded. "I can't."

"I can hear her crying. That voice in the night. Lost in the night. And only little brother knows," Mom's words were venom. "I hated you since you squeezed out of my factory. Useless brat then. Useless now. I should have killed you that night and saved my granddaughter the humiliation of ever being born from you."

That hit home. The words stung. And Sera raised the gun and locked her arms.

Ely could see he had lost. Mom had won. There was no way facing her mother now after the tragedies of her life, being betrayed by her mother repeatedly, that Sera would hear him. Not when there was some feeling of her daughter inside of him, some vestige of hope to hold onto.

Although he was begging and screaming at her, Sera wasn't listening to him.

She couldn't listen. Sera could only hear the poison from Mom's lips.

Beguiling her.

Sera fired the last bullet.

Ely, by the angle of his vision, could see that his sister was not aiming at him. At the last second, he used everything to jerk forward and shift in front of his mom. Straight into the line of fire.

The bullet hit Ely in the face and blew straight out the back of his head amidst a trail of blood, brains, and skull fragments, spattering Mom with the gore.

"No! I was aiming for her!" Sera was horrified that she had shot her brother.

Possessed inmates were almost upon her, and Sera was oblivious, feeling defeated in what she had just done.

Then a pulse hit Sera, and an invisible force sent her flying onto her back. Hitting the ground, she recoiled and covered her eyes against a blinding brightness.

Ely.

She saw him, body limp, but his eyes erupted with white light. His head was seeping the brightness as if his skull cracked wide like a surface fissure created by the shifting tectonic plates. White illumination of radiant lightning shot out of him, tendrilled fireworks with no exploding end snaked out, shooting into Demon-Mom and the surrounding possessed, throwing them back.

CHAPTER FOURTY

Tory and Bes were descending the hill, almost at the highway edge, to take possession of their prize when the radiant light exploded inside the diner.

Tory stepped forward, screaming in sudden loss. "No!"

Bes backstepped, being hit with the instant realization that a victory had suddenly been ripped from their grasp. Stolen. "The Elysium has been broken."

And then the light of an Elysium snaked out in all directions, blinding ribbons of pure light that spiralled outwards from their source and drove like arrows through some of the possessed horde, expelling the ones inside and leaving the natural hosts unconscious.

The two women showed no fear, ignored what was happening to their possessed ones, and charged into the Diner.

Stunned from the emittance, Mom rolled over and crawled towards Bes and Tory to kneel at their feet.

"I had him," Mom tried to justify her failure.

"Had! And not for the first time," Bes chided in disgust. "And your daughter?"

"She is Seraphim of my blood. She is alive," Mom replied.

"Stronger than you were."

Mom hissed. "My strength was in birthing a host. My strength is in my allegiance now."

The words she spoke aloud, but the fealty she had been imprisoned with for so long, cracked inside her mind with a pang of guilt. And Mom flashed back to those years of depression, the anguish she suffered after losing control and attempting to murder her family. The consequences of losing control and those actions forced her to lose her family. That flash of guilt for not having the strength back then to kill herself and save her family. She had thought she was fighting for them, fighting against the impulse to destroy them, until she couldn't hold on any longer.

That emotion of her true self fled and was whisked away, pushed down into the voided blackhole of her, locked away.

"And that allegiance is needed," Tory stepped forward. "This Seraphim of your breeding can't be allowed to live."

"She won't. We almost broke her once. She is strong, but alone," Mom smiled and extended her tongue over her lower lip as far as it would reach to glaze along her chin and lick specks of blood that were there. Elysium blood. Blood from her dead son.

But the daughter still lived.

And there was a debt to pay for what she had done.

Left on bended knees in submission, Claire tried to move as she stared at Sol bleeding a few feet from her. The possessed raced away at the command of the two women. The command that held her at bay. Then a force of pure energy pierced into her, through her, and Claire fell to the ground in unfathomable agony, screeching an unholy sound unmade by any human before.

Claire's cries, seeing her writhe in pain, roused Sol, and he crawled to her. It was hard with her flailing arms and kicking legs, but he managed to get his arms around her and draw her in close to his body. He held her tight while whispering in her ear that he was there, for her to hold on and fight through it.

He had never experienced raising a child, and his heart ached for only being able to hold Claire. Was this what it was like to hold your child through pain and sickness through the hours of the night?

Then it stopped. Claire went limp in his arms.

"I'm okay," she murmured, feeling exhausted. "Whatever hit me, it drove the demons inside me out. I'm okay."

Sol dropped onto his back with his hands clasped to his stomach wounds. He wasn't sure if he was.

Claire leaned over him and pressed her hands down to stem the leaking blood.

"We had a good run there, huh?" She gave a weak smile.

"It's not over yet," the Winemaker said suddenly at their side. He was also battered and torn and had crawled his way to them. "Here," he used bits of torn cloth from his shirt to begin applying makeshift bandages to Sol's wounds, but it seemed a vain effort as the material quickly reddened. "This isn't working." He tossed the bandages aside and created a latticework with his fingers and began adjusting the positioning of his hands over Sol's wounds.

"How is that any better?" Claire was concerned as blood seeped through the Winemaker's fingers. "We are in the middle of nowhere, and Sol needs medical attention. What are you going to do, turn his blood into a nice Chianti?"

"Let me concentrate," the Winemaker chided. "I do have more than one magic trick up my sleeve." He pressed down hard. "If I can force an accelerated coagulation...have the blood itself seal the wound..."

The Winemaker removed his hands. Sol's blood was no longer seeping from his stab wounds. Hard red scabs had formed to create a type of suture, pulling the skin taut and sealing the cuts.

"You are going to have some nasty scars, but that should hold until you can heal better," the Winemaker said.

"Look at us," Claire said. "We got taken out by them in seconds. But at least they are on the run now."

Sol strained to look up. Claire was right the possessed horde they had been fighting had left them. Those left were heading down the hill. But they weren't running away.

"They are still on the chase," the Winemaker said. "But we can't do anything in our current condition."

"No, we can't pursue them in our condition. We need to heal and regroup," Sol said. "Part of being here is finding others and strengthening our numbers. We need to build a small army."

Keep moving. Keep fighting. It was why he was here. Sol had found Claire. Found the Winemaker. The others, like the man they had tried to save in the diner. Others who had experienced this. Being obsessed and compelled against their will, in worst cases, possessed. And they will find them.

Then they hunt the hunters.

CHAPTER FOURTY-TWO

Emerging from an impulsive haze, Sera realized she was running, emerging from an impulsive haze.

Her thighs burning, chest aching from sprinting up the incline, Sera stopped and bent over with hands on knees to catch her breath. She had come up a hill on the other side of the diner and was surprised at the distance she had made, the restaurant viewed in the distance. She had run. Abandoning Ely. Oh God, her brother.

After firing the gun, the shot did not go as planned and hit Ely. Killing him, a red rage of despair had washed over her. And she had been ready to fight. Everything else was lost. Ely had sacrificed himself. And everything pure and good in the world that was thought lost was set free. And she was blinded by that grief and ready to fight, oblivious to the thought that it would have been her end.

She could see that she must have exited through the kitchen and out the back to be on this side now.

She could see bodies on the ground at the front of the building, just beyond the diner, on the highway, and scattered on the hill on the other side. A large swathe had been taken down by whatever had erupted out of Ely. Not all. And from the looks of it, not Mom. And not the two other women.

Despair was taking hold, washing over her. She wanted to go to her brother, hold him, and beg for forgiveness.

But he was dead.

A few more steps up, she hid behind a boulder amidst a grove of trees. Once concealed, she began to cry, lost to overwhelming emotion. Ely was gone. He had sacrificed himself and she was alone. She couldn't breathe amidst the grief that poured from her.

Her special brother. And with him, any tether to the daughter that Sera thought was gone forever, an aspect of her that he had felt inside himself, was being able to share.

Sera jerked to attention as something touched her hand. Looking down, it was another's. Small, young, but when Sera went to pull away reactively in surprise, the other hand gave a slight squeeze in a firm grip of assurance and held strong.

"Hello, Mom," a young girl said from beside her, holding Sera's hand in a clasped embrace.

Sera looked down, startled at a young girl who seemingly appeared out of nowhere and had taken her hand.

"Oh my God!" Sera dropped to her knees to take the girl by her shoulders and looked directly at her. "Is this really you?" Impossible. This girl was maybe six or seven years old, but inside those eyes...tears streamed down Sera's face in disbelief. "Anne? How can this be? You're older, grown."

"In your mind's eye, I have. You know it. You can feel it," the little girl touched Sera's heart with a pointed right index finger.

And that crushed Sera, falling forward, crying uncontrollably as she wrapped her arms around the girl's waist, burying her face against her. It was all impossible. And Sera didn't care.

Hands on Sera's cheek. Small, soft, gentle hands that enticed Sera to look up.

"We must keep going, Mom," Anne said. "I'm not quite strong enough yet. I wasn't in the Elysium long enough."

That tiny palm against a tear-soaked cheek drew Sera's attention towards the back of the diner. Bes and Tory were emerging with their remaining soldiers. And leading the pack, the thing that was once Sera's mother.

"We have held them at bay," Anne said. "But the gloves are off, and with the Elysium broken, I can no longer stay hidden. Time to go."

"I think you are right," Sera said while standing.

For a moment, her legs felt frozen. Abandoning Ely felt wrong. Even though there was nothing left of him, leaving his body to rot felt wrong. But now, Sera had Anne to keep safe.

She scooped her daughter up in her arms and ran.

The End

Compelled

~Not all our actions are our own~

Author Bio

Kevin Doyle is an author with a passion for exploring the edges of human resilience through the various genres of Science Fiction, Thrillers, and Horror. He lives in Calgary, Alberta, with his wife of thirty years, and is a proud father of four, where he finds inspiration in the chaos and fulfillment of family life.

His debut novel, *Mourning's Song,* is available now.